THE WINDSOME TREE

a ghost story

Eileen Albrizio

Apparition Press

First Edition
ISBN-978-0-692-10914-4

Library of Congress Control Number: 2018904730

Apparition Press
Wethersfield, CT

Acknowledgments

Wayne Horgan, you graciously gave me your heart in 1983, and every good thing I do is dedicated to you. Thank you to my mother Constance Magnan-Albrizio, the scribbler who inspired me to scribble as a child. To my father Francis Albrizio, thank you for being my dad. A heartfelt thanks to my sisters of Artemis Rising (Linda, Mary Elizabeth, Paula, Priscilla, Suzanne, Suzy, Terri, and Victoria), a group of incredible poets and authors whose eyes and sharp minds helped mold this and so many of my works. Thank you to Josh Kirn for reading a stranger's manuscript and rendering an honest critique. Special thanks to CAPA (The Connecticut Authors' and Publishers' Association) for giving me the resources and exposure needed to embark on this incredible adventure. Ann Collette, thank you for your expert editorial advice and guidance in getting this book ready for market. Many thanks to Rita Reali, the first editor of this book and to Mary Elizabeth Lang, the final proofreader. Thank you to Victoria Rivas for your amazing technical expertise. A super special thanks to Tyler Herron for the influence of your youthful spirit and for showing me how to ride a tire swing. And I am especially thankful to the untold readers who have already read this novel in its various stages and to all those about to read the book in its finished form.
Grazie.

THE WINDSOME TREE
a ghost story

CHAPTER ONE
Sometime
In the Abyss

The wolves were coming. Anastasia couldn't hear them, couldn't see them, but they were coming. They had come before. Alerted by the scent of sweat from a fever or the pheromones of her fear, they would prowl into her sleep. Monstrous creatures, trolling though her nightmares, she would see their snarling muzzles and sharp white fangs from behind leafless trees in a shadowy wood. She would hear their low, hungry growls, smell their dank fur. Sometimes they'd chase her, and the only way she could escape being ripped open and eaten alive was to wake up. Anastasia couldn't wake up, though. She was already awake.

She wrapped her arms around her stomach as heat spread over her cheeks and shakes scurried through her eight-year-old body.

"Momma?" she cried.

Certain she said it out loud, but no sound came back to her ears. Her breath hitched in her throat, but she didn't hear it and she swallowed the fear in her mouth.

Help me!

The place she was in was as dark as the deepest place in space where all the stars had died—a place so dark it swallowed sound and smell and light. Somehow she had gone to sleep in the illuminated world of Windsome, North Carolina and woke up in a massive black abyss.

She tilted her head in an attempt to hear some sign of life. Anything, a creak of a door, the weary sigh of her mother carrying the weight of a growing baby in her belly, the whir of a passing car. She closed her eyes—or thought she did—and tried to pick up the whistle of an oriole or the call of the gangly brown thrasher her older brother could never spot in the bare entwined twigs of their hedges. But she always could.

"Look for their eyes," she told him. "They're yellow."

Bobby?

She passed her hands down the front of her body to prove she still existed. The taffeta of her flower-girl dress she knew was white but couldn't see was smooth against her palms. Small fingers played with the satin bow at her waist. It was pink. She remembered. She stretched her arms wide in front of her and tried to feel anything that was once around her, perhaps her bed and the dozens of fairy dolls resting against her pillow. Fairies kept her safe in the dark. But there was no bed and there weren't any fairies. Not even Sparkle, her favorite fairy doll of all. Sparkle carried her wishes and made them come true. Sparkle was her best friend. Except for her brother. Bobby was her best friend, too, but she hadn't let him know that. If he knew, he'd never stop teasing her and he already called her "Booger."

"Want some ice cream, Booger?"

Yes.

"What's the matter, Booger, afraid of the dark?"

Yes.

Anastasia felt the whimpers escape from her quivering lips and thought if she ever saw Bobby again, she would tell him he was her friend. Hot tears fell from her eyes and trailed down her cheeks.

"Momma?" Nothing.

I want to go home.

Something blinked. From the corner of her sight, she saw it. It was like someone flicked a speck of light from his fingers in the way she saw the older kids flick cigarettes. Anastasia's heart did a cartwheel and she looked to where she thought she saw the light. She caught it, just for a second, in the far reaches of the pitch-dark universe. A point of light, a pinprick through the taut black canvas. It was there, and in a blink, it was gone. She sucked in a breath and felt a prickle of hope skid across her flesh. Until something moved.

It was the wolves. They were coming.

CHAPTER TWO
June 2014 ~ The Present

Mercy Amoretto sat on the edge of her bed clinging to the fading vestige of her dead six-year-old daughter. Lisa, precious Lisa, had come to visit her in the night. The dream had turned misty and the details evaporated, but Mercy's puffy lips proved she'd been there. It was a sign that Lisa would come to her as a specter in her dreams and leave her during the day with the nightmare of her absence. Sometimes she'd be the happy Lisa with her confection-sugar smile, sweet vanilla complexion, and burst of mahogany curls. Sometimes she would be the other Lisa, bald, sallow, the Lisa whose body was ravaged by leukemia. And after each visitation, Mercy would wake with lips numb and puffy.

The meds helped snuff out the dreams for a while. But she wasn't allowed to take them anymore.

Mercy got dressed and went downstairs.

"Mom, I need my baseball jersey," Joshua shouted the second she entered the kitchen. "Practice was moved to today because coach can't be there tomorrow."

"You're telling me this now?"

"I forgot."

"It's in the hamper. Still dirty. Sorry."

Joshua shrugged his knobby shoulders as if dirt didn't mean a lick to him and ran upstairs. Of course it didn't, Mercy thought. He's twelve.

Donovan bustled by the kitchen archway. He was dressed in his usual uniform, a dark business suit, white shirt, and a smart tie. Throwing the cell phone he had at his ear onto his chest, he said, "Don't forget our appointment at nine-thirty."

Seriously? We're scheduled to confess our nonexistent sex life to a psychiatrist in just under two hours. How could I forget that?

"I won't."

His cell phone was back at his ear as he shut himself in the room down the hall that served as his home office.

"Cripes, Kaitlyn. Hurry up. We're going to be late for the bus." A willowy teenaged blur that was Kira raced by the kitchen.

A second later, her twin blur followed. "Bye Mom. Bye Dad," Kaitlyn hollered.

"Lunch money?" Mercy called out.

"Got it," the identical teens yelled back and the door slammed.

"Thanks, Mom," Josh said, shoving his filthy Windsome Whirlwinds jersey into his backpack as he ran past her.

"I'll pick you up later," she yelled.

"'Kay." Another door slam and the house fell into abrupt stillness. She missed them already.

Leaving the wreckage of the morning behind her, Mercy walked out onto the back deck and stepped onto the plush, manicured lawn. One of Donovan's joys. On his days off, when the weather was cheerful, he would tend the lawn the way a horticulturist would cultivate a garden of delicate orchids. Mercy stepped across the cushion of grass and stopped at the majestic maple tree, the only tree in their yard. She sat and leaned against the trunk.

"We should have mortgage commitment by Tuesday and then we wait for the clear-to-close," she heard Don say through the open window of his office.

The licorice flavor of his tone was fragrant in the air. How she wanted to gobble it up. It never mattered what he was saying. She loved to hear his voice. He could be talking about fixing a running toilet or football. It wasn't the words that soothed her, but the way he said them, smooth and resonant, deep and delicious. Unfortunately, most of the talking they did lately was done in front of the therapist.

Casting her eyes upward, Mercy focused on her bedroom window. Sunlight speckled the side of the house and the breeze showed the movement of something attached there. What was it? She blinked a few times to see more clearly. Clinging to the shutter of her bedroom window and extending to the uppermost corner of the house was what could only be the biggest spider web she'd ever seen. My God, she thought. What kind of arachnid could have made such a thing? An enormous one. Or more likely a whole cluster of them. She shuddered and looked away.

The smell of rain hit her nostrils. Gusts picked up speed and danced the tarantella up Mercy's arms, lifting the hairs as it twirled up her flesh. She hugged her knees to her chest.

"Remember," Donovan said through the window, "don't purchase any large items between now and closing. The banks can use that against you."

There he was, cool and casual, long legs propped on his desk, his broad gladiator shoulders leaning against the back of his chair. As if he could feel her watching, he swiveled his chair around and his eyes caught hers. His was a tender face that wore the deep lines not so much of age—he was only forty-one—but of living with his face to the sun. Ballgames, boating, picnics, and vacations at the beach were his delights. But his most treasured time was right in their own backyard. He smiled.

Is he smiling because of his conversation on the phone, or is he smiling at me? She smiled back. He turned his chair around until she saw only the neatly cropped yet full head of black hair on the back of his head. The story of my life. One day they were going over the blueprints of the house they would build together, then the next day a shift of the wind and everything changed.

She ran her palms over the feathery grass as she remembered walking with Donovan through the thicket and bristly weeds of the overgrown park that was to become their neighborhood. What an eyesore it had been. More of a junkyard than a place to play. Officials in the town of Windsome were more than happy to sell it to Don and his people. She clung to the excitement she'd felt while weaving through the smattering of trees, helping Don pick up garbage and debris to clear the land. And that's how their lives had been, one exciting moment after another. Until a cold breath blew out the life of her daughter.

Wind gusted and the first drops of rain from the oncoming storm made their way through the canopy of leaves. It was time to go, the rain was saying. She fingered the furrow in her brow, took a deep breath, and got to her feet.

As she walked across the yard, her eyes drifted back to the corner where she'd seen the spider web. Moving closer, she saw it wasn't a spider web at all. It was just the shadow made from broken light through the leaves of the tree in her friend's yard next door. An illusion.

An oriole whistled above her. Mercy entered the house and shut the sliding door.

CHAPTER THREE
June 2014 ~ The Present

Donovan hung up the phone and swung his chair around to face the window. Mercy was no longer sitting by the tree. He had smiled at her, hoping to hide that he'd seen her tension. But he had seen it, expected it. Once a month, when they went to a therapy session, she would spend the hours before in a funk. He didn't blame her. Neither he nor Mercy was sweet on spooning out their flaws for the therapist to devour, but he knew Dr. Wright could do for them what they couldn't do on their own. Dr. Wright had helped Don to cope when all he wanted to do was deny his grief. She had helped their surviving children move beyond their feelings of powerlessness after losing their youngest sibling. Most important, she had helped Mercy climb out of the dungeon of her mind after her stay at Tower Hills Psychiatric Treatment Center just the year before.

Mercy called it Tower Hills Hell, and Don understood why. It was a callous place, where emotional sickness was treated like a contagion. Mercy blamed Dr. Wright for sending her there and for the misery she'd endured. Every day during her month-long program, Don fought the urge to get her out, just like he'd smuggled her out of study hall in high school to avoid the mean girls who picked on her. But Tower Hills wasn't high school and, in the end, her stay there kept her from drowning. And her therapy sessions with Dr. Wright afterward kept her strong. Sure, there were times when the depression clung to her like humidity, but it did to the whole family.

A knock, and Mercy cracked open the door.

"Are you busy?" Mercy's wan smile never made it to her eyes.

"I'm done for now. Everything okay?"

"Yes, fine. I wanted you to know I'm going to take a nap. I have a headache and I didn't sleep well last night. Another hour's all I need."

"Dreams again?"

She tossed back her dark curls and her failed smile vanished. "I'll get enough therapy today. I don't need more here." Her voice was sulky.

"I didn't mean to pry."

"You're not prying. I just want to take a nap. There's nothing lying underneath."

Those beautiful brown eyes revealed her. There was plenty lying underneath. "Of course. No worries. I'll wake you later."

"No need. I'll set the alarm."

"Sleep well."

She hesitated as if there was more to say, but the words were stuck. "I … Thanks." She walked away.

Yes, there was a lot lying underneath.

I love you, too.

CHAPTER FOUR
June 2014 ~ The Present

Mercy sat in the therapist's office, the persistent ping of a headache at her temple, feeling like she was sitting in detention.

"There's no need to be so dramatic," said Don.

"I meant it as a metaphor." Mercy swallowed her exasperation. "I meant we're not glued together like we were before. We're not connected as much."

"Then why don't you say that? Why do you have to talk like it's all so fatal?" His tone was not so much irritated as pained. He turned to the doctor. "This is what I mean. Mercy has a dramatic flair. It's hard to communicate sometimes through the drama. If she would just lighten up a little."

"I'm sitting right next to you. You don't have to talk about me in the third person."

"I'm talking to Dr. Wright about us. That's why we're here."

"Don needs to talk, Mercy," said Dr. Wright. "These are the things that remain unsaid at home. Best to get them out in this office." The psychiatrist peered over her bifocals with a look that made Mercy feel like she was ten.

Nervous, Mercy rolled her wedding band around on her finger with her thumb. It was a modest band, molded to hug her engagement ring. The stone in the ring was just a chip. Donovan bought it for less than two hundred dollars and promised one day to buy her a diamond that would make an heiress proud. Although they'd come to be able to afford nicer things, that ring, eighteen years on her finger, was a part of her. Taking it off would feel like an amputation.

As Dr. Wright jotted down notes, the tension wrapped around Mercy heavier than a wool blanket dunked in a November lake. She folded her arms around her torso. With her left hand partially hidden beneath her right elbow, she rolled her ring around and around until Wright lifted her head and glared over her glasses. Mercy unknotted her arms and shoved her hands under her thighs.

"Any changes in the bedroom?" Dr. Wright asked.

Bitch.

"The same," Don said.

The doctor scrawled on the pad and Mercy shifted on the leather couch, which creaked sarcastically beneath her legs.

"Want to talk about it?"

Unable to find a comfortable position, Mercy shifted again and, again, the leather creaked. She stopped shifting, kept her hands beneath her thighs, and clenched her jaw.

"My days are pretty full," Don said. "I've been working on a new condominium development for several months. I'm tired when I get home or have more work to do and when I'm done, Mercy's already asleep."

The doctor arched a beautifully sculpted eyebrow. "Bedtime isn't the only time for intimacy." She shot her eyes at Mercy, indicating it was her turn to answer.

"The mornings are spent taking care of the children," Mercy said, "and by the time they're off to school, Don's already left for work."

"Weekends?"

"Again, the children have a lot of needs."

Dr. Wright slapped her pen down on her pad and yanked off her glasses. "If every couple stopped having sex after having a child, we'd have a whole world of one-child families."

"That would solve the overpopulation problem." Don gave a nervous laugh.

Dr. Wright slid her glasses back up the bridge of her nose. "You're making excuses instead of making love." The room was silent as a monastery. "Before me, I see two attractive people in good health who love each other despite their problems. You're finding reasons not to be intimate when it should be the other way around. You didn't have this problem before you lost Lisa."

I hate you. "No," Mercy managed to say. She turned to her husband who was examining his hands. "We have a lot of mess to clean up. I know that."

"Maybe it's time you started cleaning up that mess. Begin with the physical stuff." Dr. Wright's buttery voice softened. "Get rid of the clutter you've collected over the eighteen years of your marriage. Clean out the basement, the garage, the attic, whatever. Throw away the junk, and do it together. Somewhere amid all that clutter, you may find a treasure that will remind you of how it was before things got so messy. It may even give you a chance to start over."

Don nodded at the doctor's words as if they were some insightful bits of information he hadn't thought of before.

"So, Mercy, are you sleeping?" Wright asked.

From the corner of her eye, Mercy thought she saw Don flinch, a twitch so slight it could have been a blink or even a figment of her imagination. But the thought landed in her head that he had flinched, and that made the question much harder to answer.

"Yes. I'm sleeping," she replied, knowing Don knew that wasn't true. "Sleep's a bit restless," she confessed, "but I am sleeping." Dr.

Wright stared at her. "Most nights." Mercy shifted. Creak. "Somewhat."

"Without the help of pills," the doctor added. "Even over-the-counter?"

"Yes."

"I'm glad to hear that. I know gaining control of your depression without medication was hard, but it's good for you to keep on this path." The doctor wrote something on her pad. "Dreams?"

"What's that?" Mercy asked.

"How are your dreams?"

Mercy knew she had dreamt about Lisa the night before, but there was something else. Like a whisper in a room full of barking dogs, there was a message there, but she couldn't hear it over all the other noise. Then something pushed through the fog of her mind. "The wolves are back."

"The ones you dreamt about when you first moved into the house?"

"Yes. They vanished after Lisa died. But they're back now. And almost exactly as they were before."

Dr. Wright sat up straight as if searching hard for a meaning, then said, "Well, it could be nothing, but you may want to write down your dreams for a while to see if there's a pattern. That may help you understand what's triggering them."

The suggestion made her queasy. Writing down her dreams would be like trying to remember the details of a funeral Mass. She didn't want to do it.

"It feels odd to have recurring dreams at my age," Mercy said. "Isn't that like a childhood thing?"

"Recurring dreams happen for many reasons and have no age limit."

"But why wolves?"

"Wolves are predators. They are wild animals that live on instinct and survival. They are frightening. There are countless reasons why you would manifest such creatures in your dreams. But I don't want to speculate. I believe once we explore when the dreams occur and the specifics surrounding them, we'll be better equipped to understand them."

What if they don't recur, she was about to ask but somehow, she knew they would. Heat spread over Mercy's cheeks. Her lips curled in on themselves.

"What is it?" Dr. Wright asked.

Mercy unlocked her lips and looked to her husband. His silent gaze back at her gave no relief. Relenting, Mercy said, "The wolves aren't the only dreams that haunt me." Tears threatened to spill, but she blinked them back. "I see Lisa's face in the days before she died. Lying in the hospital bed, hooked up to wires and tubes, she looks at me with this fear, like she knows she's going to die. So, I tell her what I'd told her since she was diagnosed. 'Everything will be all right. You'll get better soon.' But nothing is all right, and she won't get better and, in that moment of realization, Lisa's face no longer shows fear." The first tears of the session spill down Mercy's cheeks.

"What does it show?" the doctor prodded.

"Betrayal. In those eyes that pierce into mine, she tells me I've failed her."

Don placed his hand on her arm. "No one failed her, Mercy." His voice was gentle. "She knew you loved her. She never blamed you or me."

"Don is right. Children of such a tender age see their parents as saviors no matter how bad things are. The guilt you feel is natural.

We've talked about that. But you're clinging too much to it. You need to move past it."

Mercy gave her an obligatory "Yes. I know."

"You have an active mind when you sleep, but simple lifestyle changes could help. Do you drink alcohol?" The doctor's ability to deliver her questions without inflection was both soothing and distressing.

"Occasionally." Mercy breathed heavy.

"Do you feel you have any issues with that?"

"With alcohol? No. No issues."

"Good, because with your mother's history, you need to be careful."

"My mother was sick. She hated the drugs. It made her aware of how dull her mind was. When she drank, she was bad but she wasn't aware of it."

"Bipolar is a serious and difficult thing. You're lucky not to suffer your mother's affliction. But alcohol can be debilitating. I'm just saying, you should be aware of what it did to your mother."

I'm not my mother.

Dr. Wright directed the questioning to Don, and Mercy turned her attention to the room in an attempt to replace the image of her daughter that the doctor so indiscriminately induced. Daylight streaming through the only window in the room did nothing to brighten the bland, generic space or, for that matter, warm Mercy, who tightened under the wet wool tension. There was a gold-framed print of Monet's *Water Lilies*, one Mercy had seen in too many offices, but that was the extent of any attempt at warmth. The walls were gray. The window shades were white eighties-style Venetian, and the leather sofa, brown and creaking. Even the tissue box that sat before her on the glass-topped coffee table was of the hospital-issue type. The one thing the office was, however, was clean. A spotless, almost obsessive-compulsive clean.

Dr. Wright herself presented a profound contrast sitting in the center of the gray sterility. Always in colorful outfits that were never mixed and matched but purchased as an ensemble at chic downtown shops. The perfect splash of scarf enhanced her deep brown complexion. It was as if Dr. Wright wanted the patient to see only her and not the room around her. Narcissism? Mercy never thought so. More likely, she was giving the patient a place to focus. If she looked at the doctor, she would be less inclined to get distracted. Mercy wanted to look at her; visually, she was a warm light in a drab world. Pretty ingenious, Mercy thought. Hate the doctor for what's on the inside, love what's on the outside. It balanced somehow.

"Well, our time is up for today." The doctor placed her pad on her lap and folded her hands on top of it.

That was it. They were free to go. Open the gates. Release the prisoners. Pulling her hands from beneath her legs, she met Don's stare. He was wearing a timid smile, tilted in a dull expression of pain, but a smile nonetheless. Smiles had become rare things between them and that day she'd gotten two. She eagerly took it and smiled back.

~

*C*lean out the attic. *Write down your dreams.* The entire ride home, those phrases Dr. Wright had spoken spun around in Mercy's brain. She was a child with homework to do. But by the time Donovan parked the SUV in their garage, those phrases had taken root. She opened the car door and it clunked against a stack of cardboard boxes piled along the wall.

"You know, the garage could use some cleaning. Maybe we should take Dr. Wright's advice. We could do it now, since we're both home."

"It's a good idea, but not today. I still have work to do."

"But Dr. Wright said…"

"I know what she said, Mercy, but she didn't mean right this second."

"I kind of want to tackle this while it's fresh in my mind."

"Why don't you, then?"

"Because Dr. Wright said we should do it together."

"I can't right now. I have a deadline and need to go over those condo plans. Go ahead and start. We'll take on the basement or something next week. Or I'll help you finish up tomorrow."

His eyes were bright with sincerity and she quashed the desire to protest. "Sounds good."

Don entered the house and closed the door behind him.

Alone in the garage, Mercy surveyed the space. The shelves were overburdened with clutter and on the floor, dozens of cardboard boxes were haphazardly stacked on top of each other. Some of the boxes held memories and souvenirs of her family's life. Those were labeled with black Magic Marker. Her eyes scanned down a stack of labeled boxes in the corner of the garage.

Joshua – 2009 first sports gear

The Twins – stuffed animals/dolls

She paused when her eyes landed on the last box with one word written on it.

Lisa

She wanted desperately to open it but she had a mission. Clean the garage, not take a tortured walk down memory lane.

Mercy slipped into the Volvo and backed it onto the driveway. When she stepped out, she was ready. Going from shelf to box, she threw away the garbage and organized the rest. After what seemed like hours, the garage was so pristine, it would make even Dr. Wright proud. Only one pile of junk remained under a blue tarp in the corner.

Mercy walked over to it and flung the tarp over. Startled, she stumbled, nearly losing her balance. She grabbed a rake leaning against the wall and, holding it handle-end out like a bayonet, took tentative steps toward the pile. With the handle of the rake, she poked at the thing coiled up on top of the heap and Mercy swore it pushed back. Throwing the rake to the side, she yelped, turned to run out of the garage and landed square into her best friend.

"My goodness, Mercy Amoretto," Mary Beth said. "You act like you've seen a ghost!" Standing in the sunlight of the open garage door, Mary Beth's alabaster skin looked almost translucent.

Mercy laughed, embarrassed. "It's a snake." She gulped a deep breath. "I think it's dead, though." She pointed to the pile.

Mary Beth tsked, walked over to the corner, and scooped the coil from the ground. Mercy let out a scream that sounded like a high-pitched, dragged-out whine. Returning to Mercy, her friend held out her hand with the thing in it. Mercy threw her arms in front of her face as if that would protect her from a lunging snake attack.

"Are you crazy?" Mercy said.

"It's not a snake, silly." Mary Beth shoved her hand closer to Mercy, making her flinch. "It's a rope."

Leaning in, Mercy examined the dangling mass and saw it was, indeed, just a rope. A woven cord of natural fibers that must have been at least an inch and a half thick. Mercy snorted and slapped a hand on her chest.

"Why so jumpy, anyway?" asked Mary Beth.

18

"Don and I went to therapy today. It always makes me edgy."

Mary Beth tossed the rope in the direction of the overflowing garbage bin.

"Wait." Mercy snatched the rope in mid air. "This might be useful."

"Seriously?"

"It's got length and it's solid. Don could use if for something I'm sure."

"I suppose. One person's junk, as they say. Wow!" Mary Beth turned in a circle to take in the whole garage. "This place sure is clean."

"Yeah. It sure is." Standing in the open space, Mercy became overwhelmed by the enormity of it.

"What's the matter?" her friend asked. "I can see it in your whole body. You're deflating."

"It didn't work, what Wright said, that cleaning out the mess would make me feel better. I don't."

"How do you feel?"

"Like I've just broom swept a dirt road. I got the twigs and leaves off, but under my feet is still a whole lot of dirt."

With the tip of her index and middle fingers, Mary Beth rubbed at the furrow between Mercy's brows as if trying to wipe away a smudge. "Don't go there. And stop doing that with your forehead. You'll create premature wrinkles. Gosh, Mercy." Mary Beth stepped back. "You're so lucky to have that gorgeous olive complexion. It's like you were dipped in the fountain of youth. All your worrying is going to ruin it when you get quotation-mark crevices between your eyes."

Mercy forced a smile and opened her eyes wide with exaggeration. Unable to maintain the fake face for long, her shoulders slumped and she pinched the crinkle that again formed there, the crinkle that had been with her like an unwanted guest most of her life.

She noticed it form after her mother got sick and the yelling started. And although Mary Beth and Donovan had tried to rub it away throughout the years, the crinkle still returned.

"Okay. You're frowning more now."

"Sorry."

"Don't be sorry. Just knock it off." Mary Beth squeezed her in a hug. "You know, you are allowed to be happy. And besides," she pulled back, "you're with me. How bad could that be?"

Mary Beth's blue-water eyes glistened with waves of excitement and inside them, Mercy saw the teenaged girl with whom she used to revel so many years before. When her mother would batter her father with insults and his return verbal bullets would threaten to catch Mercy in the crossfire, Mercy would escape to her best friend. When she and Mary Beth were together, Mercy believed she could move mountains. Taking a second look at what she'd done that day, Mercy realized she actually did move a mountain. A seriously small one, not like Everest or the Alps or anything. More like a hill, really, or maybe just an incline, but she had moved it.

"Hey, get a load of this." Mary Beth lifted an old black tire from the top of the heaping garbage bin. "This looks like something off my dad's old Studebaker." She scrutinized the relic.

"Don't tell me you're going to use that thing. That tire's so bald it shines."

"I don't want to drive on it. I was just thinking… Give me that rope?" Mercy handed it to her. "You're right. This can be useful." She slipped one end of the rope through the hole of the tire, creating a loop, and held the contraption in front of her. "The rope's thick. I bet this could hold up a lot of weight."

"You're joking," Mercy jeered.

"Why not? You've got the perfect tree for it. It's like it's meant to be."

"Throw it away. I'm too old and too tired for child's things."

"Don't be a poop. Tire swings are romantic. Isn't that what your doctor said you and Don needed, a little romance?"

"No. She said we needed to clean the junk out of the house, not make more."

"We're not making junk. We're recycling it, and I think it's a swell idea. Besides, the kids will love it."

Mercy chortled. "Right. They're going to abandon their video games and cell phones to ride an old tire swing. Besides, the girls would never swing. High places don't agree with them. Remember the Ferris wheel at the town carnival two years ago? I don't know who was greener when they got off, Kira or Kaitlyn."

"So, not for the children, then. For you."

"I don't…"

"Grab the ladder. It'll be fun." Mary Beth, tire and rope in hand, darted out of the garage. "Get a hustle on it!" Mary Beth hollered from the yard. "I'm not taking no for an answer!"

"Coming." She grabbed the aluminum ladder and dragged it across the lawn.

"Set it here." Mary Beth pointed to a spot over which hung a thick branch of the maple tree.

Mercy propped open the ladder and held onto the base with both hands. Mary Beth dumped the tire on the ground and skipped her skinny body up the rungs until she stood with one foot on the top of the ladder and another on the rung below. She swung the loose end of the rope over the branch, wobbling a bit. Mercy's heart jumped.

"Careful," Mercy called out.

"I think I need a taller ladder." Mary Beth reached up and tied a square knot, securing the rope to the branch.

"Make sure the knot is tight," Mercy yelled.

"Who was the best knot-maker in Scouts? Me, thank you very much." Mary Beth grunted as she yanked hard on the rope. "That should do it." She climbed down the ladder and tied another square knot around the tire. "There. All ready to swing. You go first."

"You did the work. You go, I'll push." Mercy folded up the ladder and leaned it on the opposite side of the tree.

As nimble as a sprite, Mary Beth slipped her legs through the tire. Her bare calves and ankles peeked out of her cropped jeans, exposing pale Irish skin that turned red at the mere suggestion of sun. Next to Mercy, whose Italian genes helped her skin glisten to a caramel glow, Mary Beth looked like she came out of a winter's hibernation. It irked Mary Beth that she was so pale, and when Mercy asked why, she would whine there was nothing fun about being the color of paste.

Not paste, Mercy thought. Porcelain. Mary Beth was beyond gorgeous and no amount of suntan would ever change that. Secretly, Mercy envied her, but not so much because of her beauty. As pale as her skin was, Mary Beth's hide was slick. Nothing stuck to her. She could walk into fire and come out wet.

It was probably because she'd lived alone her entire adult life. Her parents ran off to Paris like a couple of Bohemians when Mary Beth was just out of high school, leaving her with only a trust fund to keep her company. Too much of a free spirit to settle down with any one person, Mary Beth was always somewhat of a maverick in their domestic community, someone who believed the world was created for her to embrace.

"Ready for takeoff!" Mary Beth hollered. She planted her sneakered toes in the grass, nudged backward, and set the swing in motion.

On the modest upswing, Mercy jumped behind her friend. Upon the swing's return, she pushed her palms against Mary Beth's back. She did that until Mary Beth gained enough momentum to continue on her own. Then darting out of the way, she watched as Mary Beth pumped her legs hard back and forth, forcing the swing to rise and fall with ease. Her middle-aged friend looked like she was sixteen again, wearing an open-mouthed smile as the wind blasted the wispy bangs of her bob-cut back with every upswing and flopped them over her forehead on the down. Up Mary Beth went and down she came, up and down for minutes until she dragged her feet against the grass and wobbled to a stop.

"Whew! That was fun," she said as she dismounted the swing. "Your turn. It's super solid. Don't be afraid to really soar."

Don't be afraid. A chill crept inside her and rippled under her flesh. It wasn't a chill that came from the air. It was a chill that formed in her blood.

"You okay?" asked Mary Beth.

"Thinking."

"Quit it and get on the swing."

As Mercy raised her left leg, she struggled with her balance and realized how out of shape she'd become. She still walked almost every day and possessed what she considered a decent figure for a mother of three. Yet, her inability to easily climb on a simple tire swing bothered her.

What was that? Something sneaky invaded her brain and hid just beyond the temporal lobe where memories live. What was it she had thought just seconds before? She was out of shape? No, that wasn't it. *A mother of three.* Yes. Mercy wasn't a mother of three. She was a mother of four.

Get on the swing.

Managing to arch her leg through the circle, she stood with her left leg through the hole and the right on the other side. When Mary Beth mounted the swing, she'd lifted like a breeze into the contraption. Mercy was about to clunk her way on like a walrus clambering onto a unicycle, but it was no matter. She was going to board the thing even if it twisted her into a knot.

She lifted her right foot and, hopping on her left foot for balance, she forced her other leg through the loop. She wriggled, trying to find a comfortable position on the seat, but the ridged opening of the tire kept digging into the backs of her thighs. She waggled a little more, but no amount of shuffling could help her find a spot that felt right.

"For shit's sake, Mercy. It's a tire swing, not a Lazy Boy! Kick off already!"

"Okay, okay."

Mercy inched the tire so far back she was standing on the tips of her toes. All she had to do was lift her feet and she would be off, but that icy fear kept her feet on the ground. She was just going to have a casual swing through the air. Easy. But her feet wouldn't budge.

Break your hold from the world. Ride the swing.

She released her feet from the earth and tucked her legs beneath her. The swing made a slow joggle forward. Instead of pushing off the ground or pumping her legs to build momentum, Mercy kept her feet bent snug beneath her thighs as the tire waved around in weary slow motion.

"If you looked anticlimactic up in the dictionary," Mary Beth cracked and grabbed the tire with both hands. "There'd be a picture of you on this swing." She hauled Mercy backward.

"Wait! Wait!" Stuck in the tire, Mercy gripped the rope.

Mary Beth shoved Mercy forward and her stomach hurled ahead of her as she lurched up. On the downswing, if she had any chance of planting her feet on the ground, Mary Beth's two palms pushing on her back snatched it away. Another shove and Mercy jerked up.

"Pump, girlfriend! Pump!" yelled Mary Beth.

Mercy threw her legs out in the arch of her ascent and flopped her feet back as she came down. Up, the legs went out. Down the legs came back. Out and up, under and down. Up and down and up again until she was soaring and free-falling like a trapeze artist, with the greatest of ease. The wind created by her movement fingered through her long, thick hair and beat against her eyes. Down she plunged and up she flew. Backward she fell and upward she soared.

Her eyes opened wide, the air blasted at her pupils and, instead of closing them against the tears, she let the air wash them of all the dirt of the day. Like sunlight through a crystal, she saw the world through a prism of dancing sparkles, dazzling diamonds twinkling through the leaves of the maple tree. Mercy flew up high to where she could see the brown rooftop of her house. Roaring down again, the blanket of her green yard expanded wide. And as her yard ebbed on the ascent and swelled on the fall, an old childhood poem swirled in her mind.

How do you like to go up in a swing, up in the air so blue? Oh, I do think it the pleasantest thing ever a child can do! Up in the air and over the wall, till I can see so wide, rivers and trees and cattle and all over the countryside.

As the Stevenson poem glided around in her brain, music filled the breeze. It was humming, like the songs of birds and little girls mixed together.

Hmmm, hmmm, hmmm.

Mercy hummed along with the song. "Hmmm, hmmm, hmmm." It was one of those eternal songs from the early years of rock 'n roll that lasted through the decades. A Beatles' song about love.

"Hmmm, hmmm, hmmm," Mercy hummed and another voice hummed with her

Hmmm, hmmm, hmmm.

It was Mary Beth, just like in their youth, the two harmonizing both in life and in song. All Mercy had to do was swing and sing and her worries evaporated.

Mercy sang the opening line to the familiar song and a soprano voice sang along. They sang together until, on the breeze, an odor rose, car exhaust. At first, it was just a whiff, but as she made the sweep downward, it became stronger as if someone was revving an engine somewhere near the tree. Up she rose, and her hand slipped from the rope. She clutched at it, but couldn't grasp on, as if the wind had taken the swing from her control. Down she soared, and her throat began to burn from the exhaust. Up she went with one hand flailing in a failed attempt to grip on. Mercy feared she would be thrown from the swing. Down again, and she shoved her feet into the earth, but momentum greater than her attempt to get grounded took the swing and swung it around in a wild circle. Dizzy and coughing, Mercy dug her heels into the grass. Mary Beth's hands were on her shoulders, and she guided Mercy to a stop.

"What the hell happened up there?"

"I don't know. I was swinging and singing along with you, and then I lost control. Maybe…" She gasped to catch her breath. "Maybe it was the car exhaust that threw me. It was so noxious."

"What for the love of pizza are you talking about?"

"You were singing, you know, 'All You Need Is Love.' The Beatles. It was nice. And everything was so wonderful, but then the fumes just got to me and I lost my grip on the swing. I thought I was going to fall."

"But I wasn't singing."

"Sure you were. I heard you clear as anything."

"No, I wasn't. You were singing, though. And off key, I might add. And as far as car fumes, I didn't smell anything."

"Really?"

"Yeah. I mean, maybe they came from down the street and you caught it on the wind when you were high up."

"Maybe." Mercy tried to figure it in her head, but it all came upon her so fast, she wasn't sure what to make of it. "You sure you weren't singing?"

"I would know."

"Weird." She looked down at the fat tire around her belly. "I feel ridiculous. Help me out of this thing."

Mary Beth held the tire still, while Mercy untangled her legs from it.

"By the way," Mary Beth said. "You had an audience while you were swinging." Mary Beth pointed to Mercy's upstairs window. "Don was checking you out. He looked intrigued."

Mercy turned her attention to the window, prickling with the desire to catch him. Don wasn't there and she was crestfallen. "Just what I need. Him seeing what a spaz I am."

"He knew you were a spaz when he married you."

"Yeah, right. Look, I've got to go pick up Josh from little league." She started across the lawn.

"Don't let one goofy incident stop you from swinging on this thing," Mary Beth called after her. "You had a blast. I saw it on your face. You looked like a little girl without a care in the world. I haven't seen that look since…" She raised her voice to catch up with Mercy, who was most of the way across the yard. "Since you were a little girl without a care in the world."

Mercy gave a nonchalant wave over her head and entered the house.

CHAPTER FIVE
Sometime
In the Abyss

Walker hovered in the black void remembering the pungent stink of tobacco leaves. He couldn't smell them exactly, just remembered how the wet leaves he helped harvest from the North Carolina fields gave off a sour perfume that hit the back of his throat like a punch. Some days, the nicotine smell would put a sick in his stomach that only vomiting could rid. Sometimes he did vomit. Almost all the colored men and boys who worked in the field did, including his Pa.

But that was eons ago. How many eons, he didn't know, but there in the darkness, he longed for the nauseating smell of those leaves. Yearned for the sweltering heat of a sun long dead.

"Mammaw?" He couldn't hear his own voice. "It's Walker. Can you hear me?" He doubted his grandmother could because he couldn't hear himself.

He tried to remember how he came to the darkness, but it was like trying to remember the day he was born. One moment he was reading under the crown cover of the maple near his home. Then he blinked and his world went black. And although he saw nothing, heard no life, he knew he wasn't alone. Something lived in the dark with him. It hulked, invisible and silent, in that place where time shifted and bent in wicked ways. And it wasn't human, he feared. It was bigger than that. A fiendish ghoul waiting to devour him.

He shivered from the cold dread that hunkered inside him. "Mammaw, please hear me." No sound.

She must be worried. He'd been gone for so long, what felt sometimes like a hundred winters. But then sometimes it felt like he'd just arrived. For all his faith in God and the angels, he couldn't figure it. It was because time had changed somehow. Was he still sixteen, or was he a man of ancient years? He had no way of knowing.

Lord, in all your goodness, lemme find my way outta here. He thought of his home and his favorite relaxing spot under the shade of the grand maple. *Mighty Lord, won' you please hep me get back.*

A spark appeared in the corner of the great abyss. It was there and gone so fast he thought he'd imagined it. Except he'd seen it before. Thought he'd imagined it then, too. As happened each time that he saw the fleck of light, hope filled him. The light was less than a dot of dust, more fleeting than the glint off a knife, but to Walker, it was a beacon. That's where he had to go. He knew it, but the universe here was vast and the flash of light so brief he could never remember from which direction it came. He stared into what seemed like the future, waiting for the light to return. It didn't come. But movement did: a bend in the black, not quite a ripple, just a suggestion of a wave.

Walker held his breath. It was the fiend. He felt it in the chill that jittered underneath his flesh. It was the fiend, and it was ready to feast.

CHAPTER SIX
July 1970 ~ The Past
Before the Abyss ~ The Living Time

Summer for Anastasia Madison was when everything glistened. It was a time for fairies to lift their wings to the wind, circle and swoop, flutter the petals of flowers and flit in and out of her bedroom window. Although fairies surrounded Anastasia all year round, summer was when the ones in her room brought their friends in to play. Some fairies everyone could see. Those were the dolls piled high on her pillow and lined along her shelves. They were the pictures inside her coloring books and in jigsaw puzzles. Then there were the other fairies meant only for Anastasia. Those were the ones that chirped with the birds, splashed with the falling rain, and dazzled her dreams with magical dust.

Sitting on the edge of her bed, Anastasia caressed the wings of her favorite doll, Sparkle. They were soft, like she imagined butterfly wings would feel. It was her most special fairy doll in all her collection, one that her father said Santa's elves made to look just like her, with long golden hair, blue eyes like a clear sky, and sunshine cheeks. It wasn't the biggest doll she owned, small enough to clutch in her fist, but it possessed the most magic.

Holding the doll to her lips, she prepared to make her wish. As the warm breezes flowed through her open window, she knew it was a good time to make it, for fairies soared on summer breezes when they carried off the wishes of little girls.

"I wish Momma and Daddy were happy again," she cooed. "Tell the wind I've been good and make my wish come true."

"You do know, Booger, fairies aren't real." Ten-year-old Bobby poked his head through the doorway.

"You don't know anything!" Anastasia shot back.

"I know more than you, Booger, 'cause I'm two years older. That makes me smarter. And I'll always be older than you, so I'll always be smarter than you." He stuck out his tongue.

She wasn't stupid. She may have been only eight, but she was "pre-super-cala-cocious" as her father called her. Certainly, she understood her collection of dolls was plastic, porcelain, and paper. What Bobby didn't know was that deep inside those dolls, real fairies hid and only she could bring them out.

"Leave me alone," she hollered. "And don't call me Booger!"

"Okay, Booger, but we're getting ready to play hide-and-seek, so you can sit with your fake fairies or come out with us. Your choice." Bobby disappeared down the hall, his footsteps clumping as he descended the stairs.

Anastasia perked up. Hide-and-seek was her game. She was the best hider in the neighborhood and it was her chance to show Bobby who was the booger. With tender care, she set Sparkle on the pillow with the other dolls and bolted from her bed. When she came to her parents' bedroom, she stopped and put her ear to the door. Soft sobs emanated from within. Anastasia gave a light rap.

"Momma?" she called, her voice lilting in a little squeak. "Momma, are you all right?" The sobbing halted. "Momma, can I come in?"

The door opened. Anastasia's mother stood smiling down at her daughter. Even with swollen eyes, her smile made them dance.

Sometimes blue, sometimes green, they were the prettiest eyes Anastasia had ever known.

"Come in, Anna darling," she coaxed.

"What's wrong, Momma?"

"Nothing, sweetheart. I just worry about my precious babies sometimes. Ooh!" she yelped. "Your little brother or sister kicked me. Do you want to feel?"

Anastasia sat on the bed and placed a hand on her mother's belly. Giggles of excitement escaped her as the little person growing inside made itself known. She pressed her ear against the fabric of her mother's dress.

"I can hear it, Momma. I can hear it moving. I think it wants to come out."

"Soon, sweetheart. Very soon."

Wrapping her arms around what used to be her mother's waist, Anastasia listened to the sound inside. Swooshing and tapping, pushing and rolling. There was a real person in there, she marveled. Her mother told Anastasia once that a long time ago she was inside her belly, but Anastasia didn't remember. She was too young to remember, her mother said. It was too bad, because it sounded to Anastasia like a nice place to be.

"Are you coming, Booger?" Bobby called from downstairs.

Anastasia popped up her head. She had nearly forgotten about the game. Catching her mother's beautiful eyes, which were not nearly as swollen as before, she asked, "Can I go to the park to play hide-and-seek?"

"Of course, sweetheart. But don't stray from your brother and be home in an hour. We have to get you ready for Uncle Mickey's wedding tonight."

"I will!" Anastasia bounded from the bed and ran down the stairs. Her wish was already coming true. She helped her mother stop crying and the baby was going to help, too. She knew that new babies were like fairies. They were magical, and soon the baby would come and everyone would be happy again.

She flew out of the house. There was Bobby several yards ahead of her, racing down the road. His legs were longer than hers, but she was springy. If she ran fast enough, she could beat him to the park, which was right at the end of the street. Anastasia could spend all day, every day, at the park with its swings and jungle walks and the best climbing trees in all of Windsome, North Carolina.

CHAPTER SEVEN
June 2014 ~ The Present

A frenetic barrage of explosions burst from the living room as twelve-year-old Joshua led his computer-game character into a battle against the enemy. Blasts, booms, and the pounding rat-a-tat racket of gunfire created an assaulting clamor that plucked at Mercy's nerves, as if someone were plucking hairs from her head with tweezers. Normally she wasn't so sensitive to the rumpus her children made. Most of the time she found a paradoxical sense of serenity in the middle of their high-octane lives. But the ache in her head, which had been with her since she woke that morning, made the noise difficult to tolerate.

"Will you please turn that down!" she called out to her son.

A blur of brunette, like a hurricane gale that's swept up a lake of cocoa, stormed into the kitchen. Long legs and a lean, lanky form, stretched thin like a string of bubble gum between the fingers, plopped down onto one of the counter stools behind where Mercy stood.

"I'm sick of you stealing my stuff!" Fifteen-year-old Kira shouted over the din.

"I didn't steal it!" More cocoa and bubble gum cycloned in and sat next to her twin. "I borrowed it," Kaitlyn scoffed. "And besides, those are my jeans." She pointed to the pants Kira was wearing.

If it weren't for the subtle differences in their hairstyles—Kira parted hers on the left side and Kaitlyn down the middle—it would be nearly impossible for the average person to tell the teenagers apart.

Mercy, however, could always tell who was who at first glance. Even when they were puffy-cheeked newborns and still had the hue of blue in their irises that would shift into deep brown as they grew into their first months of life, she knew. They were her daughters, her first born children. Identical twins, possessing that eerie connection that is signature of two children who share the same chromosomes. And although they were born from one star delivered from Heaven, they divided into two distinct, beautiful souls.

Their distinction had always been obvious to her, but not so much to Donovan. It wasn't until the girls were toddlers that Donovan could tell them apart. When they were babies, he was constantly calling one girl by the other's name.

"That's Kaitlyn, dear," Mercy would correct. Their uniqueness was in their eyes, she'd explain, and Donovan would stare deep into the eyes of his infant daughters for minutes at a time just shaking his head.

"Mom," Kira whined.

"Enough, girls. Sort it out between yourselves." Mercy peeled a carrot as water in a large pot on the stove showed the first tiny bubbles of boiling.

"When's dinner?" Kaitlyn asked as she sprung from her seat, snatched up a carrot chunk, popped it into her mouth, then reached for another.

"When your father comes down." Mercy slapped at her daughter's hand. "Do something useful, the two of you, and set the table, please."

The girls obeyed, continuing to shout barbs at each other loud enough to be heard over the battle on the computer and compound Mercy's ever-escalating headache. The repetitive throb kept rhythm to the song still in her head that she'd thought she'd heard on the tire swing. That same Beatles' song she and Mary Beth would belt out as teenagers when it blared from the radio or a tape deck. The swing must have reminded her of those brief moments of freedom in her youth, evoking the memory of Mary Beth singing along with her.

"Quit it, skank!" Kira hurled the insult like a stone and it came flying in the kitchen, hitting Mercy on the side of her throbbing head.

"You're the skank!" Her sister hurled back.

Rat-a-tat. Blast. BOOM the computer game fired.

Mercy grabbed a zucchini and began to chop. The girls continued their verbal onslaught as the computer battle raged. Picking up the rhythm of the bombardment, Mercy sliced the vegetable in a methodical motion. Without looking, she chopped like a chef, her slices swift and even. And as she sliced, sliced, sliced, an odd calm came over her. And as she sliced, sliced, sliced, her gaze turned to the yard outside and landed on the maple tree.

"Hmmm, hmmm, hmmm." Slice, slice, slice. *Blast. Boom.* "Hmmm, hmmm, hmmm."

All you need is love. It was such an organic sentiment, simple, grown from the seeds of the heart. It flourished in them despite their loss and helped them stay together when grief threatened to tear them apart. It grew strong like the maple tree from where the tire swing swayed its sleepy sway. A specially chosen tree from the woods surrounding the old park where their home would be built. She remembered how all the others on their property were felled except that maple. From the moment she saw it, Mercy knew the maple, with its warm explosion of foliage, would provide the perfect amount of shade to bring comfort to their love-filled lives on Pleasant Drive. Pleasant Drive, Windsome, North Carolina. Even the name of the place where they made their home was lovely.

Blast. Boom. Rat-a-tat. Rat-a-tat.

Thud, thud thud, the pounding in her temple responded as if Joshua's computer guns were aimed directly at her. Oh, have mercy on me, she prayed in her head. *Have mercy on Mercy and make the noise stop.*

Slice, slice, slice. *Rat-a—*

"Shit!" Mercy cried out as the knife sliced through her thumb.

"Language, darling." Don, still in his business suit, had silently walked into the kitchen and was standing beside her.

"I cut myself," Mercy raised her thumb to her mouth to clean off the blood.

"Is it bad?" he asked, taking her hand in his to examine the wound.

There was compassion in his gesture. The same compassion he'd had when he swept her away from her mother's suffocating house so many years before. The tenderness of his touch, his fingers gingerly curling around her palm to see the cut more clearly, was as sweet and as gentle as his lovemaking once was. She let her hand rest in the cradle of his palm and relaxed for the briefest moment in the safety of him. But, just as it had been of late, before she would let the emotion take her too far, she pulled her hand free.

She wrapped her thumb in a paper towel. "It hurts a little, but I'm okay."

Don grabbed his briefcase from the floor next to the island counter and turned to go.

"Where are you going?" Mercy asked.

"I've got to meet with a client. He wants to write up an offer."

"But dinner will be ready in ten minutes." *But I want you to hold my hand again.*

"Save it for me."

"It's pasta primavera. It doesn't exactly keep." It came out too curt. "Can't you put him off for a half hour?" she tried with more softness.

"I'm sorry, Mercy, I can't. I've been working with this guy for over a year. If I put him off now, I risk putting him off forever."

The lid on the pasta pot rattled as the water inside came to a roiling boil.

"This is dinnertime, Don. He should know better than to drag you out now. We're a family. We have dinner together." In that single moment, her desire for him to stay became paramount. Perhaps it was the residue of their meeting with Dr. Wright that morning that brought out her insecurity or maybe it was the lingering sensation of his nurturing hand around hers that made her regret ending the moment too soon. Whatever it was, he was leaving and she didn't want him to go. "Stay with us, Don."

"I can't, Mercy. I'll be back as soon as I can." And he was out the door.

Mercy unwrapped her thumb and ran it under cool water. The blood from her cut swirled in the basin of the sink, turning the water a morbid rust color. She knew that if what was taking him out of the house wasn't important, Don wouldn't leave. Still, she'd let him go and, with the closing of the door, came back an old, unwelcome feeling.

It was a feeling born on her birthday, just six months after Lisa died. There had been whispers behind Donovan's closed office door and he'd left the house without a kiss. On her birthday. Half the day escaped without a word. After leaving four unanswered messages on his cell phone voicemail, the festering began. By the time the sun sank low in the western sky, a mood had fallen upon her so dark and agitated, she felt like she was locked in a closet with a swarm of flies. In her mind's eye, she saw her husband with some pretty young pixie. Never before that night had she doubted his devotion. But when Don walked through the door with flowers in hand, Mercy grabbed the bouquet and threw it on the floor. Some of the blooms burst from their stems, scattering petals all over the kitchen tile. Any other man would have turned and walked out, but he picked up the damaged bouquet and put the flowers in a vase with water. Then with an unexpected reserve, he draped a coat around her shoulders and led her out of the house. When they arrived at her favorite dining spot, the maître d' led them to a large banquet room in the back. There, more than 100 friends, family, colleagues, and old school chums cheered a joyous and well-rehearsed, "Happy Birthday, Mercy!"

"It takes a lot of late nights and clandestine phone calls to pull off a surprise party like this," Don had whispered. He had kept a pleasant façade for the guests, but the doleful timbre of his whisper echoed his pain. It broke her heart.

Mercy placed the steaming plates of pasta in front of her children. They never knew what had transpired between their parents that night of her birthday. They were already at the restaurant waiting for her while she was at home hurling hateful insinuations at her flower-bearing husband.

When she had spoken with Dr. Wright about the experience, the psychiatrist said it was normal for paranoia between partners to exist after the loss of a child. One doesn't think the other is grieving enough, or that they are taking on most of the weight of the loss. The psychiatrist analyzed that Mercy felt Don was walking away from her grief and toward a new relief. The truth was, she said, both were grieving equally, just differently. Mercy had taken in Dr. Wright's words then, but didn't quite comprehend them. Yet there, as she lifted her eyes to her children devouring up their dinners, she began to understand.

Before her, four chairs filled around a table that seated six. If Don were home, that would fill five. One remained empty. Always to be empty. Empty on the day of her surprise birthday party. Empty as she sat before her pasta primavera. How she wished all six chairs were filled. She twirled some fettuccini onto her fork and thought of an old proverb. "If wishes were horses, beggars would ride." She pushed her thoughts away from that place.

Still, there was something about the flowers.

CHAPTER EIGHT
September 1928 ~ The Past
Before the Abyss ~ The Living Time

Walker Jacobs may have had only two years of schooling, but he possessed the sharp mind of scholar. It was his reading that made him so smart, having learned the alphabet at age eight at a Negro school in Birmingham, Alabama. By the time his family took up in Windsome, North Carolina, he had read hundreds of books. And at sixteen, he had amassed himself a small but respectable library right in his own home.

With his thin, long fingers, Walker lifted a single plank of wood from the floor of the bedroom he shared with his brothers and sisters. On the dirt below rested a row of small hardback books. The bindings, faded and cracked down the center, faced up to reveal the titles. He slipped out his favorite and replaced the board.

Out in the main room of his shanty home, he heard the creak of the rocking chair coming from the small porch. The low throaty drawl of his grandmother singing "Let Your Light Shine on Me" flowed through the screen door. It blended like church song with the laughter and cheers of his siblings and cousins who were playing chase in the yard. He stood there, absorbing the sound until the singing stopped, the creaking subsided.

His grandmother—round and strong—came into the house carrying a large ceramic bowl. "You gonna spend some time with your stories, chile?"

"While it's still light." Walker took the bowl from his grandmother and set it on the counter. "Mmm. Them fresh-shucked peas sure smell sweet, Mammaw. Love jarrin' season, but hate lettin' go a summer." Walker's voice was still filled with the chirp of a chickadee, not yet thick with adulthood, but ready to crack at any minute.

"The good Lord made autumn, too, chile. Love each day as you love the Lord." She took an empty bowl from the shelf and set it next to the peas. On the windowsill before her cooled a sweet potato pie.

There was no glass in the window, just wooden shutters hinged to the window frame and hooked to the outside of the house. The sun shone through and lit his grandmother's face. It looked as if she was washed with a beam from heaven, as if his Pa and Ma heard her singing and shone their light as she asked in the song. Walker was glad for the sunshine. On rainy days, they had to close the shutters and the house became dark like night.

When the rain beat down, his Pa would say, "One day I'll construct a house with glass in them windows." Walker closed his eyes and pictured his Pa sitting at the family table rolling a cigarette. "Then we'll see the rain. Not jes' hear it."

His Pa could have built that house if they'd stayed in Alabama. He'd done it for the man he'd worked for. But after that night when the white men showed up on their front lawn with sticks and hoods ready for murder, they packed up and moved north. Money in the tobacco fields wasn't as good as money building things, but one day, his Pa would say, they'd have that house. That day never came.

As his grandmother sorted the peas, pitching the bruised aside, keeping the best in the bowl, the gospel tune escaped her lips and her robust hips swayed to the rhythm.

"Can I hep you some, Mammaw?"

"Oh, no. This is my quiet time. Thank the Lord the weather's nice 'nough to keep those chillen out from under my feet." She nodded out the window. "There jes' ain't 'nough rooms in this house for 'em all to play inside. Oh, your Papa would've built us a dozen rooms if only he'd had time."

"You'll have your rooms. Don't worry. Someday I'll build that house Pa promised. Soon's I raise the money, I'm gonna buy 'nough timber to make rooms for everybody."

"With plaster walls so you don't have to hear me snorin'."

Walker laughed. She sure could snore, he thought, but it didn't bother him. At least when he woke up to her growls, he knew she was alive. After his Ma passed of the fever when he was so young and his Pa dropped dead from a heart attack in the fields, he clung to the sounds of his grandmother's life. He knew she worried something fierce about him working those same tobacco fields where her oldest son had died. She had a right to. The labor was hard, and he wasn't built like his father. Where his Pa held the mass of a bison with the strength of one, too, Walker was skinny as a cattail, all arms and legs, a reed standing tall in a North Carolina pond.

His determination, though, was bigger than his leanness, and he was hell bent on bringing a better life to his kin. Besides, those fields wouldn't hold him forever. He had what some called talent. He could write. And he was going to write a book, just like his favorite author, Horatio Alger. He would sell that book, then write another and sell that, too. He would write so many books they would fill one of those giant marble city stores that he'd read about in Alger's novels. It made no matter he was colored. He was going to make enough money to buy a mansion with a cool, dry basement where his Mammaw could store her peas and he could have a library with shelves and shelves lined with stories to read.

He tucked his book under his arm and set for the door.

"Bye, Mammaw," he called over his shoulder. "Love you."

"Don't you be wanderin' outside when the sun goes down, ya hear? I know we ain't in Alabama no more, but it's still not safe for the likes of you."

"I won't. Promise." He planted a kiss on her plump cheek.

"You're a good boy, Walker. Jes' like your Papa, God res' his soul." Before he could run off, she held his wrist lightly, stopping him. "Whatcha' readin' today?" He showed her. "Oh, I gave you this one for your birthday."

"Two years past."

"Haven't you read this already?"

"So many times I practically memorized it."

"And you're gonna read it again?" A knowing smile brighter than the harvest moon grew across her face.

"Yes ma'am."

She bellowed out a deep belly laugh, as rich and ebony as the tone of her skin, and patted his cheek. "You're a good boy. A good boy."

She returned to her peas, still chuckling while Walker trotted out the door.

CHAPTER NINE
June 2014 ~ The Present

Mercy sat at the dining room table with a half-empty glass of wine held in the curve of her palm. All the children were tucked in their nooks upstairs, silent as nuns. The dishwasher hummed its domestic song while shadows cast by the moonlight danced across the ceiling. Mercy had been quietly drinking for about an hour, waiting to hear the familiar sound of Donovan's car in the driveway. It would have been more prudent to allow the fiction of a book or movie to occupy her mind. But she let wine be her companion, and the more she drank, the more her personal drama swelled. And the longer she sat alone, the more she felt she wasn't alone at all. There was a presence. She couldn't see it, but it was there. It was Death.

It had come to reside there a year and a half before. Not as a tenant, aloof and snug in its own corner. Oh, no. Death had made itself a part of the family, strutting about by day and skulking through the night, taking up space in every niche and crevice of the place. An omniscient entity that hung like fog from the ceiling and crept like a panther in the hallways. It hunched in the closets and stomped around in the basement. It was in the oven and the bathtub. It was under the bed where monsters lurked in childhood nightmares. And it was sitting across the table in not one, but all the empty chairs.

Most of the time, Mercy was able to turn her back to it, but left alone with her thoughts and her wine, she found it harder to ignore. She tilted the glass against her lips and took a long drink. A tear fell down her cheek. Alcohol had a way of targeting emotion, but something told her it wasn't the wine's fault she was crying. The tears were already there, waiting to let go. The wine was only the current on which her tears were able to ride.

She downed the rest of glass number four and pulled another bottle from the rack behind her.

"What's one more," she said. "Or three."

With the pop of the cork, she filled her glass with the room temperature Chardonnay.

"You should let that chill," she said in a low voice mimicking Donovan's. "Well, you're not here, darling," she answered in her own mocking tone. "So I guess I can do whatever I want."

She took a sip from her glass. The taste was less pleasant than when it was chilled, but taste wasn't what she was after. She took another, bigger swallow. And as she did, Death lounged across from her with its feet up, drumming its sharp, executing fingers on the tabletop.

At that moment, the house became stifling and Mercy wanted to escape it, escape her thoughts. Run from the Death house, the suffocating house—

Wait. That wasn't right. Their house wasn't the suffocating one. That house belonged to her mother. The one from which her father ran for his life. The one in which her mother took her own. And with that, Mercy understood why the flowers haunted her.

She swallowed a large gulp and topped off her glass. She remembered what she had forgotten, perhaps on purpose. But sitting at the dining room table, her hand clutching her wineglass, Mercy remembered. It was a night from decades before. Her mother had been drinking much like Mercy was at that moment, one glass of wine after another, waiting for her father to come home. A crown roast, complete with the little white paper booties on the bones, had been resting on the kitchen counter for hours.

Mercy had gone to her room but couldn't sleep. Her bedside clock was ticking toward midnight when her mother started to mutter, low curdling obscenities that grew into loud, jagged curses. When her father came home at some point in the morning, the shouting began.

"Who is she, you bastard. Who's the whore you're fucking."

She couldn't make out what her father was saying. It sounded like mumbles. There was a crack and Mercy imagined that was the sound of her mother's palm landing on her father's face. After that, a door slam.

Later that morning, Mercy found the uneaten roast in the middle of the kitchen floor. It looked like it had been tramped on. The little white booties were scattered everywhere. Her father was nowhere to be found.

Her mind zeroed in on the crown roast and the white booties, and the picture morphed into strewn petals, broken roses, and powdery bursts of baby's breath.

"Oh, Lord." She began to swoon. The cure was a massive gulp of wine. The round mellowness of the vintage had disappeared, leaving the acrid harshness of the alcohol. Her throat closed. As she let the warm Chardonnay sit in her mouth, she realized how hard it was to actually chug wine. The liquid sat there until the urge to gag was gone and she swallowed. Without a thought to the recent assault on her senses, she poured another glass. When she threw back the last of it, the levees that held back her sobs let go and the tears became their own rivers, dragging Mercy under the rapids.

Thud Thud Thudthudthud

Mercy's breath hitched at the clumping of footsteps overhead. The children were up and about. Had she been loud? She could have been blubbering like a baby for all she knew and what a fine thing that would be for Donovan to come home to.

Up she stood too fast and the room spun like a carnival thrill ride. She grabbed the back of the chair for balance.

"I've gotta clear my head," she said and walked onto the back deck.

The night air flowed over her. It was cool and soothing. Turning her head to the clouds, she saw there were none. She was looking at a clear, star-filled sky. She tripped her way down the few steps of the deck and staggered to the center of the backyard. Her head tilted back, she focused on the starry sky. In a slow circle, she turned to see as much of the heavens as she could.

"You're up there somewhere, darling. You're up there making Heaven a more beautiful place. Blink for me, sweetheart, so I can see you."

Mercy darted her attention from star to star, anticipating one would shine brighter than the rest, and that star would be her little Lisa shining down on her. The moon, lustrous against the black backdrop, shone the brightest. But just below, as if attached by a string, she saw it. The most brilliant star in the sky: white, radiant, and enchanting.

"Lisa," she sighed out, soft and somber.

Staring at the star with such intensity that all the rest of the lights turned dark, Mercy became dizzy and blissful. All the chilling sorrow that had gripped her inside the house peeled away as she stared at her child in the sky. There was Lisa, hovering with grace among the heavenly bodies.

"It's Venus," she heard Joshua say.

Mercy spun around and almost crashed to the grass. Joshua wasn't there. She knew he wouldn't be. It was only his voice in her head. He had told her that earlier in the year.

"The one that shines the brightest there," he'd said, pointing to the sky, "the one that looks like it's tied by a string to the moon—that's Venus."

Bliss left her and Mercy sunk under the weight of her son's once-spoken words. It wasn't her daughter she was looking at. It wasn't even a star. It was a planet.

"Shcrew you!" she yelled to Venus. Throwing her fist up to the sky she screamed, "Shcrew you, you piece of shit! You're a planet. A peeshofshit planet!"

The drunk that started to abate returned with force. Her head spun and her stomach churned.

"It's not fair!" Mercy ran to the maple tree and kicked it with all her drunken might.

Pain from her big toe surged up the top of her foot and into her ankle, plunging her to the ground. Sitting on the grass at the base of the tree, she clutched her foot with both hands, rocked back and forth, and sobbed.

"Momma?" a little girl's voice cooed. "Momma, don't cry."

Mercy choked down her sobs and listened. Someone heard her.

"Kaitlyn?" she called out. "Kira?" No one answered.

She scanned the yard but didn't see anyone. Lifting her focus to the windows of the house, all was dark upstairs and down. *Too much wine. Too much emotion.*

Get into the house, she thought. Get in and splash some water on your face. Pushing against the ground, she moved to get up, but there was some kind of pressure on her belly that was keeping her in place. She tried again, but the pressure was great, as if someone were leaning against her.

"Momma?" a girl called, faint and floating on the blanket of night.

The voice didn't belong to Kaitlyn or Kira. It was much younger than a fifteen-year-old's. Pushing harder with the heels of her hands, she again tried to rise, but the powerful pressure kept her in place.

"What the hell?" she muttered.

Yanking her torso forward, she couldn't break free and a thread of panic wove through her. No matter how hard she tried, she couldn't pull her body from the tree. Someone had taken an invisible spike and nailed her to the trunk.

"Momma. Don't cry, Momma."

Twisting and pulling her body, the spike held her fast.

"Momma?"

"Who are you?" Mercy called out.

"Momma?"

Throwing the entire weight of her body forward, the spike finally yanked out of the trunk and Mercy crashed over, landing face down in the grass.

Little girl cries reverberated around her and Mercy lifted her head. There was no telling from which direction the cries were coming; they seemed to just float about. Could it be a child from the neighborhood, she wondered. Had her outburst frightened the little girl?

"Hello?" Mercy called out. The crying intensified and fear forced Mercy to her feet. She ran toward the house, taking a moment to shoot a look back at the tree. Running and looking at the tree, she slammed into Mary Beth.

"Whoa, honey," Mary Beth exclaimed, grasping Mercy by the shoulders. "What's the matter?"

Breathless and flustered, Mercy said, "Something really weird just happened."

Mary Beth tilted her head and raised an eyebrow. Mercy tried to follow her gaze, but it made her woozy. "More likely you've just been drinking too much. Whew." She waved a hand in front of her face. "I can smell it. How much have you had?"

"Too much, like you said, and it got the best of me."

"It always does. Come here." Mary Beth led her to the picnic table. "Let's sit for a minute and talk." She helped Mercy onto the bench and sat beside her. "I heard you yelling at someone. Was there somebody here? Was it Don?"

"No. Don's not here. He's with a client signing a deal."

"Well, that's a good thing, isn't it?"

Mercy didn't answer, but by the turn in Mary Beth's lips, she knew she didn't have to.

"He is with a client, Mercy. Don't start that crap again."

"I know. I know. I started drinking and I let my mind take me to some awful places."

"So who were you yelling at out here?"

At Venus for not being Lisa. "I had to get outside and…" The tears she could explain, but what about the rest of it?

"And what?"

"Mary Beth, I heard something. A little girl crying. And calling out my name. 'Momma. Momma.'"

"Are you sure she was calling to you? Maybe it was someone in a nearby house. I mean, no one calls you Momma."

"Lisa did."

"Oh, honey." Mary Beth put an arm around Mercy's shoulders and squeezed.

"I know." They sat silent for a moment, then Mercy told her friend about how she was pinned to the tree and couldn't get up. "I'm scared."

"Don't worry." Mary Beth leaned in a little closer to Mercy. "There's an explanation. When did you hear this voice?"

"A few moments ago. Out there." She waved toward the vicinity of the tree.

"What were you doing when you heard the voice?"

Mercy considered the question. She was pinned against the tree, but she wasn't doing that. It was being done to her. What was she doing before that? Feeling sorry for herself. Drinking herself into oblivion. Crying.

"Crying. No, sobbing."

Mary Beth lifted the side of her lips in a full grin. "Mm hmm."

"Don't look at me like that. I know what I heard and I know what I felt. I was pinned to the tree and I heard this little girl calling out to me telling me not to cry."

Mary Beth put her palm on top of Mercy's hand. "Look, you're drunk. Don is gone and you're scared and lonely. The cries are likely a result of your own drink-imbued brain telling you to calm down before Donovan comes home. And you weren't pinned to the tree. You were paralyzed by your own sadness." She gave a little snort. "And too stewed to stand up."

"Wow," said Mercy, awestruck. "How can you think so clearly at a time like this?"

"I'm not juiced."

Mercy stood and staggered back a bit.

Mary Beth caught her arm and helped steady her. "You better clean up and get into bed before Don gets home. He doesn't have to know about your little date with Kendall Jackson."

"You're a good friend." With grand flurry, Mercy threw her arms around Mary Beth's neck and almost dragged her down to the ground with her.

Mary Beth kept them both upright. "Okay. Okay. Don't you start getting all worked up again. Get inside. And for all things sacred, brush your teeth. I'll wait here until I know you're safe."

Mercy let go of Mary Beth and zigzagged into the house. From the kitchen window, she gave her friend a wave and watched as Mary Beth crossed the yard and ducked through the gap in the hedges. Without intending to, Mercy's eyes turned toward the tree. Mary Beth was probably right about most everything, but she was certain, drunk or not, she heard the little girl's voice.

Lisa.

CHAPTER TEN
September 1928 ~ The Past
Before the Abyss ~ The Living Time

Walker strolled across the patchy dirt of his front yard, dodging his cousins as they ran around him in a game of chase.

"Hey, Walker!" young Jebediah hollered. "Come join us."

"Cain't today, Jeb. Only gotta bit a light left."

"Ahh, you gonna do that dumb readin'. That ain't no fun."

"You say that 'cause you don't know how. I'll learn ya if ya want."

"Nah, learnin's borin'."

"Suit yerself."

Walker watched as his three cousins and two brothers ran around the yard in erratic circles. He couldn't tell who was doing the chase or who was being chased. He doubted they even knew, which was half the fun. They just needed to run free. Sundays were days to do that. Every other day was a day for work, and for the young ones, work and school. Even the youngest cousin, at a scant eight years old, labored in the produce fields in the dawn hours. His sisters were spared the hard labor, but they worked the chores of the house in the mornings and evenings. Sundays were a day to play and to relax under the shade of a maple tree with a fine book.

He turned from the boys and headed toward the small wooden shed his Pa erected on the side of the yard. Beside it, his little sister crouched, examining something in her palm. She was the last of his siblings born before his Ma died. He crouched down next to her.

"Whatcha' got there, Bug?" Everyone called her Bug because she was fascinated with insects. Her real name was Sophie. He wanted to call her that because it was pretty like her. But she liked Bug.

"It's a 'pillar. It's so furry. All its lil' legs tickle me when it crawls." She giggled. "Ain't it cute?"

"Not so cute when it's chewin' up the collards in the garden."

"I'll keep it away." She sat back on her heels and rested the hand with the caterpillar in it on her lap. Her eyes hit the book in her brother's grip. "Walker?"

"Yeah, Bug."

"I get feared when you go off by yerself. I heared Miss Bessie say a Negro boy got kilt right in the middle a day las' week. No reason. White kids just beat him like they was beatin' a dog gone crazed and threw him in the river."

"Don't you pay Miss Bessie no mind. She loves to stir trouble. 'Sides, just goin' up yonder." He pointed down the dirt road that led away from their yard. "Ain't but a mile."

"Mile's a long way."

"Nah, it ain't. You walk more than that to school."

"But I ain't alone when I'm walkin'. I got Jeb and the others with me."

"I ain't alone neither."

"Y'aint?"

"Nah. I got Ma and Pa watchin' over me and the Good Lord, too."

"Ah heck, Walker. You know what I mean."

She shook her head to get some of the gnats away from her face. The blue yarn that served as ribbons to hold her hair, tied in two knots on the side of her head, flapped with the motion.

"Don't you worry none," Walker said. "I'll be home 'afore bedtime."

"Promise?" He could feel her start to wilt. "'Cause with Ma and Pa gone, you's the only one left to care fer us. 'Sides Mammaw, that is."

"Promise. And I'll read you a story when I get back."

She smiled a brilliant smile. He kissed her temple and rubbed his nose against her cheek. She giggled. "That tickles like the 'pillar."

Walker got to his feet. "'Member whatcha said 'bout keepin' that thing away from the garden."

"I will," and she went back to studying the creature in her palm.

The air was warm with just a bit of autumn crisp around the edges. It would be another month before the nights fell too quickly, and Walker embraced the still-long days. He sauntered down the dirt road toward where the giant maple tree stood waiting off to the side for him. The sun cast an elongated shadow of his figure that matched his stride. The next morning he would have to return to the tobacco fields. But on that Sunday evening, he would lean his back against the tree and escape from rural North Carolina to the streets of New York City where Ragged Dick was shining shoes.

CHAPTER ELEVEN
June 2014 ~ The Present

Mercy awoke with fear in her throat. She peeled back the sheets, damp with her sweat, and gained control of her panicked breathing. Beside her, Donovan slept on his side, facing away. How she wanted to wrap her arms around him and let the heat of his body bring relief from her nightmare. Instead, she touched the back of his neck with the lightest brush of her fingertips. It helped a little. Although it was hours before sunrise, she sat up to keep from falling back to sleep. Dreams had a slithery way of starting where they stopped if sleep came too swiftly after waking. From her puffy lips and her still rapid heartbeat, she knew she did not want to return to the dream she'd left behind.

Through the open window wafted the spicy scent of geraniums from the garden below. Mercy stood and a smack of dizziness hit her hard. It seemed all the wine she'd drank hadn't quite made its way through her bloodstream. She leaned against the windowsill and inhaled deep breaths. Fresh air. That's what she needed.

As she descended the stairs, her nightgown, which fell just below the knee, swept its soft fabric against her legs. She walked through the dark rooms into the kitchen and out onto the back lawn. Cool grass caressed the bottoms of her bare feet. The night air felt divine on her skin. A few steps more through the grass and she stopped. Before her, the tire swing swayed in the gentle breeze. The backlit moonlight around the dark circle of the empty swing made it look like a penumbra around the eclipse of the sun.

So tranquil you look with no burdens to bear. No bodies to carry.

The tire swayed, coy and teasing. It had an attitude of desire in its slight motion as if to say it wanted to carry someone. That it was no burden at all. It wanted to carry Mercy.

Her family asleep and the hedges as her camouflage, Mercy approached the swing. In nothing but a thin, sleeveless nightgown and a pair of panties, she anticipated mounting it. The temptation pulled at her greater than the expected high of any drug. Mercy didn't want to just ride the swing. She ached to be a part of it.

But why? Why was she out there in the wee hours of the night, longing for the romance of a makeshift swing made from discarded parts and not wrapped around her husband? Why was she yearning to slip her legs through the hole in the rubber as if she were climbing onto the lap of a lover? When she awoke from her nightmare, she should have allowed Donovan to hold her through the tremors until the warmth of their bodies took them to that healing place of lovemaking. He would have loved her. He would have loved that she wanted him. There was still time.

She looked toward the house to see if there was any movement inside. None. The house was dark and all in it were asleep. To go in and wake Don at that point would be artificial. He would feel it, and there would be no love to be made.

She turned back to the swing. It was moving. Not just swaying from the breeze, but rising. All by itself. The wind hadn't increased and was not strong enough to push the swing that high, but there it was, lifting up as if propelled by a body. But there was no body in it.

Mercy stumbled backward. *What the hell?* What she saw didn't make sense. The swing rose high in one direction and fell back in the other. It rose up and fell back down. A yelp escaped her and she started running toward the house. When she reached the deck, she turned back. The swing was motionless, the rope pulled straight by the gravity of the tire. *First I'm hearing things. Now I'm seeing things.*

Her mind told her to go inside, but she took two steps toward the maple instead. Another careful step forward and the tire began to rotate counter clockwise on the end of the rope. She lifted her face to feel the slight breeze she'd felt a moment before, but the air was as still as fear. With her stomach churning from the effects of the alcohol she'd consumed hours before, she inched back in the direction of the house. The tire swing froze in place. She took a step forward and the tire turned in a drowsy, 360-degree circle. Another step forward and it began its journey around again. Before the tire reached halfway, Mercy moved her right foot behind her and her left behind that. The swing reversed with a snap and hung rigid, the open hole facing her as if demanding her approach.

"Oh my God," she whispered, her breath heaving. Despite her mounting terror, she made another step toward the swing. It began to rotate again. When she got right up to it, she placed her trembling hands on the tire. There was no movement beneath her palms. The swing was still. She turned it one way, then the other, and it gave no resistance. "It's just a swing." *That moves on its own.*

She stepped back. It was an illusion, she thought. She'd imagined it. She was still in a dream state or still drunk. She turned and walked toward the house. The shriek of an owl cracked the calm. Mercy jolted in an about face to see the tire swing hurling around in a cyclonic spin, so fast the tire was a blur.

She gasped and fell to the ground. *Go in the house. Run. Run!* But when the swing slowed to a gentle sway, Mercy got to her feet and went to it. Its movement was like an uncanny invitation she couldn't resist. Her heart racing, she grabbed the rope and slipped her left leg through the tire. Her grip firm enough to fire the white in her knuckles, she slid her right leg through. With her tiptoes, she nudged backward as far as she could go. "God help me." Her voice cracked and she kicked out her legs.

The muscles tightening in her forearms as she gripped the rope, she let the swing take her wherever it was going to take her. She didn't pump or kick off the ground. She just let the swing go. But when the swing wobbled forward then teetered back, she realized it had no self-propulsion. She jammed her feet in the grass and sat still for a minute. How could she believe an inanimate object held life? That would be impossible. The swing got caught in a vortex of wind, one so tight it only affected a small space. That was all it was. A freak natural occurrence. Happened all the time.

Inching backward, she set off again, throwing her legs out and shoving them back under her to keep the swing in motion. She pumped and pumped until she was soaring high into the night. And as she soared, nothing bad happened. Lightning didn't strike her. She wasn't hurled into an alternate universe. She was just swinging. Up and down. Up and down. She was flying. Up and down. Up and down.

Hmmm, hmmm, hmmm.

The sound was like static and it rang in her ears. She stopped pumping, letting the swing ascend and fall by the momentum she'd created.

Hmmm, hmmm, hmmm.

The increase in her heart rate was immediate. What she was hearing she'd heard before. It was humming, created by her movement through the air. Coming to her like the strange sounds of creatures, like frogs or crickets, who sang when darkness fell. But the melody was clear, known to her.

Mercy sang the first line of the song, and underneath her own voice she heard another, the same soprano harmony she'd heard before. She stopped singing and the other voice stopped, too. Cold spread up her arms and the back of her neck and Mercy found it hard to breathe. The first time she rode the swing, that same voice came to her, and Mary Beth said she wasn't the one singing. There, all alone in the night, that voice had come to her again.

Thrusting her legs out, she built more momentum, and the air waved around her as she rose and fell.

Hmmm, hmmm, hmmm.

She waited for the lyrics, but no lyrics were sung, just the humming. So, Mercy sang the opening lyric again. And the harmony, in the pitch of a little girl, returned. When Mercy sang, someone sang with her. When she stopped only the humming remained. So, Mercy kept on singing and the girl accompaniment was there but that time she wasn't alone. Someone else had joined them, although not in song.

His little blacking-box … looked sharply in the faces … Shine yer boots, sir?

Mercy hushed. It was a boy, but as she thought might happen, when she stopped singing, the other voices stopped. She couldn't make out all his words because her own singing covered them, but it was definitely a boy. She began to sing again and the others came back.

It could have been the sound of a distant television seeping through an open window, a boy reading aloud somewhere, a girl singing an old familiar song. But how disquieting and equally compelling it was that, except for the humming, the voices only came concurrent with hers. She wondered how long the bearers of those voices had been there, how long they would remain.

Although the presence of those voices frightened Mercy, they also beguiled her, and Mercy realized why she was so compelled to ride the swing. When she had gotten out of bed, she had come to the swing to hear the girl's voice she'd heard earlier in the night, only she hadn't consciously realized that. Only when the humming came to her, clear as it had when she rode the swing the first time, did Mercy understand. Someone was reaching out to her—and Mercy was reaching back. She sang, and the voices arrived.

All you need is love.

Our ragged hero ... I am afraid he swore sometimes.

~

What sounded like thunder crashed through Donovan's sleep and woke him. Dawn had yet to break and Mercy was not by his side. When he had fallen into bed, the night was peaceful and the air was calm. But the winds had changed and, as the sheers lunged and snapped like startled snakes, he feared a storm. He lifted his tired body from the bed and crossed to the window.

As he grasped the frame to close it, he glimpsed a sweep of motion: a bird, dipping with expanded wings before ascending up above the trees. When the motion came again, he knew it wasn't a bird. The motion came from the maple tree. Up and back it swept. It was the tire swing. Someone was riding it. Although the person was draped in shadow, he knew by the long, flowing hair and the shapely form that it was his wife.

Earlier, after coming home from the psychiatrist's office, Don stood in that very spot in their bedroom, watching Mercy ride the swing. In the light of day, he witnessed her transform from stressed and pensive to a vision of mirthful loveliness. She was the Mercy he'd fallen in love with when they were just teenagers. His first love. His only love. They were two kids lost in each other with forever in front of them.

Well, he chuckled, two kids and a third wheel. No matter how in love he was, there was no coming between Mercy and Mary Beth. Not having any siblings or family of her own, Mary Beth considered Mercy a sister, and she was always tagging along, invited or not. It irritated him sometimes, but he knew Mary Beth had also been Mercy's savior.

It was Mary Beth, not him, who kept striking the flint to spark Mercy's soul after her mother had died. Just shy of twenty years old, sophomore year in college, right before exams, and Mercy found her mother. Naked in the bathtub, an empty bottle of Smirnoff on the floor and a tub filled with the blood that had drained from her opened wrists. Mercy called Mary Beth first, and Mary Beth called him.

It pricked a little that Mercy hadn't called him directly. They'd been together three years at that point, but they weren't yet married and Mary Beth had been in Mercy's life since forever before that. He knew he couldn't give Mercy what she had needed then. Standing before the open window, watching his wife sail on the swing, he thought, go down to her. Make up for all that had been lost—Lisa, time, they'd almost even lost Mercy.

The sight of his wife so carefree on the swing swelled his heart and his penis. If she were with him, he'd make love to her. But that would be selfish. Even from his upper roost, even with the darkness shrouding her face, he knew his wife was experiencing something he couldn't disturb. Still, he shivered with unease. She was a strong woman, but after Lisa's death, he feared her emotions skated along a fragile edge.

He brushed off his apprehension and shut the window. "I love you, Mercy," his voice too soft for her to hear. "I hope you're happy tonight."

Don climbed into bed. Before closing his eyes, he looked at the clock.

2:35 a.m.

CHAPTER TWELVE
July 1970 ~ The Past
Before the Abyss ~ The Living Time

"Seventeen! Eighteen! Nineteen! Twenty! Ready or not, here I come!"

Bobby's bellow was distant and weak by the time it reached Anastasia, who was sitting on a branch high in the maple tree. Her body was snug against the trunk and her feet dangled without fear beneath her. It took her only minutes to shinny up the tree, a chimp lifting the weight of her own body as if it had no weight at all. She sat in the spot where she'd hidden many times before. There was no doubt Bobby knew where she was. Still, she felt invisible among the dense growth of leaves. Invisible because she knew she would be left alone until everyone else was tagged out.

The way they played hide and seek was that the seeker had to tag out the hiders, not just spot them. Bobby had to call out that he found Anastasia in the tree then tag her before she reached the goal. No way would Bobby call her out first or even second. Whenever she hid in that spot, aloft on a high branch, he always saved her for last. High places for Bobby were like dark forests for Anastasia. They scared him. So, Anastasia had plenty of time to sit in her magical place among the bird nests and daydream.

Peering through the many small openings in the thick puffs of green, she could see nearly her whole neighborhood. She saw the road that separated the park from her street and, even though it was several houses away, she could spy the top of her own house. From so far off, it surprised her how small her house looked. How could it look so tiny, she thought, yet feel so enormous when she was inside it?

"I found you, Dougy!" Bobby hollered, turning Anastasia's attention back to the world below.

Dougy Rogers darted out from behind a boulder and, after a short chase, scooted passed Bobby. He made it to the goal without being tagged. The goal was a drinking fountain, a metal pipe sticking up from the ground with a metal bowl and spout on top. It was one of Anastasia's favorite joys on hot summer days in the park. The water from it was always cold and tasty. How it got so cold, she didn't know. She knew ice cubes stayed cold in the freezer because the freezer was plugged into the wall. But there was no plug on the drinking fountain, just a pipe in the earth.

Someone must have put a plug under the ground, she thought, and then grew grass over it. Or maybe the water came from a stream in the woods. A bubbling stream filled with clean, pure water. It would, by its own energy, pump through the earth and up the pipe to the spout. The water would always be cold because the trees would always keep the stream in the shade. That was the answer she liked best. Looking down, she watched Dougy bend his head over the metal bowl and let the water from the fountain run into his mouth. Anastasia found herself smacking her lips.

It was just the right amount of hot outside to make the summer perfect. The faint breeze that brushed through the maple rustled the leaves enough to mask her movement as she shifted position to look around. From her omniscient seat, she could see where each of her friends was hiding. She giggled with glee as Bobby called them out one by one. And though her brother was good as the seeker, on that day, the hiders were all either too fast or too tricky. They avoided getting tagged, reaching the security of the drinking fountain. When Anastasia was the only one left, she knew her time in the tree was almost through. And there came Bobby, marching toward the maple.

"I know you're up there, Booger! It's where you always hide when I'm it. You have no imagination."

That wasn't true, Anastasia thought. She had plenty of imagination. Her imagination brought the cold water up from the stream in the wood right through the pipe of the fountain. She bet when Bobby drank from that spout he never once thought where the water came from.

"Jeepers, Anna, get down already. You're holding up the whole game!"

Anastasia didn't budge, letting out only the slightest snicker then allowing her mind to wander away from her brother below. She still had a smidge of time left before he got that annoyed face when his cheeks turned red and the muscles in his neck popped forward. That's when she would climb down.

A swirling breeze swam through the leaves and, with that imagination Bobby boasted she didn't have, among the noise she heard a voice. At first, it was like bird song, but then it sounded like a boy. Not Bobby. Bobby was yelling at her from below. The boy's was another voice, one in the air. One in the tree. Closing her eyes, she listened. In her mind, she saw a boy a little older than her brother. He looked smudged and rather shabby, and he was shining shoes on a city street corner. His clothes were baggy and worn. Anastasia didn't know how she conjured such a character, but there he was, kneeling before her in his torn pants and oversized coat.

He wore a vest, all the buttons of which were gone except two, out of which peeped a shirt which looked as if it had been worn a month.

The poor boy was homeless, Anastasia thought, but he would be okay. She didn't know what exactly was in store for him, but in her heart she knew this boy wasn't sad, just working hard. And in the boy's future, there was a happily ever after.

"Anna!" Bobby yelled. "For Jiminy's sake. It's getting layeet!" Bobby drew out the last word in a way that said his neck muscles were straining.

She peered down, but her brother wasn't looking up at her. Instead, he was looking around at the ground and she wondered whether he really saw her at all. Throwing his hands up in a gesture that said he didn't have a clue, he walked away from the tree and over to the merry-go-round. He knelt down and searched underneath.

"He knows I wouldn't hide there," she murmured to herself. "It's too dangerous."

"What are you doing," someone hollered. "She's in the tree!" It was Dougy looking typically miffed. "Holy Right There, Bat-turd. You were staring right at her!"

Bobby stood and turned toward the maple. His eyes followed the trunk up toward the leafy top and when his gaze met hers, his expression became confused. "Oh yeah," he said. Straightening his stance, he yelled, "Come on down, Booger! It's been over an hour and we have to go to Uncle Mickey's wedding."

"You've got to tag me out!" Anastasia called back.

"I'm not climbing up there!"

"You have to! It's the rules."

It was rotten, but she couldn't help it. He was so afraid of heights and she knew he wouldn't do it, but he'd been calling her Booger all day and she just wanted a little fun. With a huff that she could hear rise all the way up the trunk, Bobby grabbed a low-hanging branch and swung one leg over. He was slow and careful. As he made it to a middle branch, just to tease, Anastasia scooched up higher. To her surprise, Bobby kept going, determination splayed across his face. Higher still, Anastasia climbed, keeping one eye on her brother. She saw him reach for a branch above his head, but his arm was shaking and he snatched it back to secure himself in place. He was afraid, Anastasia realized, and guilt crept into her gut. He was her brother, and even though he called her Booger, she didn't want him to get hurt. She made her way down, a nimble dance from branch to branch, until she was just above Bobby's reach.

"Ha!" he cheered as he swung a hand out to tag her leg. Missing by an inch, he faltered, one foot slipping out from under him.

Anastasia let out a squeak and scurried to aid her brother, but his other foot slipped and it looked like he would tumble. Throwing his arms around the trunk, Bobby kicked his feet up until he was able to balance on the branch. Her body as weightless going down as it was climbing up, Anastasia planted herself on the same branch as her brother.

"Let me go first," she said. "Just follow me and you'll be fine."

"I don't need your help, Booger," Bobby snapped and with cautious step moved down the boughs until he was safe on the earth.

Seconds later, Anastasia felt the bouncy grass under her feet. She didn't blame Bobby for getting angry. She shouldn't have taunted him and he was probably embarrassed. He marched ahead of her, out of the park, across the road, and onto the street where they lived. Anastasia sprinted and caught up with him. His eyebrows curled in a glower and his lips locked in a pout. She didn't think he was going to talk to her. Though, after a few moments of walking in silence, he softened.

"How'd you do that," he asked.

"Do what?"

"Hide so good in the tree."

"I don't know."

"I swear I didn't see you at all until Dougy pointed you out. How could he see you and I couldn't?"

Anastasia shrugged. "Beat you home," she shouted, darting in front of her brother. The heavy patter of Bobby's quickening step grew louder behind her. She sprang harder, and the two raced each other up the street toward their house that, from her current vantage point, was growing larger by the second.

CHAPTER THIRTEEN
June 2014 ~ The Present

The alarm clock did its job waking Donovan from a deep sleep. He groaned and opened his eyes to the blast of sunshine that flooded the room. Definitely morning and the ruckus that was coming from his children downstairs proved it. His tongue was rough, as if dredged in bitter flour, from sleeping with his mouth open. He smacked his lips a few times, but knew only a toothbrush could cure it. He threw the sheets off his body and watched as they cascaded down onto the empty side of the bed where Mercy usually slept. After such a late night, he was certain she'd still be asleep. Although from the commotion erupting below, it was no wonder she was awake.

He hauled his body out of bed and pushed his feet into slippers. In the bathroom, he turned on the water in the sink, cupped his hands under the stream, and splashed the sleep from his face. When he looked up, he saw he couldn't splash away the crevices that had formed on his forehead or the lines at the sides of his eyes where the crows had landed, leaving their footprints behind. Forty-one and he looked like his father. He was even wearing plaid pajamas with the collared shirt like his father used to. Not a terrible thing, really. He always thought his dad a giant among men, a great businessman and provider. Don was okay with the PJs but wasn't yet ready to wear his father's face. He brushed his teeth and headed downstairs.

No more than two steps down, his son came barreling up. Don shoved his body against the railing but not before Joshua stumbled into him.

"Hold up there, Champ." Don grabbed onto Joshua's biceps. "Why the hurry?"

"I forgot my backpack and the bus will be here in like one second and I can't find Mom."

"What do you mean you can't find Mom?"

"I can't find her. She's nowhere."

"She's got to be somewhere. Did you check the basement? She could be doing laundry."

"Yup and nope, she's not there." Joshua raced his lanky, adolescent body up the stairs and out of sight.

"What about your sisters?" Don yelled after him, but there was no answer.

Can't find her, he worried. What did that mean?

Entering the kitchen, the scene was bedlam. Kaitlyn and Kira were screaming at each other, their voices like screeching tires. The refrigerator door was wide open. Cabinet doors were ajar. Strewn-about bread slices, half-filled cereal bowls, scattered papers, spilled milk, and jelly dirtied the counters. Thumping footsteps from his frantic son pounded above. And amid it all, Mercy was nowhere to be found. Don shut the refrigerator door.

"You're such a bitch!" Kaitlyn yelled at her sister.

"I didn't say anything!" Kira yelled back.

"Girls!" Don hollered.

"Then how did he know?" Kaitlyn swung at Kira, grabbing a long, thick mass of her hair.

Don inserted himself between his daughters, holding each back by a shoulder. "Settle down!"

"But she—" Kaitlyn started.

"I don't want to hear it," said Don, firm but not angry. "And let go of your sister's hair."

Kaitlyn dropped the tangle of brunette and locked her hands into fists.

"What's going on here?" he asked.

"Kira told Mark I was seeing Billy, so now Mark hates me."

"You are seeing Billy," Kira shot back.

"Am not!"

Kaitlyn lunged her body around Don, her hand thrust out to grab her sister, but Don caught her.

"Enough," he yelled. The two clamped their mouths shut, their eyes continuing to shoot flames at each other. With forced calm, he asked, "Where's your mother?"

"Don't know," said Kaitlyn.

"Haven't seen her," said Kira.

"You're still a bitch," Kaitlyn jabbed.

"Young lady." Don shot a forefinger in Kaitlyn's direction. "Use that word one more time and I'll take your phone away for a week." Kaitlyn opened her mouth to object, then shut it. "Smart girl."

Kira stormed out of the room. Kaitlyn pulled open the refrigerator door with a force that showed Don she still had a mad on, grabbed a yogurt and tossed it in her insulated lunch bag. Seeing her sister's lunch bag still on the counter, she grabbed another yogurt and threw it in like she was throwing a punch. God, Don thought, their attitudes were as big as the whole house. Fifteen. Mercy warned him the day would come when his little darlings would grow fangs, but he had scoffed at the notion. One day they were a couple of twin foals learning to walk. The next day, they're cussing and pulling each other's hair over boys. How did that happen? He shook his head and a smile tweaked at the corner of his lips. One thing was evident. They were gorgeous just like their mom. Athletic and tall with bright, brown eyes that were sure to send hearts fluttering in the chests of every teenage boy they batted them at.

Kaitlyn turned around and grabbed a couple of napkins from the holder next to the kitchen sink. With napkins in hand she stood, a look of puzzlement on her face.

"You okay there, Pumpkin?"

Staring out the kitchen window, she said, "I just found Mom."

Don looked where she was staring. "Oh my Lord." There was Mercy, still in her nightgown, swinging on the tire swing. "She couldn't have," he whispered, but knew she had. "Kaitlyn honey, finish getting ready for school."

"That's weird, Dad." She zipped up the lunch bags and left.

"Tell your brother and sister I'll drive you," he hollered. After taking in a deep breath, he stepped out onto the deck.

There he stood. Like so many times in their lives together, she stopped him. He couldn't move. All he could do was watch. Her tan sculpted legs guiding her through the air, nightgown hitched up, exposing her white, cotton panties. Under the sheer fabric of her lingerie, he could see the form of her breasts, still round, still firm, despite the many mouths that had fed upon them.

Her eyes were closed to him. She didn't know he was there. Like a voyeur, he watched her swing, took in all the curves of her body, reveled in the seductiveness of her. He could watch her all day and if he did nothing, didn't move, he knew she would swing through the hours until the moon replaced the sun and when the moon went to rest, she would still be swinging. And Don would watch her and never grow tired of the sight.

That's exactly what she'll do.

Mercy would go on swinging. She had already been swinging since 2:30 in the morning, perhaps earlier. Some five or more hours she'd swung on that tire, and Don knew without a doubt, she would keep on swinging until someone stopped her. It could be another five hours or another five days. She was trapped somewhere. Somewhere in her head. Just like she'd been trapped before. He'd seen that face. Thought it peaceful then, too. Didn't want to interfere with it. But that was a mistake. And as he watched her swing, he knew he couldn't make that same mistake twice. One cautious step at a time, he approached his wife until he was standing just to the side of where she was swinging.

In his best nonchalance, he said, "Mercy."

She rose up without a glimpse of knowledge he was there. Down she came, up again she rose, and she was singing a song.

He cleared his throat and a little louder, he called, "Mercy."

Up and back and up. No change.

Louder still, "Mercy!"

No response except for her singing. Up she went. Down she came.

As she soared behind him, he took a step in closer. When she descended, he grabbed the rope right above Mercy's head.

"Oh!" she yelped.

The swing wavered about until Don, with one hand on the tire, steadied it.

"What are you doing?" He hoped he sounded cool.

"I … I don't know." Her brow furrowed. "I was swinging."

"Yes. You were." He took a deep breath, rehearsed the words in his head, and said, "Have you been out here all night?"

She sat motionless in the loop of the tire, the crinkle between her eyebrows growing deeper. "What time is it?"

"Seven-thirty. The children couldn't find you. I saw you here late last night, and now you're here still."

"Seven-thirty?"

"Yes."

She stood up, the tire circling her waist. "I lost track of time." Lifting her left leg, she tried to pull herself from it, but her foot caught in her nightgown.

"Let me help you."

Don held the swing firm and placed his body close to hers so she could lean on him. Mercy pressed against him and using him as leverage, dismounted the swing. Her body felt warm against his side.

"Mercy." With a tender touch on her shoulders, he moved her to face him. "Sweetheart. Are you all right?" Searching her dark brown eyes, he saw a universe, mysterious and distant. "Mercy. Help me. Talk to me."

"I…" She blinked several times. "I couldn't sleep. It was my dreams. My dreams were … busy, and they woke me. And my head hurt. It feels like I've had a headache for days. I needed some air, so I came out here." She was coming back to him, re-entering the solar system. "I thought a ride on the swing would help relieve some pressure."

"Did it?"

"Um hmm." She nodded. "But…" She blinked.

He gave her the time she needed. They were cracked as a couple, but they weren't broken. "What is it?" A careful prod.

"Nothing. It's silly," and a guarded smile formed on her lips. She turned as if to go into the house but turned back. "I heard children."

She trusted him. Good. "When?"

"Last night. This morning. All the while I was swinging. A boy and a girl." She waited and he waited. He breathed and she blinked. "She was humming and … and singing. And he was reciting something."

Her smile, barely there, hardened a bit as her lips tightened together.

"What do you mean all the while you were swinging?"

"All the while. That's all." The wisp of her smile disappeared.

"Who were they?"

"I don't know, but they were near enough to hear."

"All night?"

"I know it sounds strange, but I heard them."

"But you didn't see them."

"No." It was soft, distant.

"How old do you think they were?"

She took a breath. "It was hard to tell. The girl sounded small, maybe Lisa's age when…" Her eyes drifted off to the side.

"And the boy," Don said. "How old did he sound?"

She looked back at him, swallowed. "A bit older. They weren't having a conversation or anything. It was like they were together, but not together."

"The voices are gone now?"

She nodded. She'd said she'd heard them all the while she was swinging. He'd only just stopped her from swinging. Had she heard the children even while he was standing next to her?

"Mercy, you were on the swing for over five hours." She bristled. "I'm just saying. Maybe you thought you heard them."

She put her arms across her breasts as if aware of how exposed she was. "I shouldn't have said anything." She walked toward the house. Her back was straight, head held high.

Donovan knew her posture was a shield, standing tall when she was really crumbling. She was a cat under attack, arching her back to look bigger, to seem stronger against her enemy. He had become the enemy. It didn't matter that he was trying to understand her at that moment. All that mattered was that he didn't understand her back then. That's what it always came back to, every tiff, every defensive motion, it all stemmed from what she had done to herself the year before. She never said so, but he believed she faulted him for it, for locking her up in that place. On the outside, she blamed Dr. Wright, but on the inside, in the cavern of her heart, she blamed him. He told himself he couldn't have known, but of course he knew. Mercy's mother was bipolar, and when she killed herself, it sent a message. But he didn't heed the warning and he let Mercy fall. If he had to do it again, he would single-handedly battle armies and monsters to make sure Mercy was safe.

As his wife walked away, the sun cast its rays through the fabric of her nightgown, exposing her firm legs and the curve of her hips. *My God, you're beautiful.* He stood watching as she entered the house. She had stopped him again, though he doubted she knew.

CHAPTER FOURTEEN
September 1928 ~ The Past
Before the Abyss ~ The Living Time

*D*ick's appearance as he stood beside the box was rather peculiar. His pants were torn in several places, and had apparently belonged in the first instance to a boy two sizes larger than himself. He wore a vest, all the buttons of which were gone except two, out of which peeped a shirt which looked as if it had been worn a month. To complete his costume he wore a coat too long for him, dating back, if one might judge from its general appearance, to a remote antiquity.

Walker raised his eyes from his book and considered his own attire. Examining his scuffed shoes with their flattened soles, his tattered pants rolled up at the ankles to allow the early fall air to tickle his skin, his shirt, missing three buttons, two at the top and one at the bottom, he saw in himself Ragged Dick, the young hero of Horatio Alger's tale.

Rubbing the spot between his shoulder blades against the rough bark of the maple tree, Walker relieved the itch that had been growing there. Settling back against his perch, he continued to read.

Dick's business hours had commenced. He had no office to open. His little blacking-box was ready for use, and he looked sharply in the faces of all who passed, addressing each with, "Shine yer boots, sir?"

"Heck, I could do that," Walker said aloud to the tree and the wind. He could shine shoes after work and after his chores on Saturdays. That would help some. Yup, Walker thought, there'd come a way he'd make it work. He would save enough money to get a real house with real plaster walls and a basement, just like the one his father dreamed they would one day have.

Above his head, a flock of birds diverted his attention as they dipped and darted, swooped and sailed, a congregation of synchronized specks dotting the billowy-clouded sky. Walker watched in awe at the bird's simultaneous movement, as if they were one body made up of dozens of separate parts. "'Mazin'," he whispered as the body of birds swooped into the branches of the tree under which he rested. A chorus of chattering and chirping sang out above him. Walker tilted his head and closed his eyes, letting the rapture of their hymn bless him with its beauty.

The air, fragrant with a mix of ruddy wood and goldenrod, tasted sweet on Walker's tongue. He opened his eyes and looked out onto the grass that expanded toward the dirt road. Behind him was a light-wooded area. In front of him, on the other side of the road, the wood was much denser. If he lifted his sight just a pinch, he couldn't see the road at all. He was in his own private glade.

As the sun made its relaxing decline behind him, it cast its rays through the leafy clusters of the maple, gilding the ground with soft light. Stretching out his leg to catch a snip of sunlight on his shin, he made certain to note how it felt so he could write it down when he got home. Just as Alger had painted a cityscape so clear Walker could feel the grit on the street and smell the sausages cooking at the corner market, Walker would create an autumn day perfect for sitting on the grass in the shade of the maple tree. When he finished painting the day with words, he would read the scene to his siblings and his grandmother out on the porch or in front of the stove. But first, he would return to the city.

Our ragged hero wasn't a model boy in all respects. I am afraid he swore sometimes, and now and then he played tricks upon unsophisticated boys from the country, or gave wrong directions to honest old gentlemen unused to the...

"Hey, boy!" Someone hollered from the road. It was a white boy, about his age, in a large black automobile pulled off to the side. His head and left arm hung out the driver's window, while his right arm draped the steering wheel. There were three other boys in the car. All smiling. All white.

Walker didn't respond. Should get up, he thought, head home, but he knew the boys could easily follow. *Don't say nothin'. Go back to your book.* Maybe they weren't after trouble and they'd go away. Still, Walker was well aware it would be a mistake to ignore them.

"You got a cigarette, boy?" the driver yelled out.

"Don't smoke," Walker said.

"How 'bout directions. We's lost," said the white boy and Walker could hear the others in the car cackling.

Walker remained silent, keeping his focus fixed on the car. It was impossible not to notice the sheen of the silver grill and the brilliant white stripe of the whitewall tires. It looked like the kind of automobile in which the top could come down in good weather, and though there was no better weather than what he was experiencing that day, the top was secured in place.

The driver opened the door and exited. His friends, following suit and with hands stuffed in pants pockets, all swaggered over to where Walker was sitting. About two feet away from Walker, they stopped in a row. The one who looked like the leader stepped forward; his shiny metal boot tips tapped against Walker's cracked leather shoes.

"I said we's lost," the boy growled deep in the back of his throat.

"Where ya' headed?" Walker didn't rise from his place, hoping his passive stance would prove non-threatening.

Anything could trigger those boys to pounce. He'd seen it with his Pa when they lived in Alabama outside the church one Saturday evening. There were three of them then, grown men. Walker had gone ahead while his Pa stayed behind to talk to the minister. As he was talking, Walker noticed the three white men hovering in the shadows. They paid him no mind. Their eyes were set on his Pa. Once the minister went inside, the men jumped his father and tried to wrestle him down. Big like a workhorse, his father broke free. When the minister came out to see what was going on, the men ran away. His Pa survived that night.

"Where we headed," the boy grunted to his clan. His companions let out a poisonous laugh. Turning back, he snatched the book from Walker's hands. "Whatcha' got there?" Scowling, he turned the book over and back again, as if analyzing it. There was something wicked in the boy's grimace, something Walker hadn't seen since that night outside the church.

Overhead, the birds' chirping intensified and Walker saw the boy's eye twitch. The boy was about to speak when, as if someone fired off a gun, the body of birds burst from the leaves and darted and swooped toward the southern sky. All four boys jerked at the eruption of life overhead. As Walker looked into the leader's eyes, he saw a fierce anger develop. The breathtaking wonder of nature that had moments before so delighted Walker had enraged the boy. A bead of sweat dripped down the side of Walker's cheek as he found himself looking into the eyes of hate.

Slow and careful, he rose to his feet. "Jes' a book."

The boy opened the front cover and examined the first page. "This here your name? Walker Jacobs 1926, 'tsays. That you?"

"Yessir."

"Don't tell me you can read, boy?"

"Yessir."

"Did you hear that?" The leader turned his head back to his followers, barked out a laugh and said, "The boy can read." The white instigator tossed the book to one of his friends. "You smart?" His head snapped back so fast, the spit that flew from his mouth slapped Walker on the cheek.

Walker let the drop of spit stay where it was. He didn't move. He didn't answer.

"You think you's smarter than me?"

Walker remained silent.

"I'm talkin' to you!" The boy pushed his face into Walker's until their noses were nearly touching. "I asked if ya' think you's smarter than me."

Trying not to flinch, Walker stated, "No, sir."

"You wisin' me?" the boy threatened.

"No, sir."

"I think he's wisin' me. You know what we do to apes who wise us?"

He wasn't sure if it was better to speak or not, so he just kept quiet. Keeping his eyes locked on his opponent, he didn't have to look around to know his surroundings. The place was his most frequented reading spot. Behind him, the wooded area had lots of open space. If he ran into the woods, they could chase him down and among the four of them, he wouldn't have a chance. The road in front of him was his only hope. It was long and they had a car, but other cars traveled that road. If he had to run, he preferred to run out in the open where maybe someone would see him.

The boys circled Walker like wolves circling their prey. One placed a hand inside his shirt. Walker assumed he was carrying some sort of weapon but couldn't figure what. Although the air was cool, he could feel more sweat bead upon his forehead.

"We teach 'im a lesson," one of the boys squawked through clenched teeth.

Afraid to speak, afraid any response would only feed their anger, he kept silent.

"What's the matter?" the leader asked. "You gone dumb suddenly?"

"No, sir."

"He's as dumb as a monkey," one of the other boys taunted.

"Too dumb to live," the leader spat.

Striking faster than heat lightning on an August evening, the leader had Walker on the ground and in a headlock. One of the boys grabbed Walker's wrists. Despite his intense struggles, he forced Walker's arms behind his back. A third boy wrapped Walker's wrists with rope while a fourth whipped the wide loop of a noose around his neck.

Kicking and flailing with his lower body, Walker hoped to connect a swift foot with the groin of one of his assailants. His lean, wily legs broke free from the boys' attempts to restrain him. But as soon as his legs slipped from the grasp of one, another would grab hold of his ankles again. With his arms tied, his legs were his only escape. He twisted with such fury he thought his ankles would crack in half against the boys' grip. Although the boys outnumbered Walker, their lives weren't at stake. The surge of adrenaline rushing though his body told him he could break free.

With every bit of force he could muster, Walker pulled a leg clear and, with the strength of his entire body, swung. His foot careened through the leader's legs, rushing forward through the fleshy mass of the boy's testicles. It came to a hard crack against the attacker's pelvic bone.

The power of the impact sent the boy reeling backward in agony. Screaming and clutching at his beaten manhood, the boy writhed on the ground helpless. The others, stunned by the sudden disruption, released their hold on Walker to attend their fallen commander. Without the control of the one in charge, the boys staggered around in a state of confusion.

Walker hopped to his knees and leaning forward, shook the wretched noose from his neck. Hands bound behind his back, he scrambled to his feet and charged down the dirt road.

Oh Lord, he prayed. *Most sunny days, I ask to be spared the noise of folks passin'.* He looked over his shoulder and his pace slowed just a bit. He wasn't able to see the group, but he didn't linger to try to find them for fear of slowing even more. Turning straight ahead, he lifted his legs higher and widened his stride. *Bring me some noise, dear Lord. Bring me a car full of kin on a Sunday drive.* Over again, he prayed for a passing motorist. The boys would surely not stick around if there were witnesses.

Doing his best to keep steady without the aid of his arms for balance, Walker stared straight ahead and ran as fast as he could. If the boys were behind him, he was certain he was creating distance. He could feel it. *Don't look back. Don't look back. Don't look.* He didn't need to see. He just needed to run. With tunnel vision, Walker ran down the eternal road. Soon someone would come. *Keep runnin'. Someone will come.*

Although there was no sight of a car approaching, there it was, the welcome sound of tires rolling over the gravely dirt behind him.

The vehicle slowed as it came closer. Walker stopped running, relieved at his rescue at the hands of a Good Samaritan.

Before he could turn to thank his liberator, a set of arms slipped under his armpits, while another tucked under his knees. Lifted off the ground, Walker found himself in the clutches of his would-be killers. They shoved him head first into the back seat of their black Model A. Two held him down, while a third tied his ankles. Fired up and howling like a mad dog, the leader raced the car back across the grass, kicking up clumps of sod and dirt in its wake.

Its brakes slammed, the car spun around to face the road, coming to a jolting stop under the branch of the maple tree. One threw open the back door, while two wrenched Walker out of the vehicle. The leader jumped on the hood of the Ford, while the other three lifted Walker up. Wearing an expression as mean as the devil, the leader threw the noose over Walker's head. Snarling through clenched teeth, he tightened the hangman's knot until it pushed against Walker's Adam's apple. Then with a wide arc of his arm, he flung the free end of the rope over a branch and secured it. One of the boys tossed up Walker's ragged book.

Dropping the novel into the opening of Walker's shirt, the leader hissed, "That'll teach ya' for thinkin' you's smarter than me." He hopped down and resumed his place in the driver's seat.

The car's engine raced beneath Walker's feet. With rabid fever, the followers jumped around the tree, hooting in a clamor of guttural and indiscernible high-pitched cries like a clan of Neanderthals thrilled at the kill of a wildebeest.

Walker heard the tires spin and rip into the soft earth. The stench of car exhaust made his eyes tear and he gagged on the fumes. The followers all threw themselves into the car and the leader revved the engine again. Desperate, he tried to stretch his bound arms above his back to get to the noose, but it was impossible. He attempted to jump through them to bring his arms up from below, but he had no leverage. Checking the space between the hood of the car and the ground, he knew the branch was just high enough so his feet wouldn't touch when the car took off. If he could just get his fingers between the rope and his neck, he might survive. But as the car bucked, his arms useless behind him, he knew this was the end of his life. All his dreams of family, home, and comfort were about to vanish.

"I love you, Mammaw," he said aloud as the vision of his sweet grandmother cracking open peas on the front porch filled his head. I'm sorry, Bug.

With a brutal lurch, the car sped forward. Walker's legs catapulted out from under him, his feet smashing against the windshield, splintering the glass. His body flew up. The book dropped free from his shirt. The weight of his own mass, the velocity of the vehicle kicking out from under him, and the force of gravity yanked Walker's body down, snapping his neck.

CHAPTER FIFTEEN
September 1928 ~ The Past
At the Edge of the Abyss

His back resting against the maple tree and his knees bent to prop up his small hardback book, Walker wondered about the calm that surrounded him. There wasn't a single stir in the serene glade in which he relaxed with his novel. It was silent like church after the service was done and all the parishioners had gone. As he sat in his personal sanctuary, the sun paid reverence to the tranquil afternoon and shone upon Walker with the splendor of Heaven.

From somewhere in the attic of his mind crept the remembrance of darkness. Just a whispery dream, but it left a layer of frost underneath his skin. He shivered and dropped his eyes to the open page of his book. Although he could see it in his hands, the book lacked any real physical substance. He saw the well-worn cover and the dog-eared pages, but it was like a reflection in the water, wavy and distorted. And while the story flowed through his mind as effortlessly as a stream through the forest, he wasn't actually seeing the words. Sentences weren't being lifted from the page with his eyes. Instead, they were delivered to him on the rays of the tranquil sun.

He wore a vest, all the buttons of which were gone except two, out of which peeped a shirt which looked as if it had been worn a month.

Over the pages and on the ground around him a shadow moved, and Walker recognized the unmistakable plump figure of his grandmother. The silhouette showed she was wearing her Sunday church-going hat with its giant puff of silk flowers bursting from the broad rim. A tired, throaty groan escaped her as her robust form bent down over him.

"These ol' bones a mine," she rasped, resting a stack of books and a tin box on the ground.

Unlike the watery image of the book in his hands and the veiled figure of his grandmother, Walker saw with clarity a stack of novels tied into a bundle with string on the ground beside him. They were some of the novels once tucked beneath the floorboards of the house his father built. Two dozen books, all read and reread, but none as read, none as loved, as the one he held but couldn't feel in his hands.

From the side of his eye, he saw the obscured figure of his grandmother sit next to him, and as she did, she let out a heavy whoof.

"You and your readin' chile. I always did worry about you comin' out here by yerself."

Our ragged hero wasn't a model boy in all respects. The sunrays delivered their gift to Walker. *I am afraid he swore sometimes…*

"You was a good boy. Never did no one no harm."

Now and then he played tricks upon unsophisticated boys from the country…

"You was too good for this earth, chile. So good, God wanted you for Hisself. Now you're my little angel in Heaven watchin' over me." Walker heard the crack in her voice and knew she was about to cry. "Oh, Lord, Lord." The cry came out in a pounding plea. "You already took my boy, now You have my grandboy. Soon You'll have me, too."

Heartrending, deep-rooted sobs burst into the space around him and Walker reached a hand to touch his grandmother's arm to soothe her. All he felt was the cool grass beneath his palm, so he brought his hand back and wrapped his fingers around the book that had no touch.

I ain't gone nowhere, Mammaw. Walker knew God didn't have him. She had to know that was true. He was sitting right there. *I'm right here.* Sobs subsiding, her shaking body grew composed and Walker, pleased he'd comforted her, let the story take him.

Dick's business hours had commenced. He had no office to open.

The books on the ground moved closer to him.

"Here's some of your favorites to read in Heaven." Tears gone, her voice returned to the rich, custard smoothness that always mellowed his spirits. "Read 'em out loud to your Papa. He sure loved a good story." He heard a loud honk as his grandmother blew her nose into her hanky. "I kep' some. Couldn't bear to let go of everything. Even that sickly rope they strung round your neck. Tried to burn it. So many times I tried. It reminded me of what evil those white boys done to you. But I couldn't. It's in the shed. Out of my sight. But your books, the ones I kep, they shine bright on a shelf I had Ol' Joe fix up over where you used to sleep."

He didn't understand some of what she was saying, but it was no matter. He liked the sound of her voice. Her fingers dug away the grass next to where he sat. The top dirt lifted up, a small hole widened in the earth and the tin box, its lid sparkling with the splashes of sunlight upon it, slid into the hole.

More groans, and Walker made out his grandmother's shrouded form bending her face to the ground as if to kiss the dirt that covered the box.

"This book's jes' for you. My gift to you. This here's your favorite tale, and this place was your favorite readin' spot. This spot, chile, will always hold a piece of you."

Wind ruffled through the stillness and the leaves of the maple fluttered above him.

She sniffed a mighty sniff. "Ol' Joe found a nice smooth stone in a stream and chiseled your name on it. 'Member he did the likes for your Papa? It ain't fancy, but at least you're restin' respectable."

His little blacking-box was ready for use, and he looked sharply in the faces of all who passed, addressing each with, "Shine yer boots, sir?"

Luminous sunrays dulled as clouds extinguished the shadow of Walker's grandmother. From a distant place, he heard her far-off voice say, "I love you, chile."

I love you, Mammaw.

Without warning, the wavy, intangible book disappeared and Walker's world turned black.

CHAPTER SIXTEEN
June 2014 ~ The Present

Mercy awoke to the snarling sound of wolves. She jerked up her feet, feeling the heat of hungry breath upon them. As her room formed in front of her, she heard the sound for what it was, a distant lawn mower and the treble laughter of neighborhood children. Pleasant sounds of life happening. She pulled the sheets aside and sat on the edge of her bed. On the nightstand lay a pen and a new, unmarred notepad opened to its first blank page. Fearing the impending fade of the dream, she snatched up the pen and scratched out the words: *wolves woods chasing.* She thought for a moment, then wrote: *hunting*

The sun blasting through the window was so bright it hurt and it was out of kilter with morning light. Checking the alarm clock, she discovered why. It was 1:15 in the afternoon. *He let me sleep.*

After leaving Donovan in the yard, she had gone straight to bed. The children were in a state of chaos, but with her fatigue and the dogged hammering at her temple, she just wanted to shut her eyes. Don encouraged her to get some rest, said he would handle everything. And he did. Just like before. Her toes poked at the rug beside her bed and she wondered if Don had thought of that time before, too. While he was packing the kids' lunches and carting them off to school, did it seem familiar to him? Did he think about what had happened in those months following her thirty-ninth birthday disaster when all Mercy wanted was sleep? He couldn't have known that the more she slept, the more waking became unbearable. So when two pills only helped her sleep for a while, she swallowed the whole bottle and took a swan dive into oblivion. Except, oblivion turned into a thirty-day stint at the Loony Tunes Motor Lodge. And it wasn't so much a swan dive as a belly flop.

Apparently, a bottle of pills was too scant an admission fee for Death to take her. Death was a discerning bastard. She had to prove she wanted to be in its company by a suicide that promised absolute success. A couple of handfuls of Valium might work, might not. A bullet to the brain, a jump from the top of a twenty-story building, a razor to the wrist, now those were serious acts. If it left her blood pooled and splattered around her, if it tore open her flesh and exposed her bone, then Death would surely accept her. Pills were for posers and, when it came to suicide, Death didn't take posers.

You should have used a razor like your mother did.

Mercy wrote down the date and time on the notepad then dragged her weary body into the bathroom. She turned on the shower and let it run to get as hot as she could stand. Steam formed quickly and fogged the mirror above the sink. As she slipped off her nightgown and panties, the events from the night before replayed in her head, but they were murky, dreamlike. *Did I really stay on the swing all night?*

She passed a palm over the mirror to clear the fog. Immediately it crept across the glass again. Her clouded reflection showed a thin wraith of a woman, someone sinking in. Her appetite wasn't what it was before Lisa took ill. It was evident in the hollow in the middle of her neck and protruding collarbones, the slightly wider gap between her slightly smaller breasts. The fog grew thicker over the glass, and the denser the shroud, the more Mercy feared she would collapse in on herself, a celestial star at the end of her life about to become a black hole.

She stepped into the shower and shoved her face into the steaming jet of water. Her body relaxed with the pulsing heat. She soaped up her caving-in torso and let the jet stream rinse the lather off. As she watched the soapy water spiral down the drain, she thought, there goes another piece of me.

Momma.

It was faint. Barely there. Mercy moved her face from the water and tilted an ear. After hearing nothing unusual, she shook it off and plopped a glob of shampoo in her hand. She lathered her hair and massaged through the tresses. Rinsing the shampoo from the snarls, she wove her fingers through the thick matted strands to untangle them.

Momma.

She sucked in a quick breath and thrust open the curtain.

"Hello?" she called out. "Is someone there?" No response. She turned off the water. The house was silent. She stepped out of the tub and wrapped a towel around her body.

Momma.

Twirling around, her wet feet slipped on the tile floor and Mercy fell sideways. She thrust her arm out to grab anything to keep from falling but grabbed only air. Her left foot slid outward and her head cracked hard against the towel bar. Dazed on the floor, she rubbed her skull where her head connected with the bar. When she brought her hand back, there was no blood. She'd twisted her arm in the fall, but didn't break it, and although there was a large lump forming on the back of her head, she wasn't bleeding. She clamored to her feet and went into the bedroom. Her long hair, still wet and dripping, soaked her naked shoulders. What she heard was real. She was certain of it. A girl was calling out from somewhere, calling out to her momma the way Lisa used to call to her.

She threw on a pair of jeans and a tee shirt and leaned out the bedroom window. The twittering giggles of preschool children drifted across the yards, but they were far off. The voice Mercy heard was closer to her. She checked her children's rooms but no one was there. They were at school, of course. The upstairs was vacant of life, save her own. No one was downstairs. There was nothing in the basement. Don's car was not in the immaculate and organized garage. There wasn't a soul around. *Well, perchance a soul.* But no bodies.

Stepping onto the driveway, a trickle of dread crept into her. The lure of the tire swing took her to the backyard. There it hung on one healthy branch, an old black tire tied to a sturdy braid of rope—the thing that would take her to the voices. But what if the voices weren't there? She took a step. What if the voices were? Her heart rate skipped up a notch. Her throat tightened. She took another step.

One foot in front of the other, careful as if walking on a balance beam, Mercy inched toward the swing. Taking hold of the rope, she hesitated, her heartbeat jittering—one second like a school girl waiting for the phone to ring, the next in dreaded anticipation of deathly silence. If silence awaited her, she didn't want to mount.

She lifted her left leg through the hole, then her right, and sat in its center. She held her breath, tiptoed backward, and braced herself as if building up nerve before plunging into ice-cold waters. She released her hold on the earth and swung forward. Her trapped breath escaped in a long gust of relief. She had a purpose being on the swing and with each pump of her legs, the dread sloughed away. Higher she rose until she could see over the hedge into Mary Beth's yard. Down she descended with the pull of gravity. Up she rose and down she came and, as she rose and fell, she listened. There were sounds all around her: the preschool kids, the bark of the Cunningham's dog. She coasted for a spell, disappointment beginning to swell inside her. The swing slowed to a stop.

Momma.

She yelped with elation. The girl was there! Right next to her. Was it Lisa, really Lisa calling out? Lisa, dead a year and a half. Buried whole, not cremated. Laid to rest on pink silk in a bronze casket. Interred under the magnolia tree on the south side of the grounds of Rolling Acres Cemetery, six miles from their home. If what she heard were real, then her daughter had not crossed over, her spirit was still earthbound. Still reachable.

How was it possible? Logic told her it wasn't. If she were to follow logic, the only other explanation would be a hallucination—of the auditory variety.

She had a hallucination once. The day after her suicide attempt when she woke up at Tower Hills Psychiatric Hospital. Mercy remembered seeing a man in a coat of patches standing in the corner of her room. He looked like a vaudeville vagabond, wearing a torn top hat with a little yellow daisy sticking out of the rim, and his hands were wrapped in white gloves with holes in the fingers. He appeared in the dull beam coming through the small window in the door. She thought, what was a window doing on her bedroom door. And then she remembered taking the pills.

For a glorious second, she thought she had died and was about to be with her daughter in heaven. But the thirst that had turned her spit into dust proved otherwise. The dead didn't get thirsty.

So, she studied the curious hobo and although there were smudges on his cheeks that were supposed to be dirt and grime, he looked rather dapper, like Fred Astaire about to sing *A Couple of Swells* with Judy Garland in *Easter Parade.*

So we'll walk up the Avenue
Yes, we'll walk up the Avenue
And we'll walk up the Avenue till we're there!

But he wasn't singing and he wasn't dancing. He was standing still as a lamppost, watching her.

Who are you? she had asked him, or thought she'd asked him.

His eyes narrowed and his grin grew wide and the panic that had struck her over finding herself alive turned to absolute terror. As she lay in the presence of that strange creature, whose grin had become jagged-toothed and sinister, she doubled back and believed she had indeed died. Except instead of finding Lisa, she was staring into the face of the devil.

All suicides go to hell.

"It was a hallucination," Dr. Wright had said. "That happens sometimes after a sleeping pill overdose."

The devil may not have actually paid her a visit that day, but she was certain she had received a sign. Her mind was warning her not to play with Death. Yet there she was, playing with Death again.

Don't we all do that, she thought, every time we get out of bed? *Yes, but you're not just playing with Death. You're playing with the dead.*

The Cunningham's dog yapped away. The lawn mower rumbled its low growling vibration from across the street. Mercy sat silent on the swing waiting. Her breathing so loud it was all she could hear. Until…

Momma.

Tearing her legs from the tire, she fell backward out of it. She fumbled to her feet and dashed through the gap in the hedges. She pounded on Mary Beth's back door.

"Be home. Be home. Please be home." Agitated, Mercy bounced in place. "Please be home. Please. Please." She pounded again. "You've got to be home. What's taking you so long?"

After what seemed like minutes, the door opened and a puzzled Mary Beth stood on the other side.

"My goodness, woman. What's the matter?"

"I'm hearing voices. I … I'm hearing voices but there's no one around. A little girl calling 'Momma.'"

"Like you heard last night when you were drunk."

"Yes, as clear as that, but I'm not drunk now. Not one drop drunk, and I heard her. Mary Beth, I don't know where else to turn. I tried to tell Don this morning, but I know he didn't believe me."

Mary Beth began chewing on her lower lip, her eyes searching Mercy's face. As if catching herself, she popped on a smile. "Come here." She sat on the stoop and patted the space beside her with her palm. Mercy sat next her friend. "Your hair is wet."

"I just took a shower. That's where I heard the girl again, but there was no girl. Then I heard her a moment ago on the swing."

"The tire swing?"

"Yes. I was swinging, trying to … Oh God. I was trying to see if the voice would come like it did before. I thought maybe the swing and the voice, or maybe the tree and the voice, had some connection."

"I'm confused."

Of course you are, Mercy thought and her cheeks turned hot. She brushed at them with her fingers like she could swipe away the flush. "So am I." Agreeing with her unconvinced friend bought her a moment to collect her thoughts. "All I know is that I heard the voice of a little girl calling out to her momma. Calling out to me. But there was no girl. Only the voice."

"This neighborhood is teeming with children, Mercy. It could have been any one of them."

"But the voice was so close to me. It was right there when I was in the shower and it was strongest when I was on the swing. It was also the same voice I heard last night. Not just when I was drunk, but later. I woke up and went out to the swing."

Mary Beth's gaze turned serious, like she was traveling a road of confusion through her head. The two sat in silence. It was clear to Mercy that her friend was having trouble maneuvering around all she had told her. When Mary Beth found her way back, her expression was as mellow as her skin.

Mary Beth tucked a strand of Mercy's wet hair behind her shoulder. "Mercy, I don't doubt that you heard a girl's voice, but I'm sure it's just a coincidence that you hear her while you're on the swing."

"It's more than a coincidence."

"Look, I know I was the one who encouraged you to put that swing together, but you might be getting a little lost in it, like it's some grand getaway vehicle."

The tightness in her furrowed brow softened. "Like your old Camaro."

"Now that was a car!" Mary Beth let out a squawk of laughter. "We were like Thelma and Louise in that thing."

"Yeah, and look at how that movie ended. The two taking a header off the Grand Canyon."

"Okay, bad analogy. Smokey and the Bandit, then. As long as I'm Sally Field and you're Burt Reynolds."

"You suck." Mercy leaned her tired body against Mary Beth's shoulder.

"I'm thinking, just until your life settles down a bit, you should stay away from the swing. Or maybe we should just take it down."

"No." Mercy snapped up straight.

Perhaps it wasn't logical that the voice was her dead daughter's, but if there were even the remotest chance of it, then there was a reason. To walk away would be like letting Lisa die all over again. Because she had let her die. It was Mercy's fault and she'd been living with that since the day Lisa left them.

It was Mercy who delayed the treatment, demanded a second opinion. The doctor had said the cancer had already progressed and catching it the earliest gave Lisa the best chance for survival. But Mercy said no. The eyes of her youngest child were too vibrant. Lisa's life-filled smile was too bright. There were no outward signs that a violent war was raging inside that tiny body. She hadn't displayed any symptoms at all. The diagnosis came after a routine check-up. The doctors took a little blood and found an anomaly. Mercy convinced herself a second opinion would prove there was a mistake in the tests, a mix-up of someone else's samples at the lab.

In those weeks it took to have another bone marrow biopsy, the cancer was free to take over her child. And after that, all Mercy could do was lie to Lisa. Tell her she was going get better when she would only get worse. Lisa suffered, she died in a state of suffering, and if that girl she'd heard was Lisa, she might be suffering still. The thought was crippling. She looked into her friend's blue eyes, searching for the logic that would take her fear away.

"What's happening, Mary Beth? Give me something. Anything."

"Here's what I think. Your marriage isn't quite in the toilet, but it's doing some calisthenics on the rim and your emotions are all jumbled up. You've never been able to come to terms with Lisa's death and you're groping for something, anything to make you feel better.

You heard some kids in the neighborhood and you connected that to your desire to hear Lisa's voice. Perfectly logical."

Mercy supposed that was possible, but Mary Beth didn't know about how they sang together and how ethereal the voices came to her. About the swing's unexplained motion. Mary Beth hadn't heard or seen any of it. If she had, Mercy knew she would understand that the girl, perhaps her daughter, needed her. If they took the swing down, she wouldn't be able to help.

Mary Beth nudged her with her elbow. "Lose the worries, kiddo."

She kept her thoughts concealed. "Yeah. I know. Still, I don't think I'll tell Don about it."

"He's more understanding than you give him credit for."

Shaking her head. "I think I'll hold off saying anything just yet. I can work this out on my own."

"Right," she said in a way that told Mercy she was full of crap. "That's why you're here with me."

Mercy plunked her wet head on her friend's shoulder. "I'll think about talking to him."

"Good. Now go dry your hair."

CHAPTER SEVENTEEN
July 1970 ~ The Past
Before the Abyss ~ The Living Time

Anastasia fussed as her mother straightened the oversized pink satin bow on the front of her crisp white dress.

"Stop fidgeting, sweetheart, or else the bow will be crooked."

"Why do I have to wear this dumb dress anyway?" Anastasia whined.

"It's a wedding. We want to look our best because it's a formal occasion."

"What does 'formal occasion' mean?"

"It means it's a special day for your uncle and you want to show him how much you love him by dressing pretty." Grabbing hold of her daughter's hips with both hands to keep her from squirming, Anastasia's mother settled her down long enough to run her palms over the skirt of the dress to even out the ruffles. "That's better," she said and took a step back.

A rose blush, like pale fruit punch, spread across her mother's face. Her lips opened in a smile that showed all the pearls of her teeth. But when her lips closed over those pearls and the blush turned pale, Anastasia knew something was wrong. Her mother sat on the bed, sinking deep into the mattress. She draped her arm across her large belly as if to protect the life inside.

"Are you sick, Momma?"

The corners of her mother's lips curled up, but there was no longer fruit punch in her cheeks. "No, darling. Just tired." Anastasia placed a hand on her mother's protruding stomach and rubbed it the way someone would rub a lantern with a genie in it. "Feel anything?" her mother asked. Anastasia shook her head. "He or she must be sleeping."

"Is it warm in there, Momma?"

"Yes, darling. Warm and snug."

"That's good."

"Yes, it is."

Something stirred under Anastasia's touch. Not a kick, just the slightest wave. "I think the baby's dreaming," she told her mother.

"You might be right."

"Sweet dreams, I bet."

"Yes. Very sweet."

"Do babies have nightmares, Momma?"

Soft, caressing fingers brushed along Anastasia's cheek and settled under her chin. With a gentle nudge, her mother lifted her daughter's face.

"No, darling. Babies don't have nightmares. Their dreams are filled with rainbows and the songs of nightingales."

Ooh, Anastasia thought, *how wonderful!* And she conjured a nightingale song in her head, one that sounded like her mother humming a bedtime melody. She tried to remember if she ever dreamed of rainbows and nightingale songs, but couldn't recall. In her efforts to remember her dreams, the one from the night before crept into her brain and darkened her thoughts. There were wolves. Dozens of them, hunting her in the woods, hoping to eat her.

She shuddered. "I'm glad babies dream about rainbows," she said just above a whisper. "Nightmares are scary."

"Run along, now," her mother said. "Go get your brother so we're not late for the wedding."

Anastasia jumped from the bed and leapt around to face her mother.

"Do I look pretty?" she chirped.

"You look like an angel."

Stomping a foot on the ground in protest, she pouted, "Not an angel. A fairy."

"Yes, darling." With a bit of effort, her mother lifted her weighted body from the mattress and cupped Anastasia's face in her palms. "A beautiful fairy princess." And she kissed her on the forehead.

There was a twinkle in her mother's eyes that sparked glee in Anastasia's heart. It was going to be a grand day, she decided, and pirouetted around to leave the room, tumbling into her father who was entering at the same time.

"I'm a fairy princess, Daddy!"

"Yes you are." He tweaked her chin. "The prettiest fairy princess in all of fairy land."

She scurried out the door and into her room. Before scooping up Sparkle from the many other dolls that rested against her pillow, she closed her door and stood before the full-length mirror attached to the back of it. Running her fingers over the bow that her mother had so carefully straightened, she felt the soft satin of the fabric. As she examined her image in the mirror, hair pulled back in a band that matched the bow on her dress, a hem of ruffles so frilly they practically floated, white tights and black patent leather shoes, Anastasia truly saw herself as a fairy princess. She spun around and the hem of her dress twirled up.

She had never been to a wedding but imagined it would be just like what she saw in the movies. The bride would wear a glorious gown and a sparkling crown, and the man would wear a white suit trimmed with gold and brilliant white gloves to match. Together they would dance and swirl into happily ever after. Anastasia, in her white fairy tale dress of dreams, twirled and twirled, watching the hem fly up and out, fancying the someday when she, too, would dance into happily ever after.

Spinning round and round, her head grew dizzy and she tumbled to the floor. The room kept spiraling as she sat motionless, waiting for it to settle around her. In the quiet of the steadying room, Anastasia could hear something coming from the other side of the wall. She slid her body to it and pressed her ear against the plaster. Her lips began to quiver from the sound of her mother's low weeping.

"Everything's going to be all right," she heard her father say. "I'll find work soon."

"I know," her mother choked through sniffles. "It's just, I worry about the children. Anna senses there's something wrong. And with the baby on the way…"

"I promise you, I'll find work. Now dry your eyes and let's enjoy the day."

Anastasia pulled her head away from the wall. Her mother didn't need to worry about her and Bobby. They were fine and she would prove it. She snatched Sparkle from the bed and ran from her room. Pausing by her parents' closed bedroom door, she heard no more voices or crying, only a little rustling, like they were getting ready to leave. The moment of sorrow had passed, and that was good, because they were going to a wedding.

A joyful jump into one last hem-raising twirl and she bounded down the stairs. When she reached the car, Bobby was already sitting in the backseat reading a comic book. Into the station wagon she climbed. Hoisting her leg over the back bench seat, she plunked down in the way back. Legs thrown out in front of her, she leaned against the corner, her back to her brother.

Knowing her mother and father would be another minute, Anastasia took the time to make a wish to the fairy that lived inside Sparkle. Holding the doll close to her lips, the silken hair tickling her, she whispered the words she heard her father say to her mother.

"Everything's going to be all right." Then, in the way of making promises, she said, "We just have to love Momma and Daddy more and they will be happy again."

"What's that?" Bobby asked, cocking his head toward her.

"Just making a wish." What did it matter if he made a snotty comment about fairies not being real? They were going to a wedding and nothing could ruin how splendid it was going to be.

"Oh," was all he said, and Anastasia turned to the sunshine pouring through the car windows.

"Everybody ready?" her father called out as he took his place behind the wheel.

Her mother closed the passenger's door and they backed down the driveway and drove onto the street.

As they rolled down the road, Anastasia bounced about, the blanket that draped the floor of the way back doing little to cushion her. It didn't trouble her, though. The way back was her special space that she had all to herself. Behind her, Bobby lounged with his shoulders against the door and his legs stretched out onto the seat, engrossed in the adventures of Amazing Spider-Man. The back seat belonged to Bobby. But the way back was all hers. It had always been that way.

The breeze flowed through the halfway open rear window. Warm-weather days were the best days for riding when the window was open with the air rushing through. Sometimes, she would sit right up against the tailgate door, her face to the open air and the wind blowing into her eyes.

Sitting, carefree and whispering wishes, she felt the speed of the car increase down the road, and the movement of air through the window grew stronger, rippling through her hair. Mmm, she thought. How tasty it was. She kissed Sparkle and let the wind carry off her wish.

A Beatle's song rang from the dashboard radio. Anastasia's ears perked. "Turn it up, Daddy. I love this song!" The Beatles sang and Anastasia hummed along. "Hmmm, hmmm, hmmm."

"Oh no!" her mother cried from the front seat.

Shifting her body to see her mother, Anastasia was anxious that it might be the baby. Her mother had told her the baby would let her know when he or she was ready to come out by knocking on her belly, like someone would knock at the front door. If the baby were knocking, they would miss the wedding.

Wait a little longer, baby. Knock again tomorrow. "I just want to dance in my dress today," she whispered to her doll.

"We forgot the camera," her mother moaned.

Anastasia smiled with relief.

"We're too late to turn back," her father's frustration apparent.

"Honey, we can't go to your brother's wedding without the camera."

"Yes, Daddy," said Anastasia, her little voice straining to reach the front of the car. "You have to take a picture of me dancing!"

The car slowed and the wind slowed with it. The Beatles crooned and Anastasia relaxed, stroking the hair of her doll the way her mother had often stroked hers.

"Doesn't that feel fab," she quipped to Sparkle. "Hmmm, hmmm, hmmm," she hummed with the Beatles, and her body tugged a bit to the left as the car swerved into a U-turn.

Glancing up, she saw they were in front of the park at the end of their street. On any other day, she would rather be playing there than doing anything else. But not this day. Turning her focus back down to her doll, Anastasia sang along to the song on the radio.

Horn blast and a piercing scream threw her attention up. Filling her sight was a wall of red and silver that was the front of a pick-up truck barreling toward them. The car jerked hard to the right. Anastasia knew her father had whipped the steering wheel around to avoid getting hit, but the truck smashed into the side of their car, sending it careening in a circle.

Shrieks from her mother filled her head, the Beatles song blaring in warped competition on the radio. The car spun, throwing Anastasia across the floor where she cracked into the metal side wall. With her fairy doll tight in her grip, she lurched to the other side as the car continued to spin. Bobby roared in a voice Anastasia had never heard before. It curdled her core more than any nightmare had ever done.

"TOM!" her mother screamed.

Anastasia was hurled to the other side, her head crunching against the window. Stinging came to her eyes and a film of red covered her sight. She was bleeding. Yanked by centrifugal force, she flew to the other side of the way back, her elbow crushing into the wheel well.

"Sweet Jesus, Sweet Jesus," shot from her father.

The car spun faster, sending Anastasia smashing from one side to the other. Another crack and she thought she screamed but heard only the terror of the others. The car spun and Anastasia spun with it, until, with a massive impact, the car crashed sideways into the same maple tree in which she had hid from her brother just hours before. It spun and crashed again, but Anastasia didn't know where, only knew it felt like the impact had sent the car flying though the air. Another violent crash and Anastasia's body propelled through the rear of the car.

"Momma!" she cried as she smashed through the partially open tailgate window. Like a missile, she shot into the tree. The center of her body slammed against a thick limb, cracking her spine in two. Anastasia's doll fell from her grip.

CHAPTER EIGHTEEN
Sometime Around the Present
After the Abyss

There was once a swallowing darkness. A place so dense with dark Anastasia thought it would crush her. Before the darkness, there were bright and inviting days, but they were long over. There were no days at all anymore. No nights. Time had been turned inside out. The world as she knew it had become deformed and unpredictable.

Without knowledge of how, Anastasia had moved from the darkness to a place known to her, but not entirely there. She found herself on the ground, at the base of the maple tree in the park. She recognized the trunk, but that was all she could see. Her universe appeared to be confined to a small circumference surrounding the base of the tree. Everything beyond that circumference was encased in a thick fog. Only where she knelt did the fog thin, just enough to expose the layered bark of the trunk and the ground from which it sprung.

A boy was with her. He was crawling around the tree, searching for something. She didn't know him. He just appeared much like she felt she had. She watched him for a while as he pushed his fingers into the grass and soil, examined the exposed roots, put his nose to the ground and took in the scent. He was searching for something he'd lost. She had lost something, too. Had to find it. She searched as the boy searched, circling the tree and exploring the ground. It may have been hours she'd done that, or only minutes, but it felt like years. A quiver of fear skittered underneath her skin. It wasn't there. That one thing she needed most of all was lost forever.

I have to find it.

"Don't worry," the boy said. "'T's here. I can feel it."

"I didn't say anything." She didn't. How could the boy respond to what she only thought in her mind?

"Ain't no need to speak. I heared what you thought."

"That's not fair. I can't hear what you think."

"Yes, you can."

"No, I can't."

"Yes, you can, 'cause I ain't spoke a word."

"Oh." She sat back and looked the boy in the face. "I'm Anastasia. What's your name?"

"Walker."

"That's a funny name. But kind of nice, too."

"Thanks," Walker said. "Do you live 'round here?"

"Over there, I think." She pointed in front of her.

"I'm from just up yonder." Walker nodded to his right. He sat silent for a moment, pondering. "Come to think of it, I ain't sure how I got here."

"Not sure how I got here either. It was like I closed my eyes and when I opened them…" Her voice broke.

Walker put his hand on top of hers to calm her. "I know it's scary, but it's better than the darkness."

"You were in the darkness?"

"For a long, long spell."

"Me, too. Why didn't I know you were there?"

"Maybe you did. I think I felt you sometimes. I thought you were a fiend waitin' to kill me."

"A fiend," she whispered.

"The space 'round me moved, and it felt so big. In my mind, I imagined some frightful beast. But it musta been you tryin' to push through the dark like I wuz."

"I thought you were the wolves." Her lower lip quivered.

"Wolves?"

"I used to dream about them. Over and over. I would be alone in the dark woods. It was always night and always after the leaves had fallen from the trees, but it was never cold. A fog covered the ground so I couldn't see them, but I knew they were there, hiding behind the trunks of trees, smelling me. There were many wolves."

"A pack."

"That's right. A pack. I would stand frozen at first, hoping they would disappear and the sun would come up. But they wouldn't, and the sun never came. And so I'd run, and they would run after me. That's when I would wake up." Tears dropped onto her lap. "Momma calls them recursing dreams."

"You mean recurring."

"Yes. She said I was having them because my life was changing. She's having a baby, you know. She said change, even good ones, can be scary. But I wasn't scared about the baby. I was happy for the baby. It was another change that scared me."

"What was it?"

"Daddy lost his job and Momma was sad. I couldn't make her happy and I was scared that she would always be sad and that it was my fault."

"It wadn't your fault, though. Everybody gets sad."

"I know." She shook her head to change the thoughts her new friend could hear. "She said the dreams would go away."

"Did they?"

"Yes. But I don't really sleep anymore." She wrapped her thin arms around her shivering body. "Anyway, that's who I thought you were. The dark was so scary, like my nightmares about the wolves. Whenever I felt the space move, all I could think of was the wolves were waiting to eat me."

"Jes' like I thought a giant beast was out in the deep black. But it wadn't a beast. Not a fiend. And it wadn't the wolves. It was jes' you an' me tryin' to reach each other. And we did. Now you don't need to be scared no more."

His voice in her head was kind and her shivers subsided.

Walker returned to his search, crawling around the circumference of the tree. When he came to a spot where a tire, detached from its car and still in the rim, rested against a tree root, he stopped. "This here's the queerest tire I've ever seen. It's huge. Must have come from some kind of truck."

"It looks like one of the tires that are on my daddy's Chevy."

"Chevy? Is that like a Model A?"

Anastasia shrugged. "I guess, but it must be bigger, from what you say." She sniffed at the ground as an animal would to find what's buried beneath. In the dim light that shone on the ground, she saw the shadow of something. She looked up, but couldn't see through the fog. The shadow looked like a rope tied with a loop on the end. It was swaying about, as if in a breeze, but the air was still as a rundown clock. "What do you think that's for?"

Walker shuddered. "Best you don't know." He crawled around the tree to move away from the shadow. As he circled the base, the shadow of the rope circled around on its own end.

Anastasia followed the boy named Walker until the hem of her dress got snagged underneath her knee. She hopped up and brushed off the grass. "I have to be careful. Momma told me not to get my dress dirty. I'm going to my Uncle Mickey's wedding." She twirled around, the skirt of her dress flying up and out. "I'm going to dance when I get there."

"Sure is a pretty dress. You look like a princess. I read about 'em in one of my books. You look like I pictured 'em in my head."

"I'm a fairy princess," Anastasia said and plopped back on her knees next to Walker.

Walker watched her for a long minute, a mournful smile coming to his lips.

"What's the matter?" she asked.

"You remind me of my sister is all."

"Is her face light, like mine?"

"No. She has my skin, but she's sweet as pecan pie like you are."

Anastasia giggled. Back to her search, she began to hum.

"What's that song?"

"The Beatles."

"The what?"

"They're a singing group. Paul is so dreamy. I'm going to marry him one day." She looked into the fog overhead and thought of the Beatles posters on the walls of her bedroom. "If I ever get back to my family."

"You will. So'll I. We've got to stick together, though. Like flies to flypaper." Anastasia nodded. "We stick together and we'll get back."

"We'll get back," she repeated, and the two continued to crawl around the base of the maple tree.

While he searched, Walker began reciting strange words, as if from an often-told bedtime story he'd remembered. There was a boy in his story. His name was Dick and he was poor. Anastasia found it a curious and familiar story, but couldn't recall how she knew it. She was going to ask him what it was, but the sound of his voice was so smooth and comforting, like a lullaby, she let him go on reciting. And as he did, she began to hum.

CHAPTER NINETEEN
June 2014 - The Present

The children were settled in their bedrooms for the night and Donovan was behind the closed door of his office making his end-of-the-day business calls. Mercy walked through the empty kitchen. She was heading to do what she had resisted doing since she had talked with Mary Beth that morning. Leaving behind the quiet habitual murmurs of her family that pulsed like a heartbeat through the house, she stepped onto the deck.

The air, so calm it couldn't provoke the puffs of the dandelions that had gone to seed, portended a storm. Before her, the swing hung patient in the thick night. Should there be a child, perhaps more than one, perhaps her own reaching out to her, she needed to know why. All it would take was one last ride. If nothing happened, then Mary Beth was right. If no voices came through the night, Mercy would take down the swing.

From an arm's reach away, she stared at the rubber of the tire and it began to turn. Mercy sucked in a quick gasp of breath. The sight shocked her despite her omniscient expectation of it. It rotated, not herky-jerky as if hit by a sudden wind, but smooth and bewitching. She spun to face the house. The light was on in Donovan's office, but the shade was drawn.

Get him! It was her proof. *Get him out here so he can see what I'm seeing.* She ran to the deck and when she looked back, the swing hung motionless. One foot on the deck step, the other on the grass, she stood, deflated. There was nothing to show. Even if she dragged him out, she was confident nothing would happen.

Mercy inched toward the swing. Another step and her trembling legs gained strength. Another still. When she was upon it, the swing began to sway left and right. Mercy wrapped both hands around the rope. The swing stilled under her touch. She slid her hands down the rough braid, and then spread her palms over the rubber of the tire. The treads were wide, yet worn. One leg lifted and no longer quaking, she arched it through the loop. With the other through, she backed up the swing with her feet. "Okay," she sighed. And she let go of the earth.

Gripping the rope, Mercy pumped her legs and soared out over the yard, creating her own wind in the otherwise windless night. Back into the leafy mass of the maple she retreated. She could smell the richness of the bark and the fresh green foliage. Crickets, tree frogs, and other nocturnal sounds played in the air. Far away, thunder rolled. A light wind came at her from the side, disrupting the stagnant night. A smattering of raindrops tapped against Mercy's face. Within seconds, the rain fell more steadily and the wind gained force. Still Mercy swung.

Momma.

Yes! Mercy thought. "I'm here!"

Momma? It came out inquisitive, as if the child had heard her and was responding.

"Lisa? Is that you?"

The girl began to hum.

"Lisa? Where are you?"

The girl only hummed and Mercy remembered if she sang, the girl would sing with her. Mercy began singing the lyrics to the Beatles' song, and the girl, who Mercy grew more and more sure was her daughter, did join her. But Mercy wanted more than music. She wanted to talk to her. She tried summoning Lisa again, and sometimes the voice would answer simply with "Momma" but nothing more. She tried singing again and there was Lisa, singing along. The voice was innocent, delightful.

Dick's business hours … no office to open … blacking-box was ready for use.

It was the boy. She strained to hear through her own voice what the boy was saying. Maybe inside those words was a message from her daughter. Mercy continued to sing to keep the voices coming. Rain pounded harder and rumbles of thunder grew nearer, but as long as Mercy sang, the voices never ceased. As she pumped against the mounting wind, her heart swelled with renewed hope. The swing had brought Lisa to her. It was Lisa who made the swing move. It was Lisa who had begged her to ride. She rose and descended and the lightning flashed.

CHAPTER TWENTY
Sometime Around the Present
After the Abyss

On the ground under the shadow of the rope, Walker kneeled. "This right here 'swhere it is," he said. He pushed his hands against the grass, but couldn't penetrate the earth. It was as if his sense of touch was remembered more than felt. He circled the tree, trying to push his fingernails into the ground but was unable.

"Why can't I dig," Anastasia asked.

"Not sure. I think we need someone to hep us. We can't do stuff the way we used to."

"We're trapped."

"Maybe not. We thought we was trapped before in the dark, but we wadn't. We got out. We can get outta this, too."

"I don't remember how I got out of the dark."

"Me neither, but we did. You know, now that it's lighter, maybe someone will come passin' and see us. I thought I felt a presence close by … at some time. Time is so peculiar now."

"I heard someone crying. It was far off, like it was coming from deep under water. I think it was my Momma. I held on to that someone who might be my Momma with my mind as hard as I could. I thought, if you felt me in the dark, she could maybe feel me, too. I held and I held with all my might, but then she was gone. There are other times when I think I hear singing. Don't know if it's the same person or not, though."

"But it is someone. That means there's someone else here. That means we'll get out."

"But my doll. She's carrying my wishes. If she can't deliver my wishes, how can we leave?"

Walker thought about it. He wasn't sure about the wishes part, but Anastasia was right. She had to get her doll. It was attached to her, like her pretty, yellow hair and her blue eyes. He'd never seen eyes that blue before. They looked like the sky.

"Someone will come. Someone will hep you get your doll." And his book. That precious gift from his grandmother was as much a part of him as grits was a part of Sunday breakfast. He reached deep in the chambers of his mind and drew forth the dulcet sound of the spirituals his Mammaw would hum while snapping peas. Walker nudged closer to Anastasia. "Will you hum that tune you was hummin' earlier? It sure was pleasin'."

Anastasia hummed and Walker let her song float through his head. As it did, the words from his favorite book laced through the music as natural as spring air through sunshine. For some time, for how long neither was sure, the two sat beside the maple tree, sharing their thoughts, waiting for someone to arrive.

CHAPTER TWENTY-ONE
June 2014 ~ The Present

It was the middle of the night and the sky exploded with light. Wind blew at near-hurricane speeds and lightning obliterated the darkness with brief, apocalyptic attacks. Thunder shook with the force of a bull stampede and Mercy, soaking wet, swung high into the storm. Although aware of the tempest around her, she held her face up to the rain as if holding it up to the warming rays of the sun.

The song flowed from her lips, while her ears captured snippets of the phrases spoken by the boy. At first, Mercy's longing for more than what they were giving was powerful, but after awhile, just knowing she'd found a way to make contact was enough.

She didn't know who the boy was or why he was there, but he possessed no threat, and if he was keeping her daughter company in that unknown world between life and death, then Mercy was glad for it. Lisa was singing and she had a friend. Death was never able to get its bony grip on her daughter. Death wasn't the champion it would like the living to believe it was. It had limitations. Lisa and the boy were proof of that. Their spirits stuck around, happy as can be, and Death couldn't do a damned thing about it.

Take that, you prick. Take that straight to hell.

Rain drummed against the leaves, beat against her body. Lightning fired its trumpet blast across the sky and thunder clashed its cymbals. Still, Mercy swung. She wasn't swinging in the midst of a carnivorous storm. She was reveling in the raptures of a symphony.

Down she came and something snatched at her toes. Kicking it away, she soared back up into the air. Down again, and a brash voice, like a car horn, cut through the torrent. High into the rain she rose, but the interruption changed things. The children's voices ceased. She continued to sing, but no one accompanied her. "I'm here!" she yelled, but the children didn't reply, and the storm became furious and brutal against her flesh.

The wind, which had been nothing more than an idle threat moments before, took hold of the swing, sending it wildly spiraling. Gusts blasted her cheeks with open-palm slaps and ripped at the fabric of her clothes. The rain, a nonstop volley of pellets, stung her eyes and skin.

Someone grabbed her ankles, stopping the spiraling of the swing. Another hand took hold of the rope and she came to a jarring halt. Arms clamped around her waist—strong arms, a man's arms—and although Mercy was too slight to fight him, she twisted and struggled anyway.

"Mercy!" The yell came out jarring and throaty.

Turning her face, she stared into her husband's eyes. His pupils were huge, like he had just woken up in a dark, foreign room.

"What are you doing?" His shouts shredded in the sawtoothed wind.

Lightning shocked the air, scattering little static charges across Mercy's flesh. Thunder boomed dynamite explosions. Don yanked at Mercy's waist to lift her out of the swing, but Mercy fought him. She needed to get back up in the air. She needed to be with Lisa.

"Let me be!" she yelled. With all her force, she yanked her body free and pushed back with her feet. The swing made a feeble ascent. She just needed a little more push.

Don grabbed at her again, but she wriggled around, sending the swing in a circle. He yelled something she couldn't hear then ran toward the house. She kicked off with her feet, and the swing took flight, but the storm, angry and threatening, made the ride wild and dangerous. Upon the second erratic descent, Don was by her side. He grabbed the tire and forced her to a stop. Gripping the rope with one hand, he produced a large kitchen knife with the other. It startled her to see him with such a large blade. He raised his arm above her head and sawed through the rope with the knife, severing the swing from the tree. The tire, with her in it, dropped to the ground.

Screams of unnatural pitch ruptured the storm, the piercing wails of children being torn apart at the limbs.

"We've got to get inside!" Don yelled. "Mercy, please! Help me free you from this thing!"

Mired in the suction of the wet soil, she struggled to disentangle her legs from the tire. Donovan clutched Mercy's upper arms, freed her from the contraption, and got her to her feet. With one grip on her wrist, he ran ahead of her, practically dragging her behind him. His strength and speed greater than hers, Mercy tripped and stumbled as she tried to keep up.

The screams, which sounded as if they were following them, grew louder. She turned her head to see what was making such a horrible noise. The moment she brought her focus to the tree, a jagged bolt of lightning struck it, tearing off the top and severing the limb on which the tire swing had hung. Mercy froze and the momentum from Don pulling her sent her crashing to the ground. Sprawled on the grass, rain pummeling her with bare knuckles, she saw two great globes of red burst from the broken end of the tree limb.

"What is that," she yelled. "Don! What's happening?"

Don tugged at her arm. "We've got to get inside."

She watched in horror as the red glowing balls hovered, collided with each other, then spiraled apart. Howls harsher than the roar of the angriest god filled the air.

"Do you see that?" She pointed to the globes. "Do you hear that?" But her voice was lost in the deluge.

With one arm, Don lifted Mercy from the ground and dragged her to the deck. She craned her neck to see the globes, which appeared to be on fire. Ball lightning. That could be it, but what about the noise and the way they moved? They jumped about erratically and they didn't just appear and strike as she imagined ball lightning would do. They lingered.

Don flung the door open. The globes rushed forward. No longer aimless, they were coming for Mercy and Don. Like homing missiles, they had a target.

Don leapt into the kitchen, yanking Mercy in with him. A great force crashed into her back, propelling her to the floor. Don was several feet in front of her, splayed on his stomach. The door slammed shut and the howls stopped. The interior of the house filled with a freakish red glow. Mercy started hyperventilating, convinced the lightning had made it into the house and had set it on fire. But the fear of fire was silenced by a greater fear. It was the absence of smoke. And it wasn't hot. If there was fire around them, there should have been heat. Instead, the air was cracked with a bitter chill that sent Mercy into uncontrollable shivers.

"Are you all right?" Don asked.

"The lightning," she gasped.

"We're safe now."

"But I see it. It's in the house."

The red glow condensed into a fog of amber that drifted into the living room and rose up the stairs. As the glow moved away, the chill moved with it and the downstairs rooms, except for the dull light above the kitchen sink, went dark.

"It's a reflection," Don said. "But I'll make sure."

Mercy took Donovan's hand and together they clambered to their feet. Don hurried up the stairs. Mercy took a few rubbery steps across the living room. A door opened overhead and she knew Don was checking in on one of the children. Low, heavy moans drifted down to her. It wasn't Don's voice and she heard no urgency from him, but the fear was in her anyway. Steps heavy and awkward, Mercy made it up the stairs. She entered the twin's room and flicked the light switch.

Whoomph. Like a vacuum sucking in sound.

Kira was lying in her bed on the farthest side of the room near the window. Her back was to Mercy, her tanned arm tucked under her dark curls. The smooth tempo of her body's rise and fall showed she was sound asleep.

When she turned to Kaitlyn, Mercy went weak. Her daughter was sitting straight up with hands over her mouth as if to hold back a knife-wielding scream from slashing through her teeth. Eyes, massive dark saucers, pinned open, unable to blink. The bed was shaking.

Mercy dropped to her knees by Kaitlyn's side. She laid a careful hand on the mattress and realized it was Kaitlyn who was trembling, not the bed. Mercy guided her daughter's hands off her lips. That's when she felt it. Frigid cold. It started from the touch of her daughter's cheek and spread through the entire room. Someone had opened a window to winter. Despite her shaking and the frost of her skin, sweat bubbled up on Kaitlyn's forehead.

"Kaitlyn, sweetheart," Mercy said, wiping away the clammy moisture from her daughter's face. "What's wrong?"

"It wasn't ... hhh ... a dream," Kaitlyn said through timid breaths.

"What wasn't?"

"What I saw." She was more gasping the words than saying them.

"What did you see?"

Kaitlyn pointed to her sister, who was, regardless of the clamor and the cold, still sleeping.

"You saw Kira do something?" asked Mercy. Kaitlyn nodded. "When?"

"Just now. I mean, right before you came in the room." There was the gravel of fear in the back of her voice.

"Kira's asleep," Mercy whispered.

"She wasn't a moment ago. She just fell that way when you came in."

Mercy studied Kira, waited for an interruption in her calm, but there was none. In a careful tone, she said, "Are you saying she's faking?"

Throughout their lives, Mercy had witnessed moments of fear in her children: residue from frightening movies, shadows after waking from bad dreams, spooked by power outages or Halloween legends. Never, though, had she seen a fright so severe as she was seeing there in Kaitlyn. She stroked her daughter's hair and Kaitlyn's shaking lessened.

"No. I don't know," Kaitlyn said.

"It's okay, Sweetheart. I'll check on her." Mercy stood.

"No." Kaitlyn's voice was harsh but low. "Don't wake her. It's better that she's asleep."

"Tell me what happened."

Kaitlyn took in several audible breaths and closed her eyes in a way to settle herself. "She rose up from the bed."

"She got out of bed?"

"No, she rose up, like lifted up. Her whole body lifted up off the bed."

"What do you mean?"

"She … levitated. It wasn't very high. Just a couple of inches. I mean, she was under the covers so I couldn't really tell, but I swear her whole body was off the mattress."

Mercy became wavy, the way someone felt when stepping off a boat after sailing for while. "I'm sure…" She breathed out the panic. "I'm sure you were dreaming or just waking up or something." But she wasn't sure of that at all. "I'm going to check on her." She pointed to Kira's bed. "I'll be quiet. I promise." Mercy took the three steps across the room to get to Kira's side. The covers moved over her daughter but only from the soft rhythm of her breathing. Mercy wanted to touch her, but didn't want to wake her. She thought of the red glow that had traveled up the stairs and wondered if it had come into the room. Even if it had, how would that and what Kaitlyn saw be connected? Mercy stepped toward the hall, Kaitlyn's stare sawing into her. "I'll be right back."

She heard movement from Don in their bedroom. He had checked on Josh already, she assumed, but crossed into Josh's room anyway. He was asleep with nothing unusual surrounding him. She checked her room. The light from their bathroom shone under the closed door.

"Everything okay in here?" she called to Don.

"Yes. I saw you were with the girls, so I decided to get out of these wet clothes."

Back out in the hall, she scanned around. No red glow. It had vanished, dissipated like steam. She went to the twins' room and stood beside Kaitlyn's bed.

"All appears fine, sweetheart. No need for you to worry." Her daughter didn't let go of the distress in her eyes. "I know the storm is frightening. It could have provoked a kind of night terror and woke you."

"I wasn't asleep." She paused. "I had to pee. When I crawled back into bed, I couldn't shut off my mind. There was so much noise from the storm ... and..." Her worry-filled gaze fell on Mercy. "I closed my eyes, but this cold came into the room. And I heard something. I thought it was the wind, but when I opened my eyes, I saw Kira rising up off the bed. That's when you came in."

Mercy stepped toward Kira.

"Mom, please," Kaitlyn whispered.

Raising an appeasing hand, Mercy bent over the bed where Kira lay. The relaxed demeanor of her daughter was enhanced by the little snores that purred from her nose. Mercy crossed back to Kaitlyn and knelt beside her bed. She brushed her lips against her daughter's cheek. "I think what might have happened, sweetheart, is that you did drop off to sleep, although it didn't feel like it, and the storm crept in and gave you a nightmare that woke you."

Kaitlyn's eyes traveled back and forth as if thinking about that for a second. "Maybe." She shimmied under the blankets, her pained look not quite erased from her face. "Mom?"

"Yes, sweetheart."

"You're all wet."

The statement rattled Mercy. She took a second to form an answer. "I was outside."

"I know." Kaitlyn rolled over to face the wall.

Mercy, mouth open, took in air, but let out no words. There were so many, yet they were a tangled mess and Mercy didn't have the capacity to straighten them. She drew out the only thing that made sense. "Get some sleep. Things will be better tomorrow."

She sat on the floor beside Kaitlyn for many minutes. Rain beat hard against the roof, drummed against the windows. A fierce flash of lightening preceded a crack of thunder. It gave Mercy a start, but didn't seem to disturb Kira or Kaitlyn, whose breathing had softened. She clutched her arms trying to hold together her emotions, but mostly to get a grip on the guilt. Had Kaitlyn seen her on the swing? If so, what must she have thought? But it was more than that. Mercy knew she could have been hurt out there, and whatever followed her in—be it lightning or some kind of heat mist—could have hurt her children.

Don's head ducked into the room. "The house is secure and Josh is asleep," he whispered. "I didn't want to wake him. How's things in here?"

"I think the storm scared Kaitlyn, but she's sleeping now. They both are."

Don's worried stare lingered on Kaitlyn before turning to Mercy. "When you're through here, will you meet me in the living room?"

"Yeah." She watched him walk away. She was a child about to be scolded. But just like a child, she knew she deserved it. She got up and put her hand on the light switch.

"Hmmm, hmmm, hmmm."

Her head snapped in the direction of Kira. She was still on her side. Mercy walked with slow step toward her daughter's bed.

"Hmmm, hmmm, hmmm," Kira hummed.

Mercy gasped.

"Mom?" It was Kaitlyn. "You okay?" She was groggy.

"Do you hear that?"

"Hear what?"

The humming had stopped.

"From Kira. She was humming. Did you hear it?"

"No, but I was just starting to drift. Humming's good though." She gave a sleepy moan and closed her eyes.

"Yes. Go back to sleep."

For minutes, she listened, but all was silent except for the storm. Mercy turned out the light and headed downstairs. Making her way into the living room, she saw Don sitting on the couch in front of the television. He looked comfortable in his pajamas. Despite her saturated clothes, Mercy sat next to him, leaving a space wide enough for a great body of silence to sit between them.

Don muted CNN and sat for a moment as if collecting his thoughts. When he spoke, his voice was cautious. "I know you found some kind of joy in riding that swing, Mercy, and I'm sorry I cut it down."

Tears welled, spilled over her lids.

"Mercy." His eyes were drooped with exhaustion. "You know I had to. The storm. The hour of the night."

"And the lightning." She trembled.

"There was a lot of lightning," Don said. "The air was absolutely charged with it."

She found his eyes. "I'm sorry I worried you."

"You didn't worry me, Mercy. You frightened me. Why were you out there? What is it about the swing that's got you?"

She dug into the tangle of her mind. Pulled out something safe. "I went out to think. The storm hadn't started yet. I got on the swing and got a little lost."

He touched her hand. It felt good. "What you were doing out there was reckless. The danger to you was serious."

"I didn't realize it was so dangerous. I wouldn't have stayed on the swing if I'd realized. I just didn't know."

"I think … I think that's what scares me the most."

"Don, please. Don't think that way."

"I'm not thinking anything. But maybe…" She saw him swallow the words that were on his tongue.

"Maybe what?" They were even. She'd scared him. Now he was scaring her.

"Maybe we should talk to Dr. Wright about this at our next session."

Yes, that definitely scared her. "Sure."

He stood. "We'll find something else for you to enjoy. Okay?"

She nodded, but it wasn't okay. Grappling with the image of Kaitlyn's frightened face, she knew Don was right. But she'd lost her connection to Lisa. It tore at her inside.

"I'm going to look in on the kids again and then hit the sack," Don said. "Although, how Josh was sleeping, I don't think a freight train could wake him up. He was so far under he was talking in his sleep. Something about some kid called Dick in a vest with missing buttons. It was kind of cute."

Mercy stopped breathing. *Could it be? Could they have heard the voices?* Kira and Josh, maybe even Kaitlyn, if they'd heard what she'd heard, that meant Mercy wasn't alone. And then Don would believe her. Don moved toward the stairs and, without quite figuring out why, Mercy closed her throat to keep any admission from slipping out.

"Goodnight, Mercy."

"'Night," she managed.

As he ascended the stairs, she could barely hear the soft thud of his step. He was being quiet not to wake the children and she understood why she hadn't told him. The children were asleep. They couldn't confirm what she'd heard. But they could in the morning.

Mercy unmuted the television and lay her head against the sofa pillow. Tears flowed silent and steady from her until Wolf Blitzer's chestnut voice pushed her into sleep.

CHAPTER TWENTY-TWO
Sometime Around the Present
At the Edge of the Abyss

The soft light that had illuminated the base of the tree had been snuffed with what seemed like a snap of a finger. A boom of thunder snatched Anastasia's voice and she could no longer hum the tune that had pleased her new friend. Walker bit off the end of the words he'd been reciting. Anastasia felt fear overtake his mind. Sheets of haze poured over them. From the cold inside her, Anastasia thought it must be rain, but it had no texture. Thunder exploded, but no streaks of lightning relieved the growing darkness.

"Something's wrong," Anastasia cried. "What's happening?"

A deeper layer of gloom fell over them swiping away the haze that could be rain and Anastasia found herself existing inside a shadow. The word dark screamed in Walker's thoughts.

"We're going back," she roared. "Walker! We're going into the black!" She grabbed her companion's hand and squeezed with all her might.

"Stay, with me, Anastasia. Keep holdin' my hand. Don't let go no matter what happens. Jes' keep a hold on me. We'll be okay. It will pass."

"How do you know?"

"It feels like a storm. All storms pass."

"But there's no rain!"

"I think there is, we jes' cain't feel it."

She didn't know if he really believed that or was just trying to sooth her. His mind had become too agitated. But he was right. They couldn't separate. They had bonded in that bizarre place where time and space were broken. Like siblings separated as infants who had found each other years later, they were connected. Their connection was their only way out of the dark. Thunder boomed.

"I'm scared Walker. I'm scared!"

"Don't let go of my hand!"

A sweep of darkness extinguished all remaining light. Anastasia screamed.

CHAPTER TWENTY-THREE
June 2014 ~ The Present

Fitful wasn't the word for the sleep Don had experienced throughout the night. Plagued was more like it. Filled with ghostly images of Mercy that flashed before him in strikes of lightning. He saw her as a skeleton, riding the tire swing in the raging storm, mouth gaping in rapture.

He got out of the bed that Mercy had not shared with him the night before and stood by the open window. His sight landed with a thud on the garden in the northern corner of the yard. He'd planted that and the other little pockets of flowers in the months after Lisa had died, hoping to give Mercy a place to breathe. In each, he'd taken particular care in picking the perennials he thought would please her—bright bell tulips and teacup daffodils for the spring, delicate aster and bold red and pink Gerbera daisies for the summer. Three little areas around the rim of the yard, each just large enough to harbor a deep-seated Adirondack chair. Three gardens with three chairs, and Mercy never once sat in any of them. But the tire swing. Although Mercy was never diagnosed with the disorder that split her mother's mind, Donovan feared her recent obsession with the swing had the same effect that bipolar would. Manic highs while riding to avoid the crumbling lows when not.

He turned away and went downstairs. As he dragged his body through the living room, for the first time in all the years they'd lived in the house, the floorboards creaked beneath his feet.

He stopped before the sofa, which was vacant, except for the faint indent in the cushion where he'd left Mercy before going to bed. He touched the fabric. It was damp. Mercy had slept there in her wet clothes, he thought. He looked around and didn't see her. *Where is she?* And as he stood there, he realized he was standing in the middle of a palpable silence. For a family of early risers, that was on the warped side of bizarre for a Saturday morning.

He walked into the kitchen to find Kaitlyn seated alone at the island counter, a barely nibbled piece of toast in front of her. Chin propped up by her palm, she didn't seem to notice him.

"Hey, Pumpkin." He picked up the empty coffeepot and filled it halfway with water. "How are you doing this morning?" She gave a shrug of her shoulders and Don saw worry in her. "Mom tells me you had a bit of a fright last night."

"I guess."

"Want to talk about it?"

"Had some nightmares is all." Her chin bobbed in the cup of her hand. "I forced myself to wake up, but the second I fell back to sleep, the nightmares just kept going."

He dumped two scoops of ground coffee into the filter. "What kind of nightmares?" With another scoop of coffee in his grip, he looked over at his daughter, who had lifted her chin from its prop and was rubbing one puffy, dark-circled eye with the back of her hand. He dumped the coffee in the filter and was about to refill another scoop, but he had forgotten how many he'd already fed the machine. He shoved the coffee canister aside and sat next to Kaitlyn.

"It's not important." She fiddled with the uneaten toast.

"Don't be afraid to talk to me. I know dreams can be disturbing sometimes. Talking about them helps take away their power. Trust me."

In a slow exhale, she said, "It started out with Kira acting strange."

"Strange how?"

"I thought I saw her doing stuff like floating in air but when I woke up this morning, it seemed more like a dream."

"So why still so glum?"

"I dreamt all night, Dad. Real dreams, like the kind you can touch and remember. Sometimes I dreamed about Kira doing things that normal people can't do. Like float. Then there were the dreams with Mom in them. They were creepy."

"Creepier than Kira floating?"

She put her lips around the edge of the toast and nodded.

He felt the floor tilt a little under his chair. Kaitlyn had come to him in the night and told him she saw Mercy riding the swing in the storm. She saw her through the bathroom window. If she hadn't told him, Mercy would still be on the swing. He was certain of it. After everything they'd been through, Kaitlyn had been through, he knew they were sitting in dangerous traffic.

"Pumpkin, I didn't tell your mother you were the one who let me know she was on the swing last night. But if you want to talk to her about it, I don't see a problem with that. If you don't want to talk to her, that's fine, too. But, I would like you to talk to me."

Her huge dark eyes drifted up to meet his. "In my dreams Mom was searching for Lisa. She kept calling out to her. And Kira kept answering, but it wasn't like Kira was Lisa or anything. She was this weird zombie kind of thing, answering back like it was automatic, like a robot." Her face was a child's afraid of something under the bed. "Dad? Why do you think Mom was riding the swing last night?"

He wished he had a cup of coffee, something to poke at his mouth while he thought. "She told me she needed to think. The swing was a good vehicle for that."

"Do we need to worry, you know, like before?"

"No, Pumpkin. No need." But he was worried.

He didn't know if Kaitlyn had seen Mercy's expression of bliss while she was riding during the ferocious storm, but there was a good chance she could sense it. Mercy wore that same joyful expression she'd worn right before her suicide attempt. The same mystifying elation that seemed to come out of nowhere.

In the months after Lisa died, Mercy had walked through the house as if walking though a mausoleum. Her despondency sucked the buoyancy out of the whole family. But right at the first sprout of spring, Mercy's eyes lit. Her smile got the children chattering again and the vigor returned to their bodies. Mercy seemed to find pleasure in every nuance of every moment and didn't back away from Donovan's touch. The days were full of life and the nights were calm and normal.

On one of those normal nights when the twins were at a sleepover down the street and Joshua was at a Scouting trip, Don took his wife up to their bed. He undressed her, caressed her, and entered her in the flickering glow of candlelight.

The next morning, in the kitchen making breakfast, Kaitlyn popped through the back door. She'd forgotten her cell phone and scurried up to her room and Donovan laughed, wondering how she'd made it through the night without it. That's when it happened. In a beat, he took off up the stairs. The scream tore through the walls and ripped at the light, and Donovan thought he saw the stairwell bend around him. It was a long, harsh scream, like there was broken glass at the back of her throat and somewhere inside was the garbled scratch of the word Daddy.

He followed the scream into his bedroom. Kaitlyn was bent over her mother, shaking her shoulders, trying to rouse her. He guided his daughter aside. Mercy's skin was yellow. Eyes set in deep, dark hollows. Around her opened mouth, in her hair, and on the pillow were vile chunks of vomit.

"Call 9-1-1," he yelled to Kaitlyn and lifted Mercy from the bed and placed her on the floor. With his fingers, he scooped the vomit from his wife's mouth and throat. It was oatmeal thick. He blew long, slow breaths into her mouth. He positioned the balls of his hands in the center of her breasts, the same breasts he had kissed just hours before.

One. Two. Three. Four. Five. He pumped until the paramedics came.

As he rode in the ambulance, he thought of Lisa. Mercy was on her way to see her. Then, miraculously, Mercy opened her eyes and breathed.

Don moved his chair in a little closer to Kaitlyn. "Your mother is fine. And your dreams were just dreams."

She shook her head in short, quick jerks. "If you could have seen her face."

"It wasn't a real face, Kaitlyn. It was a dream face."

"It was real to me."

"Pumpkin. Your mother has been struggling to deal with losing Lisa. We all have. But for mothers, sometimes the loss of a child can hit especially hard."

"This is different, Dad. She's different now. Everybody's different."

"What do you mean?"

"It could be nothing, but Kira was not like herself this morning. She wouldn't even say 'hey' to me. But it's more than that." She picked at her toast with her fingers, breaking it into tiny bits.

"It's okay. You can tell me."

"Maybe Kira's upset because she saw Mom riding that dumb swing in the storm, although I don't think she did. It's just weird that after what happened with Mom last night and me having those dreams about Kira floating that this morning she's acting all strange. Usually we get up and yap at each other for a couple of minutes then get ready together for the day. But she was dressed before I woke up and when I tried to talk to her, she didn't talk back. She just walked out of the room all focused like."

"She's fifteen. You go through a lot of changes at your age. Even though you're twins, those changes might not be happening to you at the same time."

"Maybe."

"Just to be sure, I'll go talk to her."

"She's not here. She went out with Josh. I don't know where. And that's exactly what I mean. It's Saturday. There's usually some kind of plan. But it's like the rest of the family just went off somewhere and forgot to leave a note."

He kissed her on the top of the head. "Put it out of your mind. We'll figure it out. And you don't have to worry about the tire swing anymore, either. I cut it down last night."

"You did?" Kaitlyn lit up a little.

"I did." His daughter's lopsided grin reminded him of Mercy. "I'll tell you what. I've got a couple of things to do this morning, but afterward, I'm yours for the day. Anything you want. A movie. A trip to the mall, anything."

"That sounds good."

"You okay?"

"Yeah. I'm cool."

Yes, you are. He left Kaitlyn to her crumbled toast and went out into the backyard.

At the base of the maple tree, the tire swing lay in a lump, like a dead opossum, or maybe it was just playing dead. It did seem to have a life of its own. He lifted it from the ground. There was something about the weight of it, the wide tread, and the faint raised imprint on the side that indicated it was made a long time ago. It was a tire from decades past and not something he would have bought. He must have picked it up off one of his properties and neglected to throw it away.

"Time to do just that." He walked over to the garbage bin and lifted the lid.

"What are you doing?"

It blasted him like a Taser. He whipped around to find Mercy there. "You scared me." He chuckled, nervous.

"What are you doing with the tire swing?"

He examined the object in his hands hoping it would tell him how to answer. "I ruined it when I cut it down last night. I was going to throw it out."

Lips sealed in a thin line. Her jaw moved as if she were chewing her words.

"It's okay, Mercy. It's just a thing. We talked about this last night."

She nodded, lips still sealed. He placed the tire swing in the trash bin. When he looked back at her, Mercy was staring at the bin like a child watching a parent bury a pet gerbil. She turned toward the tree, but mid turn she recoiled.

"What happened?" she asked, her head reeling toward Don then back at the tree.

"What do you mean?"

"The tree. Last night. I thought … the lightning. It struck the tree, but … It's whole again."

"I don't remember lightning striking the tree."

"Of course you do! You were there. The lightning hit the tree and snapped it practically in two." Her voice rose and the spill of words quickened. "It cut that branch right off. You saw it. And the red balls of fire, or whatever they were, came out of it and chased us into the house."

Donavon swallowed hard. "Mercy, the storm was pretty bad, but—"

"No! The tree was hit by lightning and broke apart. Now it's whole again. You saw it. You said you saw it. And the globes, the red balls that came flying out, you saw those, too. You grabbed me and protected me. You protected me and the children!"

"Mercy, I'm doing everything I can to protect you and the children, but there were no red balls of flame. And the tree, it was never struck by lightning. You can see that for yourself." His arm extended toward the grand maple, with its enormous burst of intact leaves on their assuredly attached, healthy branches.

Eyes locked on his, she appeared to be looking for something other than the proof of his statement. He took her in his arms and she began to weep.

"It was the storm, Mercy." His tone was mellow. "It was a bad one, and there was a lot of confusion."

"It was a bad one," she repeated.

"It's all right now."

"You don't understand." Her voice quivering. "You just don't."

"No, but maybe Dr. Wright can help us through this." She stiffened and pulled away. His mind back peddled. "There was a lot of lightning last night and the wind was bending those branches almost in half. I'm not suggesting you imagined it. I'm saying it looked exactly like you thought it looked. Like lightning hit the tree and broke off the branches."

"Then why did you suggest we talk to Dr. Wright?"

"Because she has a way of unraveling these things. Putting them into perspective." He tried to smile away his concern.

"I'm exhausted and I have a headache," she said. "I'm going to lie down." There was fear around her eyes.

"It was only an optical illusion, Mercy. No need to worry."

"I'm not worried." She started walking away. "You are." And she went into the house.

CHAPTER TWENTY-FOUR
June 2014 ~ The Present

The cut rope hung from the branch of the maple like a dismembered limb. Outside, at the edge of her house, its severed extremity the tire sat in the garbage bin. From her bedroom window, Mercy could see how wrong it was. That tire belonged on the tree. That tree that had been blown apart the night before and had mysteriously become whole again by morning.

Don blamed the lightning, the red glowing balls, on an optical illusion brought on by the storm. But Mercy had her doubts. *Blame it on the boogie.* You got that right, Jacko.

Soon, though, the children would be awake and tell Don what they heard and she'd get the swing back. Once they reattached the swing, they would all hear the voices together.

Observing the dangling scrap of rope, Mercy was slammed with a sudden dread. What if the swing couldn't be reattached? The rope was cut and too short. Would another rope matter? Did the connection she had with Lisa and the boy really have something to do with the materials of the swing? Could she still contact Lisa without the swing as a conduit? The bedroom door opened. She jolted.

Don's handsome face poked in. "You okay?"

"Yeah. Tired. That's all. Head's still achy."

"Come on downstairs," he said. "I'll fix us some breakfast."

"That will be nice."

He left her. With a weight in her heart and a throbbing in her head, she grabbed a couple of pain relievers from the bathroom, swallowed them without water, then followed her husband into the kitchen. Kaitlyn was sitting at the island counter alone. She was slumped slightly, like she was in a funk, her fear from the night before lingering into the morning.

"Hey, sweetheart," Mercy said, sitting next to her daughter. "How are you today?"

"Okay, I guess." Kaitlyn gave a sideways look over to Don then turned her eyes back at Mercy. "How 'bout you? How are you doing?"

"I'm fine. Last night was a rough one for all us. The storm was fierce and frightening, but it's over now. Today is a new day."

"I hope so."

"Kaitlyn, I want to ask you something, and I don't want you to be afraid to tell me the truth."

"Shoot," Kaitlyn said.

"Last night, during the storm, in your dreams or when you were awake, at any point, did you hear anything unusual?"

"I heard commotion downstairs, right before I closed my eyes. Sounded like you and Dad."

Mercy found her wedding band with her thumb and began rolling it around on her finger. "I'm sorry about that, sweetheart. I'm sorry we kept you awake. But besides us, did you hear any strange voices, like the voices of children?"

Kaitlyn scrunched up her nose and a crinkle formed between her brows. "No, Mom. I didn't hear any voices."

A whirlwind rushed through the back door in the form of Kira and Josh. There was pink in their cheeks as if they'd been running around in the open air. Kaitlyn perked up and the gloom surrounding her vanished.

"I'm starved," Josh said in an effusive burst.

"You're always starving," Kira shot back, heading for the fridge. "You're a bottomless pit."

Josh threw open the refrigerator and began rummaging with a mission through the crisper drawers and racks.

"Hold on, Champ. How about I make us some breakfast."

"Sounds great." Josh shut the refrigerator door, grabbed an apple from the bowl on the counter and chomped a huge bite out of it.

Mercy chuckled. He certainly was a bottomless pit. By definition, that's what twelve-year-old boys were, able to consume voluminous amounts of food and turn it into lean muscle and energy. To look at him, he seemed nothing more than a twig. But those arms had enough brawn to make him a star on the little league field. *One day you'll be a strong man, just like your father.*

"How's pancakes sound." Don's voice was full of cheer and Mercy's heart lightened at the scene around her.

"Oh, great," Kaitlyn scoffed. "I have to make myself boring toast and they get pancakes."

"I'm sure you have room for one pancake." Don flicked her a wink.

"Well, maybe just one." She smirked.

Kira dropped into the seat next to her sister and Josh sat across from them. Don pulled the milk from the refrigerator. Milk in one hand and the eggs in the other, Don turned to his wife and stood as if posing for a portrait—right down to the too-broad smile that looked like he was saying "cheese" behind his teeth.

"Pancakes for you, hon?" he asked.

Hon. A term of endearment. When she'd woken up that morning, she couldn't have imagined she would be sitting among her family celebrating a happy Saturday as if life hadn't stalled and needed a jumpstart. It was almost perfect, except for the elephant she was about to let into the room.

"Josh, Kira," Mercy said. "Last night, did either of you hear any peculiar voices?"

"What kinds of voices," Josh said through a mouthful of apple.

"While you were in bed, even in your dreams perhaps, did you hear children talking or singing?"

"I don't get it," Kira said. "You mean like voices in my head?"

"That's dumb," Josh said.

Kira said, "I didn't hear anything. I slept like log last night. Or is it a dog? I slept like a dog."

"You look like a dog," Josh quipped.

Kira punched him in the arm. "Shut up!"

A hint of vanilla scented the air as Don stirred the batter. "Knock it off, Champ. And Kira, don't hit your brother."

As the children babbled among themselves, Don approached Mercy. He leaned down to her and whispered, "What's up with these voices?"

In a matter of seconds, her children's denial had taken a sledgehammer to her credibility, and all expectations for understanding from her family disappeared.

"I'm sorry." It was genuine. She was sorry for causing so much trouble. And there was a happy moment going on around her. One more push from her, and the happiness would fizzle and Mercy would, again, be off center of the others. "I thought I heard something in the night. I was exhausted and a bit muddled. I was just checking to see if anyone else heard anything. Stupid."

Don whisked the batter in the bowl wrapped in his arm. "It's going to be a good day, Mercy." His response was kind with just a hint of a directive in it.

"The batter smells delicious," she said.

Straightening into Dad pose, he walked to the stove. "Hey, Champ. Where were you and Kira this morning?"

"Dad, can you put blueberries in the pancakes?" Kira interrupted.

"We don't have blueberries."

"Strawberries?" Kaitlyn said.

"No strawberries, sorry."

"Raspberries?" Joshua said.

"No luck. So, what dragged you kids out of the house so early, huh?" Don asked again.

"Blackberries!" Kira shouted, sending Kaitlyn and Josh into uncontrollable snickers.

"No berries. Now where…"

"Boysenberries!" Kaitlyn squealed and the laughter grew.

"Not boysenberries, not strawberries. No berries of any kind." The laughter settled a bit as the buttery sizzle of the pancakes on the griddle popped at the air. "Kira, sweetie, did you go to the park?"

Kira looked at Josh, the smiles on both their faces dropping to a serious line. Mercy saw it, thinking they were bummed their father was ending their fun.

"Huckleberries!" Mercy shouted with an exuberance she didn't think she had in her. When the children screamed and cackled with glee, she let loose with them, doubling over in laughter that cramped her belly. When she sat up, the children were still giggling and Don's gaze was locked on hers with the laugh still in his eyes.

They gobbled up their berry-less pancakes and talked about what they wanted to do that day. After some discussion, it was unanimously decided a movie was in order. Something funny.

They piled into the SUV, the children frolicking in the back as they headed to the theater. When they got there, they bought gobs of popcorn, red licorice strings, and sodas and munched and slurped and laughed like happy families do when they go to funny movies together. And when the movie was over, they all agreed they should do that more often.

"That was so much fun," Kaitlyn said as they walked to the car.

"Crandall's a funny dude," Joshua added.

"And really cute," Kira said.

Josh made barfing noises. Kira punched him in the arm. As he continued to walk, Josh kicked a small stone across the parking lot. "Hey, Dad?"

"Yes, Champ."

"What's a blacking-box?"

"A what?" Don said.

"A blacking-box. I think it's got something to do with shining shoes, but what is it?"

"Was that something in the movie? Because I think I missed it."

"No," Josh said. "It's just something that popped into my head."

A blacking-box. Mercy knew what it was. *He had no office to open. His little blacking-box was ready for use.*

"It's a shoe-shining kit," Mercy answered, and vertigo slipped into her ear and her sight began to spin.

"That's right," Josh replied. "Dick said, 'Shine yer boots, sir?'"

Shine yer boots, sir. Shine yer boots. Shine yer boots. Mercy gulped some air and swallowed hard and the air in her throat felt like too much ice cream going down. Josh had said that he hadn't heard any voices, but there he was quoting the boy from the tree.

"Josh," she said, her mind settling.

"Yeah, Mom?"

"Where did you hear about a blacking-box?"

"I didn't hear about it. It just popped in my head."

"Things don't just pop into people's heads. You must have heard or read it somewhere."

"I guess," Josh said, shrugging. He headed toward the car, the girls following not far behind.

She thought back to what Don had said the night before, how Josh had been talking in his sleep. Maybe, she reasoned, he'd heard it in his sleep and that's why he doesn't remember. She looked at her husband who was cross-examining her with his stare. She flashed a smile and met up with her children at the car.

She ducked into the passenger's seat and shut the door. In the vacuum of the vehicle, she heard it. Humming. It floated around inside the car. She opened the window and instead of the music escaping, the humming ballooned to fill the entire capacity of the space. Mercy spun around and saw Kira bobbing her head back and forth to the music. The humming was coming from her daughter.

On an impulse, Mercy sang and as she uncannily expected, Kira joined her on the next line. Mercy stopped singing and Kira began to hum again, leaving the lyrics behind. "Kira," Mercy said. But she didn't have time to answer.

Don had picked up the song and joined in, and Kaitlyn followed. They were singing the Beatles' tune as innocently as a family would do on a road trip. It should have been a cozy interaction, but Mercy was chilled. She didn't even know the girls knew that song. It may have been familiar, but to know the words? What crept under her skin and attacked her nerves the most was Joshua. He wasn't singing at all.

"Don?" But he just looked at her with eyes that said *Come on, join in. It's fun.* She looked back at Kira, who was still bobbing her head, a blank smile on her face. Kira was focused on her hands—the fingers of her right hand making a strange waving motion toward the left.

Don gave Mercy a nudge with his elbow, prodding her to join them. And she did. There wasn't much more she could do. They all sang, all except Joshua, the same song over and over. Once they hit the end of the first refrain, they started again from the beginning. Like "Row, Row, Row Your Boat" without the scattering of voices. And with each new round, Mercy fought the tears that would reveal her.

She expected her son to start reciting the words she'd heard the boy recite, but no words came. He sat quiet, contemplative, as if internally genuflecting to the ceremony that was going on around him. For reasons not fully realized to Mercy, it was heartbreaking. They went on that way, all of them singing except Joshua, and Mercy held the pieces of her heart together as best she could until Don pulled the SUV into their driveway.

As Don eased into the garage, they came to the close of the refrain. Don put the SUV in park and turned off the engine. In unison, they stopped singing.

The seconds crept forward without as much as an audible breath between them. No one moved. They all remained frozen in a moment in time. Mercy sat in the soundless car, waiting for the next torture to strike. Then Don opened his door.

"That was such a fun movie," Joshua said, bright and sparkling as ever.

"Crandall's so dreamy," Kira chimed and exited into the garage.

Unable to break from the spell she felt was cast upon her, Mercy sat and watched the children enter the house. Don, the last at the entryway, looked back at his wife.

"You coming?" he said.

Mercy exited the SUV and followed her family inside.

CHAPTER TWENTY-FIVE
Sometime Around the Present
After the Abyss

The black never quite took Walker and Anastasia. Their tie to the earth had become too strong, but Walker wasn't sure why. Perhaps it was because he and Anastasia had found each other, connected, and there was strength in their coming together. But it had tried to take them, that oppressive, consuming darkness with no beginning and no end, and he was bent on making sure it never happened again.

"Do you recollect anything?" he asked Anastasia.

"I remember being pulled and everything going dark, but not all the way dark like before. After that, I don't remember anything. Just kind of opened my eyes and I was here again, by the tree."

"Same's with me. 'Cept I recollect people. It's muddy, though."

"Oh my gosh. I thought I imagined that." She smiled and hope sprang from behind her blue eyes. "It was so fast, though. I couldn't make them out."

"Felt not so fast to me. Felt like a season'd passed."

"Time's funny now."

"Sure 'nuff is." He leaned his back against the tree, and it reminded him of when he would read there in the sunlight, except there wasn't any sun and he couldn't really feel the tree. Just knew he was leaning against it. "Now that we know for sure there's folks around, we should try harder to reach 'em."

"Like talk to them?"

"Talk to 'em. Touch 'em. Anythin' to get 'em to hep us."

"What about the dark place? What if it drags us in the next time?"

"I think things is different now. Somethin's changed. Things keep shiftin'."

"I can hear you thinking and you don't know for sure that the dark won't come back."

"Not for sure, no. That's why we need to get those folks to come to us."

"How?"

"Think, Anastasia. Remember you said you held on with your mind to the crying woman you think is your Ma. Think real hard about those folks you recollected when we was being pulled back to the darkness."

"I don't really remember them. It's fuzzy, like I made it up and I didn't really see them at all."

"But you did, because I saw them, too. Felt them."

"Yeah. Felt them."

"Think 'bout what you felt. Think hard, Anastasia. Think 'bout the folks who shared the space with us. Think so hard that no other thought comes in your head. And hold on. Hold on to them."

She closed her eyes and he watched her for a bit. There was some fright in the pucker of her lips, but after a moment, it softened. Walker closed his eyes and thought about the vague people they'd seen. He thought harder than he'd ever thought in all his life, and the haze around his thoughts began to clear.

CHAPTER TWENTY-SIX
June 2014 ~ The Present

Mercy's armpits and the back of her neck were damp with sweat. She'd been sweating since she'd returned home from the movies, and it wasn't the kind of sweat that came from heat. She walked under the archway that separated the kitchen from the living room. Resonant murmurs of Don's deal making came through the closed door of his office. Indiscernible chatter of her girls seeped down from the second floor. In front of the television screen, Josh sat playing his video game. Mercy sat next to her son.

"Josh?"

"Hmm." He cocked his head but kept his attention on the screen in front of him. "Josh. Look at me."

He turned his head. Mercy reeled backward. His eyes were solid white. No irises, no pupils. Just white. She clutched his shoulders with both hands.

"Mom?" It was Kira.

Just seconds before Mercy had heard Kira and Kaitlyn babbling away in their room overhead, and in a blink, there was Kira standing at the bottom of the stairs. In the next seconds, Kaitlyn descended the stairs and stood by her sister. Mercy looked to her son, whose eyes were back to their chocolate brown, except the pupils were slightly dilated.

"What's the matter, Mom?" Kira asked.

"It was … I saw… Josh." She examined his naturally brown eyes. "Are you all right?"

"You're hurting me."

"What's going on out here?" Don was standing over her.

She released her white-knuckled grip from his shoulders. "I'm sorry." Her voice was wispy and she swiped the sweat from her forehead.

"Why did you grab me?" He was a child who'd been punished for no reason. "What did I do?"

"Nothing. You did nothing. I'm sorry. I made a mistake." She sat back and collected her emotions. "You looked troubled. A mother overreacting, that's all."

"Well, I am troubled," he said. Mercy held her breath. "These Vortons are destroying my village and I don't have enough cosmic energy to defend them." He returned to his computer game battle, his thumbs beating against the control panel.

She exhaled and touched his forehead with the back of her hand. There was no fever. The opposite. His skin felt like a frozen lake. He wriggled out from under her touch, trying to stay focused on the video screen. Kira and Kaitlyn went into the kitchen, carrying with them the babble they had apparently started upstairs. Don moved back toward the hallway. He motioned Mercy to follow. She did.

In a low voice he said, "Why did you grab him, Mercy?"

"I saw something in his eyes and it scared me." *I saw nothing in his eyes. That's what scared me.* "It looked like he was going to faint. But he's fine."

He fixed on her face for a second as if trying to read what she wasn't telling him. "You've been tense, and it's starting to spill over. Why don't you rest for a while?"

"Mom," Kaitlyn called from the kitchen. "When's dinner?"

"I'm starved," Josh said.

Mercy cocked her head and smiled at her husband in a way that said, Don't worry, Darling. "About forty minutes," she answered her daughter. "Snack on something." She, in fact, hadn't given a single thought about dinner. She started for the kitchen.

"His little blacking-box was ready for use, and he looked sharply in the faces of all who passed, addressing each with, 'Shine yer boots, sir?'"

She whirled around. "What did you say?"

"The blacking-box," Josh answered.

"What about it?"

"You said it's a shoe shining box. In the parking lot after the movie."

"Yes. Yes. But…" She pinched her lips together and scanned the faces around her. Don's head was raised higher on his neck; his look was of cautious anticipation. Josh had turned away from his game, his eyes on hers. The girls stood identical in the kitchen, staring at Mercy.

"I'd better get dinner started." She went into the kitchen and stood by the sink. Behind her, she heard the explosions of Josh's video game, the chatter of her girls, the light latch of Don's office door closing. Had her children caught that intangible something that Don had tried to throw away without realizing it? Had they heard the voices, and were those voices playing in their heads, like a code? If so, the big question was how could she get them to help her decipher it? Looming behind that question was the worry that those voices would somehow hurt her children. Or, she thought, would her tampering with those voices do more damage than good? She considered it for many minutes with futile results. At least for the time being, her children were fine. She turned from the window and resolved for the moment to answer the small question: What's for dinner?

~

Slate gray of the predawn hung over the yard like a vampire's cape. Its grim shield against the pending sunrise was a warning to all mortals to stay indoors because evil still had time to do its handiwork. Even the birds knew to stay concealed in the safety of the trees. Only one cat was brave enough to saunter through the smoldering gloom. Mercy watched from her kitchen window as the shadowy contour of the cat slunk across the yard. The evening before, she had decided on chicken piccata with steamed broccoli for dinner, a meal that sounded gourmet but was rather easy to prepare. It placated her family and they all retired full and happy, except for Mercy, who had eaten little and had been up most of the night with a mind filled with phantoms.

As the sky peeled back another layer of night, she observed the cat amble to the maple tree and disappear behind it. That's when Mercy saw him.

Joshua. He was sitting on the ground, his back against the tree, a wrist propped against each bent knee as if he were holding something. She opened the kitchen window and turned her ear to the outside. Low murmurs from her son made their way to her, but the words were indistinct. It was a monotone murmur that attached itself to the air. She looked at the clock on the microwave. 6:04.

She walked out onto the yard. Like the cat, she tried to stay low and slow, one carefully placed step after another, moving toward the side of the yard to stay out of her son's direct line of sight. He wasn't looking at her anyway. He was stone set on his hands. Lifting her left foot, her heart tripped inside her chest. She set her foot down and put the right foot in front of that.

It doesn't matter that I can't hear the words. I know what he's saying.

Another inch closer and the words began to form. Flat, without inflection, Joshua dropped the words like pebbles onto the grass. They didn't bounce as if dropped onto the pavement or ripple as when hitting the water. They dropped with a little thud over and over again.

"Dick's business hours had commenced he had no office to open his little blacking-box was ready for use dick's business hours had commenced he had no office to open his little blacking-box was ready for use dick's business hours…"

Quick and even the words fell without a hint of breath between them. Of course, hear it or not, he had to be breathing, but there was no pause for it. How she wished Donovan was home. He'd left the house not fifteen minutes earlier to make a 6:30 walk-through at a condo development he'd been working on in Durham. Mercy fibbed and said she had woken early to help him off. She made coffee and as he headed out, she kissed him goodbye. When he pulled out of the driveway, she was glad to have the time to think without him observing in the background. But standing before her son, she wanted nothing more than his presence. If he were there, he would hear and he would believe her. Mercy moved in closer.

"Joshua." He kept droning. "Joshua." Her voice was dry, like her throat.

She knelt and placed her palm on his chest and her ear near his mouth. There came the slightest intake and exhale of breath, but it was as even and short as the words that fell from him.

Above her head, the leaves rustled, too much for a squirrel or a bird. A flock, maybe. The robins clustered in the tree when they slept and they would wake together and cause a stir. Mercy looked up. Her eyes fell on the soles of white Keds sneakers. Tucked inside them were the bronze, slim ankles of one of her daughters. Mercy's face went numb as if all the blood had drained from it.

It was Kira. Those Keds were her cheerleading sneakers and she had a rip on the side. It was on Mercy's to-do list to get her a new pair. High above Mercy's head, Kira sat on the branch, kicking her legs back and forth. But it wasn't a nimble kicking; rather it was mechanical and stiff. A life-sized marionette whose legs were attached to strings. And she was so high, if Mercy had a ladder she couldn't reach her. Droning monotone buzzed around her, and down through the leaves she heard the humming.

"Jesus in Heaven."

The melody didn't drift. It dripped, one drop at a time, a leaky faucet that would make you go mad in the middle of the night. It dropped like the stones from Joshua's mouth. It held the tune of the Beatles' song, but it was broken. There was a separation between the notes, each note hummed and stopped, hummed and stopped. Josh continued to drone and Kira mechanically hummed and Mercy thought her mind would explode.

Shooting a glance at the house, she cursed Don for not being home. Kaitlyn is. She didn't want to bring Kaitlyn into this strangeness, but what else could she do? Get Mary Beth? No, Mary Beth was biased toward Mercy. Kaitlyn would be believed.

"Momma?"

The word hit her like a dart. Up in the tree, her daughter leaned so far forward a breeze could send her plunging down. But Mercy saw no fear on Kira's face. Only bemusement.

"Momma?"

She chirped the word like a small child would. Her long, curls waved and splashed at her shoulders as she cocked her head from side to side, her wide, dark eyes saying, "What are you doing here?"

161

What are YOU doing THERE?

Before she knew what was happening, Kira pushed her body from the branch as if leaping into a lake. Mercy let out a yelp, jumped to her feet with instinctive agility and thrust out her arms to catch her daughter. If Mercy had come between Kira and the ground, her daughter would have broken both of them, but it didn't happen. Kira landed firmly on her feet on the branch below the one on which she sat. Mercy slapped her palm on her chest and let out a huff of relief. The respite, however, was brief as Kira sprung to the next branch below. Mercy's heart rocketed against her ribs. From branch to branch her daughter jumped until she landed like a gymnast on the ground. Kira may have been a cheerleader, but she wasn't a flyer. She was the catcher and was always at the base of the human pyramid, never at the top. She wouldn't have been able to climb to the first limb of that tree for her fear of heights.

Taking a step closer to Mercy, Kira leaned her face forward and peered into her mother's eyes. "You're not my Momma."

"Of … Of course I am, sweetheart." She looked at her son who was still in the same pose, reciting in monotone.

"Where's my Momma?" She had that little frightened lilt that Dorothy in the movie version of the *Wizard of Oz* had when she said she wanted to go home.

"Kira." Fear gripped Mercy from her genitals all the way up to the swell at the back of her tongue. "What are you doing?"

"I'm not Kira."

"Of course you are. What kind of joke is this?"

Kira shut her eyes and shook her head like a cat shaking off a sneeze. "I'm not Kira." Her voice rose and the lilt was gone. "And you're not my mother."

In that moment, the giant, sharp-toothed mouth of horror took a bite out of Mercy's senses. Those eyes, the mirrors of the soul, as the adage went, the dark chocolate that were her daughter's eyes had turned, right before her, to the color of dust. From dust, they faded to white with no distinction between the pupil and the iris. The entire expanse of her eyes was white, just like she'd seen in Josh's eyes the evening before. Nausea gripped Mercy as the irises in her daughter's eyes rose back to the surface and brightened to the color of a blue sky.

"Help me find my Momma. Please." The age left her daughter's voice, at least five or more years. "I want my Momma." It was the voice she'd been hearing. The voice she believed belonged to Lisa. It was deep with longing and Mercy started to cry. All the hope that had filled her when the swing was intact, when the voices were disembodied and she could respond to them with pure faith seeped out like water from a slow leak. Mercy wasn't in the presence of her daughter, alive or dead. She was in the presence of someone unknown.

Mercy took a breath and asked, "Who are you?"

"Anastasia." Soft from a girl lost. "Anastasia Madison."

"How old are you, Anastasia?"

"Eight. Do you know where my Momma is?"

The question floated around her and Mercy could only say, "No."

Once her answer cut the air, the droning from Joshua stopped, and Mercy could feel his hot breath against the center of her back. She spun around. Unfazed, Josh walked past Mercy, his hand reached out to his sister. Kira took it. Mercy stood, mouth agape. Joshua would much rather take a punch to the side of his head than hold his sister's hand, and it was the way he was holding it, full-palmed, fingers entwined in a firm grip. The two walked across the yard and, when they reached the back deck, the siblings' arms began to swing slightly.

Mercy followed her children as they entered the kitchen, walked up the stairs and, their fingers unraveling, separated into their respective bedrooms. Leaning through the open door of her daughters' room, she saw Kira pull down the lavender coverlet, slip her legs beneath, and pull the coverlet back up to her chin. Kira lay straight on her back, closed her eyes, and appeared to fall asleep. Her sister, who had yet to wake to what was quickly becoming the sunlit world, was rolled on her side, facing the wall. She hadn't witnessed a thing. Hope fell from Mercy like a dump truck dumping its load. She crossed the hall to Joshua's room. He was already tucked into bed, on his back, his blanket crumpled at his feet, but with a sheet hooked right up under his chin.

She left the door open and crept across the hall again. Before entering her daughters' room, she was overcome by the need to pray.

"Dear God…"

She felt sinful saying it out loud. She'd stopped praying after Lisa died, and she feared God would find her petition selfish. But what was He going to do about it? Send her to hell? Mercy let that thought finish its foxtrot, then prayed, "Dear God. Forgive me for being a hypocrite, but this prayer isn't for me. It's for my children. Something is wrong with them and I need You and Your divine goodness to help me help them. Amen." There. Sent. Disclaimer and all.

Entering her daughters' room, Mercy sat on the purple area rug beside Kira's bed, her knees tucked under the skirt ruffle, which was a shade lighter of lavender than the coverlet. Purple and lavender were the girls' colors of the moment and it pervaded every corner of the room. Examining Kira's face, there was no twitch of the eye or break in the rhythm of her breathing, no crinkle of her lips, no wiggle of her nose, nothing but the slow, patterned respiration of a young girl deep in slumber.

As she observed her, the possibility that Josh and Kira had been playing a joke on her grew slim. Her daughter's eyes changing color, the pitch of her voice, the tire swing moving on its own in the middle of the night. It wasn't logistically possible for them to do that. Most of all, she knew her children would never do something so treacherous. After all they'd been through, the thought was too diabolical. But something was happening, and she was going to figure it out.

She leaned her head against the mattress and, though the plan was to stay and watch for hours, it was only minutes before Mercy grew drowsy and the purple of her daughters' room turned to soot.

When Mercy opened her eyes, pools of morning sun came through the window. Her neck ticked and creaked like her head had been taken off and put on backwards. The covers of Kira's bed were thrown back in a sloppy heap. Her daughter would have had to crawl over her mother or down to the end of the mattress to get out, as the other side of the bed leaned against the windowed wall. Kaitlyn's bed was also rumpled and empty. From downstairs rose a hubbub of voices and the unmistakable aroma of bacon and eggs. Wafting through the meaty, buttery scent were the cheerful voices of her three children.

Mercy made the slow descent down the stairs, crossed through the living room and into the kitchen. Don, still in his business clothes, with his tie pulled down and white shirt sleeves rolled up, stared right into her with a cautious, observing expression. She sat at the island counter, resisting the impulse to smooth with her fingers the crease between her brows.

"Some breakfast?" Don asked.

Mercy gave a nod and he placed a plate of bacon and eggs in front of her. Outside and distant, the Cunningham's dog barked. Banter about boys between Kira and Kaitlyn and chatter about baseball between Don and Josh boomeranged around her. Everyone acted as if it were a perfectly ordinary morning. Except it wasn't.

"Who's Anastasia Madison?" Mercy asked.

The girls kept on talking as if the question wasn't for them.

Don paused his conversation with Josh. "What's that?"

"Kira." Mercy focused. "Who's Anastasia Madison?"

Kira turned toward her mother and said in a sedated tone, "Anastasia Madison."

Mercy stared into her daughter's eyes, which were their natural brown. She turned to her son. "Josh. Do you know who Anastasia Madison is?"

In the same tone as his sister, he said, "Anastasia Madison."

"This morning at the tree, you said to me, Kira, that you were Anastasia Madison."

"No I didn't."

"At the tree. You and Joshua…" She gasped.

Josh slipped his hand in Kira's and their fingers entwined.

Mercy regained control of her breath. "This morning," she said, "you and Joshua were at the tree."

Josh and Kira's heads turned at the same time to face each other. They exchanged a long stare before zeroing in on Mercy.

"I was in bed," Josh said.

"I was in bed," Kira said.

"Kira was in bed," Kaitlyn said.

There was something creepily robotic, like the Stepford Wives, in their alibis.

"This morning," Mercy tried again. "Early. I saw you, Josh, leaning against the trunk of the maple and you were reciting words from some story. You know, about the blacking-box. And Kira, you were in the tree. Sitting on a branch."

"What?" Kaitlyn said as Kira inched closer to her brother.

"You had climbed the tree and were sitting on a high branch."

"Climbed a tree? Mom. You know she can't do that."

"Yes, I know, Kaitlyn. It was illogical, but she was there and she didn't seem afraid."

"I don't climb trees, Mom." Kira pinched her lips together the way she did when she was younger before a cry came. "Me and Josh…" Her eyes were twitching back and forth as if she were thinking and talking at the same time. "…weren't at the tree this morning."

"Maybe you don't realize you were. Maybe you were sleepwalking and don't remember."

"Sleep walking?" Kaitlyn said. "Both of them?"

"Well, I don't know why," Mercy said, "but they were there. You were there, Kira. You and Josh."

"We weren't," Kira said.

"We weren't," Josh said.

Stepford.

Don moved next to her. "Mercy, what's going on with you?"

She let out the air in her throat. "This morning, Kira was up in the tree and Josh was sitting on the ground reciting something about the blacking-box."

"Again with the blacking-box." He sounded irked.

"It's not just that. Kira's eyes. They turned color somehow and her voice changed, and she claimed she was someone named Anastasia Madison."

"Mom, that's crazy," Kira said.

"It's not crazy. It's what happened."

"No, it didn't," Josh said. A tear fell down his face.

"No, don't cry." Mercy reached for him, but he drew back. She turned her focus to Kira. "You were in the tree. I swear."

"Oh, Mercy," Don said. "Come on now."

Kira moved in closer to her brother. Their arms were touching. Mercy saw it and knew she stood alone. Don stepped closer to his children, leaving Mercy farther off to the side, and she felt as if some ploy was going on and it was all of them against her.

"Kira, please. Anastasia Madison. Who is she?"

"I don't know." It came out panicked.

"Tell me!"

"Back off, Mercy!"

Don touched her arm and it felt like a scream. She jerked back. Something vicious was being played out and Mercy was on the outside of it. Or maybe she was the brunt of it. She had the sick feeling that she was the last Billy Goat Gruff crossing the bridge under which the troll sat, waiting to devour her.

She placed her hands on her daughter's shoulders and pleaded, "I just want to know who Anastasia is."

"Enough, Mercy!" Don yelled.

"They're playing a game, Don. Can't you see?"

"Let go, Mom! You're hurting me!"

"Tell me." She gave Kira a shake, and Don grabbed her arm and pulled one hand free from their daughter.

"Tell me," Mercy yelled.

Kira wrenched her other arm free and stumbled backward. "Leave me alone, you crazy bitch!"

Without thinking, Mercy threw her right hand back and swung, her open palm landing flat and hard against Kira's cheek. The red imprint was immediate, but Kira's reaction took a moment.

Tears poured down her daughter's face. "What's the matter with you, Mom? What did we do?"

Mercy moved toward her, but Don grabbed her arm. A terrifying swell of regret grew in her like a giant parasite, and Mercy thought it would explode right through her chest.

Josh's ears were bright red from the heat of his fear, and his face was streaked with tears. Kira sobbed into her sister's shoulder, who was embracing her as a mother should. Together, the three trudged through the living room.

At the bottom of the stairs, Kaitlyn turned. "It's happening again, Dad." It was an accusation. "Do something."

Mercy heard the lumbering steps of her children as they moved up the stairs. She was wrong. She wasn't the last Billy Goat Gruff. She was the troll. Turning to her husband, she opened her mouth, but he threw up a hand to stop her.

"I have to think," he said. "I'm going to check on them," he pointed above his head, "and then I'm going to think." There were no tears in his eyes, but she heard them in his voice. For an eternal minute he stood, chest heaving. The silence was like a handsaw, its serrated edge slowly carving away at her nerves. And then he opened his mouth to speak, and Mercy opened hers to consume the words. Anything was better than the silence.

And his words came. "Stay away from the children." He turned from her and went up the stairs.

Mercy closed her mouth and swallowed.

CHAPTER TWENTY-SEVEN
June 2014 ~ The Present

The tea was tepid with a metallic aftertaste. Mercy stared at the tea dust that had settled to the bottom of her cup. She wondered if there were portentous messages in the dust that seeped out of tea bags, just as some found messages in tea leaves. All she saw was a dark mess. She pushed her chair away from Mary Beth's kitchen table, crossed to the sink, and tossed the tea into it. She'd been at her friend's house the whole day and half the night, not willing to go home until she made sense of things.

In all her life, she had never laid a hand on her children, not a spank or even the threat of one. No level of distress, no amount of anxiety could justify hurting her children. That was something her mother would do. Not her.

The battered become batterers. No. Not Mercy. She was never really battered. Not really. Not on purpose. It was a mistake. Always a mistake. Never on purpose. And only after her father left. Only when her mother was drunk. She drank because she was sick. It wasn't her fault she was sick. She only hurt Mercy when she was drunk. And only because Mercy got in the way.

The image of Kira's frightened eyes monopolized her brain, and she thought of the times when her mother had frightened her. She remembered her mother standing before the stove, one oven-mitted hand on the cast iron handle of the frying pan, the other wrapped around a coffee cup half-filled with vodka. Her mother was shaking the pan with eggs in it and cursing her hangover.

Mercy did something—touched her mother's sleeve, spoke her name—and her mother spun around. Mucous-like eggs flew across the kitchen and the frying pan whacked Mercy smack in the middle of her forehead. The force lifted her off the ground and she landed hard, her back slamming against the radiator in the corner of the kitchen. Mercy wanted to believe it was an accident; convinced herself of it for a good three minutes, but it was her mother's slurred words that ultimately brought doubt.

"You know better than to bother me when I don't feel well."

Fear filled her that day. From the frying pan incident until the day her mother died, Mercy lived with a quaking fear for her life. It wasn't a fear that her mother would deliberately set out to kill her. But her accidents were frequent and unapologetic and when she was drunk, anything was possible. That afternoon, Mercy had caused the same fear to appear on her daughter's face.

"...work out."

"What?" Mercy said as she climbed out of her thoughts.

Mary Beth put her teacup on its saucer. "I said, everything's going to work out."

"Oh."

"What is it?"

"The stove," Mercy said.

"What about it?"

"It wasn't on."

"What stove?"

"My mother's." Mercy looked into her friend's ocean eyes. "The day she hit me with the frying pan. She was frying eggs at the stove, shaking the pan like she was keeping the heat even, but the stove wasn't turned on. It was stone cold when I touched it. She would have stood there for hours drinking vodka and shaking the raw eggs if I hadn't interrupted her with my head."

"Oh my gosh, Mercy. Why are you remembering that now?"

"Don't you get it?" She clamped her fingers together on her lap to keep the trembling at bay. "When I struck Kira, I was stuck in that same place my mother was stuck in when she hit me with the frying pan." Briny tears burned her eyes and she blinked them out. "Help me, Mary Beth. Something's happening. Something really fucked up."

"Honey, you've got to think about this straight. There's logic here somewhere. We just have to find it."

"I've tried. If it's somewhere, it's doing a damned good job hiding."

"It's not hiding. You're just associating things in the wrong way." Mary Beth stood, retrieved the tea kettle, and poured steaming water over the half-spent teabag in her cup. Sitting back down, she said, "Take the Beatles' song. It was one of our favorites when we were kids. You were singing it when you rode the swing for the first time and it brought you back to the past. It opened up a whole can of nostalgia and you attached a child's voice to it. Logical. Then you were probably unknowingly humming it around the house and that's how Kira picked it up."

"What about the blacking-box and Josh quoting that passage?"

"Again, maybe you repeated it aloud and he overheard."

"I thought of that, but where did I get it from? I've never read that anywhere before."

"Not that you consciously remember. It could be a long-forgotten memory that's been brought to the surface by some trigger event."

"Trigger event?"

"Something that happens in your life that triggers a response or memory or something like that. The tire swing, for example. All of this happened after we put together the tire swing. The swing has childhood etched all over it. That may have triggered the memory of the passage from the book that was hibernating in your mind."

"If I remembered the passage, then I would have remembered reading it. I have no memory of ever reading that passage before in my life."

"It's strange, I'll admit. But strange things happen. It doesn't mean anything."

"You're wrong," Mercy said. "There is meaning here. I heard it. There are voices. Real voices. And at least one of them was speaking to me."

"Mercy." Mary Beth stopped, as if kicking out the bad words in her mind and replacing them with kinder ones. "I don't know how to work with that. If nobody hears or sees these things except you…"

"Josh and Kira heard them."

"It's more likely Josh and Kira heard you, like I said."

"And won't admit it? Listen to me. I heard voices and I'm standing alone here. I need help. I need to find out what's going on."

"I just don't know how I can help with this," Mary Beth said.

"You can start by believing me."

"I believe in you."

"That's not the same thing."

Skepticism hung at the sides of her friend's downturned eyes. How could she expect Mary Beth to trust her ghosts were real? How could she expect Don to have that kind of blind faith? She couldn't.

"I need proof and I don't know how to get it," Mercy said. "Please, just say you'll help me." Her friend put on a guarded smile. "If only to humor me."

"I suppose out of all the half-baked shit we've done together, this isn't so bad." The words were light, but they came out heavy. "I'll humor you."

"Thank you." A tiny sweep of relief helped to clear her head. "I think we should start with why I can hear the voices now and never before."

Mary Beth sat forward. "You claim you initially heard the voices the first time you were on the swing. So, I guess the swing is where we start." Mercy nodded. "But you also heard the girl's voice in the shower."

"Yes, but not the boy's. I only heard the boy when I was on the swing. I think the boy and the girl are together, but it's the girl who is reaching out to me."

"Then if it is the swing, where did the pieces come from?"

"The garage. You were there with me when we found them."

"No, I mean originally. How did they get in the garage?"

Mercy thought, and it was right there. There was no fuzz around the edges or blur in the details. Mercy found the tire and the rope while she was helping to clear the land of debris prior to the development of their neighborhood. The tire was lying in a patch of trees, partially hidden by the overgrowth, and—she took in a shock of breath—one of those trees was the maple. Don had set the tire aside to recycle it. The rope was left coiled on a wooden shelf in an old ramshackle shed at the other end of the development. It was the only built structure on that particular piece of property at the time. The shed had belonged to someone, at least that's what the dozens of Mason jars stacked in rows three jars deep indicated, but it had been long abandoned. The shed still stood because no one cared to break a sweat to tear it down.

She remembered Don had used the rope to tie down a tarp over debris they'd piled in the bed of his truck. The rope and tire had somehow ended up in the garage and were eventually forgotten. Mercy wondered if she knew to keep them, instinctively knew that they possessed a power she would eventually call upon. Or, more likely, a power that would call upon her.

She told Mary Beth of how she collected the items. "They weren't found together," Mercy said, "but they were close enough."

"So it is feasible that there is a connection between the rope and the tire."

"And the tree," Mercy added. "Now that I've thought it out, I believe it's the connection of those items to the tree that's sparked this … whatever it is."

"So, what does it mean, and who's this Anastasia girl?" Mercy spread her hands open to indicate she had nothing. Mary Beth nudged her head toward the stairs. "Come on."

The two went up to Mary Beth's den and settled behind the computer.

"What do you think we'll find?" Mercy asked.

"We'll soon know." Mary Beth flicked on the computer monitor. "I have to say, I think it's terribly strange that Josh and Kira would be involved in any kind of prank like this."

"I'm not sure they're involved by choice."

"What does that mean?"

"I don't know. But like you said, it's not like them and that means something's wrong. Start typing."

Mary Beth began pecking at the keyboard with her index fingers. "Our only information so far is the name, Anastasia Madison. Let's start with that."

With her two-fingered hunt-and-peck technique, Mary Beth typed in the name and hit enter, sending their query out into that complex labyrinth of invisible signals known as the Internet. Amazing technology, the Internet. A person could ask almost anything and get an answer. Type a few words and presto, you can drywall your basement, learn how to fly fish, get a recipe for perfect peach cobbler, and find a little dead girl who loves the Beatles.

In just a few seconds, the results were there, all thirty-three hundred twenty-four of them for the name "Anastasia Madison."

"Shit," Mercy spit.

"Might as well start from the beginning," and Mary Beth clicked on the top result.

First up, Anastasia Madison on a social networking site. Fifty-seven years old, lives in Los Angeles, California. Enjoying a raison scone, according to her latest status update.

"Why do people take pictures of their food?" Mary Beth shook her head and clicked on her bio. No connection to their girl. Next, same social networking site, nurse practitioner from Wisconsin. Drank too much tequila the night before and called in sick.

"If I can see this," Mercy said. "I'll wager so can her boss."

"Bet tomorrow's status update will say 'unemployed.'"

"I doubt our Anastasia is going to have a social networking page. First of all, for all intents and purposes she's dead, and judging from the song she was singing, she probably lived before the Internet existed."

"True, but maybe her namesake is here. You know how people love to post family history stuff."

"I suppose," Mercy said.

And so it went. Anastasia Madison, stay-at-home mom from Arizona with pictures of her toddlers naked in the bathtub. The comments underneath said, "Too cute!" and "What darlings!" as if those innocent personal shots weren't really fodder for pedophiles. Anastasia Madison, retired social worker from Tennessee. Anastasia Madison, Michigan State College student whose cleavage took up most of her profile picture. Some of the site pages locked out Mercy and Mary Beth from seeing their posts, but the feeling was strong that none of those people were connected to their Anastasia. Websites also proved futile and there were no Anastasia Madisons in all of North Carolina listed in the online phone book. Searching phone numbers for just Madison in North Carolina brought up hundreds of hits, and a search through those showed no Anastasia as a relation.

Mary Beth fell back in her chair. "Ugh. This is getting us nowhere."

"There's got to be something." Mercy stood and crossed to the window. She could see her bedroom window across the way and all appeared dark and quiet there. She sat back down.

"Maybe," Mary Beth said, "instead of a name, we should be searching the area. If this whole thing revolves around the tree, then maybe that's the link."

"But this is a newer development. Our house was the first to be built here. It was nothing but an abandoned park before."

"Right. Did the park have a name?"

It did have a name, ordained unique upon its inception but utterly forgettable once you walked away. It had a name like Windsome, filled with the illusion that the town was named for its whimsy, or maybe because it got windy sometimes. But really it was named after the first mayor, George or John or Henry Windsome. And like the town, there was once a park with a name, but when Donovan and his crew broke ground so many years ago, the name was washed down the sewer grate.

Mercy leaned over Mary Beth and typed "Parks in Windsome, NC," and hit the enter button. Scrolling down, she found it. Woodland Park. A park named for woods. How utterly unremarkable.

Mary Beth typed in "Anastasia Madison" and "Woodland Park" in separate quotes next to each other. Nothing.

"Maybe it wasn't called Woodland Park back then," Mercy said.

"Back when?"

"When Anastasia lived."

"Or died." Mary Beth spoke out loud what she typed. "Deaths in Windsome, North Carolina since…" She stopped typing. "Since when?"

"Well, we figured somewhere around the time that Beatles song was popular. Sixty-eight? Sixty-nine?"

"But we were singing that song in the eighties. She could have died anywhere within the span of forty plus years." Mary Beth scrunched up her shoulders and stretched out her arms until they were quaking with cat-like tension in front of her. "We're coming up blank here, Mercy, and I'm exhausted."

"What about those ancestor sites?"

"You have to pay for those, and I'm beat. Maybe tomorrow." She looked at the bottom corner of the monitor and pointed at the time. "I mean later today." She stood and bent the crick out of her back. "Go home. You don't need any more trouble."

"You're right."

Mercy got out of her chair and shot a glance at her house. As she did, a flicker of light hit the side of her sight. Not from her house. It came from outside. A car passing down the street, its headlights reflecting off the vinyl siding? Probably.

She leaned on the sill and stared into the dark window of her bedroom. From the outside, no one could know they were so scratched as a family that they were constantly blotting the bleeding. It was just like those months when no one knew Mercy was crumbling under the weight of Lisa's death. It wasn't until the Cunninghams and Mendozas peered through their curtains to see Mercy carted from her home on a gurney that the truth was revealed. But a little time with the shades drawn was all it took to create the illusion that everything was fine again.

If she could do that with the neighbors, make them forget the trauma of that day, why couldn't she do the same with Lisa? Lock her death away behind a padlocked, heavy steel door, and, every time she passed by, all she had to do was turn her head in the opposite direction. Yes, she could do it. Except there was that short story she had read once about a man and woman who fell into a forbidden love and they communicated solely by knocking on the wall that separated their living quarters. One day the woman died and forever afterward, the woman's spirit would knock on the wall, haunting the man for the rest of his days. Sure, Mercy could close the door on Lisa's death, she could padlock, bolt lock, chain lock, and nail that sucker shut, but her young, dead daughter would knock, knock, knock on the echoing steel all day and night for the rest of Mercy's life.

The flicker of movement disturbed the corner of her eye again. Something from the yard behind her house. Mercy turned to see, but all was calm. It was just her brain playing with the padlock.

"Hey, wait a minute." Mercy pushed away from the window. "You said something about Anastasia dying here. If she died in Windsome, maybe she's buried here. We could find her grave. That might tell us something."

"It might. But not tonight. Go home."

"Okay, but I think if she is buried locally, the caretaker might be able to give us more information."

"Awwl right." Mary Beth spoke through an enormous yawn.

Mercy wrapped her in a hug. "Thank you for staying with me on this." When she pulled back, her heart sank from the woeful brown sags under her friend's eyes. There was deep worry in those eyes. Of course, it was stupid o'clock in the morning. She was probably just tired.

The bushes pricked at her arms as Mercy passed through the gap. Although the night still held dominion over the neighborhood, it wouldn't be long before dawn broke. As she crossed the yard, she became wrapped in the opaque stillness of her surroundings. Despite the clouds, the tree gave no rustle, the wind held no whistle, and a stab of fear slashed through her. Like a child running up the basement stairs to escape the monsters below, Mercy scurried across the lawn and into the kitchen. Fatigued, she stepped up the stairs and entered her bedroom.

Don lay on his side facing away from her. According to the soft growl of his snores, he was adrift in deep sleep. She readied herself for bed and crawled in beside him. With a space between them, she lay on her back and let the mating song of the crickets wash over her. As she relaxed into the mattress, she thought, I bet no cricket ever tried to kill herself when a frog ate her kid.

Momma?

It was fuzzy and far away.

Momma?

Mercy's eyes snapped open. The room was aglow with the intrusion of morning. She'd slept, but it sure didn't feel like it.

"Mom?"

Kaitlyn was standing in the doorway. She was dressed for school, but it felt too early.

Mercy squinted against the daylight. "Kaitlyn. Honey. What time is it?"

"Six-thirty."

That was all she said, but her face told her there was more. She wore Mercy's crinkled brow.

Good going. You gave her that. "What is it?"

"Kira and Josh are missing." There was a sting in Kaitlyn's curtness. A you're-on-the-top-of-my-shit-list jab. "Dad wants you downstairs." She didn't wait for a response. Having delivered her message, she left the room.

Mercy threw her legs over the side of the bed and thrust her feet into slippers. Kira and Josh were missing. What did that mean, she wondered as she rushed down the stairs.

When she entered the kitchen, Don was there dressed for the day, like Kaitlyn already was. Mercy looked down at her own attire—nightgown, bathrobe, and fuzzy slippers. It was like those dreams when she walked around naked and didn't know anything was wrong until everyone was staring.

"What's going on?" she asked, tightening the belt on her robe.

"We can't find Kira and Josh," Don said. "Their beds are made, and Kaitlyn doesn't think her sister slept in hers last night. I'm going to look outside."

"Did you check throughout the house?" Mercy asked.

"Yes. Every room. They're not here." His body rigid and distressed, he cut past Mercy and met Kaitlyn out in the yard.

Mercy followed, carrying her own fear with her. "Maybe they're at the bus stop."

"I already walked to the end of the street," Kaitlyn said. "They're not there."

Mercy clawed at all the scraps in her brain to try to make sense of it. "They may have gone to school early."

Don said, "It's much too far to walk." He ran to the hedges and stuck half his body through to Mary Beth's yard. Mercy heard him call out their children's names. No answer.

Mercy ran to the opposite side of the yard. "Kira! Josh!" Nothing. *Dear God.* "They could be hiding." She was grasping.

Don ran to the back of the lot. "If they were hiding in the house, I'd have found them. Not in the house, not in the garage, not in the cars. Nowhere. They're out here somewhere."

"Do you think they ran away," Mercy asked. "I mean, after yesterday?"

Don looked at her with lips tightly locked, as if he didn't know what to say.

"Not a chance, Mom." Kaitlyn started walking toward the maple tree. "If Kira ran away, she would have told me she was leaving. There's no way she would go without letting me know."

They're not hiding. They didn't leave on their own. Dread filled her and Mercy's chest grew tight. *They were taken.* "Anastasia." It came out soft and accidental, but Don heard it.

He raced over to her and whispered, "What's going on, Mercy? What do you know?"

"Daddy?"

Mercy turned. Kaitlyn was standing in front of the maple tree. She didn't know why, but the picture was off balance. The dimensions were wrong. Kaitlyn was looking at the ground, and when Mercy brought her gaze down, she understood why. Mercy couldn't see

Kaitlyn's feet. They looked like they were sunk into the earth. Beside her was a pile of dirt.

Donovan started walking toward the tree. As he got closer, his walk turned to a trot, then a full-out run. Reaching his daughter, he dropped to his knees. Mercy hurried across the lawn. The slickness of her slippers on the dew-covered grass made her slip and nearly tumble. Kaitlyn knelt next to her father. They both shoved their hands into loosely packed dirt.

"What's happening?" Mercy yelled.

"Dig," Don said.

Mercy dropped next to him. At the spot where they were digging, the grass had already been pulled away and it appeared a hole had been dug and then refilled with the same dirt that had been removed from it.

"Hurry," Donavon yelled.

It couldn't be, Mercy thought as she scooped away mounds of earth. It was just an animal that dug up the ground. A large dog must have dug up a large hole and dropped in his bone and refilled the hole to cover his stash. The neighbor's dog buried a ham bone graciously gifted to him by his owner. Then she remembered the flicker. That flash of light in the early morning hours she saw at the side of her eye from Mary Beth's window, the one that wasn't the reflection of passing headlights on the vinyl siding.

A low, ominous moan came from Donovan. Mercy looked over. There was her son's face, pasty against the deep brown soil. Joshua was buried in the dirt. Not a ham bone. Her son. In the next second, Mercy uncovered Kira. A terrified wail fell from Mercy's mouth as she pushed the dirt away from her daughter's face.

"Remove the dirt from her mouth," Don ordered, "and breath into her. Pinch her nose and blow long, even breaths into her lungs."

Don parted Joshua's lips with his fingers and scooped the dirt from his mouth. While Mercy did the same for Kira, she remembered that Don had told Dr. Wright in one of their many sessions after her suicide attempt that he had to scoop the vomit from her mouth. He'd said it had haunted him in his dreams and in his waking hours while driving down long stretches of highway or when mowing the lawn. And there they both were in a painfully parallel position, scraping away the suffocating mess from Josh and Kira's tongues in an effort to resuscitate them.

"Kira, please. Wake up, please," Kaitlyn cried.

As Mercy was about to breath her life into Kira, it didn't escape her that Kaitlyn was the one who had found her on that dreadful morning, unconscious and lying in spew.

Mercy blew into Kira's mouth, but there was no stir from her daughter's body.

"Do it again," Don hollered, and he blew his breath into Joshua.

Mercy blew all the breath from her lungs into Kira's mouth. Still nothing, so she did it again and again until she became light headed. Joshua gave the first sputter. Mercy blew another long, agonizing breath into her daughter and her eyes fluttered open. Kira hacked and spit up partially swallowed soil. Mercy lifted her daughter's head up in her arms and leaned her forward to help her cough out the remaining dirt from her throat.

Kaitlyn cried and grabbed for her sister. Don lifted their son from the pit and sat him at the edge. Josh hunched his body over and breathed quick, desperate breaths. After Kira stopped coughing, Mercy helped her straighten. Propping her daughter up in her arms, Mercy looked into Kira's eyes, which were fearfully glaring back at her. Don was by their side, his large gentle hands ready to lift Kira from the earth.

Before he did, Kira, with her eyes still attached to her mother's, said, "What did you do to us?"

Alarm spread across Donovan's face as he settled his gaze on Mercy.

"No," Mercy said, hammering back the panic in her already-pounding head. Kira had spoken out of shock, that's what it was, and the rest of them would know that, too, soon enough. The most important thing was to make sure her children were safe. Without worry of how her daughter would respond to her touch, she took hold of her arms. "Help me," she said to Don.

Don held Kira by the waist and the two lifted her out of the hole. Kaitlyn threw her arms around her sister and sobbed into her neck.

"You're going to be all right," Don said to the children. They all looked at him as if trying to absorb his words. "Do you know what happened to you?"

Kira moved her frightened stare over to Mercy and Josh followed her eyes. Don bent over so his face was aligned with Kira's. "Look at me," he said, and Mercy was grateful for it. The children looked at their father. "What happened?"

Both children shook their heads.

"We should get them to the hospital," Mercy said.

Without washing up or changing clothes, they all climbed into the SUV. With a death grip on the wheel, Don drove. Though he kept repeating "Everything's all right," and "Don't worry," his eyes held the horror and fear that Mercy knew was in all of them.

CHAPTER TWENTY-EIGHT
June 2014 ~ The Present

The emergency room doctor walked down the center of the hospital corridor with his focus on the chart in his hand. Don knew the doctor was coming to them, but his eyes were deliberately aimed away. That's right, Don thought. Look at the chart and not at the dad with his hope dangling from a fraying thread and it won't hurt a bit.

As the doctor neared them, Kaitlyn unwrapped her arms from around her chest and moved away from the wall on which she was leaning. Too antsy to sit, too unsteady to stand without a brace. Don put his hands out low in front of him to indicate she should stay put. She folded her body back into her arms and let the wall keep her from slipping to the floor. Mercy stood next to him, still in her bathrobe and slippers, her tension as charged as electricity from a live wire.

"Doctor Andrews," Don said. "How are they?"

"They are lucky." That's when the doctor looked up. "They couldn't have been buried for very long, and the dirt was loosely packed, so the weight on their lungs was minimal. That's what saved them. However, it was apparent that there was enough dirt in their airways to show they would have suffocated if left there even a few minutes longer."

"Oh my God." Mercy placed her hand at her mouth.

The doctor put on a reassuring face. "They're fine and resting now. You'll be able to take them home shortly."

The double doors at the end of the corridor swung open and Dr. Wright came through, accompanied by two people Don didn't recognize. One was a short, pear-shaped woman, smack in the heart of middle age, a skullcap of straight, short black hair painted on her head. As they moved closer to him, Don noticed the NCPD badge on the black belt that held up the woman's khakis. He'd called the police as soon as the children were safe in the hospital's care. Next to the officer was a man whose face showed him to be about Don's age, but the shock of pure white hair on his head indicated he may be older.

Don turned to Kaitlyn. "Stay here."

"But Dad..."

"It's okay. We're just going over there." He pointed to the other side of the hall. "We'll only be a moment."

She stayed, like a puppy obeying a command, with sorrowful eyes that wouldn't let go of him and a scarcely perceptible whimper hovering inside her throat.

Don led Mercy and the others several feet down the corridor. When they were far enough away so Kaitlyn couldn't hear, he said, "Dr. Wright. I'm glad you came."

"We'll get through this. Don't worry."

He turned to the woman with the badge. "Officer." He stuck out his hand.

"Detective, actually. Lucy Bachman. Special Victims." She took his hand and Don felt the firm squeeze of hard living.

"Did you see the children yet, Detective?" She let go of her grip and Don could still feel the phantom pressure linger against his fingers.

"Yes. We've spoken to them. They weren't able to give us much. Both said they went to bed and don't remember anything until after you found them."

"They are understandably confused," said the man with the white hair.

Dr. Wright turned to her companion. "This is Doctor Clarence Cooper. He's a child psychiatrist. I know, Don, when you spoke to the NCPD on the phone earlier you gave them permission to speak to the children. I think it would be best if Dr. Cooper had a chance to speak with them as well. They've been through quite a trauma."

"Absolutely," Don said.

Dr. Wright looked at Mercy.

"Um ... of course," Mercy stammered.

"I know this is a difficult time for all of you," Dr. Cooper said, "but I think it would be best if I spoke to them alone. At least at first. When a parent is present, children tend to hold some things back if they think they might get in trouble."

"What would they hold back?" Mercy asked.

"All kinds of things. Perhaps they got into some kind of scuffle at school that they don't want to talk about. Or they made a friend they feel you may find objectionable. It's usually nothing serious, but every bit of information is important in this situation."

Mercy looked at Don, the crinkle between her brows pronounced.

Just agree, he thought. Why the hesitation? He turned to Dr. Cooper. "We understand. That would be fine."

"Thank you. If you'll excuse me. I feel it's best to talk with them immediately while their memory is still fresh."

Mercy looked shaken. "But the detective said they have no memory of it."

"Not that they know of. When it comes to trauma, memories tend to hide behind a lot of curtains. Sometimes it takes someone from outside the mind to help pull those curtains back." Dr. Cooper gave a slight nod and retreated through the double doors.

Detective Bachman took a little notebook from the front pocket of her khakis. "Your children, do they have any enemies?"

"Oh goodness, no," Don said. It was true. They didn't. They were all spunk and cheer. Got great grades. Had diverse friendships.

"Are you certain? This could have been a hoax gone bad."

"No. I mean, yes, I'm certain. They never complained about anyone. Never talked about being bullied or anything like that."

"How about either of you?"

"What?" Mercy asked, defensive.

"Any enemies? Could this be some kind of retaliation?"

"I don't see how," Don said. "I've had clients in the past who weren't always happy, but nothing that would lead to this."

"Clients?"

"I'm a Realtor and developer."

"And you?" She nodded at Mercy.

"Stay-at-home mom."

"So, you're around the children more than your husband is."

"I suppose."

The detective's stare lingered a little too long on Mercy and Don felt his skin go clammy.

"How is your relationship with your children?"

"What do you mean?" Mercy asked.

"It's just a question, you understand. I have to cover all the angles."

"Yes, I understand." Mercy's voice cracked. "We're very close. All of us are." Mercy shot a glance at Don.

"Your son's twelve, I believe? And your daughter is…?"

"Fifteen."

"Fifteen, that's an interesting age. Rebellion. Boys. Hormones. Conflict between a mother and a teenage daughter is pretty much a given."

"Nothing more than any normal family."

Don felt wavy, like he'd just gotten off a roller coaster. He could read in the way the detective was side-eyeing Mercy that whatever the children had revealed to her showed a family situation pretty far south of normal.

And then there was Dr. Wright. What had she revealed? That they were flaking apart more than they were very close. Whatever may have been said to the detective, she couldn't possibly consider any of them responsible. Certainly not Mercy. Sweet, romantic Mercy who scooped spiders from the bathtub in tissues and set them free outside, alive and well to continue their lives catching flies. His stomach began to rumble.

It had to have been a stranger. That was the only answer. His children were victims of a lunatic attack. Like that poor little Walsh kid, whose dad had later become a TV star by capturing fugitives, kidnapped and decapitated. Or Polly Klaas, twelve years old and snatched right from her bed. Kids grabbed from shopping malls, public parks, walking to school. Thinking about all that, terror struck. If it was a stranger, that person would have done more than try to kill his children. A stranger would have done the abominable first. His stomach rolled over and his bowels threaten to undo him.

"Mr. Amoretto?" The detective's eyes were on him. "Do you know something?"

He tightened his stomach muscles and said, "Was there any indication that it could have been…" Saying it out loud was more painful than thinking it. "You know … a predator."

"We don't know that yet, but I can say our team informed us there was no sign of a break-in at the house and no signs of struggle."

"And, you'll be glad to know," said Dr. Andrews, "there were no signs of sexual assault and no serious abrasions or bruising."

"That's good," Don said. "That's good."

"And due to the fact that they were apparently unconscious when they were buried—" Dr. Andrews was cut off by Mercy's gasp. "I'm sorry, Ma'am. I just want you to know we did toxicology tests, and we'll have the results in a few weeks."

Mercy slipped her arm through Don's and closed the space between them. "But someone did this," she said. "Someone buried our children."

Detective Bachman pulled two business cards from the back of her notebook. "Yes, Mrs. Amoretto. And it's my job to find out who did." She handed Mercy and Don each a card. "If you think of anything, please call me right away."

"We will," Don said. He examined the card in his hand.

> *Detective Lucy Bachman*
> *North Carolina Police Department*
> *Special Victims Unit*

His children were special victims.

"Dr. Andrews." Mercy sounded as weak as he felt. "When can we see them?"

"As soon as the psychiatrist is done talking to them."

The detective and Dr. Andrews walked away.

"We'll figure this out," Dr. Wright said, and she followed the others out the double doors.

"Oh, Don," Mercy whimpered and shoved her face into her husband's chest.

Don held her in his arms while his mind circled around every nuance he'd registered from the detective. He then kissed the top of Mercy's head and said, "Let's get back to Kaitlyn. Ease her mind."

"Mercy!" Mary Beth's high-pitched cry came from down the hallway. She was running toward them with arms spread wide.

"I was wondering where she was," Mercy said to Don. "I called her right after you got off your cell with the police. That was an hour and a half ago."

Mercy unfolded her arms from Don, and Mary Beth swooped in and wrapped her in a hug. When she released her embrace, Mercy said, "What took you so long?"

"The police came to my door! Oh Mercy, I was so frightened. I know you said the children were okay, but, Jesus. The police!"

"Mary Beth, please," Don reproached, casting an eye over at Kaitlyn. The wall was still holding up his daughter. Don could feel her terror and despair. It came to him warm and steamy, like piss running down his leg.

"I'm sorry. I'm sorry, Kaitlyn." Kaitlyn's mouth gave a weak smile, but her eyes stayed woeful. "It's just they kept pummeling me with questions. I don't even know what I said to them. It was all so shocking." She took a deep breath. "How are they? Are they going to be all right?"

"They're fine," Don said more for Kaitlyn's benefit than Mary Beth's. "The doctor said they can go home today."

"Thank goodness. Do they know anything? Do they know who did it?"

"Not yet, but they're investigating."

Don dragged a couple of chairs up from down the hall so there were three. Kaitlyn immediately dropped into one of them. Mercy and Mary Beth took the others. Don paced back and forth in front of the nurses' station while his wife filled in Mary Beth on everything that was said to them.

After many minutes, the double doors swung open and Dr. Wright along with Detective Bachman and the child psychiatrist entered the hallway. They hovered out of hearing range, huddled in a conversation. It appeared to Don the two psychiatrists were doing most of the talking, while Detective Bachman stood listening, arms crossed over her rather substantial bosom. Mercy and Mary Beth were locked in a tête-à-tête; neither seemed to notice the detective and her entourage come into the area. With as much nonchalance as he could manage, Don walked to the drinking fountain halfway between them. He ran the faucet and dropped his head. He could barely hear what the group was saying, but he was able to catch fragments. He hoped he was far enough away so they wouldn't suspect. Oddly, it seemed they didn't notice him.

"She'd been violent toward the children," Dr. Cooper said. Something, something he didn't catch.

"…Her mother's mental illness," Dr. Wright said. Something, something, "after her suicide attempt…"

They're talking about Mercy. He wanted to yell to them that she's better now. Not perfect. The depression was still there, settled in the way fog settled in the dip of a highway. You still needed to tap the brakes before you drove through it. But she was better. He cast a glance at his wife, who was still lost in her conversation with Mary Beth. Kaitlyn was staring at the floor.

He lowered his lips back to the running water and the detective's stoic voice hit his ear. "From what the neighbor said…" Something and something else.

Then Dr. Wright. "…delusions … depression … possible psychotic break."

Don's head sprung up and he shot a look over to Mary Beth. *What did you tell them?* His colon gurgled like a rankled ogre and the cold sweat that accompanied the need to evacuate beaded on his forehead and the back of his neck.

"Probable cause," the detective said.

Don spun to face them and the talking stopped. The detective was heading his way. With a quick look at Mercy and the others, he was relieved that none were paying any attention to him. He met the detective in the middle.

"Is everything all right, Detective?"

"Mr. Amoretto, we're in a difficult situation here." She was speaking low, and Don appreciated that. "Whenever children are harmed, the first place we look is inside the family. It's standard procedure, really."

"I understand that, but…"

She held up her hand. "In our investigation, we've uncovered quite a bit that concerns us. And what we've uncovered has been corroborated by several people, including Dr. Wright and your children."

"What are you saying?"

"You care about your wife."

"Very much."

"You'd do anything for her."

"Of course."

"Cover for her."

"Cover?" *Fuck.* "No. I mean, there's no reason to cover for her." A bead of sweat slid down the side of his face.

"Then I'm going to ask you to be honest with me." Her broad shoulders softened and her demeanor warmed. It amazed him how such a tough exterior could suddenly morph into someone who resembled a beloved aunt. An interrogation tactic no doubt. Who would dare deceive a beloved aunt? "Your wife has a history of mental illness."

It worked. The words came at him sideways and he failed to duck. He turned his sight toward Mercy who was focused on Kaitlyn and not them. Kaitlyn was still staring at the floor.

His mind wobbled. "No. That's not true," he said. "She was depressed, that's all. Our youngest child died of leukemia. It's to be expected."

"Her mother was bipolar, committed suicide. Your wife attempted suicide. I'd say that's more than just depressed."

"How do you know this?"

"Dr. Wright informed us."

"She had no business—"

"It was not only her business, it was her obligation. There are children involved here. Your children. And their safety is at risk."

"My wife is better now." The detective let a pause grow between them. "She suffered a great loss."

"So did you."

"It's different for mothers."

"Is it?" The detective stared into him as if examining the crime scene that was pulsing right under his skin.

"She's better now."

"Kira told me your wife struck her after claiming she saw her do things she says she didn't do. Your son claims she grabbed him quite hard for no reason. He told Dr. Cooper he was afraid your wife might be slipping again. Slipping. Again. As if she's slipped before. Mr. Amoretto, do you think your wife is slipping?"

"No. No, of course not." *Fuck. Fuckfuckfuck.* Was she? He didn't know. He wanted to balls out lie, but he couldn't. The detective had made him. He'd never be able to get away with it. The detective not only had ten years on him in age, she had a lifetime on him in bullshit. Lies were like windows to her, he could tell. She could see right through them. He could try to cover up Mercy's dubious mental state, but his stammering and sweating and his growling colon, they were his Benedict Arnold, his Judas.

The detective shook her head. "Look, we'll find out what we need to know. Right now, what we have is probable cause to bring your wife in for questioning, but more so…" She took a beat to look over at Mercy and the others, who were now all staring at them. "We have a confession."

"You have what?" he yelled, and Mercy stood from her chair.

"My partner tells me your wife called your neighbor from the hospital right after you called us. She told my partner Mercy claimed she'd done it."

"That's impossible!" A sick surge of nausea erupted in Don's stomach and it danced the rumba with his Judas colon.

"In about thirty seconds," the detective said, "two police officers are going to come through that door. They're going to arrest your wife."

"No, please. You can't do this. You're wrong."

"It's going to be done."

Mercy, with timid step, was walking toward them. Detective Bachman lowered her voice. "Is that your other daughter?" She pointed to Kaitlyn.

"Yes, and our neigh— Our friend."

"Your neighbor friend. The one Mercy talked to?" Don nodded. "You may want to ask your neighbor friend to take your daughter to the cafeteria for a snack. I hear the fruit cup is quite good."

Don turned and met up with Mercy before she reached the detective. He didn't say anything to her. Didn't want to frighten her in front of Kaitlyn. He did what Detective Bachman asked, and Mary Beth, who had appeared more than a little nervous, led Kaitlyn down the corridor and around the corner. The detective was on them with two uniformed officers standing beside her.

"You're mistaken," Don said.

"Mistaken about what?" Mercy asked.

Detective Bachman said with remarkable calm, "Mrs. Amoretto, we are going to have to place you under arrest."

"What!" she yelled. The tears were immediate. She looked at Don. "What is she saying?"

"They're just going to take you in and talk with you," Don said.

An officer pulled handcuffs from his belt.

"What are those for?" Mercy cried out.

"It's just…" Don couldn't think.

"Procedure," Dr. Wright answered.

A police officer took one of Mercy's arms and forced it behind her back. Mercy jerked and twisted, trying to release his grip.

Detective Bachman told Mercy she was being arrested for attempted murder and began reciting her Miranda rights.

"Stop saying that," Mercy yelled. "I haven't done anything. I didn't do this! Don, why?"

"They say you confessed."

"I did no such thing!"

"To your friend," Detective Bachman said. "According to my partner, you told her on the phone that you did it."

"No. No. It's not what I meant."

"But you did say it, and your friend thought it credible enough to tell us."

"That can't be. She wouldn't. She'd never betray me."

Don knew she didn't mean that the way it sounded, but it sounded bad. "Mercy, please, stop talking. We'll straighten it all out."

"Let go of me." Mercy wrenched her body around until she yanked her arm free from the officer. He grabbed her arm with obvious force and twisted it behind her back. Pain flashed across her face.

"Officer, please. She doesn't understand. She's afraid."

The officer snapped the handcuffs closed and Mercy kicked and contorted her upper body, staying upright only by the officer's hold on her arms.

"No! Don! Don't let them take me!" she screamed through grating sobs. Kicking and flailing, her legs tangled in her nightgown.

"Please, do you have to be so rough?" Don pleaded.

"It's her, not me," the officer yelled.

"No. No!" Mercy's shrieking created an unhinging echo in the hall. She kicked harder, throwing off her slipper and landing a frenzied foot on the officers' shin.

"Shit," he spit. "Look lady, you're dangerously close to being charged with assault."

She twisted against the officer's grip. "Let me go! Don, help me. Why aren't you helping me?"

Her look was that of a puppy being beaten with a stick, frightened and in terrible pain. A piece of his heart tore away like a calving glacier.

He moved toward her. "It will be all right. We'll work everything out." He took another step, but the detective put a palm on his chest. He stood there stunned while his wife kicked and screamed. He just kept repeating, "I'm so sorry" over and over. Mercy's pleas grew to hysterics, her eyes large and pained. When a doctor stepped forward and pulled Mercy's robe away from her shoulders, a rush of relief washed through him.

Against Mercy's twisting and writhing, the doctor lowered the top of her nightgown just enough to jab a needle in her arm. A nurse was behind her with a wheelchair and a panting, yet calming Mercy was lowered into it. Soft weeping trailed down the hallway as one of the police officers wheeled her away.

"What's going to happen to her?" Don asked the detective.

"She'll stay in a holding cell until she's lucid and then we'll book her."

"Detective," Dr. Wright urged and walked away from Don. The detective followed and the two talked for a moment and when they returned to Don, Dr. Wright said, "They're taking her to Tower Hills."

"That will kill her."

"It won't kill her. Better there than a cold jail cell."

He wasn't sure about that. "Why, Detective? Why would she do this? What did Mary Beth say? About the confession. What did she actually say?"

Detective Bachman retrieved her notebook from her pocket and flipped it open. "Mary Beth told my partner that your wife said, 'I did this.' That's the quote I have here. She said she was responsible. The interesting thing, Mr. Amoretto, is my partner tells me she wasn't even prodded. Your friend flat out told him that Mercy confessed."

From the look in the detective's eyes and the tone of her voice, Don felt what he knew Mercy felt. Like Mary Beth had betrayed them. "Is that all she said?"

"It's enough." The detective turned and walked through the double doors.

"She's not a murderer," Wright said to Don. "She's sick. We'll figure this out. In the meantime, take care of your children. They're going to need your strength and support."

"What about Mercy? I need to be with her."

"She's going to be sedated for a while. I'll be there when she wakes. I'll make sure she's okay."

With that, she left him. The nurses, doctors, patients, and orderlies who had stopped to watch what must have looked like a freak show began to resume their business. In the middle of the hall, Don saw the slipper that had been thrown from Mercy's foot. He picked it up. So fuzzy and warm, something worn by a relaxed person, a happy person. His bowels roiled, cold sweat erupted all over his body, and the squeezing pain in his lower intestines told him to run or lose it right in front of everyone. He ran to the men's room and made it just in time to explode in the safety of the stall.

CHAPTER TWENTY-NINE
June 2014 ~ The Present

Someone had put sand in Mercy's eyes, little sharp particles gouging at the vulnerable flesh with each twitch of her lids. Unable to open them for the pain, her lids fluttered about involuntarily, the sand grating against the delicate soft tissue. After an agonizing minute, tears washed out the grit and Mercy feared if she wiped those tears away, her fingers would be covered with blood. When she fully opened her eyes, she was met with an unnatural blinding light. A few blinks and her surroundings came into focus.

Above her, the smooth, white ceiling of her bedroom and the low-profile black-bladed ceiling fan with the tempered glass globe wasn't there. Instead she saw pocked, industrial dropped ceiling tiles edged with nicks and water stains, intermixed with metal louvered fluorescent bulb coverings that did nothing to diffuse the callous light screaming from behind them. She tried to lift her hands to cover her eyes, but they were numb and immovable, as if she'd slept on them. Nausea-creating pulses hammered inside her skull.

Pushing her elbows through the thin mattress, they met with the hard slab underneath. Despite the leverage the effort should have provided, she was unable to sit up. A determined jerk of her upper body produced a crushing blow from the restraint around her chest and she snapped hard back down on the bed. With a tug of her arm, the restrains on her wrists allowed only an inch or so of movement, and the metal rails, raised on both sides of the bed, trapped her like a pig prepared for slaughter.

The ceiling tiles, the straps, the stinging reek of ammonia. If she had been in hell, she wouldn't have been more terrified. Turning her head from one side of the room to the other, she found her surroundings cold, clinical, and frighteningly familiar. A framed photograph hung on the wall, the only picture in the room, confirmed her fear—it was a photograph of Tower Hills Psychiatric Treatment Center, a massive one-story labyrinth that wrapped around countless acres of land. As if being committed there wasn't bad enough, some depraved sadist got off by hanging a picture of the place on the wall for the patient's enjoyment. She groped in the darkness of her muddled mind for any memory of how she got there but came up with nothing.

The door swung open and a woman in blue scrubs entered, rolling a hospital cart.

"Good. You're awake."

She was tall, skinny, maybe approaching six feet, but it was hard to tell because she was hunched over so far she looked like she was going to pick something up off the floor. The curve in her back was so pronounced, Mercy didn't believe the woman could straighten up if she wanted to. Deep crevices down her cheeks and across her forehead suggested she'd been doing this job way too long. When she lifted her head to see in front of her, Mercy was alarmed at how much she resembled a vulture. And that face. It was freakish and distressing.

"Who are you?" Mercy asked, but then the answer came through, wavy and contorted in her doped-up stupor. She remembered coming to. She remembered being scared, panicked. Dr. Wright was by her side and, hovering above her, was the craggy face of the vulture.

"Nurse Fowler." As if to defy her crooked body, her voice was straight and pointed as a pencil. "How are you feeling?"

"Like sludge," Mercy said. "I've been drugged."

"You can blame your hysteria for that."

"I'm not hysterical."

"Not anymore."

It was coming back. When the drug from the hospital wore off and Mercy saw where she'd been taken, she'd lost it. She might have even hit someone. That part was still murky. "I didn't do anything wrong," she said.

"The police say you buried your children alive."

"That's not true. I didn't. I would never hurt my children." And she recalled slapping Kira. "It wasn't my fault," she muttered in response to her memory.

"What wasn't," the nurse asked.

"She was humming that song." Her tongue was dry, her throat sore. She desperately wanted water.

"What song is that?"

Her mind still soupy, she was having trouble focusing. Worse, her thoughts seemed to find their way to her tongue without permission from her brain. "Beatles. 'All You Need is Love.'"

"Is there something about that song that bothers you?"

"No. But, it's the song from the girl in the tree."

"The girl in the tree?" The nurse's intrigue held no sympathy, just a punitive undertone. Mercy pinched her lips together. "Girl in the tree?" the nurse repeated.

The disembodied dead girl. "Ignore me," she said. "I'm confused from the sedatives."

The nurse unfastened Mercy's restraints and lowered the side rails. Mercy rubbed her wrists. They didn't hurt. It was a mindless action, as if that's what you were supposed to do when someone binds you then sets you free. She sat up and lowered her legs over the edge. The tile was like ice on what she realized were her bare toes.

From the cart, the nurse pulled a pile of clothes, gray sweatpants, maroon sweatshirt, socks, and sneakers, and dropped them on the edge of the gurney-like bed. With perverse calm, she said, "Put these on."

That's when Mercy became aware she was still in her nightgown; her bathrobe had been removed and she didn't see it anywhere in the room. Her sheer nightgown left her feeling exposed, but the clothes the nurse put in front of her didn't look like they would bring much comfort. Faded sweatshirt with stretched-out cuffs and fraying around the neck, dulled treads on the soles of the sneakers—the clothes looked like they'd been worn by at least a dozen different people.

"I'm sure my husband will bring me some clothes."

"You're to wear these."

As Mercy touched the fabric of the sweatshirt, foreboding crept along her skin, like the many tickling legs of a centipede. It was once soft cotton, she supposed, but years of wear and washing had turned it rough.

"What happens to me now?"

"You're going to your room where you'll stay until given further instruction."

"How long will I be here?"

"Until the evaluation is complete."

"Evaluation? How long does that usually take?"

"Could be days. Could be weeks. Hard to say."

Weeks. Any spit that had remained in her mouth vanished. "May I have a glass of water?" she croaked.

The nurse pulled a small bottle of water from the cart and handed it to Mercy. It was warm, but it didn't matter. Mercy cracked the lid and raised the bottle to her lips.

"Wait," the nurse said, and she retrieved a little paper cup. She held it out to Mercy, who took it.

Inside the cup were two red capsules. "What are these for?"

"To keep you calm."

"I'm not supposed to take any meds."

"Dr. Wright gave her approval because you are under hospital care."

"I want to see Dr. Wright."

"She'll be in momentarily. Take the pills."

Mercy flung the pills into her mouth and gulped down the entire bottle of water in one long drink.

"Open," the nurse ordered. Mercy opened her mouth. "Tongue." Mercy lifted her tongue. The nurse seemed satisfied.

"When the evaluation is over, will I go home?"

"Not sure."

"Who would know?"

"The detective would be my guess." The nurse left the room, taking the cart with her.

As Mercy pulled the nightgown over her head, she shivered, not from the tickling crawl of the centipede, but from what felt like the pressured, poisoned step of a tarantula. She dropped the nightgown on the bed and threw her arms across her bare chest attempting to squeeze out the chill and creeping sense of doom.

"This is a nightmare. And I'm the star of the show." *Shh,* her mind said. Someone was listening. Didn't someone always listen when suspects were left alone?

Keeping her thoughts to herself, she lifted the sweatshirt and raised an arm to pull it through the sleeve. In the glass of the framed photograph, she saw a ghastly image of herself superimposed over the façade of the institution. The place had become a part of her. Or worse. She had become a part of it. Mercy shoved her arms through the sweatshirt, pulled on the sweatpants and socks, and sat on the bed and waited.

CHAPTER THIRTY
June 2014 ~ The Present

Don had a fair amount of strength that came with his six-foot frame, and his bulk was as tight as a quarterback. Yet, as he held that first shovel full of dirt over the hole that had come too close to being his children's grave, he could feel the strain in his arms from the weight of it. Piled behind him were dozens of shovels full of dirt someone had excavated to create the hole. It took effort to do that monstrous act and there was a method to it. Whoever dug out the hole didn't put all the dirt back over the children. Just enough to suffocate them. They wouldn't need to pack a ton of dirt over them if they had been drugged because there would be no fear that they'd awaken. That's what had saved their lives, but it also meant this was no prank.

Never could he have imagined Mercy capable of such horror. But reality had time to pull out a chair and sit for a while, and for the first time, he considered it. If it were true, like Dr. Wright suggested, it couldn't have been an act of malice or cruelty. It had to have been some kind of mental break, like that woman who drowned her five children in the bathtub so they would go to Heaven while they were still pure. But why Kira and Joshua and not Kaitlyn? What was Mercy thinking? *I'm going to bury my children alive, but just two of them. I'll keep one as a souvenir. A reminder that the others were once here.*

He dumped the dirt into the hole, but before he retrieved another, he turned his eyes upward. Above his head, he saw the limb of the maple tree where the tire swing had hung, the swing Mercy had ridden with obsessive fervor, the swing he had cut down. The position of the hole to that particular limb was grimly coincidental.

He thought of the voices Mercy told him she'd heard while riding the swing. Mary Beth had confirmed that Mercy thought one of the voices was of a girl named Anastasia Madison. That is who Mercy had accused Kira of claiming to be. And Josh. *She heard the voices of a girl and a boy.* He was starting to see what Dr. Wright might have seen. Mercy believed two spirits had somehow possessed Kira and Josh. Had she buried the children to cast out the ghosts?

He threw the shovel aside and placed himself in the hole. It was a visceral reaction, a need to feel the earth in order to try to understand how something so horrible could have happened. With legs too long to stretch out, he bent them at the knees and lay back in the hole. He filtered the dirt through his fingers while staring up into the bountiful leaves that tufted from the maple's limbs. He let the coolness of the earth seep through his clothes. It was soothing and comfortable, like a welcoming bed. Brushing his hands through the soft earth, he thought he could easily fall asleep there. With a start, he sat up. That hole wasn't meant as a place for rest. It was meant as a final resting place.

He thrust his hands into the dirt and pushed himself to his knees. Just below the soil, he felt something hard, like a smooth rock. Don uncovered the rock, which wasn't a rock at all but a small box made of tin. Perhaps some kind of time capsule, he thought. Don pulled off the lid. Inside he found a small hardback book. Like picking up a baby bird from a nest, Don removed the antique-looking book from the tin. There was no dust jacket. The brown linen cover had an etching of a boy in a coat and a cap. The words across the top read *Ragged Dick*, and on the bottom, *by Horatio Alger, Jr.* Don opened the book to the first page. At the top right corner, in neat penmanship, he saw the faint pencil inscription, *Walker Jacobs, 1926.*

He inspected the cover again. The author's name, Horatio Alger, fluttered around in his consciousness on a spectral level. He knew he was a successful American author in the nineteenth century, his books focusing on underprivileged boys, but he only knew that by reputation. He'd never actually read any of Alger's works. Don turned to the first chapter and read through the opening paragraphs. Simple language but descriptive, and the words instantly put a picture in his head. A precocious, older homeless boy, sleeping in a wooden box filled with straw, known on the streets but working hard to get off them. Don saw the appeal right away and turned the page.

"What the heck." He read the section again and continued further down.

Dick's business hours had commenced. He had no office to open. His little blacking-box was ready for use, and he looked sharply in the faces of all who passed, addressing each with, "Shine yer boots, sir?"

Blacking-box. It's just something that popped into my head, his son had said that night after the movie. Something to do with shining shoes. Mercy had questioned him about it.

Placing the tin and the book carefully to his side, he dug some more around the hole. What else was hidden below the surface, he wondered. His fingers discovered something like a tree root that turned out, when he pulled it up, to be a plastic doll. It was small, the size of a Barbie. The dress was torn and filthy, the hair clumped and partially eroded, and the doll's wings, once magical to a little girl, he imagined, were frayed and decaying. These were children's things, a child's book and a child's doll, things for a boy and a girl.

He rummaged around again in the dirt, threw out more soil, dug deeper, but found no more. He placed the doll next to the book and wondered where they'd come from. The garage maybe, when Mercy and Mary Beth were cleaning it. Could it be that she'd found them and conjured up some image of lost children in her head? Was that where her delusion began?

He pulled himself from the hole and sat at its edge. For the first time since he disinterred his children, composure escaped him. He wept hard and long, his heart pounding as if it couldn't pump enough blood to sustain him. After many minutes, he struggled to his feet and grabbed the shovel. When he was done filling in the monstrous hole, he picked up the book, the tin, and the doll and walked into the house.

Kaitlyn was sitting on the overstuffed chair in the living room. Her chin was leaning on her fist and she was staring at her brother and sister, who were on the sofa. Don saw only the backs of Kira and Joshua's heads, but could see that they were sitting close together, as if there were invisible people on the couch scrunching them in. He placed the items he'd found on the kitchen counter and walked through the archway. When he circled around the sofa, a little bark burst from his throat. The fingers of Kira's left hand were interlocked with the fingers of Josh's right. As if hypnotized, they both stared at the television screen, unflinching. The television wasn't on. Kaitlyn's gaze was fixed on her siblings, an outsider in their newly formed clique of two.

Don sat next to Josh, and his son responded by moving closer to Kira. Their grip on each other's hand appeared painful, as if to let go would mean one or the other would fall off a great cliff.

"How are you both holding up?" he asked, but was met only with silence. "It's good to have you home. Do you want something to eat?"

"They've been like that since we got back," Kaitlyn said with grim resignation. "Huddled next to each other, not saying anything. Just staring. Mom really messed them up, didn't she?"

"Just because your mother's been brought to the treatment center doesn't mean she's responsible for this."

"How can you be sure? You've seen how she's been acting on that stupid swing and the way she grabbed Josh and attacked Kira. She's having another breakdown, Dad," Kaitlyn choked out. "Like the last time, when she tried to off herself. She barely survived that. Now this." Kaitlyn threw her face into the chair pillow and breathed out raspy, uneven cries.

Don crossed over to her and knelt beside the chair. Her arms flew around his neck and she cried heavy, tortured sobs into his shoulder.

"Don't go there, Pumpkin. Your mother loves us and would never hurt us." In his heart, he held that as truth.

Kaitlyn responded with her tears. Across the room, her siblings sat without emotion. It did not appear as though they were ignoring their sister's broken sobs; they just couldn't hear them. They weren't being cold to their sister's pain, rather they weren't in the presence of it. Kaitlyn might as well have been crying in the Mendoza's house across the street.

With startling coordination, Kira and Josh rose from the sofa and turned to their father.

"Help us," Kira said, her voice flat.

If Don had an emergency brake on his heart, someone had just pulled it. Kaitlyn lifted her head from his shoulder.

"Please, I'm pleadin', won' ya hep us," Joshua said. Although the tone was flat, as if he were saying he wanted a sandwich, it held a strange dialect.

"Dad," Kaitlyn breathed out. He turned to her and in that moment, she let out a scream so piercing it made him reel. Her death grip around his neck was the only thing keeping him from falling to the floor.

"Kaitlyn, honey," he tried, but she kept screaming.

She gripped tighter. He tried to unwrap her arms, but she held on. Whatever was making her scream was apparently all she knew.

"Kaitlyn, what is it?" he pleaded, and the screaming stopped. She released her grip. "What happened?"

"It was her eyes."

Don stood and looked into Kira's eyes. They were sad, a bit confused, but otherwise normal. "What happened to her eyes?"

"They lost all their color. I mean all of it. There was nothing in the sockets but white."

Don searched Kira's eyes. "Are you all right, sweetie?" he asked.

"I … I'm so tired," Kira said, and she blinked several times.

Joshua wobbled on his feet and let go of his sister's hand.

"Kids, we all need some rest. It's been a long, awful day, but the worst is over. Sleep will do us all some good."

"But what about Kira's eyes?" Kaitlyn asked.

"I'm sure they just rolled back in her head. You can see your sister can barely stand." As those words hung around in the air, he thought about what Mercy had said when she grabbed Joshua. She said she thought he was going to faint. Something about his eyes. "Come on. Let's all get some sleep."

Kira and Josh started up the stairs first. Kaitlyn stood, but made no effort to follow.

"Dad," she said when her siblings were gone. "Are you scared?"

Petrified. He wrestled down those thoughts before answering. "Yes, Pumpkin, I am. But I also believe that with time, everything will work out." He could tell by her pout that she wasn't buying it.

"I just don't see how when everything's so strange. I don't mean just because of today, which is bad, but ever since Mom started riding that swing. And it's not just Mom. Kira and Josh…." She looked at the floor.

"They've been through a terrible ordeal. We've got to give them some time."

She shook her head and lifted her eyes to meet his. "Kira hasn't been herself since the other night when the big storm hit. I felt it first with her, you know. I told you that. But then I noticed it with Josh, too."

"What do you mean?"

"Half the time they're normal. Like Josh is chattering about baseball or has his face in some video game. Or Kira's trying on six outfits before stealing something of mine. Then there are times when it's like someone pushed a button. They shut down, like they're going into their own heads, and they walk around all quiet and weird."

"The past few days have been stressful. They didn't tell me, but it's possible they saw your mother on the swing and were confused by that just as you were. They may have been responding to that in their own way."

"Dad, don't you understand? Kira wouldn't talk to Josh if she was feeling stressed. She would talk to me. I mean, Josh is our brother and we love him and everything, but he's twelve. I'm Kira's twin. We're best friends. And then this horrible thing happens today. Is it a coincidence?"

It sure didn't feel like it. Mercy had accused Josh and Kira of acting strangely. Not acting like themselves. She was adamant about how their behavior was off, but he had dismissed it. Now Kaitlyn was saying the same. Something had happened to them—before they were buried.

Don thought about what the child psychiatrist had said at the hospital about kids not always telling their parents their troubles. "You know your sister better than anyone. Do you think someone's hurt her, pushed her around at school?"

"I don't think so."

"Maybe something happened to Josh, and Kira was trying to protect him."

"She would have told me."

"Apparently she didn't tell you something." They both fell into thought, a hulking, hideous mystery standing between them. He started to ache from the strain, so he said, "After we all get some rest, I'll talk to them. They might not open up to me, but I'll try. Meanwhile, I'll talk to Dr. Cooper. He's a great therapist who will be working with your brother and sister to help them through this. Together, we'll figure it all out. Does that sound good?"

She gave a meek nod. "I guess."

He wrapped an arm around her shoulder and gave a squeeze. "Come on, Pumpkin. A little sleep will do us all some good."

She searched his whole face, then asked, "You really don't think Mom did it, do you?"

The answer came without forethought. "We have to have faith."

"I'm not sure what that means," she said and headed up the stairs, her gait dragging like the weight of all their misery was wrapped around her ankles. There was no effervescence left in her.

Don gave her a minute to settle in before lugging his laden self upstairs. He checked in on each of them, then sat, drained of all strength, on his bed. As much as his body demanded it, he didn't lie back. Instead, he called Tower Hills. He was told, without elaboration, that Mercy wasn't allowed to receive phone calls at that time. The sweet-enough sounding woman on the other end did say his wife was awake and that Dr. Wright had been with her. She assured him she was doing fine, and he hung up.

For several minutes, he sat, feeling uneasy. If only he could have heard from Mercy's own mouth that she was okay. Don abandoned his bed and went downstairs.

CHAPTER THIRTY-ONE
Sometime Around the Present
Outside the Abyss

On her knees beside the tree, Anastasia pushed her hands against earth she couldn't feel. There was no movement beneath her fingers, no change in the dirt.

"I can't dig, Walker. I can't break open the ground. Are you sure this is the only way to see my Momma?" Anastasia asked.

"I got an awful strong feelin' they're on the other side. We jes' gotta get there."

"It didn't work the last time. And it got dark when we did this. It's scary in the dark. Are you sure? Really, really sure?"

"It'll only be dark for a short spell. Only dark until we cross over."

"How do you know it will work this time?"

"I don't. But I know we gotta keep tryin'. And you gotta get your doll back."

"And your book. The man took them. We were so close to having them and he took them away. Why did he do that?"

"Don't know, but we gotta get 'em back. We need 'em 'cause they was with us when we left. They're a part of us."

"You know, Walker, if that woman really is my momma, don't you suppose she would help us for sure. She would want me to get to the other side, because that's where she is."

"Do you think you can reach her, with your mind?"

"Maybe. I wasn't really trying to reach her before. I was just calling for her and she was there."

"Then that's what you need to do. Call to her. I don't think she can see me, 'cause I cain't see her. So, it's up to you, Anastasia, to reach her again. Think real hard like you did before, and your Ma will come back."

"I'll try." Anastasia pushed her small fingers as hard as she could at the ground, but couldn't dig through. She plopped back on her heels and the whimpers bubbled out of her.

"Please don't cry, Anastasia. I'm beggin' you. It hurts my heart somethin' awful to hear you cry."

"I can't help it. I miss her so bad." She sniffled, trying to stifle her tears. She didn't want to hurt his heart.

"We'll get there," he said. "I promise. I'm sorry we gotta go by way of the dirt, but I know deep in my gut we can only get out this way."

"The same way we came in."

"'At's right. Same way we came in."

CHAPTER THIRTY-TWO
June 2014 ~ The Present

Through the porous cinder block wall that separated Mercy's room from the next seeped the low, sunken wails of a woman. It wasn't the kind of wailing that anyone did standing. It was the bereft of strength, body-hugging, tormented ejection of sound that came from a spirit too broken to exist in life's light.

Mercy found herself folded into a knot on the hard cot, knees bent to her chest, letting out her own little moans. Trapped in the small locked room she'd been moved to after her initial arrival, where even the bed was screwed to the wall, she had no escape from the woman's inexorable suffering, which had tortured her for more than an hour.

"Shut up. Shut up. Shut up," Mercy chanted in between her moans. She pushed the flattened pillow over her ears. It didn't help.

Down the hall, a man hacked out a wet, phlegm-filled cough. Over the intercom, several sharp pings rang out intermittently, followed by requests for doctors and nurses and, at one point, a code blue blared, causing a fevered flurry of feet and yelling outside Mercy's door. Considering where she was, the barking of the code sent a shake right through to her fingertips. Code blue. It wasn't right, and a giggle fell from her mouth. Not because she thought anything was funny, but it was a reflex that came from thinking nothing was funny at all. Outside her door, an authoritative voice yelled for something indiscernible followed by "Stat!" and Mercy found herself drowning in the pandemonium.

It was the code blue that put it all in perspective. It wasn't like she was in a medical hospital where Death was always hovering about the halls ready to snatch a mortal from his coil. When people died at psychiatric hospitals, it was because something went terribly wrong. Someone was overmedicated into cardiac arrest, or some poor clod used the cinder block wall to bash in her brains because the woman in the next room wouldn't stop wailing.

I don't belong here.

How did it happen that she went from making turkey sandwiches for her kids' school lunches to being locked in a padded cell? And if only the padded part weren't metaphorical, then the sound of agony wouldn't have clamored through the concrete like storm troopers on a rampage.

The man hacked, the woman wailed, carts clattered against desperate shouts, and the intercom pinged for this doctor and that. Mercy took her hands from the pillow and let the lump of cloth fall to her lap. She hugged her arms close to her chest to keep herself from falling apart. She hadn't remembered the place being so replete with madness before. Then again, she was in a different ward of the institution back then, the sympathetic section, if there was such a thing. In that other ward, where mothers who tried to commit suicide were diagnosed with depression or anxiety or some other forgivable affliction, the doctors at least acted like they cared. But in this section, where they kept the rapists, kid killers, and other societal scum, the doctors were demons and the nurses their minions, and they feasted on the psychosis of the degenerate minds they pretended to treat.

She heard the bolt on the door slide back and Nurse Fowler entered, accompanied by an aide carrying a tray. The aide put the tray on the table beside the steel cot and stepped back. Next to a plastic wrapped sandwich, Mercy noticed the miniature paper cup with two red tablets in it. The nurse and the aide stood silent, watching her. Mercy waited for instruction, but they stayed mute. The nurse picked up the cup and handed it and a bottle of water to Mercy.

Mercy stood. "More pills."

"They'll help you stay calm," the nurse said.

"I am calm."

"These will help you stay that way."

The nurse jerked her claw-like hand toward Mercy and, for a moment, she thought the sharp bone of her knuckle would smack her right in the nose. Mercy took the cup, tossed the pills in her mouth, and washed them down with water. She opened her mouth without having to be told and lifted her tongue.

Without a word, the nurse and the aide, in unison, turned to leave. From the other side of the wall, the woman's screams hit a pitch that would have blown a whole cabinet full of glasses into smithereens.

"I think she needs some help in the next room," Mercy said.

The nurse and the aide looked completely unaffected.

"That's not your concern," the nurse said and closed the door behind her. Mercy heard the thunk of the deadbolt.

The unrelenting screams were like knives cutting through her skin. She lunged at the locked door, her forehead thumping against the small rectangular Plexiglas window. No nurse, doctor, orderly, or anyone acknowledged what Mercy was hearing. People in white coats walked down the hall as if everything was as it should be. Nurses behind stations kept their cell phones to their ears, carrying on their benign conversations with their boyfriends or lovers or the plumber or their mothers, with not so much as a flicker of attention toward the woman's agony.

She pounded on the small window with the heel of her hand. "Somebody," she yelled. "Somebody help me, please." But no one did. She was not their concern.

She walked back to the center of the claustrophobic room and tried to ignore the woman. If everyone else could do it, then she could, too. Just redirect your attention, she thought. She turned her eyes to the tray where a sandwich in plastic wrap sat wilting. That was dinner. Two red pills as an appetizer and a white bread sandwich for the main course. She pulled back the plastic from the top of the sandwich and bit into the bread. Bologna and mayonnaise, or something that may have once been bologna. The meat was tasteless and slimy and the mayonnaise was acrid, like it was off. She put the food up to her mouth to take another bite, but decided it was better to go hungry than get sick in that place and threw it back on the plate.

The screams persisted and Mercy, unlike the doctors and nurses, couldn't ignore them. She climbed back onto her cot and put her lips to the concrete wall.

"Are you all right?" she called to the woman. "Hello. In the other room. Are you all right?" The screaming stopped. The woman heard her. It was a miracle. *Thank God.* "Can I help you?"

An uncanny peace fell like large snowflakes over the place. Even the bustle in the hallway seemed to soften. Mercy put an ear to the wall and heard not the slightest stir. Could it be the woman had screamed herself to death? No code blue announcement, but there wouldn't be if the woman wasn't hooked up to anything that would monitor her life. She would simply lie there on her cot or on the floor until someone came to give her a pill or her next meal.

"Hello?" Mercy called through the wall. "Are you there?"

"Momma?"

Mercy leapt backward. It was the woman from the next room. The voice was old, cracked, almost ancient, but the patient was using the same lilt Mercy had heard the girl named Anastasia use. She clutched the fabric at the neck of her sweatshirt and let her mind unwrap what she'd heard. The sedatives, or whatever it was she'd been given since her arrival at Tower Hills, had put a cloud over her thoughts. Of course. What had come to her ear was an aberration of what was actually said, warped by the medication. Mercy took the two steps needed to get back to the wall. With her hands flat against the concrete, she pressed her ear against it again.

"Huh ... hello," Mercy said.

"Momma?"

The air in the room turned icy. "You, there." She saw her breath. "Do you need help?"

"Momma. Momma."

Her throat grew tight and she began to gasp for the frozen air. "Who are you calling to?"

"Momma. Momma. Momma. Momma. Momma."

She'd longed to hear the little girl again, connect with the children. But this old woman, she wasn't Anastasia. That she would repeat that word to her had to be a coincidence. If not, then her cries were cruel, as if someone on the staff had told the old woman about what Mercy had heard at the tree and was playing a vicious game. After all, what else was there to do locked up all day and night except torment the neighbor?

"Momma. Momma. Momma. Momma. Momma. Momma. Mommamommamommamommamommamomma."

Mercy slapped the wall with her palms. "Please. You in the next room. Please don't do that."

The cracked voice of the ancient woman continued to cry out the word in an endless string of wickedness. Mercy pounded a fist, but unlike plaster or wood walls, the concrete allowed no vibration to penetrate to the other side. She pounded anyway. It didn't matter if it was a coincidence or if the woman was deliberately torturing her, Mercy couldn't bear it. The woman's cries, unlike the moaning and wailing of before, scratched like thistle across her skin.

The more Mercy yelled and pounded, the louder and longer the woman cried out. With both clenched fists, Mercy pounded. "Stop it!" she yelled. It didn't stop and Mercy pounded harder. "Stop. Stop!" She barely felt the impact of her flesh smashing against concrete. "Stop it. Please, stop. Stop. Stop." She pounded and screamed into the wall.

The woman kept crying out and Mercy pounded and yelled until, like a dog running on a chain until the chain ran out, her body yanked backward. The small of her back hit the tile first and she thought her head was next to connect, but a pair of hands caught her shoulders and she was eased to a soft surface. Above her face, the vulture hovered. She was on her knees and was holding Mercy's head in her lap. Next to her stood a doctor she didn't recognize with a syringe in his hand.

"No," Mercy pleaded. "You don't understand. The woman. She wouldn't stop yelling. 'Momma.' She kept yelling 'Momma.' She wouldn't stop."

"The only one yelling is you," the pencil-sharp voice said, and Mercy twisted against the nurse's attempt to restrain her. "Don't fight me. You're just making it worse."

"I didn't do anything," Mercy cried, and the doctor came at her with the needle.

"No?" The nurse reached over Mercy's head and grabbed her wrists. "Look at your hands."

She lifted Mercy's hands so she could see. They were covered with blood, the skin torn at the knuckles. There was no pain and Mercy didn't have an answer for that, but the sight of the blood and exposed tendons in her fingers put a twist in her stomach. Mercy looked at the wall. Blood smeared the concrete.

"She wouldn't stop yelling." The words came out hoarse and broken. "She wouldn't stop yelling 'Momma.'"

"I don't hear anyone yelling that," the nurse said and the doctor pushed the needle into Mercy's arm. It burned like it had been put under a flame. "As a matter of fact, I don't hear any yelling at all."

She was right. The wailing, the crying, the screaming had stopped. There was silence in the adjoining room. There were no sounds at all, except for that of her own wheezing breaths and the rapid-fire hammering of her heart.

Tingling skipped up her arms, which were still in the tight grip of Nurse Fowler, and her head grew light. Whatever the doctor had injected into her arm was fast in taking effect. The doctor shoved his hands under Mercy's back and, with Nurse Fowler's help, lifted Mercy to her feet. Her legs were worthless, her strength, evaporated. The nurse on one side of her and the doctor on the other dragged her across the floor and, by the time they got Mercy to the door, the room had turned black.

CHAPTER THIRTY-THREE
June 2014 ~ The Present

In his home office, blinds closed to avoid distractions, Don tapped away at the computer keyboard as he searched through the government's national sex offender registry. Dr. Andrews had said there was no sign of sexual assault, but maybe, for some sicko, burying children was a twisted fetish-type thing. He scrolled through the site looking for anyone in area neighborhoods who may have been capable of hurting his children. Until it was proven, he wouldn't believe his wife had done what had been done and, with Mercy in custody, he doubted if the police were ferreting out any other suspects. It nagged at him, too, that Mercy might not even be where she was if it weren't for Mary Beth's talk of a confession. He couldn't help feel she'd betrayed them. The hairs on his neck bristled thinking about it.

He had started his search after he'd called the middle and high schools and talked with the principals there. Without giving any details, he asked if they'd noticed anything unusual with his children, and the answer from both was a certified nothing. More than an hour later, after shifting his focus from one possibility to the next, he was still without answers. Stress knotted up inside him, but it was eased by the sounds he subconsciously heard coming through the door. It was the familiar noise that often drifted casually around him during any normal day. Someone's feet padding on the floor above or a television thumping out the theme music to *Law & Order*, the dull thud of a kitchen cabinet door closing or the echoing giggles of teenaged girls.

He'd taken the sounds for granted. He expected to hear them and so he did.

He sat back in his chair, wanting to drink the sounds like a tall glass of cold water, but when he listened for them, really listened, they weren't actually there. They were sounds he desired to hear, so he'd heard them. But in reality, there was only silence. When he last checked, Kaitlyn was up in her room reading, small iPod earbuds sending light music into her head. She was lost in her own private world. Mercy wasn't home. She was shut in a room at Tower Hills Center for the Terminally Grieving, and his other children, Kira and Joshua, last he saw, were sleeping.

Last he saw.

Hands against his desk, Don shoved his chair backward. It jettisoned on its wheels and hit the wall behind him. With a pit in his stomach, he leapt from the chair and tore up the stairs. He checked Josh's room. He wasn't there. In the twins' room, Kaitlyn was still reading, but Kira was no longer in her bed.

"Your sister?" he asked.

Her somber eyes met his. "Left. Don't know where she went. She's in a state again."

He gave her a reassuring wink and went down to the kitchen. On the counter, he found a small dusting of dirt next to the tin box. The lid was removed and the box empty like an unused coffin. Instinct told him to look out the window. There they were, Kira and Josh standing before the maple tree.

He walked out onto the deck and across the yard to where the children stood. They were looking down at the freshly mounded dirt. On top of it rested the doll and the book. The children had told the detective they couldn't remember being buried, but the child psychiatrist, Dr. Cooper, said they did have memories of it. And there those memories were, placed on the tomb that was once meant for them. It was as if they were trying to put the items where they belonged. And because of that, Don understood, there were memories of other things, but those things were still hiding behind their trauma.

With caution, he placed a hand on his daughter's shoulder. She turned to him, eyelids fluttering in rapid blinks as if noticing him for the first time, then she threw herself into his chest. Her slender body heaved in his arms as her blistering cries spilled out onto him. Josh's body wracked from his own silent sobs. One arm wrapped around Kira and the other around Josh, with all his gentle love, he began to guide them back toward the house. Just a few steps across the lawn, Josh turned and walked back to the tree. From the ground, his son picked up the doll with the rotted hair and the old book.

"Josh," Don said. "Those things." He pointed to the objects in his son's hands. "What do they mean to you?"

Their crying had stopped, but their faces were drawn, pale. Josh took a rigid step to his sister's side, gave her the doll then tucked his hand in hers. The two turned and walked across the lawn. Don realized, even as a dad who loved his children more than his own life, he wasn't qualified to bring out whatever was suppressed inside them.

He observed his children holding hands and wondered about their newfound need to connect with each other. But how new was it really? He could no longer consider that their behavior was a result of their trauma from being buried. Mercy had put them both together at the tree on the morning she slapped Kira. Said they were in some kind of collusion with each other. And Kaitlyn said her brother and sister formed a peculiar bond after the night of the storm. That all happened before. Then there was the book and the doll. What was it about those things that they needed? Was it the same thing that Mercy needed when it came to the tire swing?

His thoughts turned in directionless loops. He plodded back into the house and up to the twins' room where Kaitlyn was still sitting in bed. She plucked out one headphone and let it drop on the open page of her book. She nudged her chin toward Kira, who was already under the covers and seemingly asleep. "She just crashed. She's so out of it, Dad. I'm worried."

"I'll take care of it, Pumpkin. How are you doing?"

"Breathing." She plugged the headphone back in her ear and turned her eyes to her book.

Don stood in the doorway for a moment, uncertain how to react to her terse response. Was she trying to be sarcastic, or was that all she could really do for the time being? Breathe. Get to the next breath and then the next, until the world became normal again. If the latter was so, it was a start.

Across the hall, Josh was asleep under the covers. For now, his children were comfortable, so, like Kaitlyn, he breathed and moved onto the next moment. From his bedroom, he called the child psychiatrist and told him about the objects and his children's reaction to them. Dr. Cooper said the children were likely subconsciously aware of what had happened to them and were trying to take control of their emotional distress by returning to the scene with the things that had been buried with them. He advised Don to let them sleep and if he was still concerned in the morning to give him a call.

As he hung up the phone, Don wondered what the children had said to Dr. Cooper in the hospital. Would it have been enough to arrest Mercy without the confession that Mary Beth so willingly proffered?

A muddy quiet surrounded him as he crept back across the hall into Josh's room. On the covers over his sleeping son was the old book, *Ragged Dick*. With care not to disturb him, he lifted it and sat on the floor beside the bed. Josh's mention of the blacking-box had bothered Mercy and after reading a snippet of the book in the yard, he knew this was where Josh had gotten the reference. He opened it and began to read.

"Wake up there, youngster," said a rough voice.

Ragged Dick opened his eyes slowly, and stared stupidly in the face of the speaker, but did not offer to get up.

"Wake up, you young vagabond!" said the man a little impatiently. "I suppose you'd lay there all day, if I hadn't called you."

As he read the words silently, he could hear the voice of the narrator in his head. It was the voice of a boy a little older than his son but not yet possessing the thick richness of a full-grown man. It was smooth though, mellifluous.

He wore a vest, all the buttons of which were gone except two.

What was it about that line that struck him? The vest with missing buttons. Yes. Josh had said those words on the night of the storm. He had been talking in his sleep. Don thought back. He hadn't found the book yet. Hadn't dug it up. In fact, the ground hadn't even been disturbed at that point, so it wasn't like it was dug up and reburied. How did Josh know?

He read further.

Dick's business hours had commenced. He had no office to open. His little blacking-box was ready for use.

The voice in his head was clear, almost audible. Don took his eyes from the page. Was that what Mercy had heard? A sick fear invaded him and he noticed his hands were shaking. Like the piper's song, however, he needed to follow further.

Our ragged hero wasn't a model boy in all respects.

Don closed his eyes and placed the book on his lap.

I am afraid he swore sometimes, and now and then he played tricks upon unsophisticated boys from the country, or gave wrong directions to honest old gentlemen unused to the...

He snapped open his eyes and looked at the page. In black print on the old beige paper, he read the words that had just danced on their own in his head. They were the exact words. How could he have known them so exactly? And the voice—so clear, confident, as if the reader wasn't him, wasn't a forty-one-year-old real estate agent who sounded more like he was from Connecticut than North Carolina, but a boy on the edge of being a man with the round, casual drawl of the country.

I'm pleadin', won' ya hep us?

Josh had said "hep" instead of "help." He had that same dialect as what he'd heard in his head. Could Josh have heard the voice, too, when he'd read through the book? Don read further. It wasn't logical. This boy, Dick, was from the city, not the country. Josh must have read the book at some point for school. Put that voice on while reading out loud, just for fun, and Don heard it without realizing.

Or maybe there was a voice. The same voice Mercy heard while riding the swing. Mercy's ghost. Cold hit his skin like the snap of an elastic band.

"Whoa." *Think. There's no such things as ghosts, remember?*

He was the most rational one in their brood, so why was he so quick to buy into the presence of the supernatural? As his rational mind tried to figure it out, he concluded it was the power of desire. Mercy wanted to hear voices in the tree, so she heard them. Don wanted to hear familiar noises in the house earlier, so he'd heard them. It was as simple as that, and it wasn't crazy. It was human. There was no voice. Just his mind playing tricks with dead words on a page.

He flipped to the middle of the book. Closing his eyes again, he tried to imagine the words there, but nothing came. He was able to recall the words before because he'd scanned ahead on the page without being consciously aware of it and the words were already in his head when he shut his lids to them. He captured the words with his eyes and replayed them with his mind. Made sense.

He read a bit further and his head started to bob, the weariness of the day taking over. The phone ringing jolted him upright. He delicately replaced the book on the bed and went into his own bedroom. He answered the phone. It was Dr. Wright. She was at Tower Hills. There had been an incident.

CHAPTER THIRTY-FOUR
June 2014 ~ The Present

When Kira was younger, it was the tomatoes she loved best from the garden she'd helped plant with her father. Cherry tomatoes were her variety of choice, bite-sized and round and as sweet as their namesake. In her mind, Mercy saw her little girl sitting cross-legged on the perfect lawn, plucking the fruit from the vine and popping them into her mouth one by one. Her daughter was barely seven in that particular memory. Mercy saw herself standing on the back porch, holding her belly with Lisa inside, tasting the tomatoes vicariously through Kira. How the nectar from her rumination played on her tongue, a sense memory so delicious she never wanted it to end.

But it did end with a surge of acid reflux that Mercy, with great effort, swallowed back down her burning throat. The lights were off in the room where she lay restrained on what felt like a gurney. The dull beam of light weeping through the narrow window in the door diffused the dark into a marsh-like mist. She was back in the sickroom, the place where she'd woken up when she had first arrived that time ago. The wistful image of her daughter snacking on cherry tomatoes was lost in the shadows that crouched in corners and crawled along the floor.

The pickaxe chipping at her knuckles had awakened her some ten minutes prior from a thick, sedated sleep. She could see the bloodstained gauze on her bandaged hands and remembered banging on the concrete wall. She remembered the vulture face of the nurse hovering over her and the doctor jamming a needle in her arm. After that, she remembered nothing. The only window in the room was the slit in the door that led to the hall, so there was no telling if it was day or night. The grousing rumbles of starvation coming from her stomach, however, declared more than a little time had passed.

Someone flipped a switch and the fluorescent lights buzzed and flickered overhead. As she turned her sight away from the ceiling, Mercy wasn't sure what hurt her eyes more, the accosting lights or the person at the door.

"Sleep well?" Nurse Fowler asked as she propped open the door with the kick-down doorstop.

"What choice did I have?" Mercy looked around and saw she was the only patient in the room. A door to her right obviously led to the bathroom, which had a flip sign on the front that read "unoccupied."

The nurse stepped to the side of the bed, loosened the end of Mercy's arm restraint and, lifting her arm by the wrist, observed the bloodied bandaging. "You really did a job on yourself. Keep acting like that and this may become your permanent residence."

She doubted it. There was a good chance jail was in her future. If it were, she'd prefer jail to Tower Hills in a New York second. Her stomach gurgled a loud, hungry call.

The nurse lifted her vulture head. "Feeling peckish?"

"Yes."

"You were left a sandwich in your room."

"I didn't eat it."

"Well, then, that's your fault, isn't it."

"It tasted off."

"It was good enough for the other patients. Little Miss Priss would prefer what? Filet mignon?"

"I'm in pain," Mercy said.

"I would imagine."

"It's not just my hands." The last word from Mercy's mouth came out as a squeak. "My throat feels as if someone scoured it with steel wool. What have you done to me?"

"I haven't done anything to you. You did this to yourself. From what the woman in the room next to yours said, you were screaming like the place was on fire. She thought she would go mad from all your screaming." The nurse unlatched the other restraint and picked up Mercy's left arm to clock out the ticking of her heartbeat.

Like a mosquito at her ear, Mercy heard something, but from where was unclear.

"What is that? What are you're doing?"

"Checking your pulse."

"No. No. The other thing." The sound. "Did you say something?"

"Not a peep."

Momma.

It came from out in the hall. At least Mercy thought it did.

"Did you hear that?" Mercy asked.

"Hear what?" The nurse kept a sharp eye on her wristwatch.

"Momma." It was a man's voice. Clear this time.

Mercy turned her head and caught a glimpse of a man in a lab coat passing by her door. She slammed her eyes shut and tried to make sense of it. It was the drugs. For someone who wasn't supposed to be taking meds, she had enough dope in her to supply a small pharmacy. Between the little red pills and the impromptu injections, her brain had turned to mud and was making up shit that wasn't there.

"Momma." A woman that time. Not the old crone that was her neighbor, but someone Mercy's age.

Eyes flung open, she twisted her head around, but only caught a scrub-clad ankle and a clogged foot with a bright print sock sticking out.

The nurse blew a blast of air out her nose. "You need to settle down so I can check your heart rate, which, by the way, has jumped like a spooked cat."

"I'm sorry." She tried to steady her breathing. "I'm sorry." It was her junked-up mind, that's all.

"Momma. Momma." A different woman. At the door stood a thin white woman maybe in her late twenties, straight mousy hair tied in a ponytail lopped over her right shoulder. Blue scrubs. Probably a nurse. She was looking at Mercy.

"There!" Mercy jerked her head toward the door. "Did you hear her?"

Nurse Fowler turned her head and observed the woman standing under the threshold. "Oh, good. You're here. I need a urine culture for Mr. St. Pierre in room sixty-three." The woman in scrubs nodded and clopped down the hall.

"Tell me you heard her. You heard what she said."

"She didn't say anything. Quietly obeyed my orders, just the way I like it. The way I'd like you to be, at least for one minute."

"Momma." A man.

"Momma." A woman.

Mercy's head swung around trying to catch the bearers of the voices, but they were just passersby and they couldn't be saying what she thought they were saying. "Do you hear those people?" Her voice was frantic. Her throat raw. "Do you hear what they're saying?"

"You are really starting to test my patience." Nurse Fowler dropped Mercy's wrist. "There's no point in trying to get a heart rate when you're so worked up."

"But those people. They keep calling out. I don't understand why you don't hear it, too."

"When you've worked as long in a place like this as I have, you come to block out a lot of things. It's a matter of survival, really."

"Don't block them out. Listen. Do me this one favor and listen."

The two fell silent. There was some shuffling out in the hall and a bit of unintelligible hubbub, but nothing more.

Nurse Fowler stepped toward the door. "I'll be back in ten minutes to try again. Hopefully you'll have calmed down by then."

"No wait." Mercy grappled for the lever to lower the rail on the opposite side of the bed. The bandages only covered her knuckles and palms, so her fingers were free. She fumbled around, found the lever, and lowered the rail. Twisting her body, she lurched over the edge of the bed. Her legs, still strapped down, refused to follow and her upper body snapped toward the floor. Thrusting out her hands, she landed hard on them and fiery pain shot up her arms. Mercy cried out, scorching her already damaged throat.

"Guess you had to learn that one the hard way," the nurse said and, with remarkable strength, helped Mercy upright. She lifted the bed rail and secured it back in place.

"You don't understand." Tears tripped over Mercy's lower lids and streamed down her cheeks. The nurse had Mercy's wrists back in restraints. She tried to jerk away, but it only made Nurse Fowler use more force. "You don't have to be so rough," Mercy said.

"You're doing this to yourself."

"I'm not doing anything." She was crying harder.

"Momma."

"You heard that," Mercy rasped. "I know you did." She jammed her arms up, snapping at the restraints.

"Are we going to have to sedate you again?"

"No. No. That's the point. I'm not supposed to have any sedatives and you keep giving them to me."

Like a rubber ball bouncing around the hall it came at her.

"Momma."

"Momma."

"Momma."

Mercy shook her head wildly back and forth. "You're doing this to me. You and your sedatives."

"Momma."

"Please, help me." She closed her eyes against the stabbing fluorescent lights and howled.

"See what I mean? She's in a complete state of hysteria," the nurse said.

Someone else was in the room. Eyes still closed, Mercy felt the push of hands on her shoulders, forcing her to a lying position. She choked back her cries.

"There, there, dear." The sugar in the nurse's voice was so thick, Mercy knew it was only for her visitor's benefit. "Calm yourself, now," and the nurse patted her shoulder.

She opened her eyes and turned her head to see who was there. Her sight landed on a belt buckle. Simple and silver on a black belt holding up a black pair of trousers. She knew that waist. She'd wrapped her arms around it more times than she could count, although not so often as of late.

"Don," she squeaked.

He bent over her, his face sympathetic, consoling, the way someone looked at a pet right before it was to be euthanized. A man wrought with sadness over having to kill the animal, but able to keep his composure knowing he was putting it out of its misery.

"Oh my God, Mercy." He looked at her hands. "May I speak with her alone," he asked the nurse.

The nurse scowled. What did she think would happen, Mercy thought, with her arms and legs shackled to the gurney? Mercy lifted her hands as high as she could against the leather straps to emphasize those thoughts.

"Only for a minute," Nurse Fowler said. She turned toward the door and with her back to them, raised a finger of warning in the air. "Don't get her worked up, Mr. Amoretto. I just calmed her down." She left the room.

The shit you did, you lying hag.

"Mercy…"

"It wasn't my fault."

"You don't have to talk. Dr. Wright told me what happened. It seems you had some kind of an episode."

"It's this place. I swear, Don. They've got me so doped up I'm hearing things. The woman in the room next to mine and people in the halls. And Nurse Foul Breath—"

"Foul Breath. Really?" His eyes smiled as his lips turned up in a grin.

"She looks like a vulture." It was meek but genuine and Don's laugh gave her strength.

"Jeez. You're right. I couldn't put my finger on it, but, damn, that's it." It was a glimpse of light before the clouds rolled in. His body sank and he brushed with one hand the hair from her forehead. "Oh, Mercy. I know this is frightening for you. It is for all of us, but … especially for you. We'll get through this. You need to deal with it for just a short time more. You've got to stop these outbursts. They'll only make your stay here worse."

"I can't take it, not for another minute." Her words were only able to escape as a whisper. "They've got me tied up like a beast. I can't even go to pee without permission." She bobbed her head toward the bathroom. She could feel him thinking and his smile turned to a worried frown.

"Just a short time more," he said.

"Mr. Amoretto," Nurse Fowler's crooked body stood in the doorway.

"Jesus," Don whispered. "When she said only a minute, she meant it."

"May we see you for a moment?" the nurse said.

We? Who's we? Dr. Wright. It must be.

Don kissed her forehead. "I'll be right back," and he walked into the hall.

Nurse Fowler released the doorstopper, allowing the swinging door to come to a close on its own. No need for locks when leather straps will do the trick. Through the small window, she spotted the side of Dr. Wright's face with her bifocals resting on her nose. She heard her say "Detective Bachman" and although she couldn't see her, she recognized the detective's no-nonsense voice. Mercy imagined her beady eyes, plucked into her pudgy face as if by a taxidermist, staring right at her through the door. Mercy strained to see more, but the restraints made it impossible. Only grabbing snips and snaps of their conversation, it was clear they were discussing what to do with her. Was she ready for jail or did she need a longer stay with the cuckoos? Or... There was another possibility. She could go home.

Mercy closed her eyes and allowed her mind to drift back to her yard where Kira sat plunked on the ground eating cherry tomatoes. She replaced the buzz of the fluorescent lights with the sound of cicadas and turned her bed into a hammock hung under an August sun.

"Momma."

She broke from her daydream with a start.

"Momma." It was a man's voice from the hall. The hall where her husband was standing.

"Don!" She tried to yell it, but it came out cracked. "Don. Come here!" It was like yelling in a dream. The harder she pushed, the less sound came out. She opened her mouth, her throat closing against her panic. Mercy yanked her arms up, but they snapped back against the restraints. "Don!" she was able to scream and then there was screeching. It was coming from her.

CHAPTER THIRTY-FIVE
June 2014 ~ The Present

It was like driving in night rain down a lampless country route, lined on both sides with dangerous dips, and the high beams didn't work. Don had to depend on instinct and the will of God to get him over the hill and around the corner. He navigated his SUV with caution while the flashback of Mercy's screams bounced around in his head. He worried about the nurse's concern that Mercy was hallucinating, hearing voices. The word "Momma" coming at her like a weapon. *Momma.* When the nurse had told him that, he recalled hearing a doctor say that word. He was in the hall with the detective and the others. The doctor had a cell phone to his ear. Don thought the doctor was talking to his mother. When he really tried to remember, though, he just wasn't sure. It was like a mirage, a desire to hear what Mercy had heard so he could understand better what was happening.

Without knowing how, he made it up his driveway and into the garage. He didn't want to leave her, but they wouldn't let him stay overnight, and he had to get back to the children. He sat in the driver's seat and breathed in deep, full breaths and thought, it wasn't supposed to be like this.

He remembered all the way back to that day when he'd seen Mercy for the first time—the two of them partnered in junior-year biology class. Even as a high school teenager, he foresaw their beautiful future together. It was the adorable way Mercy squinched her eyes shut before slicing into the frog they shared that set his heart on a faster beat.

"My friend Mary Beth thinks dissection is fun," she'd said to him.

He told her, "So do serial killers."

As he escaped the SUV, he mourned how tragic that future he'd once dreamed of had become. Leaning against the open door of the vehicle for support—his body had taken on the feebleness of an old man—he scrambled through scenarios of what may have provoked his children to go out into the yard in the inky dark of the early morning. *No sign of a break-in. No sign of a struggle.* Could it be they didn't consider themselves in danger?

The driver's side door closed with a heavy thud and Don blindly followed his feet into the house. When he crossed into the living room, Mary Beth snapped off the television. The children were old enough to stay home alone, but considering everything they'd been through, he'd called on Mary Beth to watch over them.

"How are they?" Don asked.

"Kaitlyn's upstairs. Kira and Josh went outside to play."

"Outside?"

"Yes. In the yard. Is that okay?"

"I'm not sure."

In a step, he was at the kitchen window, but the shadowy twilight acted like amalgam behind the glass, bouncing his reflection back and preventing him from seeing outside. He stepped onto the back deck and scanned the yard. Out there, where the beguiling place of gardens and plush green lawn had become a nether world of heinous possibilities, that's where his children were.

The maple tree stood tall before him. He rushed over to where his children had been buried. The hole was back and he felt his blood slow like muck through his veins. It wasn't as deep, but someone had been digging there. Don looked over the dusky yard, but couldn't see his children. Mary Beth said they were outside, but they could have gone back in without her noticing.

"Josh. Kira," he called and nothing came back. He ran back into the kitchen. Mary Beth was standing by the door. "They're not out there."

"They could have come in, I suppose."

"You suppose? You were *supposed* to be watching them." There was anger. He didn't want it there, but it was.

"I was watching them. They wanted to go outside. I didn't think it was a bad idea. They were together and seemed fine."

"They were together when they were buried alive as well, and they weren't fine then."

"I didn't mean … I'm…"

He pushed passed her, ran through the living room and, finding his strength again, took the stairs up a few at a time. He didn't have the patience to hear it. The children were not where she said they were and, except for apologies, she had no more information to give him. If they were safely in their rooms, he would offer his own apology to her, but first he had to find them.

He landed a quick rap on the girls' bedroom door.

"Come in," a sober Kaitlyn answered.

He stepped in and saw Kaitlyn awake and back inside her book, earbuds still hooked to the sides of her head.

"Do you know where your sister and brother are?"

"Beats me." Not looking up, her voice grim and preoccupied. "She woke up, walked out of the room. I tried to talk to her, but she wouldn't talk. She was in that weird zoned-out place."

He was going to ask her more questions, but her mind was safe inside the story of her book. She didn't want to leave it and he wasn't going to force her.

Across the hall, he opened Josh's door. Neither he nor Kira were there. No one was in the bathroom and they weren't in his bedroom. He stepped into the hall and shot another look in Josh's room. The old book wasn't on top of the bed. He searched around Kira's side of the room she shared with her sister. No sign of the doll. He asked Kaitlyn about it, but she said she never saw it.

He galloped down the stairs and noticed night was making a crash landing and if his children were outside, he only had minutes to find them. He burst through the back door and out into the yard.

"They weren't upstairs?" It was Mary Beth.

He jumped and his skin tingled from the adrenaline from being startled. "You're like a cat." And he wasn't angry with her anymore. Worry had taken over that emotion.

"Sorry."

"You didn't see them go inside?"

"No. Not now and not before you came home. I didn't hear anything either."

"Then they are out here." He stepped into the center of the yard and put his opened hands around his mouth. "Kira. Josh," he yelled.

The Cunningham's dog barked two quick yelps. He walked over to the hole beneath the tree. Night pulled down another shade and he was on his knees without knowing it, pawing at the dirt in the hole. Mary Beth dropped down beside him.

"What are you looking for," she asked.

"A doll and a book." *But that isn't really true, is it?* A quick sweep of the back of his hand across his forehead and the pebbly grains of dirt scraped over his skin. He shoved his hands into the earth and felt something.

Mary Beth spoke, but it came to him like a distant train whistle. Her hand was on his arm and he looked at her. A ghastly expression crept over her face. She was pointing into the hole. "I think it's a shoe," she said.

It was. Blue with a flat sole. Kira's shoe. He'd seen her skipping around the house in those blue flat-soled shoes on many occasions.

"Dig," he yelled, and he could see Mary Beth from the corner of his eye already digging. A weak cry escaped her. She'd uncovered Josh and was straining to get his body up. "His head is most important. Lift his head from the dirt. Clear his mouth and blow!"

From the earth, he lifted his daughter's head and opened her mouth. It was filled with dirt, packed like she'd been eating handfuls of it and had yet to swallow. But, she hadn't been eating it. She'd been breathing it, and from the amount in the cavity of her mouth, he knew there was more down her throat. He cleared away as much as he could, pinched her nose closed and blew a long breath into her body. Her face was gray in the last sprinkles of dusk. Again he blew. No rising chest. No gasp for breath. He wanted to yell to the night to save her, but he blew into her instead.

Sputtering and coughing, but it wasn't from Kira. It was from Josh. Mary Beth had gotten him to sit up and she was holding him while he spit out the dirt. It was his turn. If Josh could live, so could Kira. He breathed into his daughter twice more.

"Please, Kira. Wake up. Please wake up." Kaitlyn's soft voice drifted from above him and landed in his heart.

He blew again into Kira's mouth, hoping if the precious oxygen he was delivering to her lungs couldn't wake her, the pleas of her twin sister could. Again, again, again he breathed into her, but there was no reward of life. There was trembling in his arms and he thought it was Kira awakening, but he realized with sunken suddenness, the trembling was coming from him. In the thickening dark, he could just make out the clusters of dirt on the lashes of his daughter's closed eyes. He watched his own tears drop onto her lids. The moan crept out of him like a slow roll of thunder.

"Breathe!" Kaitlyn yelled.

"She can't." He was crying. "I'm so sorry." He was saying it to all of them, including the lifeless child in his arms.

"Breathe, goddammit. Breathe!"

"She can't, darling," and he couldn't believe the words slipped from his lips.

"Not her. You! Breathe into her, Dad. Breathe!" Kaitlyn was on her belly, her head leaning into the hole, as if she were ready to take over where he had stopped. "Breathe, Dad. Do it!"

Like an ensign following orders from his captain, he did. He breathed into Kira, but no life filled her. He let another long, slow, full breath of oxygen flow into her mouth and down her throat, and Kira's eyes fluttered open. She burst a cough of dirt that spit into Don's face. It was the most exquisitely beautiful spit of dirt, and he held his daughter as she coughed up the rest.

Kaitlyn was sobbing, her hands grasping at her sister's shoulders. "Thank God," she cried. "Thank God. Thank God."

Beside him, Mary Beth gulped cries and Joshua coughed and gasped for breath. They sat in the dirt, Don with Kira in his arms, Mary Beth with Josh, and Kaitlyn hanging over the edge of the hole. They cried and coughed and drove out the dirt and the tears and the fear from their bodies. When the coughing and the crying subsided, Don lifted Kira's legs from the earth. She was wearing shorts and her skin was cold. He leaned back and found Mary Beth's shoulder.

"Let's get them out of here," he said.

Once safely on the lawn, Kaitlyn pulled her sister into a hug while Don held his son against his chest.

"What happened?" Josh asked with a rasp in his voice.

"Mom did it." Kira pulled away from her sister and reached a hand out to her brother. He took it, leaving his father's arms and crawling into hers. "She didn't kill us the first time, so she buried us again. She buried us." It would have come out as a yell, but it seemed her throat was raw from swallowing soil.

"She tried to kill us again." Josh wept.

"You remember that?" Don asked.

"I don't have to remember. It was her," Kira cried. "It had to be her."

"No, sweetie." Don's mind spun in a thousand wild circles. "It wasn't her."

Josh looked at him with eyes as dark as the coming night, his dirt-crusted cheeks streaked from tears. "How do you know?"

"Because she isn't here," Kaitlyn said. "She's locked up in the crazy house."

Maybe it was the shadows from nightfall's cloak, but Don could see age on his daughter's face that wasn't there before. "Kaitlyn," he pleaded.

"It's true, Dad. She's locked up in a cage because she tried to kill Josh and Kira. But, she's not here now. So, it wasn't Mom who buried you. Not this time. It wasn't her. It wasn't her, Dad. If it wasn't her..."

"Who was it," Kira took over. "And if she didn't do it this time..."

"Did she do it the last time?" Kaitlyn finished.

There they were, hushed by that new revelation. Don looked into the eyes of his children. Kira and Josh were clutching each other in a desperate hug, their tears genuine and questioning. Mercy hadn't done this to them. And a stranger? There was zero logic in a stranger returning to finish such a specific crime against his children.

He turned to his wife's lifelong friend. In the cruelty of the crashing night, he could only make out the contours of Mary Beth's narrow nose and angled chin. Wisps of fly-away hair, like the jutting antennae of a dozen grasshoppers drifted up from her cropped hairdo. The fair-skinned woman, whom he'd always thought possessed a simple attractiveness, had become a strange Medusa in the gloom. While he stared at her distorted shadow, he was overcome with the irrational fear that by looking into her eyes, he would turn into stone.

Mary Beth was charged with watching his children while he was gone. She was the only other person there. But what possible motivation would she have to do that horror to them? She was like family. She always had been. Detective Bachman didn't know that, though. She thought Mary Beth was a good friend, yes, but not family. So, when the detective did as she was supposed to do, look inside the family first, she hadn't considered Mary Beth.

Don stood and helped his children to their feet. There was Mary Beth, still sitting on the ground and it came to him, sudden like a seizure; this woman who had been in Mercy's life since they were children had no family of her own. Her parents had been living the good life in Paris since Mary Beth got out of high school. She had no siblings, no spouse, no children. She had no one. Except Mercy. Always Mercy. Through childhood. Through college. That's all she had. That's all she'd ever had. *That's all she wants.*

"Kids, we'd better get inside." Mary Beth stood and, from her posture, Don felt she was going to follow them into the house. "I think

... I think we need to be alone for a while, Mary Beth. I want to get the children cleaned up and make sure they're okay."

"Let me help you," Mary Beth said.

"No." He checked his tone and kept it calm, despite the terror that had stampeded over him. Mary Beth's forehead puckered and her eyes drooped with confusion. "No," he said with deliberate softness. "Thank you. You've been so..." He swallowed. "Helpful." The words jammed like a quarter in his throat. "We'll be fine."

"Are you sure? It's no bother, you know. I have nothing else I have to do."

No you don't. You have no family. "I'm sure."

Her lips tightened into a hard line and he could tell she was clenching back anger. He led the children across the yard, his pace deliberately slow. He wanted to make certain Mary Beth was on the other side of the hedge before he entered the house. When she disappeared through the gap, he brought the children inside.

He checked them over to be certain they were in no danger. Their breathing was even and, except for being filthy, they were physically unharmed. He let Kira shower in the bathroom off his bedroom, and Josh showered in the main bath. While they cleaned off the dirt from their bodies, Kaitlyn sat on her bed. Her eyes were wide, mouth agape as if there were utterances of dread waiting to fall from it.

"We'll figure this out," he said.

Her eyes moved to meet his, but her head stayed in place. She closed her mouth. The possibility hung between them that she suspected him of this horrid wrongdoing, but he would deal with that later.

Downstairs, Don checked the locks on all the windows and doors, pulled down the blinds and turned out all the lights, except for the light over the kitchen sink. He sat at the island counter, his head a mess with thought. He'd known Mary Beth for twenty-four years, as long as he'd known his wife. He trusted her, loved her even, because Mercy loved her. She was always there when they needed her. She was always there. Always. Hovering, interloping, interfering. It was no coincidence she'd built her house right next door, created that ugly gap in the hedges from bursting through into their lives so many times. Whenever Mercy had a crisis—her parents' divorce, her mother's suicide, Lisa's death—Mary Beth was there. A chronic sympathetic shoulder.

Then when Mercy tried to kill herself things changed. Don had snapped back to Mercy. They started going to therapy together. Had Mary Beth felt Mercy betrayed her by preferring to be with her dead daughter over her? And betrayed her again by preferring her husband's comfort over that of her friend? Don had once heard on a hack radio talk show some holier-than-thou pundit spitting out nonsense about how we don't so much desire to be loved as to be preferred. He never subscribed to that bullshit, but maybe Mary Beth did, and the one way she felt preferred was through her offerings of solace.

Look how much compassion she offered when Lisa died, how much Mercy needed her. Burying the children could have been a way to replicate that. Like a form of Münchausen syndrome by proxy, that strange thing where mothers hurt their babies to get sympathy from others. Except she'd turned it around. She was hurting the children to give sympathy to Mercy.

And she pointed the detective's suspicions toward Mercy why? To keep her fragile, vulnerable. Break her mind wide open so Mary Beth could crawl in and make herself at home. Especially when her husband left her and there was no one else to lean on. After all, what husband would stick around with a wife in jail for trying to kill their kids?

Oh, you clever girl. You clever, awful, horrible girl.

Mary Beth was behind everything. She was the one who goaded Mercy into building the tire swing, so antiquated a thing no one else but Mercy would want to ride: a swing that would take Mercy on a blithe journey into the dangerously fanciful world of her own mind. Mary Beth was behind the voices in the tree. She produced the doll and the book from somewhere: tangible proof that ghosts exist. *But only crazy people believe in ghosts, Mercy. Your mother was a crazy bird and everyone knows you're a nickel short of a dollar from being crazy, too.*

"Mercy." Her name came from him in a cry. Don went into his office and closed the door. From his wallet, he pulled out a business card. He picked up the phone and dialed. "Detective Bachman. It's Donovan Amoretto. There's something I think you should know."

CHAPTER THIRTY-SIX
Sometime Around the Present
Outside the Abyss

Unwanted tears burned Anastasia's eyes and snot dripped from her nose. It was eerie to her how some things she could physically feel and some things she couldn't. She sniffed and blinked, trying to hold it all back. She didn't want to make the boy sad with her crying. She just couldn't help it. The tears came. She felt like a baby. That's what Bobby would call her whenever he caught her crying.

"You ain't no baby," Walker said. "You're jes' scared. I didn't mean to scold you before for cryin'. That wadn't fair."

"Please stop reading my mind."

"Cain't hep it. Besides, you're readin' my mind, so we're even."

"That's different. You're thinking strong thoughts. Like how we're going to get out of here and back to our families. Except it's not working, Walker. It's not working. Every time we dig ourselves into the dark, someone digs us out and we're right back where we were."

"It's the man. He don't want us buried."

"But we have to be buried. That's what you said. It's the way we came in. We can only get out by the way we came in. I've tried to reach my momma, I know I got close to her, but I think she's stuck, too. I think all of us are stuck, but just in different places. I've got to find her so we can all get unstuck."

"The boy and girl will hep us. They know. I jes' don't know how they know, but they know. They're the ones who'll make it possible."

"Do you think they'll help us again?"

"Yes. I think they will. Concentrate real hard like. Send your thoughts to the girl, I'll send mine out to the boy, and they'll come to us. This time, though, when they come, don't let them leave. Hold onto them as tight as you can until we get to the other side."

"What about my momma? What if she can't get to the other side? We have to bring her with us, Walker. We have to." She read his mind. "Don't say that. Don't say you don't know. You have to know. You're older. You can figure things out better than I can. What do we do, Walker? What do we do?"

His jumbled thoughts danced behind his huge golden eyes until he settled on one.

"First, we get the boy and the girl to hep us to dig. If the man tries to stop us, we find a way to talk to him. Through the boy and the girl. Once we find a way to the other side, you work real hard to reach your Ma. Do everything in your smart head that you can to get her to come to you. Once she's here, all of us will get to the other side together."

"I don't feel so smart."

"You is. You's mighty smart indeed."

"This is going to be hard."

"Yep. But it's the only way I can figure. Now do what you done before. Concentrate so hard on the girl that she fills up your whole head."

Anastasia shut her eyes and directed all her energy on the girl. She could see her sleeping on her bed. The bed looked warm and cozy, like her bed used to be. She wanted so badly to be home under the covers surrounded by her fairies. And there were the tears again. And she wept so hard she thought she would die from it. Walker came to her in her mind, not with words, but with a guiding hand. He helped her turn around her thoughts. Remembering her own bed took her away from the girl, making her fuzzy and distant. Anastasia swept her hands through her hair to help find her focus. The tears she felt, but her hair, it was like sweeping through vapor. As hard as it was, she pushed back the thoughts of her home and pointed every bit of concentration on the girl. The fiercer she concentrated on the girl in the bed, the closer she got to her. Anastasia knew she was still by the tree with Walker, but she was also moving closer to the girl. Closer and closer until she was right beside her. Closer still, and she was inside her head. It was kind of the way she could get into Walker's head, except inside out. It was confusing in the girl's head with lots of thoughts mixing around all at once. She sifted through them until she came to one about her mother. She was remembering a summer party outside in what must have been her back yard and her mother was happy. That was a good thought. It made the girl calm and easier to talk to her.

"Help us," Anastasia said. "Help us dig so we can get to the other side." She repeated it like a song refrain until what seemed like curtains opened and Anastasia could see the light of the girl's room. The girl had opened her eyes.

CHAPTER THIRTY-SEVEN
June 2014 ~ The Present

The detective was cool on the phone, the kind of cool that got Don squirming like a suspect in an interrogation room. He pictured her on the other end: her jowls bobbing as she delivered terse answers, straight bangs bonded to her forehead as if drawn on with black Magic Marker, eyes glaring straight through the phone into his conscience.

He was resolute when he dialed the number, determined when he delivered his opening line, but once he got her icy reply, his voice took a hiatus into his stomach. Silence loitered between them while Don tried to find his voice, and the detective gave no relief, waiting patient as a London guard, as if interpreting the white noise in the background.

When he managed to speak, he told her how he had to again dig his children from the ground and how Mercy couldn't have committed the crime because she was locked away at Tower Hills. The detective responded with a frost-coated "I see." When he voiced his suspicions about Mary Beth, another "I see" dropped through the earpiece. When he asked if they would release his wife from the hospital, she said she'd look into it. He shifted with discomfort in his leather office chair and was glad she couldn't see.

It was different when the detective had talked to him under the bright overhead lights of the hospital hallway. The detective held pity in her eyes then. *Poor guy,* those eyes said. *He's gone through so much, and look how he's holding it together.* On the phone, however, there was apparently no longer a need to sound like the beloved aunt. She was in pure cop mode, and when he hung up, he felt completely screwed.

Don left his office to check on the kids. He rounded the corner into the living room and there were Josh and Kira heading into the kitchen. They moved like phantoms, making no sound, floating through the kitchen as if being carried on wheels. They were holding hands, eyes laser beams on the slider door. Don thought about what Kaitlyn had told him, how they sometimes go into their own heads.

...and they walk around all quiet and weird.

They glided through the open door and melted into the dismal smoke of night. Don hadn't looked at their feet and wished he had, not knowing how they could skate across the ground like that.

He flipped on the outside light and followed them to where they stood at the precipice of the hole. In the swat of a cat's paw, the children dropped in. Don lunged to the edge, his mouth dry, his flesh pocked with perspiration. The children were on their knees digging at the dirt.

"Kids." The word fell from the desert of his mouth. "Can you hear me?" They dug, and a low grumble of thunder threatened in the not so distant sky. "Josh. Kira. Listen to me." They didn't. "Listen to me." Lightning set the sky ablaze, and its sibling thunder responded with booming applause.

As if reacting to nature's signal, the children stopped digging and leaned back on their heels. Kira put her right hand in Josh's left and shoved her other hand into the earth. From it, she pulled up the decrepit fairy doll. Josh lifted his right hand. In it, he held the old hardcover book. A drop of rain tapped Don on the shoulder.

"We should go inside, now. A storm's coming."

Still holding hands, the children shifted their bodies so they were sitting length-wise in the hole. Kira rested the doll on her lap; Josh rested the book on his and with their free hands, they began scooping dirt over their feet, lower legs, and knees. Rain pattered down, large drops of warning falling from the sky.

Don jumped into the hole. "What are you doing," he shouted while trying to clear the dirt from their bodies.

They piled on more dirt, which started to thicken from the moisture of the rain. They piled the dirt on. He scooped the dirt away. They showed no emotion, except for a resolute need to bury themselves. The rain stopped teasing and came down in an onslaught. Their hands moving unnaturally fast, they grabbed mitts full of what was quickly becoming mud and slapped it over their bodies. Don tried to lift Kira from the ground, but she lunged at him, scratching his neck. It stung and he jerked back. An act of survival. An animal scratching at a threat.

The mud had become heavy, plaster-like. In trying to clear it away, Don grabbed the objects off his children's chests and threw them out of the hole.

Thunder crashed. Lances of lighting sliced open the dark. From Kira burst a hawk-like screech that pierced the wind. A growl churned deep within his son and rose to a roar, and the night became a battlefield of assaulting rain and explosive thunder, screams and ungodly howls. The children's chests where the objects had rested began to glow. Dull for a second, like the electric burner on a stove set on low, then bright red, a bonfire blazing beneath their flesh.

Don threw his body over both his children in an attempt to douse the fire, but below him he felt no heat. With his hands shoved underneath his son to gain leverage, he pulled. When he had his son's body mostly out of the mud, the red glow from beneath Josh's clothes began to pulse. Painful howls ejected from Josh's mouth. Screams came from his daughter; the glow inside her keeping the same beat as the one inside Josh.

Petrified, Don's blood raged through him, ramping up his strength. He yanked Kira from the mud, and in that instant, the red globes exploded from both his children's chests, knocking Don backward. Josh and Kira fell limp and silent in the grave and in one heart-stopping second, Don thought his children were dead. But there were no rips in their clothes, no shredding of flesh, no heat, no wounds, no sign of violence to their bodies. He'd seen the globes of light burst from them. Yet his children were whole and, where the fiery orbs had left, came the rise and fall of even breathing.

Above, the zipping whir of fast-moving objects. He shot his sight up to see the red globes spinning around him, two out-of-control cannonballs of heatless flame. They crashed into each other, fused together, then broke apart. They ricocheted off the tree, shot into the high limbs, and plummeted down, striking the doll and book, shooting them back into the hole. When the doll and book hit the ground, the globes stopped their frenzied flight—a sudden halt as if put on pause. After a moment, they lithely floated over the hole. One globe hovered over the doll, the other over the book.

Don reached for the one over the doll. When he grazed it with his fingers, a shiver of static trickled up his arm, shimmied up his throat, and landed with a zap on his tongue. The orbs drifted over the children. Don tried to swat them away, but his hand went right through them. Terror-stricken, he watched as those strange orbs, like butter melting into a hot biscuit, sunk back into the children's bodies, leaving no imprint of their passing.

Josh and Kira's eyes shot open and their irises were red flames. Each took hold of their objects and placed them on their chests. Two-fisted, they shoveled mud over their bodies. Moving as fast as possible,

Don cleared what he could away, but the children's hands were moving at physics-defying speed. For every five piles of mud the children slapped onto their necks and faces, Don was able to get one, maybe two handfuls off. He focused on the mouth and nose, moving from one child to the next. He could tell they were beginning to breathe in the mud.

Kaitlyn was upon him, throwing mud off her siblings.

From above, Mary Beth shouted, "What's happening?"

He didn't look up for fear of losing a millisecond of time. "The children, they're burying themselves. I don't know why." His voice was drowning in the storm. "Help me!"

She was in the hole next to him, working the mud off Joshua, leaving Don and Kaitlyn to work on Kira.

"He's fighting me," Mary Beth yelled.

"Fight back! Get him out of the hole, no matter what it takes. Break his arms if you have to."

"What?"

"Do it!" Broken arms could be mended. But there was no bringing his children back from the dead. God knows, he thought, Mercy tried with Lisa.

With his hands shoved under Kira's armpits, Don managed to get to his feet and lift his daughter up from the ground. Fast as the snap of a flag in the wind, she snatched the fairy doll from the mud. That doll had to come with her, and he was in no position to question it. Don heaved his body from the pit and pulled Kira up beside him. She plopped in a sitting position: eyes closed, hand clutching the doll, her head lolled forward like a human-sized puppet left unattended.

"Help," Mary Beth choked out.

She had Josh's head and upper body out of the mud but, with herself bogged down in the mire, couldn't lift him higher. Don's massive hands gripped his son's tender twelve-year-old arms and he yanked Josh onto the grass. Like Kira, his son's eyes were closed, his face flopped down toward his lap, his hand gripping the book. Don pulled himself from the hole and helped the others out.

The rain, having exhausted its tantrum, slowed to a few stubborn drops and the thunder and lightning ceased. Responding to the storm's quelling, Josh and Kira stood, opened their eyes, and lifted their gaze to the sky. Don followed their sight. The clouds had peeled back to reveal the heavens filled with stars.

"What the hell just happened," Mary Beth yelled, her chest heaving, her breathing coming out in audible wheezes.

"I can't believe what I saw," Don said, a terrified chill rushing over his flesh. "I swear. There was something inside them. Red lights. Like something out of a horror movie. Their chests glowed and these red lights exploded from them. Exploded!"

"I saw it, too," Kaitlyn cried. "I heard the screams and ran to the bedroom window and saw. Those red things." Her voice was rising. "Dad! What was that?"

"Your mother saw them. The red lights. She told me, but I didn't know what she meant. My God." Don turned to his son and lifted his T-shirt. There were no marks on his chest and his skin was cool.

Mary Beth said, "Is he okay?"

"Something came over them. Something unnatural. If I hadn't seen it myself…" He took his son by the shoulders. "Help me get them into the house."

Kaitlyn draped her arm around her sister and, with Don and Mary Beth guiding Josh, they all tramped across the lawn. Safely in the kitchen, Don's sight fell upon Kira's hands. Her fingernails were crusted with dirt. It was the same with Josh. On the day they went to the hospital, after that first time he'd found them buried, he saw the dirt under their nails. In that moment, he realized the dirt was there because they'd been digging at it, not just placed in it.

"We can only get back by the way we came in." The words came out of his son's mouth, but it wasn't his voice. It was the voice he'd heard when reading from the pages of *Ragged Dick*.

"What does that mean?" Mary Beth asked between punctuated gasps.

"Josh?" Don examined his son's face. Josh's eyes were closed. So were Kira's. "Why were you burying yourself?"

"We can only get back by the way we came in?"

Kaitlyn slithered next to her father. "Why is he putting on that voice?"

"I don't know, Pumpkin, but for some horrendous reason, they are the ones who had buried themselves all along."

"That's insane."

"No. It's not." And he thought about Mercy with her broken hands. "The explanation is somewhere in those fiery balls we saw."

"Do you think lightning hit them?" Mary Beth asked. "It could have affected their brains so they're confused about what they're doing."

"As far as I know, lightning doesn't float. It strikes. And there was no heat, no damage to the children. Besides, if I thought there was even the slightest chance of that, they'd be on their way to the hospital now."

Mary Beth shuddered. "Mercy's been trying to tell me something for a while and I brushed it off that she was depressed, you know, because of Lisa. I thought she was searching for castles in the sky and would get over it after a while."

He collapsed inward. "She tried to talk to me, too."

The doorbell rang. Don jumped. Gathering his nerves, he said, "Stay here." He swiped a kitchen towel from the stove handle, wiped his face and hands, then tossed the towel in the sink. He took two steps toward the living room, then turned to Mary Beth. Her face was drawn, her mouth locked open in horror. "Stay together."

The doorbell rang again.

It was all a mistake, Detective. My children buried themselves because some strange electric energy took over their bodies. Sorry to have bothered you.

His heart jackhammered inside his chest as he opened the door. Detective Bachman was there looking like she was ready to slap the cuffs on him. Beside her towered a lanky, middle-aged man with a face so pale it looked as if he'd spent his days in a cave.

"Mr. Amoretto," she said with the same reserve he'd heard on the phone, "my partner." She waved a hand at the man but didn't bother to mention his name. "We tried to pay your neighbor a visit, but it appears she isn't home."

"Is that so?" It was just a response, except it sounded like a retort, which sounded like it was covering a lie.

"May we come in?"

Like vampires, they needed an invitation to enter. He was standing over the threshold staring at these apparitions: one short and squat like a female version of Lou Costello. The other a tall piece of wire. They were the Abbott and Costello of vampires. He opened the door wider and they stepped in.

"You're wet, Mr. Amoretto." She scanned his body as she passed him. "And rather muddy."

Just get them to leave, he thought. Take the focus off Mercy and Mary Beth and get them to leave.

"Oh. Yes. I remembered I left my book out on the picnic table after the rains started falling. I didn't want it to get destroyed. I slipped in the mud on my way back in."

"Rains?"

"Just now. We had a flash downpour."

"Interesting. We must have been just behind it."

As if she were in her own home, she walked through the living room toward the kitchen, her wiry partner by her side. Don squeezed his hands into tight fists to keep from grabbing their arms. Trying not to breathe too hard, he walked a step behind them. When standing at the front door, the kitchen archway was at a slant, so the detectives couldn't see beyond it from that angle. But once across the living room, they would have a clear view of the kitchen and everything in it, including his mud-caked children. And Mary Beth.

"Detective." It came out calm, which surprised him. "Is there something you want to talk with me about?"

She stopped, but her partner kept heading toward the archway. "You called me, Mr. Amoretto. I should be asking you that question?"

It passed through him to tell the detective about the orbs of fire and how they appeared to strike his children and … what … turned them into zombies? Like that wouldn't get him a room right next to Mercy's at Tower Hills. "I … I was overly anxious when I called you. My wife is locked away, you see, and it breaks my heart. I fear I'm a bit irrational. Everyone has become suspicious to me. You understand. I shouldn't have called."

"Suspicions are good. They keep us on our toes."

The detective entered the kitchen, and in one long stride, Don stood behind her. The room was empty. Mary Beth must have taken the children outside. Maybe she took them to her house, and that thought made him more jumpy than a frog on a hotplate.

"There's an awful lot of mud in here," Detective Wiry said, studying the floor. "Lucy," he said to his partner and nodded toward the counter, which was also smeared with mud.

"Oh," Don thought fast. "When I fell, I dropped the book in the mud and put it on the counter to get a towel to wipe it off." There was far too much mud on the counter for one little book to leave. He knew that. The detective knew it, too. Bachman gave a quick survey of the kitchen as if looking for the book. "I brought it upstairs."

The detective turned her attention to the kitchen window. An anxious trail of fire ants crawled over Don's flesh. He looked out to where she was staring, but the outside lights had been turned off and saw only the reflection of himself and his guests in the kitchen. When his eyes met the mirrored image of Detective Bachman, her focus was dead set on the reflection of his face.

With a jerk of his head, he turned from the window.

"What were you reading," she asked.

"Pardon me?"

"Your book. What were you reading?"

Think. No time. "Ragged Dick."

"Ah. Horatio Alger. Lifted the spirits of many a poor boy in his day." She walked around him so she could see into his eyes. "You know, a lot of people think that Alger himself rose from rags to riches, but that's not true. He was a private school kid, even went to Harvard."

"Is that so?"

Her beady eyes narrowed in a look that said in the most understated way, don't fuck with me. "Interesting choice of literature. Alger's a bit out of your age group. If I were to guess, I'd pin you as a Grisham man."

"It's my son's. He was reading it in school and it sounded interesting, so I picked it up. You know, to see what he was learning."

"You take an interest in your children's education. That's good of you." If there was sincerity in her tone, he didn't hear it. She turned as if to walk away and a rush of warm relief ran through him. It hardened to ice when she turned back. "Where are your children, by the way?"

"Upstairs."

"Mind if we talk to them?"

"Actually, they're sleeping. They've been through quite a lot lately."

"I should say. Buried alive twice and all."

"Like I said, Detective, I made a mistake when accusing Mary Beth. It seems the children are suffering from some type of post-traumatic stress. I found them in the hole in the back yard today. They were just in the hole, not in any real danger, but I panicked. After I called you, I realized they were just trying to remember, to figure the whole thing out."

"On the phone, you said they were buried."

"I was mistaken."

"So they weren't buried in the dirt?"

"Not buried. No." *Oh, what a tangled web.*

She started toward the living room and for the first time in the minutes he'd been talking with her, Don realized he hadn't kept track of Detective Wiry. Edging toward the arch, Don saw Bachman's partner already at the front door, his hand on the knob. While Bachman distracted him, her partner had found something. Don didn't know what, but there must have been something, and he was waiting to run it through the evidence lab or pass it by the district attorney, or whatever those wiry detectives did with things they scooped from crime scenes. It skipped through Don's brain that he wished he'd read more Grisham.

"Sorry to take up so much of your time, Mr. Amoretto." She shook his hand. It was more of a hard clasp with no real shake involved. A grip and release kind of gal. She turned, then stopped, her forefinger shooting up in the air. "It seems your wife is in the right place for now." Her head turned toward him, but her body stood firm.

"I'm convinced she's not to blame for any of this."

"I see." She turned her head away and waddled down the front walk with her partner just ahead of her. "If you have any more suspicions, please don't hesitate to call," she said over her shoulder. "After all, suspicions are what—"

"Keep us on our toes. Yes." And he closed the door.

Through the front window, Don watched the two detectives duck their equally awkward bodies into the frame of the navy blue sedan. It took them forever to drive off, and the wait was insufferable, like waiting for a jury to say whether you were going to get a needle in the arm or be sent home for supper. After an excruciating amount of time, they pulled down the street and around the corner.

CHAPTER THIRTY-EIGHT
Sometime Around the Present
Outside the Abyss

W alker and Anastasia were standing beside the tree. There was a woman and a girl also standing there. Anastasia didn't know who they were exactly, but the girl was familiar, like they had a connection. Anastasia stared and stared at the girl, who was so like the girl who was helping Anastasia, but different. Nowhere around her did she see the man.

"He'll come," Walker said in his mind. "He always comes at some point when the boy and the girl are with us, he'll be back. 'Member what I told you. If the man won't let us go by way of the dirt, then we get the boy and the girl to aid us in talkin' to him. Keep holdin' onto your girl and I'll hold onto the boy, and he'll come. Then we'll talk to him. We'll show him what we need to do. Once he hears. Once he sees, he'll hep us."

Anastasia tried, but she'd never had to hold on for so long before and she found her mind filling with strange images and chatter that made her feel like she was in a room full of people all talking at the same time. "I can't think," she said. "There's too much noise in my head."

"It's the girl's thoughts. I get that, too. You know how to calm her?"

"I've done it before, but I can't do it now. I think she's scared. Did I scare her, Walker? I didn't mean to scare her. It hurts a lot to think I did. Please. How do I make her not be scared?"

"When you hum that tune, it calms me real nice. Maybe it'll work for her."

Walker slipped his hand into Anastasia's palm. She began to hum. She felt Walker open his mind to the music. He picked up the rhythm of her tune and began to recite the words from his book. The girl, who was so close to Anastasia she could feel her soul, softened like she'd come out of the cold.

CHAPTER THIRTY-NINE
June 2014 ~ The Present

Don dashed through the kitchen, flipped on the outside light, and flew out onto the deck. In a loud whisper, he called, "Mary Beth." He tore over to the tree. "They're gone."

Kaitlyn popped out from behind the maple and rushed into her father's arms.

Mary Beth appeared. "When I heard the detective's voice, I slammed off the outside light and scurried the children out here."

"How are they doing?" Don nodded toward Kira and Josh who were standing at the edge of the cursed hole.

"Calm." Mary Beth said.

Kaitlyn touched her father's sleeve. "Listen."

"What is it?"

"Just listen."

He did, and caught the quick, thumping pulse of his heartbeat inside his ears. "What…"

"Shh," Kaitlyn said.

There it was. A girl humming. Don knew the song and he started to shake. Underscoring the humming was the voice of a boy. *THE* boy. The southern boy he'd heard in his head. The boy who had found his way inside his son's mouth.

"Where's it coming from?" Kaitlyn said, her words cracked and frightened.

"Everywhere." Don stood frigid, the voices clinging to him like spider webs. When he turned his eyes to Kira and Josh, they were sitting near the hole. He knelt beside them. They were holding hands. The doll was on Kira's lap and the book was in Josh's other hand. Their mouths were moving. The voices were coming from them. But it wasn't his children speaking. It was that older boy, and from Kira, a much younger girl. It was as if his children were channeling the spirits of strangers.

"Daddy?" Kaitlyn cried out. She was on the ground beside him. "What's happening?"

Don took Kira's chin in his fingers and turned her face toward his. *Those eyes!* He fell backward. Kaitlyn screamed.

"Their eyes," Mary Beth yelled. "They're gone!"

But they weren't gone. They were changing. Right before all of them, Kira and Josh's eyes had turned solid white. His children blinked, and Kira's eyes shifted to sky blue; Josh's, almost gold.

"Impossible," Don gasped.

In unison, the children stood. Don leapt to his feet and hurled his arms around them. Without resistance, the two dropped the doll and the book into the hole. Don led them away from the edge and released them. With strong but gentle hands, he placed his palms on either side of Kira's face.

"Kira," he wheezed. "Sweetie?"

She reacted, but not with words. His hands applying only the slightest pressure, she began to rise.

"What are you doing," Kaitlyn cried.

"I'm not doing anything."

He let his hands fall from his daughter's cheeks and Kira continued to rise, lifted by an unknown power. Josh was beside her, hovering three feet off the ground.

"Holy shit." Don grabbed his son's arm, but it was as if Josh was being pulled away by some unseen force.

"They're floating," Mary Beth cried out, her voice matching the horror on her face.

"I saw Kira do that," Kaitlyn screeched. "In bed the other night. She lifted all the way off her bed as if it was nothing." She threw her body into her father's chest. "Dad! It was on the night of the storm. I knew it. The storm did something. It brought something. And somehow it got into them!"

The night of the storm. It all happened that night. The red balls of light. The change in Kira and Josh. "I don't think it was the storm that brought something." Don said. "I think something brought the storm."

Kira and Josh hovered eerily over the hole. The objects were not in their hands, yet the children did not behave with fury as they had done when Don had thrown the objects from them. They were looking down at the objects as if they were finally in the right place. They'd put them in the grave. That's where they were supposed to be. They didn't have to hold onto the objects. They just had to know where they were.

Like bricks, his two children dropped into the grave. Kaitlyn shrieked. Don thought his heart would fly out his mouth. Kira and Josh sat, still as mountains. They weren't digging. They weren't doing anything. And they weren't actually sitting on the ground. They were hovering, legs crossed, right above the earth.

"Kira," Kaitlyn quavered.

"What are you doing," Don asked.

"We can't just stare at them, Dad. We've got to figure out what's inside them." Kaitlyn jumped into the hole.

"No!" Don yelled.

"Kira," Kaitlyn said again.

"Momma?" Kira looked up, but not at any of them. "Momma?"

"Who's she talking to?" Kaitlyn asked.

Mercy.

Mary Beth stepped closer to him. "Don, Mercy told me she heard a girl calling for her Momma and felt like the girl was talking to her. It came to her while she was swinging and while she was in the shower."

"And she heard it at Tower Hills." He'd heard it, too. From the doctor walking down the hall. He went lightheaded and grabbed Mary Beth's arm to stay steady. He rocked until the fog lifted then let go. Slipping into the hole, he opened his mind because everything he'd seen and heard threatened to shut it down. He knelt next to Kira and placed his large hands on her slender shoulders.

"Kira, sweetie."

She looked at him with bright blue eyes. "I'm not Kira."

Of course you're not. Not with those eyes and that child's voice. "Who are you?"

"Anastasia Madison."

Mary Beth screamed. "Mercy said! She said Kira was Anastasia! Oh, Don!"

"Dad!" Kaitlyn cried out. "It's the girl Mom was asking Kira about. When she slapped her. But it wasn't Kira who Mom was trying to hit. It was Anastasia. She just … missed." Her arms gripped around her father's shoulders.

"Won' you hep us?" Josh said.

The stranger's voice, those pale gold eyes, they kicked Don in the heart of his senses and his mind became a manic mess.

"Is Josh someone else, Dad? Like Kira is someone else?" His daughter's frightened questions floated about them.

"Champ?" Those strange golden eyes stared with no understanding in them. "Son?"

"Yessir."

"What's your name?"

"Walker sir. I's Walker Jacobs."

"Where's Joshua? My boy. Where is he?"

"He's right here aside me, sir."

Aside. Inside? "How did you get here?" Walker pointed down. "You came here through the ground?"

"Yessir."

Kaitlyn whispered to her father, "What does he mean?"

"It was dark," said the little girl's voice. "Dark like the whole world died. It's lighter here."

"But t'ain't the right light. We's got to cross over to the other side. We's got to get back by the way we came." Josh and Kira both stared at the ground.

"Dad?" Kaitlyn's voice was trembling. "Does he mean the way they came is like through a grave?"

"Yes." He wobbled, but caught himself.

"Are there ghosts possessing them?"

"God help us. Yes."

"Are their bodies buried here? Right here in our yard?" Kaitlyn yelled.

"No, Pumpkin. There are no bodies buried here. Just the doll and the book. But it's logical to assume…"

"Nothing's logical about this," Kaitlyn said.

"You're right." He pushed hard to control the war against rationality raging in his mind. "Those objects." He nodded toward the things in his children's hands. "They belong to them." His brain skipped. "I mean, to Anastasia and Walker. Or once belonged to them."

"And the tire and the rope," Mary Beth said. "It's all connected. It all started when we attached the rope and tire together and tied it to the tree. Mercy knew that. Tying these things together must have set something free."

"It feels more like something got trapped," Kaitlyn said.

Fighting his own terror, he painstakingly removed Kaitlyn's clutch from his body.

"They don't gravitate toward the rope and the tire," Don said. "It's the doll and the book they need." *And the objects were found in the ground.* "They have to get back by the way they came," he mulled aloud. And he understood. They were thinking about it like children because they were children. Children's minds work in a different direction than adults. They see what's in front of them instead of what's beyond them.

"Walker." It sounded wrong coming out of him. "Do you know what happened before the dark?"

The boy inside Josh looked up at the maple. "I was readin'. Right by this here tree." His expression grew grave. "No, that ain't it. White boys came. Strung me up." He bowed his head to his hands.

A fearful sorrow filled Don as he realized what he was facing. He didn't want to ask the girl inside Kira; he already knew. Not the details, but the outcome. She offered it to him anyway.

"Daddy was driving us to Uncle Mickey's wedding." She was bubbling with glee. "I'm going to dance like a fairy princess."

She doesn't know she didn't make it there. "This spot," Don said to the girl. "Does it mean something to you?"

"This is the best climbing tree in the world." There was cheer. And in a blip, a change of a channel, gloom took over her face. Slow, like a cloud passing over the moon, she said, "Daddy was driving us."

No further information was necessary. This was a favorite tree for both of them, and this was the place where they both died. A cosmic coincidence that brought them together in death. And brought them to Mercy, who died a little when Lisa died.

"They lived here and they died here," Don said. "But they weren't buried here. They're confused. My guess is they had these things with them when they died. Because of that, the things became attached to their souls. It could be when their bodies were taken away and buried somewhere else, these belongings were left behind. They think they need to be buried here because this is the last place they remember. But they're mistaken. They don't need to bury their souls here with the objects. They need to bury the objects with their souls. We need to find the cemetery where these children were laid to rest and bury the objects with their bones."

"Mom isn't crazy," Kaitlyn faltered. "There were ghosts in the tree."

"Now, they're in Josh and Kira," Mary Beth added. "How did they get in them?"

"The night of the storm, Dad."

"Yes. When I cut down the swing, I severed the spirits' attachment to the tree. The spirits lost their connection and needed to attach to something else."

Mary Beth said, "Why Kira? Why not Kaitlyn? They're identical twins."

"I'm older," Kaitlyn said. "Two minutes, twenty seconds. Anastasia must be very young to have a doll like that. She chose Kira because she was the youngest girl in the house."

"Or," Don said, "it could be that you were awake at the time. You had gotten up to go to the bathroom. That's when you saw your mother on the swing."

"How do we get the ghosts out of them, Dad? If we don't, they'll bury themselves again and they'll take Josh and Kira with them!"

Acting on impulse, Don snatched the doll from Kira. She began to shake and a fierce scream harpooned from her mouth.

"Why did you do that," Kaitlyn shouted. "Give it back to her!"

Kira's chest began to glow and a fiery-colored orb pulsed through her clothes. He placed the doll on Kira's lap. The girl inside his daughter relaxed. She laid her hand over the doll and the glow from her chest disappeared.

"I'm sorry, sweetie," he said to both Kira and the girl inside her. "I needed to know." The girl in his daughter whispered something in the doll's ear. He couldn't make it out, but it sounded sweet. "Anastasia, what are you saying?"

"I'm making a wish to my fairy. Wishes to fairies always come true."

He let that settle inside him for a moment then wrapped his arms around Kira's waist and began to lift her out of the hole.

"Momma!" she cried. "Momma. Momma. Momma!" She kicked and squirmed out of his arms.

"What's wrong?" Kaitlyn yelled.

"She needs her Ma," Josh said in the boy's voice. "She'd reached her before, but couldn't get her to come to us."

"Reached her where?" Don asked.

"Here by the tree I think. Someplace else, too, far off."

Don whirled around. "Mary Beth, you said you were going to try to find the cemetery where the girl was buried. Did you?"

"I never followed through with that, but I thought to start here in Windsome. There's only one cemetery in this town."

"Rolling Acres," Don said.

"That's the one. I was going to call and see if the caretaker had some kind of registry or something. I never got around to it."

"Momma." The girl inside Kira called. "Momma. Momma." It was a chilling cry, desperate and frightened.

"Tonight, help me take care of the children. Tomorrow, call Rolling Acres."

"I'll do it first thing in the morning. What are you planning?"

"I'm not sure, but I know I need to see Mercy."

Hospital floors had a way of echoing footfalls that made Don feel like he was walking through catacombs. It was especially disturbing in a mental hospital. That it was the second time that day he'd walked the same path through Tower Hills didn't make it easier. But it did make him as unyielding in his mission as a soldier under enemy fire.

Throughout the night before and intermittently during the day, he'd witnessed Kira and Joshua spill in and out of themselves. There were long, painful spells in which his children lost their signature brown eyes to the blue and pale gold of those other children. Lost their voices to those of the dead. Periods of unbearable agony when the girl named Anastasia cried out for her mother in a relentless stream. There were times when they levitated off the ground and floated to their homemade graves, observing it as if the answers were swirling around like a whirlpool from the underworld.

Although Mary Beth had discovered the cemetery where the children's bodies were laid to rest—it was Rolling Acres as she'd suspected—the one named Anastasia wouldn't budge without her mother. And the one named Walker wouldn't budge without Anastasia. And neither, but for an occasional moment when Don saw the confused eyes of Kira and Josh return to their natural color, would let go of his children until they crossed to the other side. As he trod steadily down the halls of Tower Hills for the second time, he was determined to rid his children of those spirits in whatever way he could.

He'd arrived at the hospital earlier that morning, just a visitor coming in to see his wife. He signed in with a precise signature, neat penmanship, unlike the illegible scrawl he would use later. He counted the paces to the room where they were keeping Mercy. It was what Mercy called the sickroom. Although she was supposed to be under close watch, he discovered that "close watch" had significant gaps.

As he neared Mercy's room, he heard that same telltale calling he'd heard earlier that day. "Momma," from the lips of a nurse behind the station. It wasn't loud enough for anyone else to notice, but he did. He was tuned in to it. It passed through her like gas through a tube, a brief puff and it was gone. Then the orderly, swiping back and forth with the giant octopus mop and dipping it into the cloudy water in the bucket. "Momma." His voice low and deep like he was about to break out in a version of "Roll, Jordan, Roll." At one point, it even sifted out of the wrinkled lips of the craggy-faced Nurse Fowler.

No one appeared to notice that ping pong of the word bouncing from mouth to mouth in and around Mercy's room. But Mercy did. The first time he'd arrived that day, he found her rocking her head back and forth in torment, begging for the noise to stop. His presence had calmed her. When he was left alone with his wife, he explained all they'd learned about her ghosts. Told her he believed her. They all did. She went mute for a moment, shutting her eyes to hold back the anger he knew she deserved to have. When she spoke, only one word came out, weak, like the cheep of a bird.

"Why?"

Why did you do this to me? Why did you let them lock me up? Why couldn't you love me enough to keep me from this brutal place? That one word hammered him. He promised her he would explain everything, but at the moment, their priority was to save their children.

"After all we've been through," she cried and banged her bandaged hands on the bed. Don winced at the unavoidable pain that must have come with it. "How could you?" Her voice was as broken as his heart. "How could you think I would hurt our children? What kind of monster do you think I am?"

"I don't. I didn't." His words were stammers of uselessness.

Her cries were the exhausted kind. Tears poured down the side of her face and into her ear.

Don bent over her; pressed his cheek against hers. Whispered, "I'm sorry. I'm so very sorry."

"Oh, Don. We have to save them. Our children."

He lifted his face, stayed close. "We will."

"How? With me trapped in this place."

"That's what I'm here to figure out. With you."

She grabbed his eyes with hers and held them hostage. "Don't you leave me until we do."

He promised he wouldn't. For the next three hours he'd studied the patterns of the staff and plotted his plan with Mercy. When he left his wife, she was a little stronger knowing he was heading home to finish their plan with Mary Beth and Kaitlyn. He didn't know if it would work, but they had no choice. It's not that he was going to break

Mercy out of Tower Hills exactly, just borrow her for a bit, then bring her back. None the worse for wear. But he had to wait until after darkness fell, while still leaving enough time to return her before visiting hours ended at 9:30. It was all about the timing.

There, on his second visit of the day, with their plans mapped out, he stood outside Mercy's door and swept his vision across the area. Only one nurse sat at the station. Her head was bent over some paperwork, but he didn't recognize her. She was the night nurse. Two doors down the hall, he spied a wheelchair. He tugged on the collar of his white shirt and swaggered to the desk with what he hoped was a look of professional confidence.

"I'm here to see my patient," Don said. "I'm her therapist."

The nurse looked up. Although Mercy was awaiting an indictment, Tower Hills wasn't a jail. It was a hospital, and the rules were more relaxed. She nodded her approval. He slipped into the room and put his forefinger to his lips to indicate to Mercy to stay quiet. He swung the door shut.

"How are you doing," he whispered.

"I'll be better when this is over." Her lips were chapped, and her hands, restrained at the wrists, were wrapped in gauze bandages.

"When was the last time someone checked on you?"

"About ten minutes ago. That's when I threw another fit. I tried to make it enough so they would keep me restrained in here instead of sending me back to the locked room. The only problem is they made me take something, so I'm really dopey."

"Don't worry. I've got that covered." Don took a few minutes to review the plan with her. When he was sure Mercy was ready, he stepped out of the room and approached the nurses' station. "My patient needs to use the bathroom, may I release her restraints."

The nurse said she had to do it, and followed him into the room. She unbuckled the leather straps on Mercy's arms and lowered the rails. Mercy gave Don a sideways glance and went into the bathroom. Don flipped the sign so the "occupied" side was facing out.

"I'm just going to give her some privacy," he said and motioned toward the door.

The nurse followed him out and took her position behind the desk. It was far too many minutes that she stayed there, and Don felt as jittery as if he'd drank a full pot of coffee. He paced the hallway, trying to appear controlled. After many agonizing minutes, the ding from a call button rang out and the nurse left her station and rounded the corner.

Don scurried to the wheelchair. He rolled it into Mercy's room and whispered into the bathroom. "Ready." Mercy came out. Motioning to the wheelchair, he said, "This will help us move faster."

She sat in the chair and he propped her feet in the footrests. He left the "occupied" sign on the door, wheeled his wife out into the hall, and closed the door to the room.

"Keep your face down." And he rolled her down the hall in the direction of the exit.

The place was morgue quiet. Rounding the corner of the one-floor building, he counted the steps to freedom. He passed an orderly. One right turn. One to go. He scooted by a janitor and walked with a quickened step toward the last corner. There it was. The exit. He was going to make it.

"Mr. Amoretto?"

If he weren't gripping the handles of the wheelchair, he might have jumped straight to the ceiling. Maintaining his focus on the exit, he kept walking.

"Mr. Amoretto."

It was the vulture. She sounded about twenty paces behind him, but he could hear her feet galumphing to catch up. He ignored her with what he hoped was a "you've got the wrong guy I just look like him" attitude.

"Mr. Amoretto," her voice bellowed from behind.

He lessened his step to look more casual, but tried to keep a good clip in his pace nonetheless. Her bones were bent and his legs were longer, so he could easily out-walk her. Then again, she was a vulture. She could fly. If ghosts could inhabit his children's bodies, then vulture nurses could fly. *Keep it together and keep on walking.*

"Mr. Amoretto." She sounded closer, and he began to run. "Stop that man!"

If he didn't know better, her voice was coming from above.

Ahead, the exit loomed: double glass doors with pull handles, metal half-squares attached to the glass. The doors pulled open. No rubber grid mat on the floor, no motion detector above the jam. It was a hospital, for Christ's sake; there had to be an automatic trigger. Another pair of trampling footsteps joined the nurse's and Don cut into a full-on run. With relief, he saw a round gray button inscribed with the blue handicapped symbol to the right of the doors. Shoving his shoulder into the button, the doors began their excruciatingly sluggish opening.

"Stop," a man's voice yelled, and the stomping footsteps were at his heels.

A hand grabbed the collar of his shirt. Fingernails clawed at his skin. It ripped like the teeth of a comb tearing his flesh. Spinning the wheelchair around, Mercy's legs flailed out with the force of the turn, and the footrests of the chair cracked into the ankles of the orderly behind them. The man buckled and fell. Don spun the chair around, knocking the man in the jaw with the wheel. Instead of incapacitating him, it angered him and he scrambled to his feet.

Behind the man, the vulture nurse, panting and wheezing, ran in a clumsy gallop toward them. Don slammed the gray button on the wall again to keep the doors open and he spun the wheelchair in the direction of the man and the nurse. With full speed, he charged, feeling more than a twinge of guilt for using his wife as a weapon. In the second before barreling into him, Don whipped the chair sideways and slammed the side of it into the man's groin area. The man tumbled backward, crashed into the nurse, and the two fell in a tangled mass to the ground.

"Sorry. Sorry," Don said to both his wife and the people he'd rammed. He was desperate, but he never wanted to hurt anyone.

In a mad turn that sent his wife reeling in the chair, Don shoved her through the door. There were two male voices hollering after him, and Don assumed one was the orderly and the other was the janitor. He raced across the walkway toward the parking garage.

"Are you all right," Don asked his wife. Mercy let out a grunt and he took that as a yes.

Instead of going through the pedestrian entrance, Don ran through the open door at the front of the garage where the cars enter. From many yards behind him, he heard incomprehensible shouting. He heard the word police. He ran up the car ramp to the first floor elevator. He pushed the up button and gave a quick glance over his shoulder. They were coming, but they weren't in sight yet.

"Come on. Come on!" he yelled at the elevator door.

The welcoming chime sounded and the doors whooshed open. Don stuck an arm into the elevator and pressed a button. He didn't know or care which button he pressed. When the doors closed and the elevator rose without him or Mercy in it, he wheeled his wife around the corner and huddled in the shadows.

He gulped air in shallow spurts to squelch his distressed breathing and placed a palm over Mercy's mouth to cover her frightened moans. Footsteps echoed in the cavernous garage and shouts of chase bounced off the concrete and steel. Don huddled with his wife and waited for the giveaway sign that his hunters had caught the bait.

"Look," one yelled. "It's stopping on level three. Take the stairs, it's faster!"

The metal bar on the door leading to the stairwell rattled, and soles clacked up the concrete steps. When the door clanked closed, Don straightened and pushed the wheelchair out of the shadow. He trotted to Mary Beth's car, which was parked illegally in a "Reserved for Physicians" space not four feet away. He'd planned for what had become the inevitable breakdown in his plan that the police would be looking for his SUV, not Mary Beth's Acura. Detective Bachman and her wiry partner were likely on their way to his house now, but they wouldn't find anyone there. It was possible he could still execute his plan and get Mercy back. Not necessarily without a hitch as he'd hoped, but he could come up with some excuse. There'd be consequences, but that wasn't his main concern. He had to get them all to the cemetery and bury death once and for all.

CHAPTER FORTY
June 2014 ~ The Present

In the passenger's seat of Mary Beth's Acura, Mercy let the air from the open window cleanse away the stench of stale urine and bleach that seemed to live like mold in the halls of Tower Hills. The blast against her face did wonders in lifting the swampy mist from the drugs she'd been given during her stay there, allowing her to concentrate on saving her children. There was relief in knowing there was an explanation for what she'd heard and seen. But there was no relief from her fear. She wasn't frightened knowing ghosts existed among them. She believed in that already—every waking moment when she spoke to her daughter in her heart, every sleeping moment when Lisa came to her in her dreams. Her fear was getting those ghosts out of her children. Her knuckles throbbed, but her head pounded harder.

She turned to her husband. "Are you okay?" No answer. "Don?" His eyes were fixed on the road, nostrils flaring with his intake of breath.

"I'm sorry I didn't believe you," he said, pain coming with every word. "All of this could have been avoided if only I'd believed you."

She was angry when he first told her he'd discovered the ghosts were real, hurt that he didn't take her words as unconditional truths. But she would deal with that later. She had to focus on her children. "You believe me now. That's what's important. So, let's do this thing and when everyone's safe, we'll talk then."

He gave her a wan smile. "Deal." He turned the car onto the main road that led to their neighborhood.

"I thought we were going to the municipal lot," Mercy said.

"This is the fastest way. Don't worry, I'll avoid our street." He flipped off the lights to the Acura.

"I wish you had brought the children with you in the first place. It would have been faster."

"I couldn't risk it. We were a grip away from getting busted back there. If we weren't that half a step in front of them, we would have been caught and they would have taken the children away right on the scene. It's difficult enough having to take them to the cemetery." Don pulled the car onto Sycamore Street, which was parallel to Pleasant Drive.

"How did you figure out who the boy was, Don? We knew the girl was Anastasia Madison because she told me through Kira, but the boy?"

"His name was inscribed in the book with a date underneath it."

The book that was buried with the doll. He'd mentioned it. The book with the passages she'd heard in the wind.

"They were local kids apparently," Don said. "Buried at the town cemetery. From what Mary Beth told me, the caretaker was able to find them rather easily. Seems lots of people inquire about gravesites. He gave her a general idea where they're buried. Unfortunately, they're on opposite sides of the grounds. The boy is buried in what used to be a small segregated cemetery. It was bought by Rolling Acres when they expanded in the 1960s."

Sirens pealed from somewhere. Mercy jumped in her seat and fire burned in her cheeks. Don turned a corner and Mercy could see the municipal lot at the end of the street. Their SUV was barely visible, parked in the darkened corner. He coasted into the lot and pulled up right behind it.

"How did you get the children to come to the parking lot? You said the girl wouldn't go without her mother."

"I told her to make a wish to her fairy doll that her mother would meet her here and that it was sure to come true because we were all wishing together." He opened the driver's side door. "Let's see if it worked."

Instead of getting out of the car, he leaned across the seat. Cupping Mercy's cheek in his palm, he pressed his lips against hers. The moistness of his mouth soothed her dry lips. Funny how a kiss could cure a pain. At first, it was just a passing of their lips. Then he moved into her, and she enjoyed his mouth with intimate fullness. It was the kind of kiss lovers shared before they were about to never see each other again. When he pulled away, his gaze met hers and she forgot to breathe for the seconds in which she melted into the wonder of his deep, remorseful eyes.

"I love you," he said.

"I love you, too."

A second later, he was out of the car. Mary Beth emerged from the parked SUV. More sirens and a pulse of red and blue flashed in the rear-view mirror. The pulse was faint and far away, somewhere over the trees, like a distant disco ball. They were coming for them. Would arrest them, and her children would forever be prisoners, held hostage by spirits whose sole goal was to find Heaven and take her children with them.

"Hurry," she muttered and felt the crease in her brow deepen. The sirens moved closer. "Oh, God. Hurry."

Mary Beth opened the back door of the SUV. Mercy couldn't see in the dark if the children were in the vehicle, and when no one came out, her nerves, which were already burning, began to sizzle. Don darted over to the opened passenger door and reached in an arm. When he pulled it out, he had the small hand of their son in his. Josh stepped from the back seat and Kira came out after him. Kaitlyn popped her head out of the front seat of the Volvo and watched her father rush her siblings toward the Acura. When he got there, he threw open the back door.

"Sirens," Mercy said in a loud whisper.

"I know." Don helped Josh into the car. Even though it took precious seconds, he snapped the seatbelt around his son's lap. Kira followed Josh on her own and Don secured her in place. "Let's go."

The dark that had fallen shrouded them as they rolled out of the parking lot and onto the street. Sirens whooped nearer and Mercy held her sight on the rear window. Flashing lights, more prominent than a minute ago, dominated the vista behind them.

"They're coming," Mercy said, turning her vision back toward Don.

"I'll keep the headlights off and let the streetlights guide me."

"Cops pull people over for not having their headlights on."

"Don't worry. Keep an eye out for cars and pedestrians. I'll get us to the cemetery unnoticed. I know these streets. I helped build them."

He did. She'd studied the specs with him all those years ago. The streets were structured in a series of loops connected to square grids, some streets leading to cul-de-sacs, others, like the one they were on, fingered out to the main roads on either side of the development. Don could not only navigate them at night with the lights off, Mercy thought, but with his eyes closed and one elbow on the wheel.

He turned right on New Prospect and then left onto Cardinal. From Cardinal, he maneuvered onto a lonely road named Park Ridge with no homes on either side, only several acres of fields of grazing cows and horses. Because it was night, there were no cows or horses visible, and Mercy wondered if the animals slept as humans did when darkness fell. Were they corralled into barns to sleep in separate stalls and then released back to the fields at dawn to graze? Or did they sleep in the pasture, hiding in plain sight, as she and Don were hoping to do as they drifted without headlights up Park Ridge toward the land of the dead?

Behind them, the sirens became subdued whirs as they headed away from their pursuers. With their lights off, they made their swift, yet steady, way to their destination, hiding in the middle of the road. She made a quick check over her shoulder to where Kira and Joshua sat holding hands and, for the first time since they entered the car, she thought about the fate of her other child.

"Kaitlyn," Mercy burst. "Where is Mary Beth going to take her?"

"To a diner in Raleigh. She'll be safe there."

A diner, the kind of low-key grease pit people hid out in when they were on the lam. She envisioned her daughter hunched down low in a booth away from the window, maybe wearing a baseball cap pulled over her eyes.

"She's okay," Don said.

He'd read her mind, as he'd often seemed to do after so many years connected at the heart.

"There it is." Mercy pointed out the front window.

Ahead loomed the expansive gates of Rolling Acres Cemetery. In the early days of their courtship, those gates were a romantic beckoning for the young lovers, an entryway to a mysterious landscape of open-armed marble angels and massive sepulchers. She and Don would stroll the grounds, arms around each other's waists, admiring the magnolia blooms and the museum-like statues and ignoring the dead who rested there. But as the gates loomed closer, the dead had become her primary concern.

The enormous wrought iron fence towered in front of her like the rigid veins in a massive pair of bat's wings. They were topped with iron angels, sentries reaching across the arch warning Mercy and Don not to enter. The cemetery was closed. It was always closed after dark to keep the drunks and teenagers from desecrating the grounds with bottles and condoms, yet bottles and condoms always seemed to make their way in.

Don turned the vehicle off the main driveway and onto the patchy dirt, away from the inanimate yet watchful eyes of the angel guards. He drove to the far end of the property where the iron fence ended. Just inches away from the brick wall of the crematorium, there was a gap. It was not unfamiliar to Mercy and Don. As teenagers, they'd slipped through that gap more times than Mercy could remember.

"You ready?" Don asked as he put the Acura in park.

Mercy nodded and turned to her children in the back seat. They sat, staring ahead, with the precious objects in their laps. "This better work," she said and exited the car.

Don opened the trunk and retrieved a shovel and flashlight. With the children in tow, they all slipped through the unguarded break.

"Are those spirits inside Kira and Josh now?" Mercy asked.

"From everything I can figure, they are. They seem to trust me, though, and are willing to follow."

Based on the caretaker's description, they headed for the magnolia tree on the eastern side of the grounds. Although the blooms of the tree were long gone for the season, Mercy could almost pick up the lingering perfume of the open blossoms. It was one of the spots where she and Don would sit when their love was as fragrant and exposed as the flowers that had hung above them. To Mercy's relief, it was also far from where Lisa was buried.

When they reached the area, the flashlight beam bouncing off the glossy markers, they scanned for the name Madison. There were a surprising number of Madisons. Most were single plots for single sets of bones. That wasn't what they wanted. They were looking for a family plot, the caretaker had said. A broad stone engraved with several names. The band of light found it; black marble with chiseled white lettering. Anastasia Marie Madison. Below her name were the dates 1962 – 1970. Eight years old. The old grief that had never left Mercy crawled up her throat. Surrounding Anastasia's name were those of the family. Carol Jean Madison, beloved wife and mother, 1941 – 1970. Thomas Robert Madison, beloved husband and father, 1939 – 1970. Robert Allen Madison, 1960 – 1970. Precious Jane Madison, 1970 – 1970.

Precious Jane. Precious. An infant, or maybe not even born at all. Perhaps she died in her mother's womb, having never felt the air on her skin. Spared from knowing the agony that sometimes comes with living.

"They all died at the same time," Don said, sorrowful. The words dropped from him like tears.

"Momma," Kira said in Anastasia's voice. "Momma, it's dark here."

"We have to hurry," said Don as he thrust the shovel into the ground.

"Momma, I'm scared."

Another slice into the earth at a right angle to the first, he then lifted the triangle of sod and placed it aside to keep the grass atop it preserved. Keep it clean, Mercy thought, so the evidence of tampering won't be seen. Don dug out more dirt from the hole until Mercy heard the dull thud of his shovel hitting something.

A coffin. She figured it must be close to the surface because the family was laid to rest in stacks.

Don placed the shovel on the ground and, using his best fatherly tone, said, "Anastasia. May I talk to your doll for a moment?"

"Do you want to make a wish?" Kira-Anastasia asked.

"Yes. I want to make a very special wish."

Mercy made her own special wish. She wished with all her might to God and all the dolls in the universe that the tortured spirit of that eight-year-old girl would leave her daughter's body and find her way home. The girl inside her daughter handed Don the doll.

"How do you know where to put it?" Mercy asked. "There are several bodies buried there."

"It doesn't have to be directly on Anastasia."

"Oh, Don. That sounds so macabre."

"I'm sorry. I don't know how else to say it. From what I've seen, the doll just needs to be near enough so she knows where it is." He placed the doll into the hole. "I hope." He covered the hole with the removed dirt and replaced the patch of sod over the top, leaving no sign that the ground had been disturbed. Turning his attention to his daughter, he called, "Anastasia?" The little girl gave no response. "Kira?" She, too, was out of reach.

"It didn't work," said Mercy.

"Maybe we have to bury the book at Walker's grave before the spirits can be freed. The two may have died separately, but they were connected in death. These items were together below the maple tree since at least 1970. There must be some kind of bond between the spirits as a result."

Thunder grumbled and wind fluttered the leaves of the magnolia tree. Mercy grabbed her daughter's hand, Kira's other shoved into Josh's, and gave her a slight tug. Pain from her broken knuckles returned with the pressure, but she tuned it out. Lightning flashed. It may have been the brewing weather or her physical connection to the children, but through the bandages, Mercy felt the distinct tingle of electricity.

"This way." Don waved and started across the cemetery.

Bobbing and weaving through the maze of statues and headstones, with only a narrow beam of light to guide them, they headed toward the area of the grounds that were rumored in childhood stories to be the most haunted part of the cemetery. It wasn't a potter's field, but it was definitely lacking the ostentatious ornamentation of wealth that was emblematic of the other areas of Rolling Acres. It was obvious this was a different cemetery before Rolling Acres took it over.

Mercy never knew it was once a segregated piece of land, just knew it was rumored to be haunted. On her many jaunts to the cemetery as a young person, she'd always stayed away from this part. It wasn't that she actually believed the ghost stories back then—that came later—but it spooked her anyway. Stepping over and sometimes accidentally on top of the stones that marked the graves of the poor, she no longer trembled over those ghosts from stories past. The only ghosts Mercy feared were the ones inside her children.

As Don flashed the light over each marker, Mercy tried to make out the writing on them, but there was no shiny reflection to help her see clearly. The inscriptions were weathered and barely discernible on the modest stones of odd shapes, most no bigger than a football. Some had no writing at all. Others had rustic markings that looked like they were chiseled by hand. One of those stones had to have Walker Jacobs' name on it. He was in the registry, that's what Mary Beth told Don, which meant someone had taken care to bury him there and mark his stone. Getting on all fours, Mercy crawled from one marker to another feeling the surface of the timeworn stones with her fingertips as if reading Braille.

From the corner of her eye, she saw movement, a shadow in the darkness. A ghost. She shot a look around, but her children were standing still as brick walls and Don was crawling in search of Walker's name.

"I found it," Don said.

Mercy jumped to her feet and ran to Don's side. There it was. A simple stone, flat in the earth, displaying the name Walker Jacobs, and underneath, 1912 – 1928.

"Jesus," Don said with a touch of panic in his voice.

"I know. Only sixteen."

"No. Not that." He pointed to the cemetery entrance several hundred yards away where two flashlight beams fluctuated up and down. They appeared to be heading in their direction. On his feet, Don grabbed the shovel and, less careful than at the site of Anastasia's grave, dug up the dirt and threw it off to the side.

The beams from across the way bounced in front of two silhouetted figures, and they were getting closer.

"Where is it? Where is it," Don growled.

"What's the matter?"

"I can't find a coffin."

"You said it wasn't necessary. The book just had to be close to the boy's bones."

"I don't know." The lights grew closer. "I just don't know."

"Put the book in the ground." Don kept digging. "Put the book in the ground," she said in a sharp whisper, but he kept digging.

"What's going on here?" The unfamiliar voice was harsh.

Mercy swung around and was hit with a blinding beam of light to the eyes. She heard the shovel behind her thud against the earth. Unable to see past the stabbing light, she blinked and turned her head sideways. When she looked back, the beam of light had landed on Don, who was standing next to the open hole in the ground, the shovel several feet to his right.

"What are you doing?" the voice barked.

Details of the owner of the voice emerged as Mercy's eyes adjusted. The balding man in his sixties looked like he might be the caretaker, and he wasn't alone. A hefty uniformed police officer stood by his side, his fist wrapped around the flashlight, which was as long as a police baton. He jerked the beam from one face to the next.

"My … My wife," Don stammered, "was looking for the grave of an ancestor. We didn't mean any harm."

The officer flashed the light onto the children, who were standing over Walker's grave, staring down at it.

"What about them," the officer said.

"It was their curiosity that started our search." Mercy tried to sound blasé about it.

The officer shined the light on the shovel that was lying on the ground, then on the patch of opened earth.

"That was already like that when we got here," Don said.

"Not true," said the caretaker. "I saw them with that shovel across the way. They were on the other side of the cemetery with it. That's why I called you."

"I need to see some ID from both of you," the officer said.

"I … I left my purse at home," Mercy said.

"Someone drove here." The officer whipped the light in Don's direction.

"We walked," Mercy lied.

"Either one of you produces a driver's license or I take you all to the station in handcuffs."

"We didn't do anything," Mercy pleaded.

The officer shone the light on Mercy's hands. "What happened to you?"

"I had an accident."

His pissed-off face showed that wasn't the right answer. He reached for his belt to retrieve handcuffs or maybe a gun, both equally terrifying. They couldn't run, not with the children. She looked at her husband and tears formed hot in her eyes.

Don pulled out his wallet and removed his driver's license. As he handed it to the officer, he said, "I didn't tell you the truth."

"No kidding," the officer huffed.

"I didn't tell you the truth because I thought it would look bad."

"It does."

"We were just going to bury an item that belonged to our relative here." Don pointed to the ground. "The children came up with the idea that he would want to have it with him."

Kind of true, Mercy thought.

"This is where the black folks are buried," the caretaker said. "You don't look black to me."

A thought jumped into her head. She remembered asking Mary Beth to check into ancestry sites when searching for Anastasia. "We found out on one of those websites where you look up your ancestors that I have African blood that goes way back. That's how we discovered our relative."

You see officer, we weren't grave robbing. We were grave giving.

"You realize it's after closing," the officer said.

"That was poor judgment on our part," Don said.

The officer took several steps away from them and began talking into his shoulder radio. Mercy couldn't hear what he was saying, but if he were calling in Don's information, he was about to get one heck of a lowdown.

"What item?" the caretaker asked.

"What?" Don looked dazed, like the caretaker was speaking gibberish.

"You said you were burying an item for your relative. What is it?"

"This book." Mercy snatched the book from Joshua's hand. "His name is inscribed in it. That's how we knew it was his." She dropped the book into the hole.

Thunder boiled through the clouds.

"Donovan Amoretto," the officer said, marching back toward them. "Husband of Mercy Amoretto?" He tucked the flashlight into his belt and slipped Don's driver's license into his breast pocket.

Lightning flashed and thunder exploded. Rain beat down on them hard and wrathful. Joshua, his head raised to the sky, roared, his voice bellowing in accordance with the thunder. Kira, her hand still gripping her brother's, raised her face to heaven and let loose an eardrum-ripping screech.

"What's wrong with them?" the caretaker yelled.

Mercy threw her arms around her daughter. "They're frightened, that's all."

"Let go of the child!" the officer hollered.

"She's just frightened. My God! Can't you see they're scared." Mercy's pleas did nothing to stop the officer from approaching closer.

"Let go of the child!" the officer yelled to Mercy, but she held her daughter firm against her chest.

Screams and roars, more ferocious than seemed possible to come from such small bodies, shattered the darkness. It was as if the sound was solid and the night a wall, and when the sound hit the wall, it splintered like a windshield hit by a rock. All the parts of Mercy's body that touched her daughter tingled with skittering static charges.

"Don!" Mercy yelled.

A giant ocean of rain poured down. Lightning tore the stars away. Thunder detonated. Don raced for their son. Along the road at the far end of that section of the cemetery, a battery of red and blue lights swirled and flashed. Mercy dropped to her knees with Kira in her arms. Inside her daughter's chest, a blazing red light began to glow. It pulsed beneath her daughter's blouse and the static charges against Mercy's body grew intense. Don had hold of Josh, whose chest also pulsed with that same red glow.

The officer rushed toward her. "Get away from the girl!"

In a flash, the brilliant red glowing balls burst from both Josh and Kira. Josh's body slumped against her husband and Kira went limp in Mercy's arms. Between the aggressive rain, thunder, and her own panic, Mercy couldn't tell whether her children were alive or dead.

"What did you do to the them?" the officer yelled.

The ghost children. The balls whizzed above her and as she watched, she felt a pop inside her head and the world went black.

CHAPTER FORTY-ONE
June 2014 ~ The Present

W hat had been solid earth when they entered the cemetery had turned to mud under the abuse of the heavy rains. Mercy, unmoving on the ground, was quickly being swallowed by it. Don saw her go down with their daughter in her arms, dragged down by Kira's weight after the red globe burst from her. Kira had gotten to her feet, but Don believed Mercy had been stunned by the globe's explosion from Kira's chest. He hurtled to his wife's side and gave her shoulders a shake. She didn't respond. Her eyes were closed. Her mouth was open.

"Mercy." He shook her harder. "Mercy!" There was no movement from her.

"What's going on here?" the officer barked down at him.

Don's ear was on Mercy's chest and he heard no beating, but with the rain, he couldn't trust what he didn't hear. He moved his cheek to her mouth, felt no breath against his skin.

The officer checked the pulse on Mercy's neck, then yelled, "Call a bus!"

Don knew that meant an ambulance, but didn't know to whom he was yelling. That's when he realized there were people. They just appeared all around him: people in uniforms, people not in uniforms.

"Sir, you need to get away from your wife," the officer said.

"I know CPR," Don shouted back. All too well. It was likely the officer also knew CPR, but he let Don do what he needed to do. He started pumping her chest, breathing into her mouth.

"Is Mom okay?" It was Kira's voice.

One. Two. Three. Four. Five.

"Dad?" Josh cried.

His children's utterances hung about the periphery of his awareness as he worked to jump his wife's heart. *One. Two. Three. Four. Five.* He felt no life in her.

"What happened?" a voice yelled.

"Did you see those fireballs?" Another voice.

"I think she got struck by lightning!"

Don knew she hadn't been struck by lightning. It had been the spirit of Anastasia escaping Kira. But the spirit wouldn't have hurt Mercy. Don had felt the same thing before in their yard. Just in case, he checked his wife's body and as he suspected, there was no tearing in her clothes. No burn marks. Just Mercy unconscious, drowning in the downpour. He pumped her chest and breathed into her, with the sounds of his children crying in his ears.

Someone touched his shoulder. He jumped.

"Sir." A man in an EMT jacket was bending over him.

Don put his lips over Mercy's and prayed into her mouth. "Come back to us." If he lingered there long enough, she would move, kiss him, open her large, dark eyes, and reveal the stars of life.

"Sir." The EMT had his hands on Don's shoulders. "We need to get her in the ambulance."

He crawled over to the side and the EMT put an oxygen mask over Mercy's face. Another brought over a stretcher. Don kept his eyes on the mask, waiting for the plastic to fog from her breath. It didn't. The rain turned hard, like a storm of pellets beating against all of them, pounding at Mercy's body as if in punishment, and he wondered if she could feel it. He got to his feet and followed the EMTs as they rolled Mercy toward the ambulance.

"Mr. Amoretto." It was Detective Bachman.

"I need to go with my wife," Don said.

"You need to come with me." The detective's beady eyes were intense with suspicion.

"My children." He tossed a look toward Kira and Josh who were both clinging to each other and shivering in the heartless rain.

"We'll take care of them, make sure they're safe."

Before the EMTs could shut the ambulance doors, Don called in, "How is she? Is she breathing?"

The paramedics gave each other a not-so-furtive glance. The one who attached the oxygen to Mercy said, "We need to get her to the hospital. They'll take it from there." He pulled the door shut.

The ambulance rolled away and Don started to run after it, but the detective caught his arm.

"What's happening, Dad?"

He turned to see Kira's dark brown eyes wide with fear.

"Is Mom okay?" his son asked, clutching his arms across his chest.

Those were his children's voices. Not the voices of the spirits, but the voices that belonged to Kira and Josh. Their pupils, although enlarged in the darkness, reflected the rain, and it was his children's eyes. The spirits, at least for the moment, had left them.

He jerked his arm, which was still under Bachman's tight grip. "Detective, please. Let me talk to my children."

She ignored him and pulled off the handcuffs hitched to her belt.

"My children are frightened," Don pleaded. "Let me at least reassure them." Of what, he didn't know, but he would find the words.

Detective Bachman slapped a cuff on Don's wrist, forced the other behind his back, and clamped his wrists together.

"Are you a mother, Detective?" The slight lift of her chin revealed her answer. "Then you know I can't leave them alone, not with Mercy in God knows what condition and me being dragged away in handcuffs."

She shifted her eyes to her wiry partner and gave a nod toward the children. The partner went to Kira and Josh and led them back to Don.

Mustering up his composure, Don bent at the waist to better meet his children's eyes. There were tears in his own. He knew that. Fighting them only made him want to cry harder. They spilled out and Don hoped the children thought it was only the rain on his face.

"I'm not sure why your mother collapsed," he said. "But I do know they'll take good care of her at the hospital. As soon as I know how she's doing, you'll know. Okay?"

They each gave a timid bob of the head.

"Dad?" Josh asked. "Why are you in handcuffs?"

Don peered up at the woman detective. She gave him no help. "These folks are with the police department and they need to ask me some questions about what happened here tonight."

"What did happen, Dad?" Kira asked.

"It's a long story, sweetie. I know you're confused, but I promise, I'll explain everything later. The first thing we need to do is get you some place warm and dry."

"You're not coming with us?" His daughter's panicked voice tore at his heart.

"I'll be home soon."

Dr. Cooper had arrived with gray blankets. He draped one over each child. "Come with me, kids," the psychiatrist said.

"Dad!" Josh yelled. "Where are we going?"

"It's okay, Josh," Dr. Cooper said. "This fine detective and I," he pointed to Bachman's partner, "are going to take you and your sister to see a doctor, just to make sure you're okay. After that, we'll take you home."

"I'm scared, Dad," Josh cried.

"Don't worry, Champ. Do as they say, and I'll be with you soon."

The psychiatrist and Detective Wiry led the children toward the police vehicles waiting along the cemetery road. As they traipsed across the muddy earth, the children kept throwing frightened looks over their shoulders. With each look, Don mouthed words like "It's okay" and "I love you."

"Detective Bachman," Don said. "I need to know about Mercy. I need to be with her."

"We will be in contact with the hospital."

"We've done nothing wrong."

"You've done plenty wrong. Just how much more wrong you were planning is what I intend to find out." She turned him toward the cruisers, where his children stood waiting with the other detective.

By the time they reached the patrol cars, the downpour had softened to a drizzle and the wind had quieted to a breeze. Clouds rolled back to reveal a bright moon.

"Dad, look!" Kira was pointing over his shoulder to the area from where they just came.

When he turned, he saw, hovering over the place that marked Walker Jacobs' grave, two red orbs. They were suspended several feet above the ground. They stayed suspended there, in a state of reflection.

"What do you think it is?" Detective Bachman asked to no one in particular.

The two red globes—two fallen stars that couldn't quite touch the earth—lingered peacefully. All stood watching in reverent silence. Don turned to his children, who were watching awestruck. Each had a palm to their chest as if they knew.

He turned back to the red globes. They had begun to move. Slow and with the fluidity of an eagle's turn, the globes looped around each other, fused together, but not with the violence that Don had witnessed before. With the grace of a dance, the orbs separated and moved upward in a slow ascent toward the stars. They all watched the globes rise higher and higher until they were no bigger than specks of light among the celestial masses. Higher still they rose and disappeared.

"I'll be dipped," said Detective Wiry.

Bachman removed her grip from Don's arm and swiped a hand across her wet bangs. "Twenty years on the force and I thought I'd seen everything."

Kira inched toward her father and whispered, "You know what that is, don't you."

"Yes, sweetie. I do. Do you?"

She shook her head. "No, but it doesn't scare me."

"Mr. Amoretto." Bachman's hold was back on him. "It's time to go."

Don resisted just long enough to see his children climb into the back seat of the dark sedan. Detective Bachman opened the back door of the cruiser next to it, and Don got in. The sedan with his children in it eased forward, the children shifting in their seats so they could see him out the back window. Don watched as they rolled away. He tried to keep their faces in his mind. But in his children's eyes, he saw Mercy.

News came to Don about Mercy while he was in the police interrogation room. Detective Bachman had first spoken with the doctor then handed the phone to Don. Doctor Andrews, the same doctor who had taken care of Kira and Josh, told him they couldn't determine definitively what had caused Mercy's death but suspected a burst aneurysm in the brain. An autopsy would confirm it, but that was the most likely cause. The words were like a great shove to the chest, sending Don stumbling backward. Molten hot anguish burned him from the inside, and for several seconds he thought he would faint. He grabbed the interrogation table and the sobs came up, pouring from him like vomit. The doctor's assurances that her death was immediate and that she didn't suffer did nothing to ease his agony.

"But she did suffer," he yelled, dropping the phone. His wails took over his words and he tumbled into a chair, sobbing for what felt like a lifetime. When his cries lulled to a whimper and his head slumped into his hands, it wasn't because he had actually calmed. He simply expended every ounce of energy on his grief.

Gaining a modicum of control, he straightened his body and swept the tears from his face. "Please, Detective. I need to see my wife."

"I need to ask you some questions first."

"How can I answer your questions? I can't even think."

"I understand."

"No, you don't."

"Mr. Amoretto, I am very sorry for you loss. I know this is a difficult time."

"This isn't a difficult time."

"It's not?"

Don's eyes met the detective's. "When I was installing a new bathroom sink and accidentally cut the water line and flooded the first floor, that was a difficult time. When my parents decided to live with us for two months while waiting for their home to close in Florida, that was a difficult time. This, Detective, isn't difficult. It's unbearable."

There was no pause, no real sympathy from her. "Mr. Amoretto, that you had nothing to do with your wife's death is good for you. What's not good is this nasty business about your children being buried in your backyard and you breaking your wife out of the hospital and ending up at the cemetery with shovels and said children."

"I didn't mean to break Mercy out. She just needed to be home."

"But she wasn't home, was she? She was at Rolling Acres Cemetery."

"Yes."

"What were you planning to do?"

"What difference does it make?"

She slammed her palm on the table. "I'm not playing games here. I can last all night. You tell me what you were planning or it will be a very long time before you see your children again."

"My wife is dead. Don't you get it? Our children have lost their mother, and I've been arrested for being at the cemetery after dark."

"You're not arrested yet. You're being questioned, and for more than being at a cemetery. Your children were buried. The doctors who had previously examined them confirmed that. And according to you, they were buried in your own back yard. You've also committed a serious crime when you wheeled your wife out of Tower Hills. This doesn't look good for you."

"I don't care how it looks."

"We care. Were you going to bury your children at Rolling Acres?"

"No. Of course not." *Only the ghosts inside them.* Gravity took his shoulders a little closer to his knees.

"Who buried your children in the yard?"

"Nobody. It was a mistake."

"It was no mistake. Someone buried them."

"You said I'm not under arrest. So, I don't have to answer any more questions. I want to call my lawyer."

The pear-shaped detective got to her feet, shook her head in disgust, and left the room. She returned with a cell phone. Don called the only lawyer he knew he could trust, Daniel Paul, a real estate lawyer Don had worked with since the early days of developing their neighborhood. When his friend arrived, he looked every bit the part of a criminal lawyer, with his black leather briefcase, tailored suit, and shiny Prada shoes, but it was just show. Paul's most challenging cases were dealing with foreclosures and litigating bad real estate deals. Defending someone for attempted murder wasn't within his skill set. But his presence was enough to shut down the interrogation.

Throughout the next several months, the investigation continued, but eventually fell away, as no evidence was ever produced to indicate Don or Mercy had anything to do with interring their children. He was charged as an accomplice in breaking Mercy out of Tower Hills and vandalizing cemetery property, but those charges brought only a sentence of probation because there was no proof of any other crime. That wasn't the worst sentence, though. He and his children were sentenced to live for the rest of their lives without Mercy.

CHAPTER FORTY-TWO
Sometime
Away from the Abyss

It began as that tiny dot of light in the corner of the universe, the one Anastasia saw each time she was thrust back into the darkness. How many times she had been in that complete and lonely darkness, she couldn't remember. It was too many times to count. One thing she did know was that for all those times she'd been there, she'd been afraid. But something was different now. The light at the far end of the black had begun to move. Not closer—it still stayed far out of reach, like the sun or the moon was out of reach—but it began to break into flecks.

First, one dot of light popped from it, then another and another. And she could hear it when it happened. Way off in the distance, she heard the dots as they sprung forth. *Ping. Ping, ping. Ping.* More dots popped from the first, as when popcorn started to burst from oil in a pan, slow and steady at the beginning then building until the room was filled with the overlapping drumming of kernels bursting open.

But it wasn't popcorn Anastasia was seeing. It was hundreds, thousands, even millions of little glowing specks filling the space in front of her and then around her until she was in the center of millions and millions of radiant glimmers of light. And they weren't just white. They were every color she could imagine. The dots blinked and twinkled like a universe filled with colorful fireflies. Floating among them, she realized the pinging she'd heard was really sparkling voices that swam and cascaded in musical harmony.

> *sweet child, you smell of sugar*
> > *there, a sunset of gold and pink*
> > > *ruffling breeze against my face*
> *streams of cool and bubbling water*
> > *fields of fragrant waving violet*
> > > *giggles are wiggles inside out*
> *toes are for tickling when you sleep*
> > *wings help lift me in the air*

"It's fairy dust," Anastasia said in awe, and she heard her own voice. She giggled and she heard that, too. "Giggles are wiggles inside out," and she giggled again.

When the sparkles brushed against her, she tingled. She swam weightless in the cool pool of glimmering lights, and the voices sang around her. It was a little like when she was sitting high in the maple tree at the park looking out over her neighborhood. She had no fear. Her light body poised in the thicket of leaves, which sang their own song while rustling in the breeze. She felt as if she were floating among the birds and the squirrels when she was in that tree. And far below, Bobby would be calling for her to come down.

Hey, Booger.

"Oh," she exclaimed and whirled around in a circle, scattering the sparkles in all directions. But Bobby wasn't there. She peered below her, but there was no below. No below and no above, just a universe of twinkling, singing fairy dust.

I bet you can't catch me, Booger.

The voice was definitely her brother's. She couldn't see him, but he was there somewhere.

Whizzing past her, so fast and close she felt its wind, flew a radiant indigo ball of light. It was bigger than the flecks. Much bigger, the size of a baseball, but fuzzy, like a deep blue twinkling baseball-sized dandelion puff, and she laughed because she wanted to play with it.

Come on, Booger, I'll race you.

It was Bobby. The blue fuzzy ball was Bobby and he wanted her to follow him. Anastasia had only to think and off she went, chasing Bobby through the scattering flecks. She spun and dipped like Peter Pan's Tinker Bell, a fairy with gossamer wings and as light as magic.

With Bobby in the lead and Anastasia close behind, they soared through the ever illuminating space until they came upon a swirling loose cloud of mixed pastels: lavender, pink, and mint green, circling around and around in a fluffy whirlpool. It was huge, maybe the size of their garage, she thought, and it appeared to be growing, much like cotton candy did as it wrapped onto a paper cone. Bobby stopped and Anastasia slowed to his side.

This is it.

"What is it, Bobby?"

As the cloud spun around itself, it began to swirl apart and then disperse, revealing behind it an expanding opening of pure white light. The light was magically warm and cool at the same time.

The indigo ball that was Bobby swooshed up to the edge of the opening and shimmered. Follow me. And he disappeared into the white.

Anastasia floated to the opening. She could no longer see the indigo ball. She couldn't see anything but the white light, but she wasn't at all scared. Bobby had zoomed into the light and he would never lead her anywhere dangerous. Besides, she thought, light was opposite of dark, which meant it was the opposite of scary.

She eased her hand into the portal and her whole body, from her toes to her nose, filled with bliss, as if every wish she'd ever wished to her fairies was coming true in that moment. And as she waded in that bliss, she felt something else. Love. The comfortable kind, like when she was cuddled in her momma's arms right at the brink of sleep. Anastasia hugged herself and rocked from side to side, she was so happy. And with a simple thought, she floated deeper into the light.

Anna, darling.

"Momma?"

Yes, sweetheart.

Anastasia let out a rapturous squeak. "Where are you, Momma?"

I'm right here.

A dazzling golden star, a fireworks star that had yet to dissipate, glided forward and stopped right in front of her.

"Momma, is that you? Are you the star? Bobby's a fuzzy blue baseball."

Her mother laughed. *Yes, Anna. It's me.*

"Why can't I see you as you?"

You can. You just have to wish it.

Anastasia wished and the star glistened and sprinkled apart into a shower of golden confetti, and when the confetti winked and disappeared, the beautiful form of her mother emerged. For so long, she'd called to her, and now there she was, her mother, as perfect as ever. Anastasia threw her body into her mother's outstretched arms.

"Oh, Momma. Momma. You found me. I knew you would. I knew. I knew."

She nuzzled her face into her mother's breast and inhaled a deep, consuming breath that smelled of lilacs and cookies. All around her, the light began to taper and shift until it evaporated away, revealing a bed covered in a pink and purple quilt, its pillows heaping with fairy dolls, and pink walls covered with Beatles' posters. On a plush, pink shag area rug beside the bed, Bobby sat cross-legged, reading a comic book. It was her bedroom. Bobby had led her out of the dark and into her own bedroom.

She did a princess twirl, the hem of her clean, white dress lifting up as she spun around. When she stopped, she saw her father leaning against the jam of her bedroom door. He had that crooked smirk on his lips he always had when he was about to reveal a surprise.

"Missing something?" her father asked.

She didn't know what he was talking about. Everything that had been missing for so long was right there. Her father drew his arm from behind his back. In his fist, he held Sparkle. Her golden silk hair and pristine gossamer wings begged Anastasia to caress them. She snatched the doll from her father's hand and clutched it to her chest.

"Oh, Daddy," she cried. "She's like she used to be. How did you do it?"

He scooped her in his arms and smothered her cheeks with kisses. She giggled and wriggled against him, but not enough to escape, just enough to play. His kisses were as bubbly and sweet as root beer.

"I have to kiss those cheeks because they're so delicious," he said.

"Oh, Daddy." Anastasia playfully swiped a hand over her face. "You're getting me all wet."

The cooing sound of a morning dove came from across the room. It rose from a bassinet next to the window, a white wicker basket, lined in lace, on a base that rocked. Anastasia's mother glided to the bassinet and lifted a pink-cheeked baby into her arms. The baby was as small as one of her dolls. Her little legs peddled as if she wanted to walk, but she was too small to walk, even Anastasia knew that. She knew she was a girl, because she had on a frilly pink dress and little pink socks.

"Come here, sweetheart, and meet your little sister."

Her father released her from his arms. It was the baby from her mother's belly. She knocked and was finally born.

"This is Jane," her mother said. "Isn't she beautiful?"

"Oh, yes, Momma. She's more beautiful than any of my fairies."

"Welcome home, sweetheart," her mother said.

Around and around, Anastasia twirled, arms outstretched, the hem of her clean, white dress with the pink satin bow rising up around her. She was home.

CHAPTER FORTY-THREE
Sometime
Away from the Abyss

Walker awoke to darkness, but it was different than what he'd known before. A haze surrounded it, as if the darkness were some kind of overlay and light was peeking out from under the edges. And it was moving. Like the chiffon of ladies' Sunday dresses billowing in a jaunty wind, it ascended and descended in lapping waves. It soothed him because it was moving.

From the undulating fabric arose soft-white clouds, tumbling about as if at play, puffing together and separating into smaller puffs that puffed together again to make larger ones. A breeze didn't propel them; they moved by their own doing. As Walker drifted among them, he could hear each one had a voice. Separate voices played off each other, bouncing to the rhythm of a stroll through the woods. They were singing. Their song reminded him of the songs his Pa would sing when working in the tobacco fields. His Pa had said singing made the day pass more pleasant-like, and although the song of the clouds was similar to his Pa's, it was a song Walker had never heard before.

It's a good day for fishin'. And plantin' in the garden. Sun smilin' on the chillen. Grass soft 'neath my feet. Molly's singin' in the kitchen. Papa's playin' his guitar. It's a good day for fishin'. And plantin' in the garden.

In his mind's eye, Walker saw the enormous garden that he and his Pa had planted alongside their shanty home. Both wide and high, it was a gorgeous plot, producing enough vegetables to last them the entire year: okra, collards, turnips, mustard greens, and the tender peas his grandmother would rhythmically shuck with her plump fingers. He could taste the peaches from the bountiful tree they'd cultivated, smell the mix of herbs from the garden, and, on top of that, he caught the wafting aroma of tobacco. Not the caustic punch he'd smelled in the fields, but the warm smoke of his father's freshly rolled cigarette.

The trick, son, is don' pinch too much and don' pack too tight.

"Lord Almighty!" Walker spoke out loud and he heard the words that slipped from him. "Pa?" he called out, and his own voice came back to his ears. It didn't get swallowed like before in the deep dark that wasn't so dark anymore. "Is that you, Pa?"

It's me, son. You made it like I knew you would. Jes' a matter a time.

Walker turned in the buoyant gray, but he didn't see his father anywhere.

"Where are you?"

Right before you, son.

Walker watched as a cloud rose from the fabric of space, a little brighter than the others, a little larger, and glistening from within. Walker touched the cloud, and it puffed apart like vapor. He let out a gasp, but the misty tendrils swirled back together again, and a hearty, from-the-soul laugh came from the cloud's center.

Follow me, son. I got somethin' to show you.

The cloud with his father's voice brushed by him and, when the misty edge swept across his arm, Walker felt like he had just passed through a cool sun shower. The cloud glided through the brightening gray toward the edge of the chiffon, and Walker followed. When they reached that place at the edge, the gray began to peel away until it was completely gone. After so much time, Walker found himself in the presence of sunshine.

You're here, the cloud said, and disappeared into the light.

Walker hesitated, not because he was afraid, but because the joy that had consumed him rendered him motionless.

Come on, Son, his father beckoned.

And Walker sailed into the light.

The sunshine softened to the glow of a September afternoon at just a breath away from evening, and all around him Walker saw shapes form. The rectangle of a table, the square of a window, the round, squat protrusion of a fat-bellied stove. And the scents came, the warm tobacco he'd picked up earlier and the unforgettable delight of cooling sweet potato pie. At the end of the table, Walker's father sat, rolling a cigarette: a hard-muscled man, with a thick, strong neck, a chest as solid as a train car with a heart as tender as a calf inside it. His pa looked up and smiled. He gave his cigarette a lick and stuck it in the corner of his mouth.

In the front doorway stood the tall, slender figure of his ma, gleaming in the late afternoon sun. Walker was only twelve when she left them, but there she was, as youthful and as daylily-beautiful as he remembered. From behind her, the gleeful chirping and chattering of his siblings and cousins roamed in from the yard.

With his two long legs, Walker leapt into his mother's arms.

"I missed ya', Ma. I missed ya' somethin' bad."

"We missed you, too, my strong boy." She held his face in her hands, kissed his cheek, and said, "But you're home now."

He was. There was his Pa rolling another cigarette for later and the window with a sill where the sweet potato pie rested to cool. But the window wasn't exactly like the one from the home he once knew.

This window had sliding panes with real glass in them. It was halfway open, staying in place all by itself. And in front of that window, he saw his grandmother, her back to him, plucking peas from a pod, her broad hips swaying, humming the tune of a Sunday church song.

"Mammaw?"

She turned her head in a smooth motion, her hips still swaying to the tune rolling from her lips.

In one long-legged leap, Walker went from his Ma's arms to his Mammaw's, squeezing her in a long, tight hug, sobs of joy spilling from him.

"Oh, Mammaw. You smell's good as molasses."

"That's 'cause I was workin' on that pie all afternoon, and now I just plucked these peas from the vine to get 'em ready for jarrin'."

Releasing his grandmother, Walker looked around the room. What a warm, joyous reunion! Only the Good Lord could have made it happen. And as he was thinking that, he realized he was just like the character from his favorite Horatio Alger book. He hadn't risen to riches, but to a wealth of peace and love.

Beneath his feet, there was a little give in the floorboards. He looked down and noticed a small latch in an indent in the wood. It was a door. He stepped aside, looped a finger through the latch, and pulled the door open. There was a stairway leading down to a softly lit room.

"We have a basement now, son," his father said. "With block windows to let in a little bitta day."

"Windows with glass in 'em?"

"'At's right." His father lit the cigarette that had been sitting in the corner of his mouth, took a long drag and let a plume of smoke pour from his lips.

"How'd you do that—make a basement?"

"Why, you can do anythin' here, son. Go ahead," he prodded.

Walker descended to the bottom of the stairs, where he was met with a chain coming from the ceiling. He pulled the chain and the room lit up with electric light. In that light, he saw rows and rows of shelves filled with hundreds, maybe thousands of books, a library full of beautiful books of every size and kind. Walker was about to get one of the books, but stopped. Instead, he pulled the chain that shut off the light and went back up the stairs. He closed the hatch door and stood near his Mammaw. Outside, the children were playing in the yard. Over by the garden, his little sister scooped something off the leaf of a collard plant. She shook her head to scoot the gnats away, and the blue yarn that tied her two pigtails flapped about. Bug carried the insect over to the shed, where she crouched and studied the thing in her palm. He could hear her giggle at it tickling her.

Walker picked up a handful of peas and began to crack open the husks.

"Ain't you gonna go read some a your new books?" his grandmother asked.

"Nah," Walker said. "I'm happy right here." He'd leave his books for later. He had forever to read.

CHAPTER FORTY-FOUR
December 2014 ~ The Present

Long ago, for Don and Mercy, time was infinite. Hours, minutes, and seconds were theirs in boundless quantities. Like a lottery winner who never believed he'd run out of money, Don and Mercy never thought they'd run out of time. But like the lottery winner, they were wrong.

It had been six months since Mercy dropped dead in Rolling Acres Cemetery and the unrelenting shock still clung to the Amoretto family. The autopsy proved what doctors had suspected; a burst aneurysm was to blame. Doctors told Don that there was nothing he could have done. The guilt came anyway. She'd complained of headaches. A lot of them. He remembered that only after the fact.

He hid his guilt from his children. Told them their mother was in a good place, at peace. When he spoke those words, they weren't hollow, as when they came from others who lived outside the pain— those words from others spoken right before they went home to their own living, breathing loved ones and washed their hands. After what his family had experienced with Anastasia and Walker, the meaning of life and death had shifted. The soul lived, and so they believed did little Lisa and Mercy. Just not with them.

Around the dining room table, he and his children sat in front of white cardboard boxes stuffed with cold, uneaten Chinese takeout. His stomach turned queasy at the greasy food. There was a rap at the slider door. Mary Beth's face peered through the glass. Without getting up, he waved a hand for her to enter.

"I was feeling lonely and thought I'd come over and bug you guys for a while." She crossed to the island counter and picked up the white carton in front of Kaitlyn. "Uck. What is this?"

"I think it was once General Tso's chicken," Don answered, "but I don't know what it is now."

Mary Beth opened the refrigerator door. "Is that what you've been living on?"

No, he thought. They were living on grief and faith.

"Let me make you something edible." She scanned the contents of the refrigerator. "On second thought…"

"Yeah, I know. I need to go shopping."

"I'm not hungry anyway," Josh said, and his shoulders slumped.

"Hey, sweetie," Don said to Kira, trying to lift the mood. "Tell Mary Beth about your short story."

"Come on, Dad. It's not a big deal."

"Like heck it isn't. It won first prize in the school writing contest. It's going to be published in the high school annual journal."

"That's fantastic!" Mary Beth said. "What's it about?"

"It's not about ghosts in trees," Kira said, defiant. "It's just a dumb story. The judges were dumb for picking it."

"I doubt that," Mary Beth said.

"It is about a tree, though," Kaitlyn chimed in.

"Tattletale," Kira shot at her sister.

Kaitlyn ignored her. "A tree that lives with a brain and a heart and protects the family that plays under it. It's a really good story. I read it twice."

The corners of Kira's mouth tweaked up in a smile.

"Sounds wonderful," Mary Beth said. For several seconds, everyone sat in what appeared to be their own contemplative bubble. Mary Beth pulled a small box of Twinings tea from her purse. "Did you know," she said, "your mother and I were tea aficionados?" She picked up the tea kettle from the stovetop and filled it with water. "Whenever things got too difficult to talk about, we would make a cup of tea. We'd sit across from each other and just drink one sip after another with no words in between. It would preoccupy our tongues long enough for our thoughts to settle, and by the time the tea was gone, the words would come."

When the kettle whistled, she poured everyone a steaming hot cup. She took the first sip, and Don could feel a ritual about to begin. The children each lifted their cups, blew on the fresh brew, then sipped the hot tea with delicate caution.

When Kira's cup was empty, she said, "What was Mom like when she was our age?"

"She was beautiful, just like you," Mary Beth said, "and full of spunk too. That's what I tell Francis when I try to describe her to him."

"You and that lunkhead seem to be hitting it off," Don chuckled.

"He's not a lunkhead. He's a podiatrist. That takes too much schooling to be a lunkhead. And he's crazy about me, so he's got great taste."

"I've seen your feet. It must be your witty banter that attracted him."

"Funny. All I know is he listens when I go on and on about Mercy, and that's all right with me. I wish she could have met him."

"She would have approved." Don looked into his children's faces, which had brightened a little. "Even though he is a lunkhead."

They all laughed.

CHAPTER FORTY-FIVE
Sometime
Away from the Abyss

Eyes closed, her mind coming awake, Mercy thought she heard the electric buzz of the fluorescent lights that had become a familiar horror since her stays at Tower Hills. With lids squeezed shut, she predicted the pain that would come from the jabbing light and from knowing she was again committed.

Her lids fluttered and she opened her eyes. There were no harsh, accusing fluorescent bulbs. Any trace of the buzzing was gone, replaced by what sounded like the languid push of waves against the shore on a lazy dawn. She wasn't in Tower Hills. She wasn't inside at all. She wasn't outside. She was in a cool gray mist, suspended as if buoyant in a deep lake, and it smelled sweet, like freshly picked cherry tomatoes.

Infinitesimal particles of mist effervesced on her flesh then rose in the air in clusters. They floated around her, carrying her through the indefinable gray. And as she was carried through a sky with no beginning and no end, she heard a voice. It was coming from the mist, and she could only discern that it was the mist itself speaking.

When you entered here
the barbs in your heart
were plucked and discarded
and those once departed

no longer apart.

The mist was speaking to her in a voice she knew.

When you entered here
you overcame death.
We heard every prayer
and joy is the air
you take with each breath.

She breathed in and tasted sugar and it sparkled on her tongue like soda pop.

When you entered here
you left behind fear.
You're bathed now with grace.
In this loving place
lives all you hold dear.

She came to a stop and a sensation grew inside her. She'd had the sensation before on the shores of Cancun, Mexico, in the seconds before dawn, when the sky, still wearing a lace curtain of night, teased the horizon with the coming of the sun. It was the sensation of something magnificent about to happen.

And it did. It began as just a crack, and from that crack burst a brilliant beam of light. Wider it opened, until the light absorbed all the mist, evaporated the gray, and Mercy was basking in the warmth of divine sunshine.

Mercy first saw the outline of her house, and as it filled in, she saw the twins' bikes toppled on their sides near the hatchway. The yard grew up beneath her feet, and the soft carpet of Don's handiwork brought comfort to her entire body. The maple tree where the children of another time once lived stood magnificent and protecting over the yard. Birds were singing, a chipmunk chirped, and a little girl giggled.

Mercy turned. From the middle of the yard bounded Lisa, just as she was when she was healthy and rosy at four years old, her mahogany curls bopping about. Her arms were spread as wide as her open-mouthed smile. Mercy went weak with joy. How could it be? But it was. It was Lisa. She lifted her daughter into her arms without effort, twirled her around, and kissed her soft cheeks again and again.

"I missed you, Momma. I missed you, missed you, missed you." And she returned the kisses, giggling with each smack of her lips against her mother's face.

"Lisa! Lisa, my girl. I missed you, too. Oh, my darling. I don't know how you're in my arms, but you are." It was some kind of miracle, or maybe it was a dream. But holding her precious girl, taking in the fresh scent of her hair, it was too real for dreaming. She kissed Lisa again and felt her smooth skin against her lips.

"I am an angel, Momma."

"An angel?"

Lisa bobbed her head up and down. "And so are you."

That should have puzzled Mercy, but somewhere deep in her soul, she knew. It wasn't a dream. There was only one way she could be holding her daughter.

"We all are." It was the voice of a woman, an adult voice that had been inside Mercy for all of her life. The voice of the woman in the mist.

"Mom?"

In the archway of the open sliding back door, Mercy's mother stood, slender, tall, with shiny dark hair and a smile blooming with love.

"Nonna's been taking care of me while we waited for you," Lisa said.

"Nonna?"

Her mother moved across the velvet lawn to Mercy. "It's what you would have had the children call me."

"Yes, it is."

Mercy looked into bright, healthy eyes, deep brown, with radiance hinting just underneath. Her mother's skin, smooth and youthful, as if never ravaged by mental illness or alcohol abuse. Her face, genuine with compassion, elicited a smile from Mercy, one that held on her lips the words I love you. With Lisa balanced on her hip, Mercy wrapped an arm around her mother and held her in a long embrace. It felt warm: a soft cotton afghan on a cool fall evening. She released her and could still feel the lingering warmth.

"What happened to me?" Mercy asked, and her mind reached around for the answer. She found it. Saw it, really, in a soupy memory of that night in the graveyard, where she hovered outside herself, looking down at her own body from above. "I died."

"Only in the sense that you are no longer trapped inside a world of pain."

"Neither are you."

"I was sick, Mercy. All those times I hurt you, hurt your father, my mind was broken. The sickness, it took away my control. And the drinking—I was just trying to numb the sickness. I never truly meant to hurt you."

"I know, Mom. I know because I was sick, too. Not the same as you, but I understand." Mercy looked around. "Where are we?"

"We're in a place where all is forgiven and our souls are washed clean."

"Don, the children?"

"It's not their time yet."

"But this house. The yard."

Mercy's mother pointed off to a place beyond the maple tree. There was her house, her yard, identical to the one in which she was standing. Don was tending a newly planted garden. Kaitlyn and Kira were climbing aboard their bikes, while Joshua was fiddling with some handheld computer game at the picnic table.

"We can see them, but they can't see us," her mother said. Mercy wondered if that would always be true. "I've been watching over you, Mercy. You and your beautiful family. I'm so proud of you."

"I've made so many mistakes. How can you be proud?"

"Mistakes are of no matter here. What matters is what's in your heart. You have love in your heart, my daughter. That's all you need."

All you need is love.

"Isn't it pretty here, Momma?"

"Beautiful," Mercy said and spun around with Lisa in her arms.

Lisa squealed. "Do it again!"

She whirled around again, her daughter laughing with excitement.

When they came to a stop, Lisa's cherub voice chirped, "Momma? Is this your home now?"

Mercy looked over to the other place where the world still spun on an axis, then into her daughter's chocolate brown eyes.

"Yes, my darling. You and Nonna and I. We're home."

The End

EILEEN ALBRIZIO is a former ABC and NPR radio news host and journalist. During her tenure, she earned numerous first-prize honors for her news and features from the Associated Press and the Society of Professional Journalists. She's a graduate of the CT School of Broadcasting and has earned a BFA in Theatre and an MA in English. She has published numerous volumes of short literature, which include poetry, plays, and short stories. Her writing has won many awards and has been nominated for many more. Her book *The Box Under the Bed* won the 2015 Paranormal Poetry and Prose Prize. She's a two-time recipient of the Greater Hartford Arts Council fellowship for poetry. A freelance creative writing teacher, she's taught at conferences and institutions across the Northeast, including at the York Correctional Institute, CT's maximum-security prison for women. She and her husband Wayne Horgan have owned and operated Heroes & Hitters, a comic book store in Rocky Hill, CT, since 1989.

THE BOX UNDER THE BED: Haunting Tales and Tidbits.
These compelling little poems and stories explore
the dark side of the human psyche
and the ghostly side of life.
Available on Amazon.com

www.facebook.com/EileenAlbrizio

36469504R00188

Made in the USA
Middletown, DE
17 February 2019